LOST RIVER

Stephen Booth

Published by Westlea Books

First published in 2010 by HarperCollins

ISBN 978-0-9572379-9-5

Westlea Books
PO Box 10125, Tuxford, Newark,
Notts. NG22 0WT. United Kingdom

www.westleabooks.com

Stephen Booth's LOST RIVER:

A May Bank Holiday in the Peak District is ruined by the tragic drowning of an eight-year-old girl in picturesque Dovedale. For Detective Constable Ben Cooper, a helpless witness to the tragedy, the incident is not only traumatic, but leads him to become involved in the tangled lives of the Nields, the dead girl's family.

As he gets to know them, Cooper begins to suspect that one of them is harbouring a secret - a secret that the whole family might be willing to cover up.

Meanwhile, Detective Sergeant Diane Fry has a journey of her own to make - a journey back to her roots. As she finds herself drawn into an investigation of her own among the inner-city streets of Birmingham, Fry realises there is only one person she can rely on to provide the help she needs.

But that man is Ben Cooper, and he's back in Derbyshire, where his suspicions are leading him towards a shocking discovery on the banks of another Peak District river.

A number 17 *Sunday Times* bestseller in the UK, LOST RIVER is the 10th novel in the award-winning Cooper & Fry series.

PRAISE FOR THE COOPER AND FRY SERIES:

"Suspenseful and supremely engaging. Booth does a wonderful job." - *Los Angeles Times*

"Simultaneously classic, contemporary and haunting."
- *Otto Penzler, Mysterious Bookshop, New York*

"Makes high summer in Derbyshire as dark and terrifying as midwinter." - *Val McDermid, award-winning crime novelist*

"Intelligent and substantive crime fiction, rich with complex characters." - *Library Journal*

"Booth has firmly joined the elite of Britain's top mystery writers."
- *Florida Sun-Sentinel*

"Crime fiction for the thinking man or woman, and damnably hard to put down." - *January Magazine*

"Highly recommended - a great series!" - *Seattle Mystery Books*

"Ben Cooper and Diane Fry are the most interesting team to arrive on the mystery scene in a long while." - *Rocky Mountain News*

"One of our best story tellers." - *Sunday Telegraph*

"There are few, if any, contemporary writers who do this as well as Stephen Booth." - *Arena magazine*

"Booth is a modern master of rural noir." - *The Guardian*

"Booth delivers some of the best crime fiction in the UK."
- *Manchester Evening News*

"Booth's aim is to portray the darkness below the surface... in this he succeeds wonderfully well." - *Mark Billingham, crime novelist*

"If you read only one new crime writer this year, he's your man."
- *Yorkshire Post*

LOST RIVER

1

Monday

On the banks of the river, Ben Cooper was running. His breath came ragged and hot in his throat. The sweat ran into his eyes. All around him, water rushed over stones, pale rocks gleamed under the surface, wet slabs of limestone caught the glare of sunlight trapped in a narrow valley. As he splashed at the edge of the water, he saw shimmers of steam rising from the wet grass, bursts of foam on the edge of his vision. And he saw long streams of blood, swirling in the current like eels.

A hundred yards away, someone had started to scream. The noise echoed off the limestone cliffs, and shrieked among the caves and pinnacles of the dale. He wanted to put his hands over his ears to block out the noise, to stop the pain of the screaming.

But he knew it would never stop, would never be out of his head again.

Behind him, other people were running. He could hear them stumbling and gasping, crashing into trees, cursing each other. The outlines of the Twelve Apostles swayed against the sky above him, jagged stone spires bursting from the hillside like teeth.

Cooper stopped to swipe the sweat from his eyes, wondering whether he was seeing anything properly. The sun reflecting off the water created impenetrable shadows and glittering fringes of light, caught strands of grass waving below the surface like hair. A fish popped up to the air, another jumped and splashed across the river. Water foamed around an obstruction, a shape lying deep on the gravel bed.

Cooper shook his head. Who was screaming? Why didn't someone tell them to stop? There were enough people here by the river. Scores of people. Dozens of families had been drawn into Dovedale by the hot May bank holiday weather. Sensing the sudden burst of excitement, they milled aimlessly on the banks like panicked sheep. In the distance, he could see them lining the stepping stones in a dumb row.

Nearby, a man stood on the bank, his hands raised, water dripping from his fingers. Cooper had the mad impression that he was some kind of priest, performing a blessing. High on an arch of rock another figure hunched, silhouetted against the sky, his face invisible. A predator on its perch, scanning the valley for prey.

In the water, Cooper saw another rock. More rocks everywhere, lying half in and half out of the river, worn as smooth as skin. Pale, wet skin, everywhere in the water. What chance did he have of distinguishing anything? No chance. No chance, until it was too late.

He looked up again. Was it really someone screaming? Or was it just a bird, startled from its roost in the birches on the limestone edge? A whole flock of birds screeching to each other, over and over, a cacophony of despair. It felt as though the rocks themselves were screaming.

He breathed deeply, tried to focus, forced himself to be calm. Now wasn't the time to lose his head. He was a police officer, and everyone was looking to him to do something. He lowered his eyes, and kept running. Still there was too much light glaring off the water, too many shadows, too much random movement. The roots of an ash tree covered in algae crouched at the edge of the water. A broken branch lay like a severed limb.

There were shouts up ahead now, and the sound of an engine. Voices calling questions, and shouting instructions. Finally, someone was trying to take charge of the chaos. He stumbled into the water, splashed spray in a wide, glittering arc. The coldness of the water was a painful shock, a blast of ice on his hot skin. He missed his footing on a wet stone, slipped, found himself crouching low over the water, staring at a broken reflection of his own face.

No. Not his own face. It was smaller, motionless – a white face, hair floating, the blood washed clear by cold, crystal streams, a green summer dress tangled on the body like weeds. A green shroud of weeds barely stirring in the water.

He plunged his hands into the river and grasped the limp arms. With a heave, he drew the body up out of the water, into the air, and held the cold form in arms, hardly daring to look at the white face. The limbs flopped, her head lolled back on her neck. Water

2

cascaded from the folds of her dress and oozed from the sides of her mouth.

Finally, Cooper raised his voice.

'Here,' he called.

And then the screaming stopped. The limestone gorge fell silent. And there was only the roar of rushing water – the endless sound of the River Dove, never stopping, continually washing clean. A torrent of water, purifying death.

Cooper turned towards the bank. And that was when he saw them. They were standing close together, but apart from the crowd, as if the onlookers had instinctively drawn away. Two adults, and a boy of about thirteen. He stared at them in despair, his mouth moving but no words coming out.

Their isolation, the tense attitude of their bodies, the desolation of their expressions – they all told him the same story. This was the dead girl's family.

Well, the tourist authority would love it. They'd be sending out the ice-cream vans and unfolding the awnings at the tea rooms. For once, summer had come early in the Peak District.

The thought was no consolation to Detective Sergeant Diane Fry, as she sat in her car on a hot street in Edendale. The windows were open, but there wasn't enough breeze here to ruffle her hair, let alone to cool the clammy interior of a black Audi. She cursed herself for having parked with the front seats in full sun, so the heat had been focused on the fake leather like a laser aimed through the windscreen. She couldn't even use her air conditioning without risking the battery. Now the heat was rising all around her in a mist, steaming up the mirrors. Another half hour of this, and she might spontaneously combust. That was, if she didn't die of boredom first.

She thumbed the button on her handset.

'Anything happening?'

'Not yet. It's all quiet.'

'Okay, thanks.'

Fry sighed, glanced in her rear-view mirror, and shifted uncomfortably in her seat. The Audi was a new car, since she'd finally got rid of the battered old Peugeot. But she hadn't been able to tear herself away from black. These days, everyone seemed to go for silver grey or metallic blue, but personally she tended to agree with Henry Ford – anything, so long as it was black.

Of course, it wasn't the best choice when the summer decided to start early, with a heat wave at the end of May. Black seemed to absorb every last drop of heat.

What she needed was movement. Her foot on the accelerator, a breeze whipping past the windows. The air con going full blast. She wouldn't really care where she was heading, if only she was moving. Out of this housing estate, out of the town of Edendale, and into the Derbyshire countryside for the sake of a cool breeze on the hills. She never thought she would hear herself say it.

A voice crackled.

'Still nothing. Shall we call it a day?'

'Not yet.'

'I'm dying here, Diane.'

'I'll make sure you get a good funeral, Gavin.'

In the CID car, DC Gavin Murfin and young DC Becky Hurst would really be getting on each other's nerves by now. Murfin would be dropping crumbs on the floor and sweating, and Hurst would be talking too much and spraying the interior with air freshener. One of them would probably kill the other, if she made them sit in the sun any longer. Fry pictured the contest. If she had to place a bet, her money would on Hurst. She was younger, faster, and meaner.

Fry looked up the street again at a suggestion of movement. An old man walking an ancient dog. Neither of them was moving at more than half a mile an hour. The dog was black, like her car. Its head drooped as it slowly put one foot in front of the other on the pavement, heading towards the corner shop at the end of the street.

They weren't what she was watching for. Her target was a fair-haired man in his late twenties, wearing a baseball cap. Intelligence said that he was living in one of these houses halfway along the street, a typical Devonshire Estate council-owned semi. But she was starting to think he might have moved home.

'I'd better start making a note of what music I want,' said Murfin.

'What?'

'At my funeral. I don't want any of this happy-clappy, celebrating-his-life sort of stuff. I want everyone to cry when I go.'

'Gavin, can we keep the chatter to a minimum, please?'

She heard him sigh. 'Okay, boss.'

In the last few months, Fry had found herself thinking about moving home, too. She wasn't sure whether it was the new car, or all the other things that she had to think about, particularly the major decisions she had to make. Decisions that she'd been putting off for weeks.

Whatever the reason, her flat at number 12 Grosvenor Avenue had begun to feel narrow and confining, as if she was living in a cell. The detached Victorian villa, once so solid and prosperous,

5

had started to flake at the edges, the window frames warping with damp, tiles slipping off the roof during the night and frightening her half to death with their noise.

'Is this him, Diane?'

Fry watched a white baseball cap emerge from behind an overgrown privet hedge on to the pavement.

'No, it's female.'

'Oh, yeah. You're right. Female, and suffering from a recent fashion disaster.'

Despite herself, Fry smiled. 'You being the expert, of course, Gavin.'

She could hear another voice in the background. Hurst, giving Murfin some earache.

'Becky says I'm being sexist,' said Murfin. 'So I'm going to have to go and kill myself.'

'Fair enough.'

Fry looked at the row of council houses, wondering about the kind of people who lived here, rent paid out of their Social Security benefits. Some of them hardly seemed to care about the conditions they brought their children up in.

When she'd first moved into her flat, there had been a private landlord – absent, but at least a real person who could be spoken to occasionally. Last winter, the property had been sold to a development company with an office somewhere in Manchester and an automated switchboard that put you on hold whenever you phoned with complaints.

It was a shame. When she looked around the other houses in Grosvenor Avenue, she saw what could be done by a responsible owner. But the present landlords didn't worry about their steady turnover of tenants, who were mostly migrant workers with jobs in the bigger Edendale hotels, and a few students on courses at High Peak College. The former tended to disappear in the winter when the tourist season was over, and the latter were gone in the summer.

Fry had been the longest surviving tenant for two or three years now. No doubt the owners wondered why she was still there. She was starting to wonder that herself. It was probably time to say goodbye to the mock porticos, and the flat on the first floor, with its washed-out carpets and indelible background smells.

But where would she go if she left Grosvenor Avenue? Well, that was yet another decision – one she wasn't equipped to make right now. She had far more important things to think about. Subjects that would dominate her thoughts, if she let them. Decisions that would change her life for ever.

Fry swore under her breath and turned up the fan to coax a bit more action out of the air con. When she first joined the police, back in Birmingham, she hadn't anticipated how much of her time would be spent sitting in cars. And always uncomfortably, too – wearing a uniform that didn't fit because it was designed for a man, strapped into a stab-proof vest that pinched her skin in awkward places because ... well, because it was designed for man.

And then, when she moved to CID, she'd been too excited to take in what everyone told her – that she'd spend just as much time in car. And when she wasn't in a car, she would be sitting at a desk, filling in forms, compiling case files, answering endless queries from the Crown Prosecution Service. Like so many other police officers, she lived for the moment when she got a chance to get out of the office. Well, maybe she had the answer to that. Perhaps she had a road trip coming up.

Recently, she'd been working hard to get back in physical condition, to regain all those skills that she'd learned under her old *Shotokan* master in Dudley. If you didn't train regularly, you lost those skills. But now her body was tuned and fit again. Her natural leanness was no longer taken as a sign of poor health. As for her mind ... well, maybe there was still some work to do.

Then her phone rang. Though she'd been getting desperate for something to happen, Fry was actually irritated. She checked the caller ID and saw it was Ben Cooper. It had better be important.

'Ben?'

'She's dead, Diane.'

'Who is?'

The connection was very bad. His voice was intermittent, crackly and fragmented like a message from outer space. Detective Constable Cooper calling from Planet Derbyshire.

'The little girl. The paramedics tried to revive her, but she was dead.'

'Ben, I have no idea what you're talking about.'

'I tried, Diane. But she was already –'

'You're breaking up badly. Where are you?'

'Dovedale. It's –'

But then he was gone completely, his signal lost in some valley in the depths of the Peak District. Dovedale? She had an idea that it was way down in the south of the division, somewhere near Ashbourne.

Fry frowned. Just before Cooper was cut off, she thought she'd heard a siren somewhere in the background. She dialled his mobile number, got the unobtainable tone. She tried again, with the same result. No surprise there. So she used her radio to call the Control Room.

'An incident in Dovedale. Have you got anything coming in?'

She listened as the call handler found the incident log and read her the details. There was no mention of DC Cooper, just a series of 999 calls recorded from the public at irregular intervals, probably as people got signals on their mobiles. Units were attending the scene, along with paramedics and ambulance. One casualty reported. She supposed it would all become clear in due course.

'Thank you.'

When she thumbed the button again, she got Gavin Murfin's voice yelling for her.

'Diane, where are you? He's on the move, on the move. Your direction. Repeat, your direction. Have you got a visual?'

'What?'

Fry looked up and saw movement on the pavement a few yards ahead of her position. But it was only the old man coming back towards her, flat cap pulled over his eyes, dog lead in one hand, plastic carrier bag in the other. The dog dug its heels in and stopped to water a lamp post.

'Nothing. Nothing in sight here.'

'He's long gone,' said Murfin. 'He was legging it. Didn't you see him?'

'No.'

8

While his dog performed its business, the old man stood and stared at her defiantly like some ancient accusing angel.

'Bloody Hell, Gavin,' said Fry. 'We've lost him.'

For the past half hour, Cooper had been listening to the yelp and wail. The modern tones of emergency response vehicles, howling up the dale one after another. The noises merged inside his head with an echo of the screaming. The noise still bounced off the sides of his skull in the same way it had ricocheted among the caves and pinnacles of Dovedale.

He still didn't know who had screamed. Perhaps it was the mother. Or it might just have been some random bystander, reacting with horror to a glimpse of a body in the water. A small, white face. Long streams of blood, swirling in the current like eels …

'Their name is Nield.'

The tall uniformed sergeant was called Wragg. Cooper remembered him vaguely, and thought he'd probably turned up at a couple of major incidents in E Division when he was still a PC. He was fairly recently promoted, and was based at Ashbourne section now. He was wearing a yellow high-vis jacket over his uniform, and had removed his cap to reveal close-cropped fair hair. He looked harassed, but it might just be the heat.

'Local?' asked Cooper.

'Yes, by some miracle. Among all these crowds, you'd think it'd be city people who suffered an incident like this. You know, the sort who've never actually seen a river before. Folk who don't think you can drown in water unless there's a sign telling you so.'

'You've seen too many tourists.'

'You got that right,' said Wragg. 'I never want to catch duty on a bank holiday again, I can tell you. Do you know how long it took me to get my car through those jams? You won't be able to move down here later.'

'That will be somebody else's headache.'

'I wish.'

Cooper was leaning against Wragg's car. He had a clear view up the gorge towards the weirs, and beyond them, the pool where he'd pulled the body out of the water.

'How old is she?' he said.

'Eight.'

'She's only eight years old?'

'Yes.'

'She was here with her parents. How the hell did it happen?'

'They say their dog went into the water to fetch a stick. A golden retriever, it is. It seems the girl ran in after the dog. Only the dog came out.'

Cooper shook his head in despair. 'Where are the parents now?'

'Gone with her to hospital.'

'They surely don't think she'll be revived. Do they?'

Wragg shaded his eyes with a hand as he watched some members of the public being shepherded away from the scene.

'You don't give up in these circumstances,' he said. 'That's the very last thing you do.'

Events had moved pretty quickly once the girl's body had been recovered from the water. Cooper had carried her to the bank and laid her on the grass. Then a woman had come forward from the crowd of bystanders, saying she was a nurse. Cooper had handed over resuscitation efforts to her, and she kept it going until the fast-response paramedic arrived, closely followed by the ambulance and Sergeant Wragg and his colleagues from the Ashbourne section station.

'We'll need a statement from you, of course,' said Wragg. 'But it will do later. We're trying to catch as many witnesses as we can among the public before they disappear.'

'Of course.'

'But there doesn't seem any doubt it was an accidental drowning.'

'There was blood, though,' said Cooper. 'Blood in the water. She had an injury on her head.'

'She probably fell and hit her head on a stone. That would explain why she drowned in such a shallow depth.'

'"Probably"?'

'There's hardly going to be any trace evidence,' said Wragg irritably. 'The stone is somewhere out there being washed by thousands of gallons of water every second. We'll see what eye-witness statements say, but I think you'll find that's it.'

'Yes, all right.'

There had been no blood on the girl when he'd picked her up. But Cooper remembered seeing the wound now, an abrasion and broken skin on her forehead. The toughest thing he'd ever done was putting that body down, handing the little girl over to someone else. It felt like abandoning her to her fate. For some ridiculous reason, his instinct had been telling him he was the only person who could save her.

It was strange what your mind could do in a crisis. Sometimes, the rational part of your brain cut out altogether and you acted entirely on instinct, with no conscious thought involved. But occasionally your mind presented you with odd flashes of information that didn't even seem to be relevant at the time.

Right now, Cooper was remembering images from the last hour or so. Paler rocks under the surface, streams of blood swirling in the current like eels. Jagged limestone spires at crazy angles. A dead, white face with floating hair. And a man with his hands raised, water dripping from his fingers.

'Anyway, the Nield family ...' said Wragg, consulting his notebook. 'Father is a supermarket manager in Ashbourne. Mum is a teacher. There's a boy, about thirteen years old, name of Alex. They're all in a state of shock, as you can imagine.'

'And the girl?' said Cooper.

'What?'

'The girl. You haven't mentioned her name. She must have a name.'

Wragg looked taken aback.

'Of course. Her name is Emily – Emily Nield. She's eight years old.'

'Thank you,' said Cooper. 'That's what I wanted to know.'

He was aware of the noise of tourist cars rattling over the cattle grids out of Dovedale. Streams of scree had spilled from Thorpe Cloud like ash from a small volcano, slithering slowly

11

towards the valley bottom. Two spaniels splashed in the water, scattering the mallards.

Many visitors were still clustered on the smooth, green slopes of the lower dale, where the limestone grassland had been grazed short by rabbits and sheep. Some were making their way down to the car park from the slopes of the dale, where they'd been exploring the woods or the limestone pinnacles and caves.

Suddenly, Cooper pushed himself away from the car.

'Just a minute.'

'Where are you going?' asked Wragg.

But Cooper didn't bother answering. He ran over to the car park and began to dodge between the groups of people, searching for a face. Some of them stared at him as if he was mad. But he was sure he'd seen someone he recognized. It was just a glimpse, a face half turned away in shadow, but the angle of a cheek and the tilt of a head were distinctive. It was a face he remembered for a reason, one that should mean something important.

He stopped two women getting into their Land Rover Discovery.

'Excuse me, did you happen to see …?'

But he didn't know what he wanted to ask them, and they hurriedly slammed their doors, fearing that he was some lunatic.

Cooper stopped, shaking his head. Maybe he *was* mad. But that face had been important, if only he could pin down its meaning.

Frustrated, he walked slowly back to the police vehicles. The River Dove was returning to its normal state after the excitement. Small brown birds with white bibs hopped from stones and plunged into the water after food. Dippers, they were called. It was said that crayfish and freshwater shrimps lived in this river. The water gave life to so many creatures. But it could take life away, too.

'DC Cooper, are you okay?' asked Wragg.

'Yes. Why wouldn't I be?'

'You're shivering.'

'Oh, I'm just cold.'

Wragg stared at him with a baffled expression. He wiped the sweat from his own face with a handkerchief and squinted up at the glaring sun.

'Oh, yeah. Chilly day, isn't it?'

Cooper didn't reply. He couldn't tell Wragg what he really felt. It sounded too ridiculous. But right now, he felt chilled to the bone.

3

And that was it. The entire operation blown in a few seconds of inattention. Fry turned off the engine of the Audi, got out and stood on the pavement, waiting for Murfin and Hurst to join her.

'What went wrong, boss?' asked Murfin. He looked exhausted and irritable, perspiration standing out on his forehead.

'I missed the signal,' said Fry.

'That's tough.'

He exchanged glances with Hurst, who stood in the background, unsure of her position, or what she was expected to do now. And who could blame her, when she was given this kind of poor leadership?

Fry couldn't stand the quizzical look that Murfin was giving her. As if she never made mistakes like everyone else. Well, she had to admit this was going to be an expensive mistake. Expensive in time and resources. And even more expensive in terms of damage to her career, when Detective Superintendent Branagh got to hear about it.

From the moment she arrived in E Division, Branagh had made it clear that she wasn't DS Fry's biggest fan. Now she had just proved to the Super that she couldn't even organize a simple drugs surveillance. Piss-up and brewery would be words on Branagh's lips. Damn it, this was the worst thing that could have happened. And it was all Ben Cooper's fault.

Emily Nield had been taken to the Royal Derby Hospital, which had a new Accident and Emergency department off the Uttoxeter Road, just outside the city. Cooper found her family sitting in A&E. Through a window, he could see a doctor already speaking to them, with that practised shake of the head that conveyed bad news. In this case, probably the worst news it could possibly be.

Cooper waited a few minutes, watching hospital staff come and go. He was unsure of his reception, and didn't want to rush in where he wasn't welcome. But he needed to know the worst. And somehow he also needed to make contact.

The father of Emily Nield had his back to the window, but Cooper could see he was a man in his forties, with short dark hair turning grey at the temples. He was dressed in the style that some politicians adopted when they were trying to look casual for the cameras. A blue shirt with the cuffs turned back on strong-looking wrists, cream chinos that were now stained around the knees. The mother's face was red and puffy, half hidden by a tissue. Cooper wondered where the boy was. Hadn't there been a teenage boy with them?

He caught the attention of the doctor as she came out and identified himself.

'Yes, I'm afraid Emily Nield was declared dead on arrival. Very sad.'

'Thank you. Can I speak to the parents?'

'If they're willing.'

Finally, he judged the moment was right, and went into the room to introduce himself.

'I'm very sorry,' he said.

There had been so many times that those three words had seemed to convey very little. They were said without sincerity, with only self-interest in mind. But right now, they seemed to mean no more than the amount of breath he'd used to inhale before he said them. What words *could* you say to parents who'd just seen their youngest child die in front of their eyes?

He always hated meeting people for the first time in circumstances like these. It was impossible to know from looking at them what sort of people they had been before they were broken, before their world was turned upside down for ever. They might have been people full of joy, the kind who took the greatest delight in life, their expressions always lit up by smiles. No one would know that from their faces now. In just a couple of hours, the pain had been etched too deeply into their faces, the light in their eyes had been dimmed too far. Sometimes that light never returned.

It was always worst for parents, too. No parent should have to be present at the death of a child. It was contrary to the natural

15

order of things. And Emily Nield had been, what – eight years old? To Cooper, it felt like a tragedy beyond measure. He had no words that could express to the Nields the way he felt.

Mr Nield stood up and shook his hand in an awkward, solemn way. Nield was a tall man, an inch or two taller than Cooper when he was standing. The slight hunch of his shoulders suggested he was uncomfortable about his height.

'We need to thank you,' he said.

'No. There's no need, sir. I did nothing.'

His thanks made Cooper's throat tighten with a surge of emotion that he struggled to hide.

'You tried,' said Nield. 'You did your best for our little girl. Yes, you did your best. No one can say more than that in this world.'

Cooper smiled. But when he looked the man directly in the eyes, his smile faded. He recognized him now. This was the man he'd seen on the bank of the River Dove, hands raised as if in blessing. Yet a few minutes later, Nield had been standing in a little group with his family. Cooper wondered if his sense of time had been distorted during the incident. He would have to find out from Sergeant Wragg how long it had taken from the girl entering the water, or from the alarm first being raised. Possibly events had seemed to happen much faster than they really did.

'I'm Robert Nield, by the way,' said the man. 'This is my wife, Dawn. Our son Alex is here somewhere. I think one of the staff took him out of the way of ... Well, they've all been very kind. They couldn't have treated us better.'

'I'm Detective Constable Cooper.'

'You're a policeman. We actually didn't realize that, did we, love?'

Mrs Nield shook her head. She hadn't spoken yet, but at least her face appeared briefly from behind the tissue.

'I'm a detective with Derbyshire Constabulary.'

'We know a few of your people,' said Nield, 'but I don't think I've come across you before.'

'I'm based in Edendale, sir.'

'That would explain it. We're Ashbourne people.'

'Yes, I know.'

16

Nield looked at him curiously, as if he too was searching for an elusive memory, a connection that he wasn't quite making. Cooper was used to that look from people he'd never met before. Often they'd known his father, a long-serving police sergeant of the old school who'd practically been the centre of the community in Edendale. Sergeant Joe Cooper was known to thousands, even now. And those who'd never met him in life knew of his death.

Well, it would come to Nield later, when he was thinking straight again. He could deal with it then.

'I don't know what arrangements have been made, but I could run you home,' said Cooper. 'My car is just outside.'

'That's good of you. I'd completely forgotten, but I left our car behind when we came in the ambulance.'

'In the Dovedale car park?'

'Yes.'

'If you like, we can drop your wife and son home, then I'll take you to pick up your car. How does that sound?'

'Excellent.'

'As long as you feel up to driving. If not, I can arrange for it to be taken care of.'

'No, I'll be fine. We'll find Alex, and we can be off.'

'I keep thinking "if only we could turn back the clock",' said Dawn Nield as they walked to Cooper's Toyota. 'Just a few minutes, or a few seconds. If only I'd been watching Emily more closely, if we hadn't been throwing the stick for Buster, or we'd chosen to go somewhere else that day instead of Dovedale. Robert said it would be crowded on a bank holiday. That was why we went early. If we'd set off a bit later, we might not have been able to park the car, or there might have been more people around when it happened ...'

'Love, there's no point in tormenting yourself,' said Nield.

'No, you're right.'

Dawn wiped her eyes and looked briefly at Cooper. He read everything in that fleeting glance. While she might tell her husband he was right, those were no more than the words that came automatically from her mouth. What was happening inside her head was a whole world away. He knew she would never stop

17

tormenting herself, could never rid herself of the endless 'what ifs'. That list of possibilities would run through her mind in a constant loop, the moments when history might have been changed, playing over and over again like scenes from a film she had never actually watched. For the rest of her life, she would still be asking herself: *What if?*

The drive back to Ashbourne on the A52 took only twenty minutes. Cooper was glad it wasn't a longer journey. The atmosphere in the car became uncomfortable as the Nields fell silent, each of them absorbed in their own thoughts. He'd tried to fill in some of the silences himself, but there was a limit to how much you could say in these circumstances without starting to sound ridiculous and insincere.

Ashbourne was a town built mostly of red brick, which made it look totally different from the limestone and millstone grit of Edendale to the north. This was clay country, softer than the White Peak, less forbidding than the bleak moorlands of the Dark Peak.

At school, in Geography lessons, Cooper had learned the significance of the boundary of Red Triassic rock which ran from Ashbourne to Thorpe, leaving the limestone gorge of Dovedale in startling contrast on the other side.

Perhaps it was all that red brick, but somehow the town felt unfamiliar to Cooper, as if he had already left his comfort zone. The Pennine hills were in his blood, and nothing could replace them. If he were ever to move, even the few miles to Ashbourne, it wouldn't feel like home.

As he drove into the town, Cooper could see the last stages of construction work taking place on Clifton Road, where a new hospital was due to open next year. He wondered if it would have its own A&E department, whether it would have made any difference if Emily had got to hospital a few minutes quicker.

But he recalled the body he'd held in his arms, the futile attempts to resuscitate her on the riverbank. Surely she had already been dead when she came out of the water?

The boy was very quiet. At least the mother had let some of it out in that burst of emotion. But Alex was dumb. He was a slim youth, a bit under-sized for thirteen perhaps. He had dark hair like his father's, but allowed to grow long, so that it fell over his face.

His mother occasionally tried to push it back into position, and each time the boy flinched away from her. Alex had dark eyes, too, that gazed into Cooper's every time he looked in his rear-view mirror.

Shock took people in different ways, of course. It was slightly disturbing, though, the way the boy kept looking at him and saying nothing. It was as if he was trying to weigh up Cooper's trustworthiness, wondering whether he could share some secret with him. It was highly likely that he found it impossible to talk to either of his parents at that age. What thirteen-year-old could? A stranger to talk to might be exactly what he needed.

But how did you communicate to a thirteen-year-old boy that he was welcome to talk if he wanted to? Probably you didn't. Teenagers were like animals, weren't they? You had to wait until they came to you.

The Nields lived on the Shires Estate, off Wyaston Road. Executive homes with a view of the countryside where the road turned into a steep hill before curving to a dead end just short of the A52. At the bottom, children were playing football in the road. You didn't see that too often.

The Nields' house looked to be ten or twelve years old, with carriage lamps and hanging baskets, an oriel bay window and two half-timbered gables. It was set back from the road behind a neatly trimmed beech hedge, and a paved driveway led up to a double garage.

A house like this was usually described in estate agents' adverts as a period-style detached residence. Cooper turned and looked at the view beyond the end of the close – Peak District hills on the horizon, including the distinctive pyramid shape of Thorpe Cloud. A detached residence in a much sought-after area, then. Lucky Nields.

He dropped Dawn and Alex off at the house, reassured to see a member of the family waiting anxiously for them on the drive. Nield explained that it was his wife's sister, come up from Derby to be with her.

'Thank you,' said Nield, when Cooper returned him to the car park in Dovedale. 'I don't know how to thank you enough.'

'There's really no need, sir.'

19

Cooper watched Nield drive away in his silver VW Passat. The car park was almost empty now, and access to the dale itself sealed off by police tape. Beyond the tape, Cooper could see Sergeant Wragg's yellow high-vis jacket down by the river. But he felt reluctant go near the water. The thought of its noise and icy coldness made him shiver. The image of water foaming over a weir caused his skin to crawl with apprehension.

Shading his eyes with his hands, Cooper gazed into the distance for the furthest glimpse of water he could get before a curve in the dale hid the Dove from view. He knew that the river rose way in the north, on the slopes of Axe Edge, close to the Leek to Buxton road. It ran roughly southwards for forty-five miles to join the Trent. For much of its course, it ran with one bank in Derbyshire and the other in Staffordshire. Which meant, strictly speaking, that his jurisdiction as an officer of Derbyshire Constabulary ended in the middle of the water, about halfway across the stepping stones.

He pictured the Dove widening as it reached Hollinsclough and flowed beneath the reef knolls of Hollins Hill, Chrome Hill, Parkhouse and Hitter into the tourist village of Hartington. It was after Hartington that the valley became a gorge, the meadows ending abruptly at Beresford Dale. Wolfscote Dale, Mill Dale, and then the northern entrance into Dovedale itself, where more than a million visitors a year came to admire the wooded slopes and white limestone rocks carved by nature into towers, caves and spires.

South of here, the Dove was joined by the River Manifold before flowing through the lowlands of Southern Derbyshire on its way to the Trent at Newton Solney.

Past those stepping stones, on a curve of the river, was a series of rocky outcrops, all with picturesque names. Dovedale Castle, the Twelve Apostles, Lovers' Leap. They were picked out on maps and photographed by tourists as they strolled along the banks of the river in the summer. Pickering Tor, Tissington Spires, the Rocky Bunster. One of the most prominent features was a natural arch on the eastern side of the dale. For some reason, whoever had named these rocks had suffered an imagination failure at this point. According to the Ordnance Survey map, this was called simply the

Natural Arch. A bit disappointing, really. You would have expected the Devil's Bow or the Mouth of Hell.

Cooper tried to sort out his memories, to clarify what he'd seen in Dovedale, and what he hadn't. But no matter how hard he tried, he couldn't get an image of Robert Nield out of his head, hands raised, water dripping from his fingers.

But the image only flashed across his memory. With it came another, much stronger recollection. The feel of a cold, limp body. Not yet stiff, but icy. The coldness of the freshly dead.

Above the weirs, the river looked too shallow for anyone to drown in. Anyone but a small child, anyway. Downstream, the water was deeper between the weirs. The current formed deceptive pools. How had the Nields managed to choose a stretch of river where the water was that bit deeper, the crowds were sparser, and everyone seemed to be looking the other way?

But that was the way it went with these things. A combination of circumstances that no one could have predicted, and this was the outcome.

Cooper started the Toyota and turned north towards Edendale. He found he wasn't even convincing himself. A combination of circumstances? Or was it something more?

The cold eating into his bones could not be explained by the weather.

4

And how do you feel about it now? It was a question Diane Fry expected to be asked at any moment. It was, after all, a question that she'd asked herself many times, trying to analyse her own feelings, to make an inventory of the emotions as they welled up inside her. Pain, fear, horror. An awful sense of loss. And some other emotions so deep and nameless that they didn't fit into any inventory.

It didn't matter what questions they asked her. No neat list would contain those feelings, no analysis could pin them down.

She recalled that rainy Monday morning in March, when she'd found Detective Inspector Gareth Blake standing in her boss's office at E Division headquarters in Edendale. She hadn't recognized him at first, as she automatically held out her hand, seeing a man who wasn't much above her own age, his hair just starting to recede a little from his forehead, grey eyes observing her sharply from behind tiny, frameless glasses.

'Diane,' he said.

And then she'd remembered him. It was the voice that did it. She and Blake had worked together years ago, on the same uniformed shift in the West Midlands. But he'd been ambitious and got himself noticed, earning an early promotion. He was more mature now, better dressed, with a sharper hairstyle. The reek of ambition still hung in the air around him, though.

So what was Blake's specialty now?

Cold case rape enquiries. Well, of course.

And then there had been Rachel Murchison, smartly dressed in a black suit and a white blouse, dark hair tied neatly back, businesslike and self-confident, but with a guarded watchfulness. A specialist counsellor, there to judge her psychological state.

Some of the phrases leapt out at her from the conversation that had followed.

'Obviously, we don't want to put any pressure on you, Diane.'

That was Blake, pouring a meaningless noise in her ear.

'It's understandable that you feel a need to be in control. Perfectly normal, in the circumstances.'

Murchison's contribution. Well, Fry hadn't wanted this woman telling her whether she was behaving normally or not. She didn't want to hear it from anyone else, for that matter.

Just the sound of her name from Blake's lips had brought back the memories she'd been trying to suppress, but which would now forever bubble up in her mind. She remembered how both of them, Blake and Murchison, had watched her carefully, trying to assess her reaction.

In the days that followed, others had seemed to be watching her in that some careful manner. But they could never comprehend the painful attempt to balance two powerful urges. The need to keep her most terrible memories safely buried now had to be set against this urge she'd suddenly discovered growing inside – the burning desire for vengeance and justice. No one could understand that. Not even Ben Cooper.

DC Ben Cooper had already been the darling of E Division when Fry had first arrived in Derbyshire. She'd been told how wonderful he was, what areas he was the expert in, the heights of knowledge he'd attained that no one else could possibly aspire to.

She'd heard his name mentioned so many times before she actually met him that she'd already formed a picture of this Mister Perfect, the detective everyone loved, the man most likely to stand in her way. The picture that entered her mind was of a six-foot alpha male with broad shoulders and perfect teeth, smiling complacently.

When he entered the CID room that first day back from leave, he could only have lived up to expectations if he'd been walking on water, or floating in a golden glow and trailing a string of haloes from his angelic backside. DC Ben Cooper had been set up for her to despise from the outset. No one liked a goody-goody.

But things had changed since then. Fry knew better than anyone that he was no Mister Perfect.

For years, her instinct had been to concentrate totally on her work. And that was a familiar story. She was no different from all the washed-up people everywhere, all the fools who'd ever messed up their lives or destroyed their relationships. Work was safe

23

ground, a place where *personal* feelings could be put aside, shrugged off with her coat at the door of the office.

The trouble was, right now she could feel the safe ground shifting under her feet. She was still as dedicated to the job as she'd ever been. But she had a suspicion the job wasn't quite so loyal to her any more.

Fry was waiting to be called into Superintendent Branagh's office, back at E Division headquarters in West Street, Edendale. She felt like a naughty school girl being sent to see the headmistress.

'Michael Lowndes,' said Branagh, when she was finally summoned. 'What went wrong?'

There was no point in trying to make excuses. Branagh had eyes that could look right through you.

'I took my eye off the ball, ma'am.'

'Obviously. You were supposed to follow him to the meeting, and take the main players out. You were in position, and so was your team. We only put together this operation so that Lowndes would lead us to the others.'

'We failed,' said Fry.

'We?'

Fry swallowed. 'I failed.'

Branagh sat back in her chair and studied her for a few moments. 'Diane, we've been patient with you for a while now,' she said.

'Yes, ma'am.'

'We've given you some leeway, allowed you plenty of space. But you have a decision to make, and it's time you made it. I believe it's starting to affect your performance.'

'I wouldn't say that.'

'Have you some other explanation?'

But Fry hadn't. She couldn't blame anyone else but herself.

'DS Fry, I want you to make a decision here and now. I don't like to put pressure on you in these circumstances, but I have wider issues to consider.'

Fry looked at her, wondering if she would be as terrifying herself if she ever reached the dizzy heights of such a senior rank. Not that it was likely.

The last time Fry had sat in this office was when DI Gareth Blake and the specialist rape counsellor Rachel Murchison had arrived from the West Midlands, bringing the news of a DNA hit that would enable them to re-open the enquiry in which she was the victim. A cold case rape enquiry. All they needed was her response, a decision on whether she wanted to go ahead with a fresh enquiry, or close the book and put the whole thing behind her.

Blake's words still echoed in her mind. She'd been turning them over and over since that day.

'When we get a cold case hit, we consult the CPS before we consider intruding into a victim's life. We have to take a close look at how strong a case we've got, and whether we can do something to strengthen it.'

'With the help of the victim.'

'Of course. And in this case …'

'In *my* case. This is personal. Don't try to pretend it isn't.'

'In your case, we had a very credible witness report from the victim. From *you*, Diane. Everything is on file for this one. We have an e-fit record in the imaging unit, and a copy of everything has been kept by the FSS. But the bottom line is, we got a DNA match.'

DNA, the holy grail of trace evidence. The national DNA database had gone live in 1995 and every week now the Forensic Science Service laboratory in Birmingham matched more than a thousand profiles taken from crime scenes, solving crimes up to thirty years old. Soon, the database would hit its target of three million profiles.

It was so easy to believe that DNA evidence was foolproof. Yet the larger the database, the greater the chance of somebody being wrongly linked to a crime. For some, it was too much like the beginnings of a Big Brother society they didn't really want to be part of.

'The time is now,' said Branagh. 'Do we have a decision?'

'Yes, ma'am.'

'Excellent. I'm granting you indefinite leave of absence.'

Branagh made a note in a file on her desk.

'Of course, since we don't know how long you'll be away from the division, there'll be an appointment to Acting DS in your place.'

Leaving Branagh's office, Fry pulled out her mobile and dialled a number.

'Dad? Will you be at home tomorrow? Yes. I'm coming to see you.'

Ben Cooper turned right and dropped the Toyota down a gear to go up the steep street.

Edendale was one of only two towns that sat within the boundaries of the Peak District National Park. At Buxton and other towns, the line on the map took wide sweeps around them and back again, to exclude them from national park planning restrictions. But Edendale sat too deep within the hills to be excluded. It lay in the middle of a valley running west to east, halfway between the Hope and the Wye. The River Eden came down from the hills and meandered its way through the town before escaping to the east. Because of its position, every road in the town led upwards, out on to the moors.

Castleton Road climbed past close-packed residential areas that spiralled up the hillsides, houses lining narrow roads that took sudden twists and turns to follow the humps and hollows of the underlying landscape.

Further out, the houses became newer as they got higher, though they were built of the same stone. Finally, the housing petered out in a scattering of smallholdings and small-scale dairy farms.

For the moment, Edendale was constrained in its hollow by a barrier of hills. But the pressure of housing demand might force it to expand some time – either southwards into the gentle limestone hills of the White Peak, or north towards the bare gritstone moors of the Dark Peak.

By the river in the centre of town, the Buttercross area was where Edendale's antique shops clustered. This was the oldest and most picturesque part of the town, including Catch Wind and Pysenny Banks, where the stone-walled streets were barely wide

26

enough for a car and the river ran past front gardens filled with lichen-covered millstones.

In this area, his sister Claire's shop stood empty now, the 'To Let' signs up, and all its stock sold off. There wasn't much hope of a sale at the moment.

It was hardly the only empty shop in town anyway. Time moved a bit more slowly here than in other parts of the country, and the recession had come along late, its ripple effects hitting the Eden Valley some months after the stone that had been dropped into the water of the UK economy.

At the height of the recession, twenty per cent of retail property had stood vacant in the city of Derby. In the north of the county, smaller market towns like Edendale had survived for a while on their tourism business – thanks to all those people who'd decided to spend their holidays in Britain rather than fly to the Maldives. And now, while the papers talked about the green shoots of recovery, the shutters were still up in Edendale's High Street.

But Claire Cooper was ready to make a fresh start. She was a 'glass half-full' sort of person, and saw it as an opportunity. Even Matt might be pushed and cajoled into adopting a more optimistic outlook than he'd expressed for a long time.

At E Division, Gavin Murfin would be retiring in a few years' time, finally able to claim a full pension at the end of his thirty years' service. Gavin's eldest was due to get married soon. He'd probably be a grandfather before long. But what would he do with himself in his mid-fifties, a career in Derbyshire Constabulary behind him, and too much time on his hands?

It was funny how that happened in someone's life. Time turned them into a person their friends didn't recognize and had no connection with. Old colleagues who'd depended on each other's support for years suddenly found they had nothing in common, no way even of sharing the office gossip. You couldn't talk about work to a civilian. And all of that could be a brutal wrench for some officers. Too cruel a rupture.

Cooper had a sudden vision of himself in twenty years' time, overweight and middle-aged, slouching around the CID room at Edendale, checking his watch to see if it was time to go home yet, setting a bad example for the younger DCs, grumbling about always missing out on promotion. He could become another Gavin Murfin.

No, surely not.

But some things never changed. Every division was still struggling to meet all its targets. Sanctioned Detection Rate, Crime Reduction Figures, PDR Completion Rate, Public Confidence Measure. The list seemed endless and unattainable.

Number 8 Welbeck Street lay just across the river from the town centre, close enough for him to walk to work if he wanted to. It benefited from a conservatory, and long gardens between Welbeck Street and the shops on Meadow Road. Unfortunately, his landlady Mrs Shelley, who lived next door, was becoming dottier and dottier, and he wasn't sure how long he had left before her acquisitive relatives took over the two houses. No doubt they had their own plans.

He did still have a cat, though. Not the original black moggy who had come with the ground-floor flat as a sitting tenant. The poor chap had died one day in his sleep, and the flat had felt very empty without him.

Cooper's new cat had chosen him one day when he visited the Fox Lane animal sanctuary. She had hooked him with her claws as he passed her cage, and refused to let go. One look into her anxious bright green eyes had left him with no option.

Now she was very much at home in Welbeck Street, enjoying the freedom of roaming the back gardens. He was gradually getting used to seeing tabby stripes instead of long black fur.

It had taken him ages to name the new cat. Naming an animal seemed such a simple thing. It wasn't like choosing a name for a child, when something that suited a gurgling baby also had to be cool enough to avoid bullying when a child reached its teens, and appropriate for a responsible adult who didn't want to sound like a porn star.

Claire had told him that a cat was the Celtic equivalent to the mythical two-headed dog Cerberus, the guardian at the entrance to the Underworld. So he'd toyed with some names from Celtic mythology. Brigid, Mari, Morgan, Rhiannon. Wikipedia had come up with a whole list. But none of them had seemed right. They sounded too much like witches.

He'd decided that the name ought to represent something of the area, the landscape that meant so much to him. Living in town, he missed the countryside, particularly his old home at Bridge End Farm. It ought to be something that reminded him of good things, the name of a hill or valley. Not a bleak peat moor from the Dark Peak, but something gentler.

The answer had come to him as he sat looking at the cat, gazing into her green eyes. He had an image of the wonderful panorama from Surprise View above Hathersage. It was a view that summed up the Peak District. On one side was the edge of the Dark Peak, with its twisted gritstone tors and the ramparts of Carl Wark. On the other side lay the White Peak, densely wooded slopes, limestone dales, picturesque villages. Ahead, there was a view right up the valley to Castleton, and on the horizon the hump of Mam Tor, the shivering mountain. The Hope Valley. Perfect. Now his cat was called Hope.

Cooper's phone chirped. He'd finally bought an iPhone, though it was a cheap one he found on eBay. He spent far more time playing with it than he ought to. He'd turned it to vibrate while he was with the Nields. Now there were lots of messages waiting for him. One was from his brother, Matt.

'Ben, can you call? I need to talk to you about something. It's … well, it's a bit of a family problem. So call, can you? Or come to the farm.'

Then there was a spell of silence before the call ended. No, not actually silence. If he pressed his ear to the phone, he could hear the sounds of the farm in the background. A dog barking, birds singing, cows lowing like a stage chorus as they headed in for milking. He pictured Matt crossing the yard behind the herd, forgetting that he had the phone clutched in his huge hand as he shoo'd an awkward beast through the gate. Cooper could have listened to it for ever. But finally there was a faint curse, and dead air.

And there was Liz. A voicemail message, simply to say *Hi, Ben. Did you get my text? Love you.*

No call from Diane Fry, which was unusual. No last-minute instructions, telling him how to do his job while she was away.

He wondered what the problem was with Matt. Or with the family. That was what he'd said. That meant Kate – or more likely one of the girls, Amy and Josie. Matt was forever worrying about them, fretting over how they were doing at school, and what sort of friends they were making. Last time, it had been some concern about the youngest, Josie, just because she had an imaginary friend and talked to herself a bit. Then, Matt had convinced himself she was in the early stages of schizophrenia, the illness her grandmother had suffered from for so long. But that seemed to have passed over now, so it must be something else.

Well, he would find out sooner or later.

A beep announced another text coming in.

'Oh, for God's sake –'

Cooper breathed deeply, surprised by his sudden burst of irritation. His anger had no apparent target. It was just a text message. But the sound of the beep had been enough to cause a momentary surge of temper, a flush that passed rapidly across his temples. He took a few more breaths to calm himself, and checked his phone.

It was Liz again. That would be the fifth or sixth text from her today. Some people had nothing better to do with their thumbs.

The previous text had said: *CU 2nite? xox*

Liz had gone on to Twitter, too. Cooper suspected she was getting a bit obsessed with it. Sometimes, when he was with her in the pub, she would tweet on her mobile phone. Just to let her friends know that she was … well, with him.

The new text said: *so? 2 busy? :o*

Cooper thought that when they invented the English language, they should have included punctuation marks to indicate irony and sarcasm, instead bothering with stuff like semi colons, which no one ever used. Subtleties of tone were completely lost in a text message. It was so hard to tell what mood someone was in when their voice was inaudible.

Recently, Liz had been complaining that he was always too busy with work. She was a civilian Scenes of Crime officer, recently transferred to B Division in Buxton, which meant they didn't see each other in working hours any more. They'd been going out together for months now, and were pretty much considered a serious item. Marriage hadn't been mentioned out in the open. Not yet, anyway. But she'd met his family, and he'd been for dinner with her parents in Bakewell. It felt like there was an irresistible impetus to their relationship, which could only end in one way.

The trouble was, when they did get engaged, he was pretty sure Liz would announce it first on Twitter.

Well, at least Liz didn't blog, so far as he knew. Blogging was a minefield for a serving police officer. All over the country, bosses were getting paranoid after the chilling honesty and politically incorrect opinions of bloggers like Inspector Gadget and Night Jack. Attempts to preserve anonymity had been rejected by the High Court. A blog could get you into real trouble.

Cooper gave in to the psychological pressure and put down his phone to open a tin of Whiskas. Everyone had their own idea of priorities.

When Hope was satisfied, he poured himself a beer from the fridge and went back to his phone. He really didn't feel like going out tonight. In fact, he felt so unwell that he might be coming down with summer flu or something. Swine flu, even. You never knew.

Sorry, wiped out. Tomorrow, ok? xxx

He knew it wouldn't suit. He waited a while, sipping his beer and stroking the cat. But there was no reply, and finally he nodded off in front of the TV. He woke three hours later, realizing it was nearly bedtime.

'This is no good, Hope.'

He lay awake that night, expecting flashbacks. He didn't usually have trouble sleeping, the way he knew some of his colleagues did. It was those who lived alone that seemed to be unable to switch off from the job. A house full of kids didn't give you any option, he supposed. A family around provided all the support and distraction you could need. Far better than a reliance on alcohol, or worse.

But that wasn't his problem. It never had been before, except on rare occasions. So why was he lying here afraid to fall asleep, nervous of the dreams that might come in the darkness?

He had an appointment for a meeting with Superintendent Branagh in the morning. Now was not the time to suffer anxiety attacks.

Diane Fry knew she was only imagining the sirens. They were nothing more than a noise inside her head, an echo of the monotonous internal shriek that had been going on for days.

Mostly, during the daytime, she hardly noticed it. As long as she kept busy, and there were people around her, provided there were other sounds, the background din of normality … well, then she was fine. Absolutely fine. It was in the quiet moments that she heard it. Distant at first, like the high-pitched hum of an electric motor.

But gradually, it would grow nearer, forcing its way to the front of her mind, until the scream was loud enough to shatter her thoughts into fragments, like a glass splintered by a singer's high note. Then her head would throb with the noise, until her brain banged against the inside of her skull and the pain was intolerable. Once her concentration was destroyed, she could think of nothing but the shriek, feel only its pounding. It took over her whole body. It had her at its mercy.

The nights were the worst, of course. Always the worst. Any bad thing that ever happened in her life – well, it was always a lot worse in the dark, in the cold hours before dawn, when the world seemed to recede into the darkness and leave her totally alone. Then she had to listen to the radio, turn on the TV for the *Jeremy Kyle Show*, anything … anything to avoid the silence. She had to drive that noise back into the distance.

Fry turned over, pumped her pillow. Well, she supposed the sirens could be real. Edendale wasn't exactly crime free. More likely, though, it was some idiot who'd wrapped his car round a tree on the bend at the top of Castleton Road.

And then there were the voices. Voices that were coming gradually nearer. Right now, they were almost inaudible in the distance, like someone talking on the other side of a hill. She knew those voices would grow closer when she arrived in Birmingham. Then they would be too close. So close that they'd be right inside her head.

Immediately, she felt the sweat break out on her forehead. She cursed silently, knowing what was about to come.

Now that she was alone, the darkness would begin to close in around her, moving suddenly on her from every side, dropping like a heavy blanket, pressing against her body and smothering her with its warm, sticky embrace. Its weight would drive the breath from her lungs and pinion her limbs, draining the strength from her muscles.

Her eyes stretched wide, and her ears strained for noises as she felt her heart stumble and flutter, gripped with the old, familiar fear.

Around her, the night murmured with unseen things, hundreds of shiftings and stirrings that seemed to edge continually nearer, inch by inch, clear but unidentifiable. Next, her skin began to crawl with imagined sensations.

She had always known the old memories were still powerful and raw, ready to rise up and grab at her hands and face from the darkness, throwing her thoughts into turmoil and her body into immobility. Desperately, she would try to count the number of dark forms that loomed around her, mere smudges of silhouettes that crept ever nearer, reaching out to nuzzle her neck with their teeth and squeeze the air from her throat. Two, three … she was never sure how many.

And then she seemed to hear a voice in the darkness. A familiar voice, coarse and slurring in a Birmingham accent. 'It's a copper,' it said. Taunting laughter moving in the shadows. The same menace all around, whichever way she turned. 'A copper. She's a copper.'

5

Tuesday

In the CID room at Edendale next morning, the rest of the team were already hard at work over their reports when Cooper arrived. DC Luke Irvine and DC Becky Hurst were at the desks closest to his, and they nodded to him when he came in, their eyes full of questions.

Irvine and Hurst were the newest members of E Division CID, and they made Cooper feel like a veteran now that he was in his thirties. After a few years as beat and response officers, they'd been rushed into CID. That was an indication of the shortage of experienced staff. An entire new generation was coming into the police service, all Thatcher's children, born between 1979 and 1991. They had quite a different attitude to the older officers like Gavin Murfin.

They were eager to impress, too – anxious to get every last detail right in their reports and case files before their supervisor saw them. He had to give credit to Diane Fry for that. She had the new DCs with their noses to the grindstone. No one wanted to get on the wrong side of her.

Cooper supposed he might have been like Luke Irvine once, when he first got a chance to take off the uniform and work as a detective. Young and eager. How times had changed.

'DC Cooper. I hear it was rather a disturbing incident yesterday. Are you all right?'

The sudden stir in the room was accounted for by the arrival of their DI, Paul Hitchens, and Superintendent Branagh. Cooper found Branagh looming over his desk dressed in a black suit and white blouse, like a funeral director. Her shoulders were broad enough to carry a coffin on her own, too.

Cooper stood up. 'Yes, ma'am, thank you.'

'Your line manager should make sure you defuse. I know you weren't on duty, but even so. Then off to HR Service Centre – Care First, or a trained colleague supporter for a de-brief.'

34

'No, really. Thank you, ma'am, but I'm fine.'

'Well, everyone needs counselling services now and then. Perhaps a little leave? No? All right. Well done, anyway. Don't forget – see me in my office at nine.'

When Branagh had left, DI Hitchens put his hand on Cooper's shoulder.

'You do have to be aware of the fallout, Ben.'

'I'm sorry?'

'The psychological fallout.'

'Oh, I see.'

'So don't bottle it up. There are systems in place. Critical incident support. DS Fry should take care of it.'

Cooper nodded, accepting the good intentions, but hoping that no one would mention it again. Diane Fry had other things on her mind anyway.

'They say it's like falling off a horse,' said Murfin a few minutes later.

'What is?'

'Trauma. Getting over a traumatic incident. The thing to do is go back and put yourself in the same circumstances again. It's like when you fall off a horse – you have to get straight back on. Otherwise, you just get more afraid of doing it. It kind of builds up in your mind, the idea that you'll fall off every time. If you leave it long enough, it turns into a proper phobia, like.'

Cooper felt a surge of irrational anger, as if Murfin's comment was the final straw.

'Gavin, you're not a psychiatrist. You don't know what the Hell you're talking about.'

Murfin looked surprised at his irritability. But then he seemed to accept it, and looked thoughtful.

'Well, it couldn't be *exactly* the same circumstances,' he said. 'Not in this case, I grant you that. But the principle is the same. Trust me.'

'Thanks a lot, Gavin.'

No matter what anyone said to him, now was not the time to be showing any signs of weakness. It certainly wasn't the time to be taking leave from work, or asking for counselling. This was his one opportunity to prove himself – and if he didn't come up to scratch, he wasn't likely to get another chance. His failure would be marked down in his personal assessment, and reflect on him for ever.

So he had to suck it up. He mustn't let anyone see that he was affected in any way. Act normal. Be strong. That was the only way.

But Cooper had to admit to himself that he didn't feel entirely up to scratch. There was a slight tremor in his hands that hadn't been there before. When someone dropped a stapler in the office that morning, he jumped as if he'd been shot. That wasn't like him at all.

Fry had only come into the office to clear her desk. She watched Cooper get up and leave the CID room as nine o'clock came round. He was off for his appointment with Branagh.

'Gavin,' she said, 'did Ben meet the family of that girl who drowned? Has he mentioned it to you?'

'Well, he hasn't, as it happens,' said Murfin. 'He hasn't talked about it much. But, yes – I hear he went to the hospital in Derby. Even drove the family home afterwards.'

Fry sighed. 'He's getting personally involved.'

'I couldn't say.'

'Very loyal, Gavin.'

She dumped some files in her 'out' tray. They weren't all dealt with, but someone would pick them up when she'd gone.

'This family. I suppose they're another lost cause of his.'

'No. A nice, respectable middle-class family, from what I hear. You should try reading the bulletins.'

Fry scowled. 'How can you tell when a family is nice and respectable?'

'When the kids are well behaved. Respectful. I like that.'

'Oh?'

Murfin seemed to sense the way she was looking at him. 'What?'

'Oh, nothing.'

'Anyway – compared to my lot, some middle-class kids are a marvel. I wish somebody would write a parenting manual telling us how to turn out teenagers like that.'

Fry looked up as Cooper came back from the Super's office.

'Acting DS?' she said.

'Yes.'

'Well, I suppose ...' said Fry, struggling to find the right words to camouflage her doubts. She wasn't sure what she supposed. And she wasn't sure whether she cared, really.

'I've got the experience, Diane,' he said, defensively.

'Gavin has more than you.'

Fry knew it was a ridiculous thing to say, even before the sentence had left her mouth. The prospect of Gavin Murfin as Acting Detective Sergeant was so bizarre that it made the choice of Ben Cooper seem all the more preferable, even to her.

'Well, look after the kids, won't you?' she said.

'Of course.'

And she supposed he would. In fact, Cooper would probably ruin them for anything worthwhile in the course of a week. He'd pollute their minds by encouraging them to empathize, improvise, trust their instincts. Some nonsense like that. She'd have her work cut out to undo the damage when she came back from Birmingham. It might take her years to get them back in shape.

Fry sighed. Oh, well. God had sent Ben Cooper to her as a challenge, there was no doubt about that.

'I need to hand over this case to you. The drugs enquiry on the Devonshire Estate.'

'To me?'

'Yes, to you. Acting DS Cooper.'

'Right. That would be Michael Lowndes?'

'He's our initial suspect. But we believe he's low level. We haven't pulled him in because we want to identify the main players. We had an abortive surveillance operation yesterday. You heard about that?'

'Yes, Diane.'

'Our information was that he was due to meet up with his bosses yesterday to make one of his regular payments. But we slipped up, and lost him on the estate. He could have had somebody waiting to pick him up, we don't know. You'll need to see if you can get another shot at it. Okay?'

'Fine, I'll give it a go.'

Fry handed him the file reluctantly. She felt as if she was handing her purse to a mugger, and advising him how to spend the money.

'Diane, is it true you're going –'

'To Birmingham, yes.'

'I hope it goes well.'

'Thanks. Whatever that means.'

'Yeah.'

Fry turned away. The trouble was, no matter how clumsily he did it, Ben Cooper was always sincere.

Before she left the office, Fry relented and went over to give him some advice. Tips on how best to handle the team while she was away. Cooper nodded politely, even made a few notes. As if he actually thought she knew what she was doing.

'And don't worry about the thing yesterday,' she said. 'I know what you're like, Ben. But it was an accident, pure and simple. Not your responsibility. Don't get involved. Turn in your statement, and forget about it.'

'Right, Diane,' he said. 'Understood. Have a good trip.'

When Fry had picked up her things and left, Cooper called Murfin over. He was munching on a chocolate bar – what he called his second breakfast.

'Yes, new boss. What can I do for you? Pick up Michael Lowndes and give him the old rubber hose treatment, or what?'

'No, Gavin. I want you to get PNC print-outs for all the registered sex offenders in the Ashbourne area.'

Murfin stopped chewing. 'Are you looking for someone in particular?'

'Yes,' said Cooper. 'And I'll recognize him when I see him.'

To reach the A515 from Edendale, Cooper had a circuitous drive across Tideswell, Miller's Dale and Blackwell. One of the pleasantest drives in the Peak District, but he barely noticed it. The A515 was the road south, down out of the White Peak to Ashbourne.

Three-quarters of an hour later, Cooper was sitting down on a rather chintzy sofa in the Nields' lounge, facing a fireplace with a polished oak surround containing a living-flame gas fire – one of those things that were supposed to provide the impression of an open fire, but without any of the mess. Photographs of the family stood on a display mantel. At one end of the room, double doors stood open into a dining room with another bay window overlooking the rear garden. And, in the distance, he had another view of Thorpe Cloud.

'Have you lived here long, Mr Nield?' he asked.

'About two years.'

'But you're local, aren't you?'

'Oh, yes. We lived in Wetton before we came here.'

Cooper nodded. Wetton was a small village about ten miles northwest of Ashbourne, close to Dovedale itself.

'And you're a supermarket manager, is that right?'

'Yes, I manage an independent here in Ashbourne, called Lodge's. Do you know it?'

'I've heard of it, I think,' said Cooper.

'Well, that's something. A lot of people don't even realize there *are* independent supermarkets any more. We're a bit of a dying breed.'

'It's good to have independent businesses. Ashbourne is lucky.'

'Times are changing, I'm afraid. That sort of view sounds like pure nostalgia from a commercial point of view. There are too many supermarkets in Ashbourne now. The opening of Sainsbury's was the last straw. We can't all survive in this economic climate.'

'Do you think you'll close, then?'

'Probably,' said Nield. 'In the next year or two, perhaps sooner.'

'And will you be able to get a job at one of the other stores?'

He shook his head. 'I doubt it. I come from the wrong culture, you see. When the big chains take you on, they want to turn you into a Sainsbury's person, or a Tesco's person, or whatever it is. They need to own your soul, to make sure you're a team player.

I've had too many years outside their culture, you see. I'm tainted by too much independence.'

Mrs Nield had disappeared into the kitchen as soon as Cooper arrived. Not because she wanted to get out of his way, but because it seemed to give her something to do. Another woman was in there, slightly younger. Her sister.

'For one thing, I'm a big believer in sourcing local produce, wherever possible,' said Nield, perching on an armchair. 'Take bottled water. The Co-op here sells its own Fairbourne Springs, which comes from Wales. Somerfield's now, they stock water from Huddersfield and Shropshire.'

'Instead of …?'

'Well, Buxton spring water. That's what we sell at Lodge's. Locally produced, you see. Of course, we used to stock Ashbourne water, but that went the way of all things, when Nestlé closed the factory. It's like everything else. Too much competition.'

Cooper was conscious that he was filling in time, besides letting Robert Nield talk about something other than the death of his daughter. But he was waiting for Mrs Nield to return before he asked his real questions.

'Where is your own store, sir?'

'Out on the Derby Road. You know where you turn off to the Airfield Industrial Estate? We're there. We used to be in the centre of town too, of course. But rents got a bit high for us.'

Mrs Nield brought a tray of cups in. Proper cups and saucers, something he never bothered with at home.

'Mrs and Mrs Nield,' said Cooper as she poured the tea, 'I'm sorry to ask you questions at a time like this. I know you've made statements for Sergeant Wragg, but could I ask you to go over again what happened in Dovedale yesterday?'

Dawn sat in the chair next to her husband, and grasped his hand for reassurance.

'We didn't really see what happened. Not exactly,' said Dawn. 'We told the sergeant. It must have happened very quickly.'

'Yes, I understand that,' said Cooper.

Nield nodded. 'I understand why you need to know, DC Cooper. Or could we call you Ben?'

'Yes, of course.'

40

'It seems that our dog, Buster, ran into the water to fetch a stick. Emily ran in after the dog.'

'Who threw the stick?'

'We're not sure. One of the children.'

'And you saw Emily go into the water?'

'Not really. We were chatting on the bank. I think I was watching out for Alex – he tends to wander off on his own, you know. The next thing I knew, someone shouted, and when I looked round Buster was coming out of the river, shaking himself, spraying water everywhere. And then we realized we couldn't see Emily.'

He paused, appeared to be doing his best to recall events accurately.

'Go on, sir.'

'Well, I suppose it was a minute or two before we realized what had happened. We thought she was just hiding behind a rock or something. Children play like that, don't they? But … she wasn't playing.'

Dawn had brought out the tissues again while her husband was speaking. Cooper was beginning to feel uncomfortable, but there was an important point here.

'If I've got this right, Mr Nield, you didn't actually see Emily go into the water, and you didn't see her fall or hit her head on a rock?'

'I suppose that's true. But that's what happened, isn't it? Well, isn't it?'

'Yes, I'm sure it was,' said Cooper, because that was what you said in these circumstances. 'One more thing – did you happen to see anyone near your daughter in Dovedale? A stranger?'

They shook their heads.

'No,' said Nield. 'Well, there were a lot of people around. All of them were strangers, I suppose.'

'But no one in particular showing an interest in her?'

'Not that I remember. Dawn?'

'No, sorry,' she said. 'What is this about? These are strange questions to be asking. I don't understand them.'

'I'm just trying to clear up the details.'

41

Mrs Nield rose unsteadily and left the room. Cooper took a drink of his tea, found it was already starting to get cold.

'She'll be all right,' said Nield. 'It takes a bit of time.'

'I know.' Cooper looked out of the window at the outline of Thorpe Cloud. 'By the way, what was Alex doing when the accident happened?'

'Taking photographs, I think,' said Nield. 'We bought him a digital camera for his birthday. He loads them on to his computer and creates effects with them. He has some software. I'm not sure what they call it ...'

'Photoshop?'

'That's it. He's very creative, you know.'

'So what was he taking photos of in Dovedale?'

'I don't really know. Rocks, water, trees.'

'Not people?'

'No. He isn't really interested in that. He likes to look for patterns. You know – the bark on a tree, moss on a stone, sunlight through the leaves. He makes images from them, and uses them as background on his computer screen.'

Nield smiled at Cooper.

'There are a lot worse things that a boy of his age could be doing, aren't there?'

'Yes.' Cooper smiled back. 'I was thinking, Alex might have caught a few people in the background. If he was taking photographs of the river, for example. There were so many people around that day, it would be hard to avoid them altogether.'

Nield frowned. 'Well, I suppose so. But he would edit them out. Why are you so interested?'

How to explain to him? How to tell the father that he would like to track down some more witnesses to what had happened? Independent witnesses, whose memories might not yet have been distorted. Well, he couldn't. Cooper hesitated for a few moments, then backed off.

'Oh, no reason. Just in case there were any loose ends.'

Nield was still frowning, but before he could ask whatever question was on the tip of his tongue, his wife came back into the room. She looked better, as if she'd splashed cold water on her facer and combed her hair. It always helped, somehow.

'How is Alex?' asked Cooper.

'A bit quiet,' she said. 'Do you want to talk to him?'

'Well ...'

'He'd be glad to see you. He quite took to you yesterday.'

'Really?'

'He said he thinks your job must be interesting.'

Cooper suspected that Alex Nield was probably just another teenager who'd watched too many episodes of *CSI* and *The Wire* to have an accurate picture of what police work was all about in Derbyshire.

'Go on up,' said Nield. 'He's in his room. Second door on the left. He'll only be playing on his computer.'

'You're sure you don't mind? He's a minor. Strictly speaking, I shouldn't talk to him without one of you being present.'

Nield laughed. 'You're not going to interrogate him, are you? It'll do him good to talk to someone outside the family. And it might get him away from that computer screen for a few minutes.'

Cooper looked at Mrs Nield, who nodded. Well, it was against procedure, but he was doing it at the request of the family. It would be a private conversation, not an interview with a witness. As long as he kept it that way, he'd be fine.

On the first floor of the Nields' house, he found a galleried landing, and counted the doors to five bedrooms. One door stood open, and when he glanced in he saw a desk, laptop, bookshelves, a small filing cabinet. Two of the others had small ceramic name plaques on them. He knocked on the door bearing Alex's name in Gothic lettering, and got a muffled 'yeah'. He took that as an invitation to enter.

The boy was sitting at a desk in front of a PC screen, his legs curled round the seat of his chair. On the screen, Cooper saw a graphic representation of a medieval castle with individual buildings inside its walls – a barracks, a stable, a granary and warehouse.

'What is it you're playing?'

'*War Tribe.* It's a morpeg.'

'Oh, okay.'

Alex snorted, as if he was used to adults just pretending they understood what he was saying. But Cooper thought he might have a bit of an advantage.

'An MMORPG.' he said. 'A Massive Multi-player Online Role-Playing Game.'

'Mm. Yeah.'

'They're usually programmed in PHP, aren't they? What browser are you using?'

'Safari.'

'That's good.'

Alex gave him a sly sidelong look. Cooper decided it was the moment to shut up. It was best not to push his luck too far. The boy would open up, if he wanted to.

Cooper noticed he was using a *War Tribe* mouse mat with a screen shot from the game.

Hanging on the side of the wardrobe was a white T-shirt with the slogan *Cranny Up, Noob!*

'Where did you get the mouse mat?'

'Uh, they have a Café Press website. You can get all kinds of stuff there.'

'Right.'

He felt like adding 'cool'. But it might, or might not, be the wrong expression this month.

Down one side of the screen was an inventory of resources – iron, wood, wheat – and a list of the troops available. He saw that this particular castle contained three thousand axemen and a thousand mounted knights.

'Are you online a lot?'

'You have to be, to build up your cities and watch out for attacks. Anyway, if you're offline too long you go yellow, and you get kicked from your tribe.'

'Right. And that would be a bad thing.'

'Of course. You've got to be in a tribe.'

'Absolutely.'

'Anyway, I'm not online as much as the big players. Some of the guys play on their mobiles,' said Alex.

'Oh, okay. But not you?'

'My phone is too old. It's rubbish.'

44

'Maybe your dad will buy you a new one.'

'Yeah, right.'

'So what's your log-in name?'

Alex narrowed his eyes. 'You're not going to ask me for my password, are you? That's wrong. Besides, it's illegal.'

'Illegal?'

'In the game. You can get banned for sharing your password.'

'Why?'

'People try to bend the rules all the time. They try anything to get an advantage. Even blackmail.'

'You're joking.'

'Oh, yeah. Big players threaten to catapult your cities unless you give them resources.'

'A protection racket.'

'That's illegal too, though.'

'Well, I don't want to know your password. I only wondered what you call yourself.'

'I'm Smoke Lord.'

'Really? But you don't smoke, do you?'

'What, cigarettes? Of course not. It means your cities will be smoking ruins after I've attacked them.'

'With your catapults?'

A lock of dark hair fell over his face as he turned to stare at the screen again.

'I'm a Gaul,' he said. 'I have fire catapults.'

'And attacking people and setting fire to their cities isn't illegal?'

'Don't be stupid. It's the whole point of the game. It's called *War Tribe*. It's a war game.'

'Yes, that *was* a stupid question,' admitted Cooper. 'I think I must be out of my depth.'

'I guess so.'

Cooper stood up. 'Do your parents not mind you playing on the computer all the time?'

Alex snorted. 'They keep a check on me, if that's what you mean. They've got a lock on it. Parental controls. And while I'm at school, Mum comes into my room and checks my browser history, to see what sites I've been looking at. Can you believe that?'

'Mum likes to be the one in control, does she?'

'Too true. You ought to see her at meal times.'

Cooper could sense the boy starting to close up. He decided it wasn't the best time to ask Alex about the photographs he'd taken in Dovedale. He left the teenager to his game and went back downstairs.

'Thank you, Mr and Mrs Nield. I think I've bothered you enough. I'm sorry to have intruded.'

'It's all right,' said Dawn. 'It helps to talk, to have things to do. You've got to keep busy at a time like this. There's no point in turning inwards.'

Cooper could see that she was the sort of woman would who put her energies into organizing things, into organizing anyone who came within her orbit. But the danger was that the grief would hit her later – perhaps at the funeral, or in the long, dreadful weeks to come. He searched for something to say that wouldn't sound too trite.

'Well, be thankful that you still have your oldest child.'

'What?' she said.

'Alex.'

'Oh. Yes.'

There was an awkward moment when they looked at each other in embarrassed silence, neither having any idea what to say.

Cooper knew that he'd been taking advantage of his position with the Nields. They would probably have reacted quite differently to a police officer who didn't happen to be the man who'd tried to save their daughter's life. They wouldn't have talked so readily, been willing to answer those questions all over again without suspicion. But he'd pushed their gratitude as far as he could. It was time for him to leave.

But Mrs Nield touched his arm as he paused on the door step.

'Ben – you'll come to the funeral, won't you?' she said.

Cooper said goodbye to the Nields, and found his way out of Ashbourne. He thought back to the few minutes he'd spent with Alex. The boy was clearly absorbed in some other universe that his parents probably knew nothing about, and wouldn't understand if

46

they did. Interesting that so many things were illegal, or against the rules in the *War Tribe* universe. But he supposed there must be plenty of people who set out to be bullies, cheats and liars. Just like real life, in fact.

On the way out of town, Ashbourne's confusing one-way system took him past the fire station. The alarm was sounding at the station. Two retained firemen jogged up the road, and a third arrived on a bicycle.

He wondered if Alex Nield's online world had an imaginary fire brigade that would rush to put out the conflagrations caused by imaginary fire catapults. He supposed not. It was far too exciting to watch your enemies burn. As any teenage boy knew, destruction was so much fun.

6

Nearly two hours after leaving Edendale, Fry turned off the M6 at the Gravelly Hill interchange, the vast tangle of flyovers and slip roads known everywhere as Spaghetti Junction. In a couple of minutes she was on the Aston Expressway, eating up the tarmac on those two final miles of motorway that led right into the heart of the city.

It was morning rush hour. That was something she'd forgotten. She was sitting in a sea of carbon monoxide all the way from Sutton Coldfield to the Bull Ring. Tasting those fumes made Fry conscious of how she'd begun to acclimatize to her new home in Derbyshire. Up there in the hills, you could actually smell the air. You knew you were breathing oxygen.

In a way, the Expressway was a perfect introduction to Birmingham. It seemed to sum up all the city's quirks and contradictions. This was the only stretch of motorway in the country with no central reservation. Instead, it had a seventh lane in the middle, which worked in opposite directions at peak times – a tidal-flow system, controlled by arrows on the overhead gantries. According to legend, one of these gantries used to contain a pipeline carrying vinegar from one part of the HP Sauce factory to another across the Expressway. Once, the pipeline had sprung a leak, and the paintwork of dozens of passing cars had been ruined by vinegar rain. Or so the story went. It could just be a bit of Brummie folklore.

It was difficult to sum Birmingham up, though. Fry had heard many clichés about the place. Workshop of the Empire, Venice of the North, city of a thousand trades. Oh, and birthplace of heavy metal. Well, that last one was probably right. It probably dated from the time when four lads from Aston decided to become Black Sabbath. Ozzy Osbourne was some kind of god in these parts. They had even preserved the terraced house in Lodge Road where he grew up and first got himself into trouble as a disaffected youth.

She switched on the radio, and tuned it to BBC WM, where the Breakfast Show was just finishing. The presenter's voice sounded familiar. He was another former student of UCE, one of the local success stories they often talked about. She couldn't remember his name.

When her phone rang, she recognized Gareth Blake's voice straight away. It was that voice, those smooth tones, that had told her they intended to re-open her rape case.

'Diane, can you talk?'

'Yes, I'm hands free.'

'Good. Are you in Birmingham?'

'On the Expressway,' said Fry.

'Brilliant. I'm really pleased that you made this decision, Diane.'

'In a way, it was made for me.'

'Oh? You're not feeling under any obligation, are you? We haven't put any undue pressure on you?'

That was typical of Blake. Covering all the bases, trying not to put a foot wrong. No one could ever claim that DI Gareth Blake hadn't gone by the book.

'No, don't worry. I'm on board.'

'That's good, Diane.' He sounded relieved. 'We've set up a meeting with the team this afternoon at two o'clock. In Lloyd House. You know where it is?'

'Gareth, I worked in Birmingham, remember?'

'Of course, of course. Well … Colmore Circus. You'll find it. The other thing is – Rachel Murchison would like to touch base with you before the meeting. Talk to her, won't you? The sooner the better. She's waiting for your call, Diane.'

Fry exited the Expressway and found her way via back streets through Aston and Newtown. Aston Cross was unrecognizable without the familiar background of the HP Sauce factory. Its old site was now just an expanse of soil and rubble.

Her last posting in the West Midlands had been here, as a detective constable based at Queens Road. D1 OCU, the Operational Command Unit for Aston.

The building still looked the same. Marked police vehicles stood out front. Round the back, she knew, parking places were marked in strict hierarchical order from the entrance – Chief

Superintendent, Superintendent, DCI, Chief Inspector, right down to the IT department.

She wondered if every cell in the custody suite still had the Crimestoppers number printed on a wall just inside the door. Somebody must once have decided that a prisoner in the cells might use his one call to report a crime. Hope sprang eternal, even in a custody suite.

Fry frowned at the boarded-up wreck of a pub under the shadow of the Expressway. She couldn't recall its name, or whether she'd ever drunk there when she worked at Queens Road. Maybe they'd tended to go into The Adventurers a few yards down from the nick. Some memories were just lost, she supposed.

Driving up Aston Road North reminded her of a snippet passed on by one of the lecturers over coffee during her course in Criminal Justice and Policing at UCE. Apparently, Sir Arthur Conan Doyle had lived on this very road when he was a poor medical student, helping out a local doctor. That was pre Sherlock Holmes, of course. She might even remember the name of the doctor, if she tried not to think about it.

This was part of her old patch when she was in uniform, and later as a divisional DC. She ought to know this area well, but things had changed. New buildings had gone up, entire streets had disappeared. Worse, every pub she remembered in this area seemed to have closed. The Waterloo in Wills Street, the Royal Oak on Lozells Road, even the Cross Guns in Newtown. All gone, and more besides.

But Birmingham had always been a work in progress. The city's oldest buildings came down faster than new ones went up. The old Bull Ring shopping centre had been state of the art, not many decades ago. The early seventies, maybe? The late sixties? But the place had already been looking tired when Fry herself had hung around its walkways and escalators as a teenager. Now the city had a new Bull Ring. Borders and Starbucks, and the rippling metallic girdle of Selfridges, known to locals as the Dalek's Ballgown. Award-winning, that Selfridges design. A sign of Brum's arrival in the twenty-first century. But how many years would it last, before Birmingham decided to move on, ripped it down and stuck up something new?

She checked her watch. She was early yet. Not that they would mind her arriving a bit sooner than expected. They would probably be delighted. She could imagine them chuckling with excitement in the hall, fussing around her, patting her arm, ushering her into an armchair while the kettle boiled. But she wasn't quite ready for that yet.

Beyond the underpass at Perry Barr, she turned into the One-Stop shopping centre and parked up. Inside the mall, she walked past Asda and Boots, and out into the bus station.

She had studied for her degree in Criminal Justice and Policing at UCE, the University of Central England, right here in Perry Barr. From the bus station, she had a good view of her old alma mater, though it had now been renamed Birmingham City University. She could see the Kenrick Library and the golden lion emblem high on the main building of the City North campus.

Instead of going back to her car, she crossed to the other side of the bus station and walked towards Perry Barr railway station, past a few shops that stood between here and the corner of Wellington Road – The Flavour of Love Caribbean takeaway, Nails2U, the Hand of God hair salon.

But there was no point in avoiding the call. She was caught up in the machine now, had voluntarily thrown herself into the mechanisms of the criminal justice system, and she had no escape.

'Diane, are you well?' said Murchison, answering her phone instantly, as if she had indeed been sitting at her desk waiting for it to ring.

'Yes, I'm fine.'

'I just wanted a few words with you, before our meeting this afternoon.'

'You just wanted to make sure I was actually on my way, perhaps?'

'No. I think you've made the commitment now. I'm sure you won't change your mind. But if you do –'

'I won't,' said Fry.

'All right. Well, I know you might be feeling isolated and vulnerable at the moment. But don't forget, you're not alone in this. We're all on your side. Any support you need is available, twenty-four hours a day. Anything you want to talk about is fine. Don't hold it back. Call me, any time.'

'Thank you. That's very kind.'

'Don't worry, Diane. It's my job.'

Fry winced, wondering if she had just received the hand-off, the subtle reminder that this wasn't a personal relationship but a professional one. She supposed that counsellors, like psychiatrists, had to be wary of relationships with their clients, and draw firm boundaries. Some of the people Murchison dealt with must be very needy.

Below her, the yellow front end of a London Midland City train whirred into the Birmingham platform of the station.

'There's a lot of noise in the background,' said Murchison. 'Where are you?'

'Perry Barr.'

Murchison was silent for a moment. Fry thought she had shocked her in some way. But Perry Barr wasn't that bad, was it?

'Diane, is there a particular reason you're in Perry Barr?'

'Yes, a personal one.'

She thought she could hear Murchison shuffling papers.

'May I ask …?'

'I'm visiting someone. Family.'

'Oh. That would be … your foster parents?'

'Well done.'

'That's all right.'

'I know it's all right. I don't need your permission to visit them.'

'No, no. Of course not.'

'I'm just calling in for a cup of tea. So you can tell Gareth Blake I'm behaving myself.'

Murchison laughed. Fry thought she heard relief in her voice.

'I'll tell him. And we'll see you later, yes?'

'Of course. After I've checked into my hotel.'

Fry watched people hurrying down the concrete steps to the platform and getting on to the train. She thought about following them, getting on the train and riding past Aston, past Duddeston and right into New Street. As if she could ride by everything, without even a glance out of the window, and start all over again.

But she stood for too long at the top of the steps, and the train pulled out, the noise of its motor dying as an echo on the brick walls.

'Diane,' said Murchison finally, 'everything will be all right.'

Fry ended the call, and looked around. Opposite her stood three tower blocks surviving from an early 1960s attempt at low-cost housing. A number 11 bus emerged from Wellington Road in a burst of exhaust fumes. A strong smell of burning rubber hung on the air from the plastics factory on Aston Lane.

She walked under the flyover and emerged on the Birchfield Road side. Kashmir Supermarkets and Haroun's mobile phones. Money-transfer services and lettings agencies for student flats. Outside Amir Baz & Sons boxes of vegetables were stacked on the pavement. Fry stopped to look at some of the labels. *Bullet Chilli. Surti Ravaiya.*

Now she felt lost. Nothing seemed to be recognizable. The street signs still pointed to UCE, but there was no point in following them. When you got there, you would find it had ceased to exist. Its name had been consigned to history.

The disappearance of so many landmarks gave her a strange sense of dislocation. Birmingham had been changing behind her back while she'd been away. This was no longer the place that she'd known. The Brum she saw around her was a different city from the one that she'd left. It was as if someone had broken into her previous life when she wasn't looking and tried to wipe out her memories with a wrecking ball and a bulldozer.

But then, it was probably true the other way round. She wasn't the same person who'd left Birmingham, either.

The Bowskills were the family she'd lived with the longest. She'd spent years in the back bedroom of their red-brick detached house in Warley. She'd been there when Angie ran away and disappeared. And she'd stayed with the Bowskills after her sister had gone. She'd needed them more than ever when she no longer had Angie to cling to.

And those times in Warley had been happy, in a way. Fry clearly remembered window shopping with her friends at Merry

Hill, touring the Birmingham clubs, and drinking lager while she listened to the boys talking about West Bromwich Albion. Jim and Alice Bowskill had done their best, and she would forever be grateful to them. There had always been that hole in her life, though. Always.

There had been other homes, of course. Some of them she remembered quite well. She particularly recalled a spell with a foster family who'd run a small-scale plant nursery in Halesowen, and another placement near the canal in Primrose Hill, where the house always seemed to be full of children. But those families were further back in her past, too far upstream to re-visit.

Jim and Alice Bowskill now lived in a semi-detached house with a vague hint of half-timbering, located on the Birchfield side of Perry Barr, the close-packed streets in a triangle bounded by Birchfield Road and Aston Lane.

As she drove towards it along Normandy Road, Fry had a good view of the Trinity Road stand at Villa Park, reminding her that Aston was only a stone's throw from this part of Perry Barr. Here, everyone was a Villa fan.

There seemed to be home improvements going on everywhere in these streets. She saw an old armchair standing by the side of the road, bags of garden rubbish lined up at the kerb.

Most of these houses had been built at a time when the people who lived in them weren't expected to own cars. So there were very few garages and hardly any off-street parking. It took her a few minutes to find somewhere to leave her Audi.

Jim Bowskill was wearing his Harrington jacket. Well, surely not the original Harrington – the one she always remembered seeing him in. It would have been worn out by now. But he was a man who had never been without a Harrington. He once told her he'd started wearing one as a mod in the 1960s, and just found that he never grew out of them.

When he reached his mid fifties, he'd thought for a while about having a change. But then he'd seen Thierry Henry wearing one in the Renault adverts, and that was it.

The current Harrington was a classic tan colour, with the Fraser tartan lining and elasticated cuffs. Seeing it made Fry feel an intense burst of affection for him. It was probably just nostalgia – a vague memory of hugging a coat just like that.

He was a lot greyer than she remembered him. Slightly stooped now, too.

'Hello, love. It's good to see you. We haven't seen much of you since you left to go to Derbyshire. Having a good time away from us, I suppose?'

He said it teasingly, but Fry felt sure there was more than a hint of genuine reproach. She immediately felt guilty. She thought of all the reasons she'd given herself over the past few years for not keeping in touch with her foster parents, and all of them seemed petty and contrived.

Fry supposed she'd only been trying to justify her reluctance to herself. But she shouldn't have made Jim and Alice the victims of her self-justification.

'No, I'm sorry. I've been so busy.'

'We understand.'

Fry knew from the tone of his voice that he saw the lie, and forgave her. And that just made her feel even more guilty.

Jim Bowskill had been sorting out his blue recycling box for the weekly refuse collection.

'How do you like it here?' asked Fry.

'Oh, it suits me. The house isn't too big, so it's easy to maintain. And there are lots of shops. We didn't have the One-Stop shopping centre when you were here before, did we?'

'Yes, Dad. It's been there for fifteen years.'

He nodded. 'And there are plenty of bus routes, if I need to go anywhere. So, all in all, it's very handy.'

The Bowskills moved from Warley to Perry Barr some time after she left home to live on her own. She wasn't sure why – though Alice's family was originally from this part of North Birmingham, so maybe it was another case of nostalgia, a woman drawn back to the past by those lingering memories.

In a way, this part of Perry Barr had come full circle. When the indigenous white community had first started selling their houses, the Indian immigrants had moved in. As the Indians became more prosperous, they'd moved on to other areas, and Pakistanis had come in. When the Pakistanis sold their houses, the

Bengalis had replaced them. And now here was Jim Bowskill, living in his double-fronted semi off Canterbury Road, explaining that it was easy to maintain and handy for the shops, and close to a bus route, if he needed it. And it was in the heart of Perry Barr's Bengali area.

Fry knew better than to talk about the Asian community round here. If you looked for an Asian community, you wouldn't find it. Instead you'd see a whole series of Asian communities – Pakistanis, Bengalis, Hindus. And even within the nationalities, the complexities of caste and locality were impossible for an outsider to sort out.

In some parts of the country, there were entire populations who had come from a handful of villages in one small region of Pakistan. The more you learned, the more you realized how undiscriminating the very word Asian was. It was a pretty big continent, after all. And she knew that no one around here would readily call themselves Asian. It was an outsider's term.

And everyone knew there was a pecking order among the different ethnic groups. The cycle that had played itself out in Perry Barr over the years was repeated in other parts of Birmingham. Newly arrived immigrants lived in the poorest streets, until they could to move on to better areas and bigger houses. These days, the leafy avenues of Solihull were full of Hindu millionaires.

Once an Asian parent had explained it to her:

'In the old days, we thought we would come here, send some money back and eventually go home. But the new generation don't see it that way. A lot of people don't consider this the host country any more, they consider it their home.'

'But sometimes the old country is home, too, isn't it?'

He smiled. 'Yes. Sometimes when people say "home" you have to ask which home they're talking about.'

Alice Bowskill looked frail. She wasn't that old, really. But time hadn't been kind to her. Nor had the years spent worrying over other people's children.

Fry hugged her.

'Mum.'

Jim smiled at them both, delighted to see them together.

'Do you still support West Brom, Diane?' he said.

'Me?' said Fry. 'I never did, not really.'

'It was just because the boys did,' said Alice with a sly grin. Fry almost felt like blushing.

'Not the Blues, surely?' said Jim, missing the significance of his wife's comment.

Of course, Jim Bowskill was another Villa fan. She wondered if that was part of the reason for the Bowskills moving to Perry Bar, so close to Villa Park? There were pubs round here where a Blue Nose would be torn apart at first sight.

But she wasn't a Birmingham City fan. She wasn't actually from Birmingham. She wondered how long it would be before some Brummie looked at her sideways and uttered the immortal phrase: 'A yam-yam, ain't you?'

There was no point in trying to deny it. People in these parts were acutely sensitive to the differences in accent that marked you out as Black Country. In a way, she was as much of a foreigner in Brum as she was back in Derbyshire. 'Not from round here' might as well be permanently tattoo'd on her forehead.

The Black Country was the name given to the urban sprawl west of the city of Birmingham. It encompassed old industrial towns like Wolverhampton, West Bromwich, Dudley, Sandwell and Walsall. And many smaller communities, too – like Warley, where Fry had lived with her foster parents, and which was nothing but a string of housing estates tucked between Birmingham and the M5 motorway.

In some ways, those small Black Country communities were far worse than the estates of inner city Birmingham. Some of them were completely cut off, isolated by the collapse of the manufacturing industries from the affluence evident in the new apartment blocks, the new Bull Ring shopping centre, stacked to the roof with consumer goods and designer labels. It was in places like West Bromwich, rather than Birmingham itself, that the BNP were getting a foothold. It was there they found the disaffected white working classes, desperate to find a voice.

Jim sighed. 'Moved allegiance altogether, I suppose. It's Derby County, then. Tragic.'

'Dad, I don't even like football.'

There weren't many people like Jim and Alice, who would be willing to take on other people's children, especially when many of those children were deeply troubled and disruptive. It took a lot of dedication and commitment. A lot of love.

She wondered about some of the other foster children who'd passed through the Bowskills' lives. There must have been many of them. She supposed that most of them kept in touch better than she ever had. It had been too easy for her to forget the debt she owed them. She'd been too quick to put everything behind her when she moved from the West Midlands, cast the good aside with the bad when she started a new life in Derbyshire.

Fry remembered the Bowskills reluctantly producing her birth certificate when she needed to register at college. They themselves had obtained it from her social worker, by special request. Only her mother's name had been on the certificate, the space to record the father left blank. It seemed her parents had never married, so the surname she carried was her mother's, not that of an adoptee.

Then she thought about the one child the Bowskills *had* adopted. Perhaps tired of saying goodbye to those they'd cared for over the years, they had fought to keep one particular boy, a few years younger than Fry. He was called Vincent, a quiet boy born to an Irish mother and a Jamaican father. He had been with Jim and Alice after Fry had left to set up home on her own and pursue her career in the police. The Bowskills' last commitment, the one final object of their love.

The children's charity Barnardos had said recently that there was too much focus on trying to 'fix' families, when it would often be in the best interests of the children to put them up for adoption straight away when there was a problem. And by 'straight away' they meant at birth.

Parents who'd failed to care properly for older children would not be allowed to bring up younger ones. It seemed to Fry that there was a definite logic in the argument.

And yet Vincent Bowskill had made the wrong friends, had been attracted to a way of life that the Bowskills deplored. Something had still gone wrong, in spite of their best efforts. So despite what the experts said, could there be some genetic influence that would always flow in the blood? Blood, they said, was thicker than water.

Or maybe it was because there was no easy way for a boy like Vince to fit into a society that liked to put everyone in a category.

Fry knew that mixed-race people were an elephant in the room – the fastest-growing ethnic minority in Britain, more numerous than black Caribbean or black African. Yet it was only in the 2001 census that they were given an ethnic category of their own. They were obvious to anybody living in a large British city, yet invisible at a political level.

In multicultural Britain, the fact that more and more people were having children across racial divides was an inconvenient truth. It didn't fit with the concept of neat communities of black, white or Asian.

And that could be a problem for boys like Vincent Bowskill. These days, black and white kids tended not to call each other racial names. But the mixed-race kids got it from both sides. Many of them were fated to spend their entire lives searching for an identity.

'So how is Vince?' she said, as Jim sat down with her.

'Oh, you know – fine.'

'Really?'

'Well, to be honest, he's always been a bit of a worry to us. But he does his best. He's a good lad, at heart.'

'He isn't involved with a gang, is he?'

'No, no. Well, we don't think so.'

Fry realized Jim Bowskill might find it difficult to tell what sort of circles his adopted son moved in. When Vincent came here to visit, he wouldn't be displaying his gang tattoos and waving a gun around. He'd be well behaved, polite.

And maybe … just maybe, he'd actually turned his life around and moved on. It was possible to do that.

'Should I look him up while I'm here?'

'Vince?' Jim looked doubtful. 'Oh, you don't have to, Diane. But –'

'I'll see if I have time.'

'All right.'

She knew she had to broach the one subject they hadn't touched on, the one the Bowskills were shying away from.

'You know why I'm here in Birmingham, don't you?' she said.

'Yes, you told us. The case.'

'You'll let us know how it goes, won't you?' said Alice. 'Don't stay out of touch, Diane.'

She sounded even frailer than she looked. Fry hoped Alice wasn't worrying herself too much about something she couldn't do anything about.

Fry looked out of the bay window into the street. All the people passing were Bengalis. She hadn't seen a white face all the time she'd been here.

'Dad,' she said, 'what's *Surti Ravaiya?*'

'Oh, it's a type of Indian eggplant. You serve it stuffed.'

'Thanks.'

'Why? Are you developing an interest in cooking?'

'No.'

Jim Bowskill looked at her oddly. 'You know, you haven't changed, Diane.'

She turned back to the room. 'What do you mean?'

'I remember you when you were a teenager. You were always a very distant girl – so self-contained. It was hard for anyone to get you to open up. No matter how hard we tried, Alice and me, we never really understood what you were thinking, or feeling. You're the same now. You're still that teenage girl.'

'I'm sorry, Dad. I don't know what to say.'

'Do you remember that friend you had at school? Janet Dyson. Your best friend, she was.'

Fry shook her head. 'Janet …?'

'Dyson. Pretty girl, with long dark hair. Her father ran the taxi firm.'

'I don't remember her.'

'You must do,' said Jim. 'She was your best friend. You used to walk out of school holding hands sometimes. It was very sweet.'

'How old was I?'

'Eight or nine.'

'It's too long ago, Dad.'

'I can't believe you've forgotten. We remember everything about you.'

'Well, you must have kept a photograph album. She'll be in there, this girl. I bet you've been getting it out to remind yourselves before I arrived.'

'No, no.' He tapped his temple. 'It's all up here. All we have are our memories. They're what make us the people we are.'

Fry was puzzled. 'Why are you bringing this girl up now?'

'Janet Dyson? Well, we wondered why you fell out with her. You suddenly stopped being best friends with her, and we never found out why. You wouldn't tell us. We thought, well … now that so much time has passed, we thought you might tell us what happened.'

'Dad, I have no idea.'

He sighed. 'Still the same Diane.'

'Dad, honestly – I have no idea. I can't remember what happened. It can't have been anything very important, can it?'

'If you say so, love.'

After a while, Fry looked at her watch and decided it was time to prise herself away. Refusing all offers of more tea, she got up to leave, then hesitated in the doorway.

'So … is there a photograph album?'

'Well, I think so,' said Jim. 'Do you want to see it?'

She thought for a moment, mentally recoiled as she imagined the album's contents. Happy, laughing snaps of herself and Angie, skinny teenagers in jeans and puffa jackets. Sunburned on holidays in Weston-super-Mare, dressed up in their best frocks for some cousin's wedding.

'Another time, Dad,' she said.

On the corner of Trinity Road stood a *masjid*, a community mosque. This was the one that had originally been named the Saddam Hussein Mosque, after the Iraqi leader donated two million pounds to build it. During the first Gulf War, the *masjid* had been fire-bombed, and excrement wrapped in pages of the Koran had been pushed through the letter box during prayers.

When the second war came round, elders had decided to change the name, and now it was simply *Jame Masjid*, the main mosque.

Just behind it, Fry could see the little parade of shops where Burger Bar Boys in a Ford Mondeo had sprayed bullets from two MAC-10 machine pistols, killing Letisha Shakespeare and Charlene Ellis as they left a New Year party, and putting the city firmly in the headlines.

She supposed it was natural for her to worry about Jim and Alice Bowskill living in this area. Everyone worried about their parents. For a moment, she wondered if she ought to check whether they were registered with the Birchfield Dental Practice or the Churchill Medical Centre, if they used the post office here, or the one in Perry Barr. But it didn't really matter.

Fry turned on to Trinity Road and headed towards Aston. In the few hundred yards drive between the *Jame Masjid* and Villa Park, she passed the Ozzy Osbourne birthplace. The mosque, football, and heavy metal. Well, that came as close to summing up Birmingham as anything she could think of.

7

On his way back from the Nields, Cooper called at the Ashbourne section station on Compton. He spotted the blue lamp over its door right next to the Wheel Inn.

Seeing the Wheel reminded Cooper that he'd once had a memorable duty in Ashbourne, many moons ago, when he was drafted in to help police the world's oldest, largest, longest and maddest football game. Several thousand people turned up every year for Ashbourne's Royal Shrovetide Football – and that was just the players.

From an objective point of view, the event was basically a moving brawl, which seethed backwards and forwards through the streets of the town, across fields, and even along the bed of the river. The game lasted for two days, with goals three miles apart on opposite sides of the town. If you visited Ashbourne on those days, you had to be careful where you parked your car.

Of course, the pubs remained open all day, all the shops and banks boarded up their windows, and some closed completely, making the town look as though major civil unrest was taking place. Which, from a policing point of view, it was. There had been intermittent attempts to ban the game because of its violent nature. But it had been going on for a thousand years now. So that was that.

Cooper remembered the Wheel Inn particularly. The two 'teams' – if thousands of people could be referred to as a team – came from the north and south sides of the town and were known as the Up'ards and Down'ards. Compton was Down'ard territory, and the Wheel one of their favourite gathering places before the match.

Inside the station, he didn't have too much difficulty persuading Sergeant Wragg to let him have copies of the statements from the witnesses to Emily Nield's death in Dovedale. There was a small sheaf of them, collected by Wragg's constables as they intercepted members of the public leaving the scene.

'Emily was a pupil at Parkside Community Junior,' said Wragg as he gave Cooper the file. 'I thought a copy of her photograph might be useful.'

'Thanks.'

The photo was clipped to the first page. In it, Emily Nield was pictured in a green sweatshirt with her school logo, and was grinning cheekily at the camera, with one slightly crooked tooth prominent in her smile.

Seeing the photograph was a shock for Cooper. He hadn't seen the girl in life, and could not have described her if he'd been asked to. Nor could he have recognized her from the photograph. As far as Cooper was concerned, she bore absolutely no resemblance to the body he'd held in his arms in Dovedale.

But that was what death did to you. In a few tragic moments, Emily Nield had become a different person. Unrecognizable.

'The son attends Queen Elizabeth's Grammar School here in the town,' said Wragg. 'But I suppose you don't want to know about him.'

The file also included the Nields' own statements. Cooper had already got their version of events first hand, but he accepted the copies from Wragg and tucked the file under his arm.

'Thank you for this. It's appreciated.'

'No problem. Is there anything I need to know?'

Cooper hesitated, decided he could trust Wragg as a colleague.

'It's just a suspicion. I thought I saw someone I recognized among the bystanders in Dovedale.'

'Ah. Someone who shouldn't have been there?' asked Wragg astutely.

'Yes. I'm going to do a check on the Sex Offenders' Register, to see if I can make an ID.'

Wragg nodded. 'Let me know, won't you? He might be one of ours.'

'Of course.'

A look of concern crossed the sergeant's face. 'You don't think this person was involved in Emily Nield's death in some way?'

'Let's hope not,' said Cooper. 'I really hope not.'

Outside, he paused to adjust to the glare of the sun, and dug out his sunglasses from a pocket.

To his right, where Compton became Dig Street, he saw two supermarkets standing side by side near the bridge over Henmore Brook – Somerfield's standing right next door to the Co-op. Behind them was the Shaw Croft car park, where the Shrovetide football game was kicked off or 'turned up'. A few years ago, Prince Charles had arrived to be 'turner-up'. He was a great lover of tradition.

Round the corner in St John Street, Cooper passed Ashbourne's famous Gingerbread Shop with its original wattle and daub frontage. He supposed the town was very attractive in its own way. But it wasn't Edendale.

Gavin Murfin had been calling him from West Street, no doubt wondering where his new Acting DS had disappeared to for so long. He wasn't used to that when he was working for Diane Fry.

'I got those print-outs for you, Ben,' he said. 'There aren't many entries on the register in the Ashbourne area. Are you sure you don't want me to widen it out a bit? Derby is only twenty minutes down the road, after all.'

Cooper knew he was right. Visitors to Dovedale came from many miles around. It was probably a futile exercise, the list too long for him to plough through in search of a half-seen profile. On the other hand, the fact that the face he'd seen was familiar meant that the individual concerned must be from this area, at least from Derbyshire.

Well, didn't it? Or could his memory be playing some trick on him, throwing up a recollection of a photograph he'd seen in a bulletin from another force, or even glimpsed in a newspaper or on the TV screen.

'We have to start somewhere, Gavin. That will do for now.'

'I still don't know what this is about, Ben.'

'Sorry. I'll explain it you later.'

Murfin's voice became muffled, as if he was shielding the phone with his hand.

'And where the heck are you? I've been covering for you. But, mate –'

'I'll be back soon.'

65

With a deep sigh, Murfin accepted his reassurance. 'I hope I actually make it to my thirty, Ben. I'm afraid Superintendent Branagh might kill me before that.'

Fry felt sure some of these Birmingham city-centre underpasses were exactly the way they'd been when she drove through them in her very first car, a white Mini. Particularly this one under the Paradise Circus island. It had grey walls, and a black roof so low that no natural light penetrated the tunnel. It was probably a metaphor for something, diving underground into this grim, lightless world, but knowing that you would emerge a minute later, out into the sunlight.

As she came back above ground, Fry caught a glimpse of the old Paradise Forum shopping centre, which was supposed to have been scheduled for demolition. And next to it was the brutalist Central Library, described by Prince Charles as looking more like a place for burning books than for keeping them in. These buildings seemed old now, though they were built in the mid seventies. Well, thirty or forty years was a lifetime in the history of Birmingham architecture. Buildings she remembered being under construction while she was growing up were already being pulled down as obsolete.

Turning into Broad Street, she passed billboards announcing the site of the new Library of Birmingham. She had been booked into a hotel in Brindleyplace, part of Birmingham's 1990s revival – a canalside development containing offices, bars, restaurants, an art gallery, a radio station, and even the National Sea Life Centre.

Arriving at the hotel, Fry entered a lobby like a piece of abstract art. Sofas and armchairs were blocks of red and blue on a yellow background. Cylindrical white pillars framed a zig-zag turquoise staircase. She felt as though she'd walked into a piece of abstract art.

The receptionist at the desk wished her a good stay, but hardly looked at her. That was the way she liked it – not as it was in Edendale, where everyone wanted to know who she was and where she came from.

66

She found herself in a room equipped with an iMac computer and satellite TV. In reception she'd seen a library of CDs and DVDs. She could always watch the latest rom-com if she got really bored.

The front of the hotel looked down Spine Road towards the Central Square of Brindleyplace, with the Italianate arcade and campanile of the 3 Brindleyplace office block filling most of the view at the bottom of the square. Fry strained her neck to look southwards, over Broad Street, but saw only more hotels and offices. Even from several floors up, there was no hope of a distant enough view to see the Lickey Hills, which lay ten or twelve miles south of the city centre.

The Lickeys had been her first experience of countryside as a child. Perhaps the only one, unless her memory was successfully blocking out the others. There had been a train ride with her foster parents through Edgbaston and out past the huge Longbridge car plant, where Rovers were still being produced then. Arrival at a small railway station in Barnt Green had been followed by an uphill walk to Lickey itself.

She recalled bluebell woods – so what time of year would that have been? She wasn't sure now. But she did remember being urged and harried to the top of Beacon Hill, where on a clear day they said you could see thirteen counties. Old counties, that would have been, though. Most of what you saw now was the metropolitan sprawl of the West Midlands.

Beacon Hill was supposed to be the highest point in a direct line west from the Urals. You'd need a *really* clear day to see Russia. At less than a thousand feet, it was half the height of many of the Peak District hills. But it seemed high enough to her.

To the north, she'd looked out over the M5 towards Dudley and the Black Country, those small industrial towns of her childhood crouching on the skyline. Then she'd turned to the northeast, and found herself gazing all the way to Birmingham city centre. Its towers stood clustered together, with the BT Tower and the cylindrical shape of the Rotunda easiest to pick out, but all of them faintly blurred, as if they were standing in a mist. There was something mysterious about the sight, a fascination that seemed to call to her. It was like the first glimpse of the Emerald City at the end of the yellow brick road. The distance and perspective had made that island of tall buildings look like some far-off promised land, a place she could reach only by hacking her way through the forest of suburbs that stretched for miles at her feet. Rubery, Bournville, Selly Oak, Edgbaston. Their very names made them sound like obstacles in her way. They were surely Munchkin Country.

She vaguely remembered hearing her foster parents' voices telling her it was possible to see beyond Birmingham, right out to the countryside at Barr Beacon and Cannock Chase. But she hadn't bothered trying. That view of the city was enough for her.

The view from Beacon Hill would be quite different now. There were more glass towers in the city centre, with the old landmark of the Rotunda almost obscured by bigger, taller, newer buildings. Most of the Longbridge car plant had disappeared completely since the collapse of MG Rover and the arrival of the Chinese. The results of large-scale demolition must have left a huge hole in the landscape of south Birmingham. She imagined that loss would be all too obvious from the Lickeys.

She checked out the bathroom and the shower in her room, turned the TV on and off with the remote. She felt quite at home in an anonymous hotel. That was what hotels were all about, making you feel at home. Being alone among strangers was comfortable. There were no painful reminders. The stresses of life were suspended, and you could lie back on your bed, rootless and free. A bed that had been made by someone else, too. Wonderful.

Stretching out on the king-size bed, Fry decided she ought to face up to what she would go through during the next few days. She didn't want anything to come as a shock.

Gareth Blake had explained it all to her that day in Branagh's office. Most of it she didn't need explained, in theory. But it was different to hear it spelled out, when you knew the 'victim' they kept referring to was yourself.

'Diane, we'll understand if you say you've moved on and you don't want to testify. But there are things we can do. A victim can agree to interview without any commitment to give evidence.'

'Don't keep calling me the victim.'

'I'm sorry, I'm sorry. Look, you might not be sure about this until you re-read your own statement. That's often what we find. A woman has tried to forget the incident, put the trauma behind her – of course. But then she goes back and reads the statement she made at the time, and she changes her mind. She agrees to go ahead and give evidence in court.'

Fry remembered Branagh's face had been impassive during the conversation. For once, she wasn't weighing in to put pressure on. And she recalled thinking there must be a reason for that. Everything Branagh did had a reason.

Fry had wiped her palms on the edge of her jacket, then tried to disguise the gesture. It was too much of a giveaway.

Blake had leaned forward earnestly.

'In court, you can have a screen, if you want. So that the accused can't see you and you can't see him. We often take victims into court to show them where they'll give evidence from, and where everyone sits. We might not need to do that for you, obviously. But you understand what I'm saying? We bend over backwards to make it easier.'

'Easier?'

'Less difficult, then.'

She ought to be better prepared than the average victim. At least she knew the jargon. Like every other area of policing, the investigation of rape was littered with impenetrable acronyms. Victims were dealt with by an STO and an ISVA. A specially trained officer and an independent sexual violence advisor. A case file would contain a ROTI, a record of taped interview, in preparation for the EAH, an Early Administrative Hearing. For a member of the general public, the terminology could be baffling.

The first stage of the actual court process would be a committal hearing at a magistrates' court. She would not have to attend that, as her statement would be enough. The case could then proceed to crown court, where the second stage would be the trial, with a judge and a jury, a prosecution barrister to go through her evidence, another for the defence to challenge what she said.

If her attacker was found guilty or pleaded guilty, the judge would be given an impact statement before sentence, to explain how the attack had affected her life. Nothing was held back.

'In every case I've dealt with since joining the cold case unit, victims have been delighted to be approached. They say that a conviction brings closure, often after many years of torment.'

'But you do need consent to go ahead.'

And Blake had hesitated.

'In almost one hundred per cent of cases.'

Well, the treatment of rape had changed in the last couple of decades. The West Midlands had a dedicated facility, the Rowan Centre, where victims could pass on information without giving a name or address, or worrying about making a statement. That option had never been available to her.

Throughout this process, she must keep reminding herself one thing. She wasn't part of the investigating team for this enquiry. On the contrary, she was the IP, the Injured Party. That was how she would be referred to in the official police documents. She was the IP.

When she left the hotel, Fry heard music coming from the direction of The Water's Edge. She bought herself a sandwich in Baguette du Monde near the multi-storey car park, and idly studied the programme for the Crescent Theatre while she ate it. *Something is rotten in an upper-crust Danish family gathered to celebrate the 60th birthday of their wealthy patriarch. The occasion descends into nightmare when the eldest son accuses his father of sexual abuse.* That would be a comedy, then. She might give it a miss.

The Water's Edge was busy with people. The development had formed a complex of bridges where three canals met, connecting Brindleyplace to the ICC and NIA. Narrowboats were moored to the towpath, one of them converted into a café. The music she'd heard turned out to be a jive group on the bandstand, playing to customers eating outside at the restaurants. Their sign said *Jive Romeros*.

It was funny how canals had become a decorative feature. They had been such a part of the industrial revolution, yet they were surviving the wholesale demolition of the factories they'd once served. They were like all those Victorian pubs, preserved in the middle of modern office developments and retail parks.

She could see some of the city centre's glass towers from here. Most prominent among them was the Beetham Tower on Holloway Circus. The huge glass panels in its upper levels made the building look as if its walls had been blown away in a bomb blast, exposing the hidden lives of the people behind them.

A full-scale crown court trial would mean expensive defence barristers being shipped into the city. Would they take accommodation at Brindleyplace? No, she guessed not. They would stay at the Radisson SAS in the Beetham Tower, and drink downstairs at the Filini Bar.

Around the corner from 3 Brindleyplace, Fry could see the entrance to the National Sea Life Centre, a fan-shaped building backing on to the canal. It boasted a transparent walk-through underwater tunnel, yet it was about as far from the sea as you could get in the UK.

She thought of all the people she'd dealt with as a police officer over the years. All the victims, all the families. And all the children, of course. Particularly the children. There were some victims she'd let down, when she ought to have been able to help them. Everyone said you shouldn't allow any of that get to you, that you should just let it go and move on to the next case, to another victim looking for justice, needing your help. But sometimes it wasn't so easy.

And she thought of all the times she'd observed the behaviour of victims and felt a lack of sympathy at their weakness, their hesitation when faced with a decision. All the times she'd wanted to tell them that it wasn't as bad as all that.

Fry had so often seen people going into court to confront their past. The worst part of the process was waiting in the witness room, and the long walk down the corridor to take the stand. She'd watched people taking that walk. It might only be a few yards, but when you were going to face your own demons, it could seem like a million lonely miles.

'So what do you say, Diane?'

'I need time.'

'Of course. All the time you want.'

71

For herself, Fry knew that the long walk down that corridor would be the most difficult thing she'd ever done in her life.

Cooper stopped a few miles out of Ashbourne and pulled off the A515 into a car park serving the Tissington Trail, close to the village of Alsop. Dovedale was just over the hill to the west – the Milldale end of the valley, up past the boardwalks beyond Reynard's Cave and the weirs under Raven's Tor.

He couldn't put off reading the witness statements any longer. And he was afraid of being distracted when he got back to the office, too caught up in other things, all those unavoidable demands on his time.

Ideally, the statements ought to be read on the ground, in Dovedale itself, so he could picture where the witnesses were standing. But it would take too long right now to battle his way in and out of the dale against the traffic, and mingle with the crowds. That would have to wait for another time.

The statements were all pretty brief. The one thing that became clear was that no one had seen everything. Some witnesses recalled seeing the dog go into the river, but not the girl. Others had seen Emily and her brother playing on the bank, throwing sticks for Buster. Then they'd looked away, absorbed in their own concerns, until all the shouting began.

A few members of the public stated that they had actually seen Emily run into the water, then fall and bang her head on a rock. He could see why Sergeant Wragg felt the results of the interviews were conclusive.

But Cooper was bothered by the wording of these statements. *'Yes, I saw the little girl fall and bang her head.' 'She was knocked over by the dog. The rock struck her on the side of the head.' 'She couldn't catch the dog. I saw her slip and float downstream towards the rocks.'* One lady believed there had been a whole crowd of children and dogs in the water, too many for her to be able to distinguish one little girl in a green summer dress. Meanwhile, her friend had seen the girl distinctly, but swore the dress was blue.

All of these people had been within a few hundreds yards of the incident. Strange that none of them had noticed the child's parents. How odd that none of them had seen what Cooper saw – the man standing on the bank, his hands raised, fingers dripping water. Robert Nield was a striking enough figure at any time. You'd think he would have been observed by at least one of these eyewitnesses.

But perhaps some of them *had* seen him. Possibly, they had just never been asked.

Murfin was waiting impatiently in the CID room, looking anxiously over his shoulder as if he expected the Spanish Inquisition at any moment.

Cooper smiled. 'It's all right, Gavin, chill out.'

'I've had Luke Irvine out on the Devonshire Estate,' said Murfin, 'to see if he can sniff out anything more about Michael Lowndes.'

'That's great, Gavin.'

'I'm glad you appreciate it. If the information checks out, we should be able to have another go at putting surveillance on him this week.'

'And what about the sex offenders?'

Murfin sighed. 'ViSOR print-outs are on your desk.'

He was chewing as usual, but he was managing to do it with an air of dissatisfaction. Murfin had that sort of face, one that had sagged enough with age and misuse to enable him to carry off two expressions at once. His eyes looked merely quizzical, but his jowls were resentful.

Cooper flicked through the file, not reading the details at first, but looking at the photographs. The Police National Computer was linked to the database for ViSOR, the Violent and Sex Offender Register. Print-outs from the database gave him name and address records, photographs, risk assessments, and offenders' modus operandi. Sex offenders on the register were obliged to confirm their registration annually, failure being subject to a penalty of up to five years imprisonment.

73

And Murfin was right – there weren't many of them, just a dozen or so. Some of the individuals could immediately be discounted on grounds of age. How did you get yourself on the Sex Offenders' Register at the age of sixteen? It didn't bear thinking about.

Then Cooper stopped turning the pages. A face was looking out at him, the usual full face and profile shots taken in a police custody suite on arrest. The face itself was unremarkable. It was the representation of a middle-aged man with receding hair and a hint of grey stubble, a man who could pass unnoticed in any street. Cooper realized it was the eyes he remembered. They were calculating eyes, watchful and suspicious of the world. In some circumstances, they might look like the eyes of a predator.

'Sean Deacon,' he said.

'Oh, him,' said Murfin. 'A nasty piece of work. He has a record of violence towards children. His partner kicked him out when she found out he was physically abusing her two children.'

'How old were they?'

'Four and six,' said Murfin.

The address given for Deacon was in Wirksworth, about ten miles northeast of Ashbourne, on the other side of Carsington Water. So Murfin had extended the search criteria anyway, and had pulled out Sean Deacon at the second attempt.

'Does he have a job at the moment? Where does he work?'

'At the Grand Hotel. He's a kitchen worker.'

'What – here in Edendale?'

'Absolutely.'

Cooper had an image of a man slouching from an interview room to a cell in the custody suite at Edendale, a man who turned to look at him over his shoulder as he passed. It was that tilt of the head he'd recognized in Dovedale, a face half turned away in shadow, but the angle of a cheek and the slope of a shoulder were distinctive. You might change your face, but it was difficult to hide the way you moved.

'I think I was involved in an arrest,' he said. 'Or at least an interview.'

'You have a good memory.'

'For faces, yes.'

'Handy.'

'If he's on the register, he must have been convicted under the Sex Offenders Act since 1997.'

'Oh, yes. He was later convicted for attempting to abduct a seven-year-old from a park in Matlock. He was given four years in prison, spent thirty months inside, came out on licence, and now he's on the Sex Offenders' Register.'

'And he was watching children in Dovedale on Monday,' said Cooper.

'Is this him, then?'

'Yes, this is him.'

Cooper was feeling quite shaky now. It would pass, he knew. If he gave it a few hours, and got a good night's sleep, he'd be absolutely fine, just as he'd told Superintendent Branagh.

Then he thought about going home to Welbeck Street. And it occurred to him that home, on his own, might be the place where he would feel worst.

At the end of the morning, he walked out of E Divisional Headquarters and crossed the road, passing the back of the main stand at Edendale FC. The last match of the UniBond League season had been played a few weeks ago, but it wouldn't be long before the pre-season friendlies started at the beginning of July. Some Yorkshire side from Sheffield or Barnsley would be the first visitors, he'd heard. Then a local derby with Buxton or Matlock.

He didn't follow the Edendale soccer that closely, but it was useful to be aware of big matches from a policing point of view. Also, it helped to know when you wouldn't be able to find anywhere to park your car on a Saturday.

Liz Petty had dashed over from Buxton, still in her blue sweater, and met him for lunch in May's Cafe off West Street, in a lane running steeply downhill to Edendale's Clappergate shopping centre.

He'd first met her when she was a SOCO in E Division, and they'd abseiled into a disused quarry together looking for evidence. She'd been bundled up in overalls and a waterproof jacket then, with a red helmet pulled over her eyes. But he remembered a conspiratorial smile as she came alongside him on the face of a quarry, the smile shared by rock climbers. Her face had been flushed with cold and excitement, and her eyes shone with pleasure from under her helmet. That was the moment he realized he wanted to know her better.

Things had moved slowly after that, as these things did. It was only on his birthday one year that he began to see their relationship differently, when among the cards left on his desk was one from Petty, signed 'Hugs, Liz'. Their initial date had followed soon after that, dinner at the Raj Mahal in Edendale, and their first chaste kiss, her skin cool and slightly damp from the rain.

He really cared for her now, and he'd always taken it for granted that he would get married and settle down one, day, probably have a couple of kids, just like Matt. Was Liz the one he would be married to when that happened?

'Acting DS?' she said. 'Wow. But a permanent promotion would be great.'

'Yes, of course it would.'

'That would help a lot.'

Cooper sensed there was something else that she wasn't saying. One of those female subtexts that he was supposed to pick up on, a message he should understand without being told. What could it be?

Liz glanced at him, and looked away. And he felt as though he'd just failed an important test.

8

Waiting in the lobby of West Midlands Police headquarters in Colmore Circus, Fry picked up a newspaper off the table. The *Birmingham Mail*. She hadn't seen the paper for years, in fact never read a local newspaper at all now.

She found herself drawn to the personal ads. To her mind, they seemed to give a more honest glimpse into people's real lives than any of the journalists' stories elsewhere in the paper. As she read the ads, with their sometimes cryptic wording, she recalled an Agatha Christie play that had once been staged by the local amateur dramatic society in Dudley. *A Murder is Announced*. Why had she been there? She'd been dragged along against her will, she imagined. Maybe some friend or relative had been in the cast. All she remembered was the bit about a silly advert in the personal column, giving the time and date and place of a murder. Then there was some business with the lights going out and shots being fired, and a body on the floor.

She stared out of the plate glass on to Colmore Circus, a stream of traffic going past into the city. This wasn't Little Paddocks in Chipping Cleghorn, and she couldn't expect to see Colonel Archie or Miss Letitia walking in through the French windows. There was no vicarage here that hadn't been turned into student bedsits. And no village shop in the shadow of the mosque.

Rachel Murchison showed her to a room on one of the upper floors of Lloyd House, through an open-plan office full of ringing telephones.

'I just wanted to touch base before the meeting,' said Murchison, arranging a folder full of papers in front of her.

'Yes, I understand.'

Touching base. One of those phrases beloved by management types everywhere. Fry's heart sank when she heard it.

Murchison was now in a navy blue suit offset with a white blouse, dark hair tied neatly back, businesslike and self-confident, but still with that guarded watchfulness. She was the specialist counsellor, there to judge her psychological state.

In any cold case rape enquiry, the police had to consult counsellors before they approached a victim, and develop a joint approach strategy. They needed to understand whether the victim had moved on and didn't want to testify.

On the day Blake and Murchison came to Derbyshire, their approach strategy would already have been developed. They had planned their tactics before Fry even heard about the hit on the DNA database.

'I'm just here to help. There's no pressure. It's all about support.'

Support. It was such an over-used word. Fry had already heard it too often. There, in that overheated room, looking out over the back of the Edendale football ground, it had the dead sound of a curse.

'It's understandable that you feel a need to be in control. Perfectly normal, in the circumstances.'

Rachel Murchison would be from a sexual assault referral centre. Fry knew the police would have examined the stored exhibits from her assault for blood, saliva or semen traces, with the help of the Forensic Science Service. They might have found the tiniest speck of sperm on a tape lift from her clothing. Without statements from independent eyewitnesses, the police were reliant on forensic science.

But here, there was a witness, wasn't there? Someone had come forward after all this time. She wondered if she would get to find out who this person was.

'I understand from our phone conversation that you were visiting family in Perry Barr,' said Murchison. 'Your foster parents? You keep in touch then? That's good.'

Fry didn't tell Murchison that she'd been guilty of failing to keep in touch as well as she ought to have done. Christmas cards, the occasional phone call. Jim and Alice Bowskill would have been justified in reproaching her, but that wasn't their way.

Instead, she gave an answer that she felt sure would tick the right box.

'They're very supportive.'

78

'Excellent.'

Murchison looked down at her folder. Fry was trying to avoid letting her eyes stray that way, afraid of seeing her own name leap out at her, preserved as a subject for psychological study.

'And there's a sister, I believe?'

Indeed there was. Angie Fry was her older sister. They'd been apart for fifteen years, but were finally reunited. If united was the right word.

'As I'm sure you know, we were both taken into care as children,' said Fry. 'I was nine, and Angie was eleven.'

'For your own protection?'

'Social Services said my parents had been abusing my sister. They said it was both of them.'

'So your childhood was spent in foster homes?'

'Yes.'

At first, they'd kept moving on to different places. So many different places that Fry couldn't remember them. It was a few years before she realized that they didn't stay anywhere long because of her sister. Angie was big trouble wherever they went. Even the most well-intentioned foster families couldn't cope with her. But Diane had worshipped her, and refused to be split up from her.

'But you were separated from your sister at some point?'

'When she was sixteen, Angie disappeared from our foster home and never came back.'

Diane had been fourteen when Angie left. It had been 1988, the year of the Lockerbie bomb, the year Salman Rushdie went into hiding and George Bush Senior became president of the USA.

The small details were impressed on Fry's mind. The last memory that she had of her sister, Angie unusually excited as she pulled on her jeans to go out that night. She was off to a rave somewhere. There was a boy who was picking her up. Diane had wanted to know where, but Angie had laughed and said it was a secret. Raves were always held in secret locations, otherwise the police would be there first and stop them.

But they were doing no harm, just having fun. And Angie had gone out that night, with their foster parents making only a token attempt to find out where she was going. Angie had already been big trouble for them by then, and was getting out of hand.

Looking back, Fry knew she had been unable to believe anything bad of Angie then. Every time they'd been moved from one foster home to another, it had been their foster parents' fault, not Angie's. And when Angie had finally disappeared from her life, the young Diane had been left clutching an idealized image of her, like a final, faded photograph. The memory still brought the same feelings of anger and unresolved pain. Feelings that revolved around Angie.

'Of course, she was already using heroin by then.'

Fry wasn't sure whether she'd said that out loud. But she could see from Murchison's expression that she'd heard it. And again, it seemed to be the right reply, although it had slipped out without any thought this time. The room began to feel like a confessional, the place to get any of those psychological hangups off her chest.

She supposed that was the theory, anyway. So along as she could talk about it, she must be all right. If only it was that simple.

'And what of your parents?' asked Murchison.

'My real parents?' said Fry. 'I remember almost nothing of them.'

'Nothing?'

'Almost nothing.'

'But your mother ...?'

'She died, they told me. My father is just a blank. He's not even on my birth certificate.'

Murchison nodded. 'And how do you feel about your family now?'

'It's all history,' said Fry.

'You're saying you've moved on, Diane?'

'Absolutely.'

'I'm glad to hear that. It's possible to get eaten up by guilt over things that are no fault of yours. There's no point in feeling guilty all the time. It has a very negative effect.'

'Why would I feel guilty? There's no reason for me to feel guilty about anything.'

'It's common to have irrational feelings that we can't explain the reasons for.'

'*We?*'

Murchison took no notice.

'During this process, we'll be trying to uncover any hidden memories that you may have, Diane.'

'Hidden memories? Something else I'm not aware of?'

'Those hidden memories are vital, both for their evidential value and for your own closure.'

Fry watched Murchison tidy away her folder. She wondered if the counsellor felt as though she'd got inside the victim's head, and satisfied herself that she was psychologically fit for the ordeal to come. Did Rachel Murchison now think that she understood Diane Fry?

Looking at the clock, Fry stood up first and shook hands. A lot of what had just been said sounded like bullshit. But Murchison had been right about one thing. She did need to be in control.

Like all the best detectives, DI Gareth Blake had a sidekick. He was an Asian detective sergeant, very smart, very bright, named Gorpal Sandhu. Though he said very little, Fry observed in him the same watchfulness. Perhaps, after all, it was characteristic of everyone in West Midlands Police. If so, she had forgotten it, had never noticed it when she served in Birmingham herself.

'So have you kept in touch with any of your old colleagues in the West Midlands, Diane?' asked Blake after the introductions.

'No, not with anyone.'

'Really? Not even DC Kewley?'

'No one.'

'That's a bit unusual.'

'Perhaps. I don't know.'

Fry thought it ought to be obvious that she'd wanted to put that part of her life behind her. Yes, it was true that her previous service with West Midlands Police was a memory she almost cherished sometimes, whenever she looked out at the primitive rural wasteland she'd condemned herself to in Derbyshire.

But that was an idealized image she'd created for herself, a long way from the reality. In fact, she had left Birmingham without a farewell to any of her colleagues. No leaving party, no

81

parting gifts, no cards wishing her all the best in the future. She might as well have said: '*I'm going out now. I may be some time.*'

Blake and Sandhu were watching her, politely waiting until they had her attention again.

'I'm sorry if I'm teaching my grandmother to suck eggs, Diane,' said Blake. 'But we do have to go through the processes.'

'I know.'

'At the evidential stage, the CPS have to be satisfied first of all that there's enough evidence to provide a realistic prospect of conviction. That means that a jury is more likely than not to convict. Normally, if a case doesn't pass the evidential stage, it won't go ahead.'

'Yes.'

'If the case does pass the evidential stage, the CPS has to decide whether a prosecution is in the public interest. If the evidential test is passed, rape is believed to be so serious that a prosecution is almost certainly required in the public interest. Okay so far?'

'Absolutely.'

'Now. When considering the public interest stage, one of the factors that Crown Prosecutors will take into account is the consequences for the victim of the decision whether or not to prosecute, and any views expressed by the victim or the victim's family.'

'Paragraph 5.12 of the Crown Prosecutors' Code. Striking a balance between the interests of the victim and the public interest.'

'Exactly. As I'm sure you know, the definition of rape was substantially changed by the Sexual Offences Act 2003. Offences committed before 1st May 2004 are still prosecuted under the Sexual Offences Act 1956.'

'And under the 1956 Act, it's a defence if the defendant believed the victim was consenting, even if the belief was unreasonable.'

'I'm afraid reasonableness is a matter of fact for the jury. Not for us.'

'You said the case was re-opened on the basis of intelligence,' said Fry.

'Yes.'

'And now you have a suspect.'

'Two suspects, in fact,' said Blake. 'Their names are Marcus Shepherd and Darren Joseph Barnes. We had an element of luck, actually. Our primary suspect had a DNA sample taken when he was arrested for robbery and possession of a firearm. Criminals don't just commit sexual offences, but other offences too.'

'Are they in custody?'

'Arrested and bailed.'

'What? They're out on the street?'

'Diane, you know we have to get all the evidence together that we need for an airtight case. Evidential value is crucial. But forensic techniques have improved. We're very hopeful.'

'We had information, credible enough to arrest two suspects,' put in Sandhu. 'We took fingerprints and buccal swabs as per procedure, and we got a hit on the database.'

'From both?'

'Just the one,' he said. 'But we believe they were together. The lab might be able to get a new DNA profile from the exhibits in storage. New techniques are available. Low copy number.'

'Yes.'

DNA techniques had advanced significantly over the last twenty years in terms of sensitivity, reliability, and speed of results. They had become really important in revisiting old cases, reviewing the evidence recovered at the time. Preservation must have been good in Birmingham, because DNA deteriorated after a while. DNA evidence had to be looked at in terms of preservation. If it was kept cold and dry, it lasted an awful lot longer. It was theoretically possible to obtain DNA profiles from samples over a hundred years old, provided it was known how they'd been preserved.

Forensically, it could all go horribly wrong before it ever got into the courtroom. The collecting and handling of evidence was so important.

There had been no witnesses to the assault that she could remember, and certainly none had come forward at the time. There had been plenty of appeals, of course. Lots of trawling from house to house in the area, hours spent stopping cars that used the nearby roads, and talking to motorists, lots of effort put into leaning on informants who might have heard a murmur on the streets. All to no avail. It was an offence with no witnesses other than the perpetrators and the victim.

Apart from her own statement, the only evidence Fry had of the attack were bruises and abrasions. And those faded with time, leaving only the crime-scene photographer's prints to pass around a jury. As for the psychological scars … well, they didn't show up too well in court.

But now they had a credible witness report, as well as an e-fit record that had been kept in the imaging unit, and a copy of the file retained by the FSS. So where had this new witnesses come from?

According to Blake, this person was on witness protection. They could be putting themselves at serious risk to testify. Someone had done some smooth talking, or exerted the right kind of pressure.

Blake was busy giving her the bad news, touching on the six per cent conviction rate for rape cases.

'I'm afraid the conviction rate in rape cases is still very low in this country.'

'Yes, I know that.'

Blake tilted his head in acknowledgement. 'Of course you do. And I'm sure you're aware, too, that there's a lot of pressure to improve conviction rates.'

'Absolutely. The inference from the poor figures being that the police don't take rape allegations seriously enough.'

'Well, that's a perception the public might take away from the statistics. We know it isn't true, though, don't we? Generally speaking. There are lots of other factors that make convictions difficult to achieve, especially in cases where the defendant is known to the victim.'

'Like the fact that it's impossible to provide objective evidence on whether consent was given.'

'Exactly. It always comes down to one person's word against another's. And juries don't like that. They want to be presented with evidence. We're handicapped by those old-fashioned notions of people being innocent until proven guilty, and having to establish guilt beyond reasonable doubt. When it's just a question of "he says, she says", there's always going to be room for reasonable doubt. One person's truth is someone else's lie. We all know that. It would take a poor barrister not to ram the point firmly into the heads of a jury.'

'Or a defendant who's not very convincing on the stand.'

Blake smiled. 'Ah, yes. There are some people who just look so guilty that jurors will convict them whatever the evidence. But that's the chance you take in a jury system, isn't it?'

He was repeating himself from that meeting in Superintendent Branagh's office. But something about their relationship had changed since then, a shifting of the dynamics had taken place, and Fry was the one at a disadvantage. She could even remember the moment it had happened.

'You know, I don't like to hear you call me "sir", Diane. It was always "Gareth", wasn't it?'

That had been a clear signal that their relationship wasn't going to be a professional one. They weren't to be considered a DS and a DI working together, no longer colleagues who could safely share information fully with each other. From that moment, from the second she called him 'Gareth', she wouldn't be a fellow police officer any more. He was the investigator. And she was the victim.

'But the six per cent figure is based on reported rapes,' he said. 'Most of them never get to court. There's a high attrition rate, as you know.'

'Attrition rate?'

'Yes.' Blake looked embarrassed, then faintly irritated. 'Diane, you know the jargon. Don't try to make me feel as if I'm personally responsible for it.'

Gareth Blake might have been uncomfortable. And she had to confess to herself that she hadn't made it any easier for him, hadn't wanted to either. She'd taken a small satisfaction in seeing him squirm, in watching that smooth demeanour crumble for a moment. It was petty, she supposed. But gratifying, all the same. Each time, it had given her a little bit of illicit pleasure.

Yes, Blake might have felt uncomfortable. But he couldn't know what it felt like to be on the other side of the table, to be a woman hearing a man lecturing her about attrition rates in rape cases. No amount of specialist training would give Gareth Blake that insight. He didn't have the right kind of eyes to see it. He didn't have the right kind of mind.

Blake shuffled his papers and closed his file.

'Right. We'll move on to the next stage. This afternoon, Diane, we'd like to take you back to the scene of the incident. If that wouldn't be too difficult for you. But we would understand, if –'

'No. No, that will be fine.'

Fry had thought a lot about this moment, the time when she would have to see the place again. Memories were one thing. They didn't have any concrete substance, and you could bury them, if you tried hard enough. But a place was real. You couldn't deny the existence of a street, the wall of a factory, the hard concrete of a pavement. You couldn't bury them in that dark hole at the back of your mind. Reality was still there when you closed your eyes.

They went to the Digbeth area in Gareth Blake's car. He drove a Hyundai. Silver grey, she noticed. Just like almost every other car on the road, except hers. But his air conditioning worked well. On the journey across town, Fry tried to steady her breathing, to clear the buzzing in her head, the faint dizziness she'd experienced when she walked out into the open air.

It was just the unaccustomed heat, she told herself. It felt so much warmer in the middle of a city than out in the wilds of Derbyshire. Concrete absorbed the heat, acres of plate glass reflected the sun on to already humid streets. And hardly a breath of wind reached this far into Birmingham. It was blocked by the miles of suburbs to the south.

She began to dream of standing on the Lickey Hills, way up on Beacon Hill. She could feel the wind up there, whipping through her hair, cooling the sweat on her brow. She could see that view of the city from a distance, its cluster of towers faintly blurred, as if standing in a mist. A first glimpse of the Emerald City. The far-off promised land.

'Are you all right, Diane?'

She jerked at the sound of Gareth Blake's voice. She'd almost forgotten where she was. But suddenly she was back in the here and now, sitting in the passenger seat of Blake's car, pulling up to the traffic lights in Deritend High Street. She saw a Peugeot dealer, the Old Crown, and the brick campanile of Father Lopes' Chapel, which now seemed to be used as a car wash.

'Yes, I'm fine,' she said.

'I thought you'd fallen asleep there for a minute.'

Fry tried a smile for his benefit.

'Wide awake,' she said.

'We're here, anyway.'

Well, this part of Birmingham hadn't altered much. Ironic, when it was the one area that she would have been glad to see transformed. But these factory walls hadn't changed, or those side streets full of workshops and warehouses. The pub was still there, too. The Connemara. How had that particular pub survived, when so many others had closed?

The arches of the railway viaduct were certainly the same. Black brick, chipped and scrawled with graffiti. It stood exactly as it had been built centuries ago. Well, except for the graffiti, maybe. The messages were pretty modern.

And the scrubby expanse of waste ground – that was still there, of course. Dense with clumps of weed, bounded by a barbed-wire fence. Even from here, she could see the gaps that had been prised in the fence. Someone still used this spot for their own purposes. Drug dealers, crack whores, sexual predators hidden in the shadows …

Fry took a deep breath. She was in danger of losing objectivity, letting her emotions run away with her.

'We have your statement, of course,' said Blake. 'But sometimes more details will come back to you, once you have some distance from the incident. Distance in time, I mean.'

Blake and Sandhu watched her carefully, noting every movement she made, everything she looked at or reacted to. Fry was trying to fill the scene with other people, apart from herself. She hadn't been alone then either. Far from it.

'This witness you have,' she said. 'Where did she come from?'

'She was on her way home,' said Blake. 'She worked for a small publisher based in the Custard Factory.'

'The Custard Factory? Does it still exist?'

'Oh, yes.'

Fry was surprised. By all the rules of logic, the Custard Factory was an idea that shouldn't have survived this long. The five-acre sprawl of industrial buildings had once been the territory of Sir Alfred Bird, the inventor of custard, who employed a thousand people there. Now, old factory buildings had been restored and converted into an arts and media quarter for Birmingham's brightest young creative talents. A bohemian community of artists, with cafés and dance studios, art galleries and holistic therapy rooms. It should never have existed. Not in Digbeth.

She supposed the Connemara would at one time have been frequented entirely by factory workers – men leaving their hot, exhausting jobs in the engineering works. Maybe employees from Mr Bird's custard factory, too – though she imagined most of those would have been women. Perhaps they would have been covered in a fine yellow powder, the way coal miners used to be distinguishable by the black layer of dust around their eyes.

'You had left your partner in the car,' said Blake. 'You were going to check the factory premises up the street here, to see if there was activity.'

'Yes, that's right.'

'Your partner was DC Andy Kewley.'

'Yes.'

That night, she and Kewley had been in an Aston CID pool car, a Skoda Fabia. The blokes hated driving a Skoda. They always used to grumble about Traffic cops getting flashy BMWs to use as RPUs, the unmarked road policing units. Since they were unmarked, they said, why couldn't they be shared with CID? Some hopes.

They had been just one of several units drafted in from the divisions for a big operation headed up by the Major Investigation Unit. Kewley was driving, and she was observer. She had responded to a request over their radio from the officer in charge of the operation.

Fry remembered being passed by a slightly battered red Mercedes truck. M. Latif & Son; *The people's warehouse – serving the Midlands since 1956*. The Latif warehouse was in Digbeth somewhere. Bordesley Street, maybe.

And then the street had been empty. Or so it had seemed. She soon learned her mistake.

She had her personal radio in her hand when the attack came. But the first blow had numbed her arm, and she dropped the handset in the dirt without getting chance to hit the red button that would have summoned assistance. She heard her radio crunch under someone's foot. *'Hey, she's a copper.'*

As if the voice in her memory had just spoken to her again, Fry turned suddenly and looked around her. A piece of wasteland wedged between a railway viaduct and a factory yard. A battered fence protecting it with rusted barbs.

It was as if this piece of ground had been preserved just for her, to create a permanent reminder of a landmark in her life.

Blake and Sandhu stood back out of the way as she walked a few yards along the fence towards the parapet of a bridge and found a flight of steps. Below her ran the River Rea, Birmingham's forgotten river, dirty brown and flowing under factories, invisible even from the bridges, overgrown with trees bursting from the walls of the factories. The Rea was hidden under the city, imprisoned in underground culverts to prevent flooding of the industrial buildings and working-class housing of Digbeth.

The sound of the water reminded her. She was standing in the exact spot now.

So this was it.

She saw five steps down to the water, a patch of weed-covered dirt. A sagging fence, a damp brick arch. And a series of jagged shadows on the corner of the street, moving ever closer.

But the day was bright, and the sun was overhead. Those shadows were in her memory.

And then she seemed to hear that voice in the darkness. A familiar voice, coarse and slurring in a Birmingham accent. *'It's a copper,'* it said. Taunting laughter moving in the shadows. The same menace all around, whichever way she turned. *'A copper. She's a copper.'*

'Diane?'

'Yes. Okay. I'm trying to remember.'

'You weren't examining the scene. You were looking towards the corner of the street.'

89

'Yes. I think …'

And then the memory came to her. From among the ghosts of factory workers and custard makers, darker figures stepped from shadow to shadow, walking into the present. Or almost the present.

'Yes, I think …' she said. 'I think at least one of them came out of the pub.'

'That's great, Diane. See, it works.'

Sandhu had taken a call on his mobile. He gestured to Blake, and they went into an anxious huddle.

'Damn it,' said Blake. 'Oh, God damn it.'

'What's the matter?' asked Fry.

'I don't believe it.'

'Gareth?'

Blake looked at her, then away. He kicked at a stone in frustration.

'Bad news. Really bad news. We just lost our key witness.'

9

There was one more important person who Fry hadn't met up with yet. She was about to put that right, but with mixed feelings. She'd spent all afternoon answering questions from Gareth Blake and Rachel Murchison, hour after hour with people watching her for a reaction every time she turned round.

She had never imagined how exhausting it would be, what relief she'd feel when she was finally allowed to escape. And this was the only first stage of the whole ordeal. She knew there was first worse yet to come.

'Not brought your farm boy with you, then? Nice Constable Cooper?'

Angie Fry sat across a table in a bar on Broad Street, close to Diane's hotel. It had to be a bar, because Angie hadn't offered to show her where she lived. And Diane hardly dared to ask. She was convinced that her older sister lived with a man, a totally unsuitable man who Angie knew she would disapprove of.

Diane frowned across the table. She had a glass of spritzer in front of her, while Angie was drinking something out of a bottle that she couldn't remember the name for.

'He's not my farm boy. Not my Constable Cooper.'

'Oh? I thought he was part of your team.' Angie held up a hand with the first two fingers entwined. 'Like that, you and him, aren't you?'

'This is nothing to do with him, or anyone else back in Derbyshire,' said Diane. 'This is just me, and it's personal.'

Angie had the grace to look faintly embarrassed.

'Okay, Sis. I'm sorry. I was just trying to keep it light, you know.'

It was obvious that Angie had cleaned up her act since Diane first made contact with her again. She seemed to have more than one set of clothes, at least, and her hair was tidier.

Diane no longer felt quite so embarrassed to be seen with her in a respectable bar. Whether Angie was clean in every sense,

Diane still wasn't sure. But then, it was a question she couldn't ask either.

Even now, she sensed a lot of unfinished business with Angie. There were so many things they hadn't talked about. A gulf still existed between them, a chasm so wide that that it could never be bridged now. The relationship they'd had when they were teenagers back in Warley – well, that was long buried in the past. It was the only thing they had in common, and it was the one subject they would never talk about.

'Besides, Ben Cooper is Acting Detective Sergeant now.'

Angie paused with a bottle halfway to her mouth. 'What? He got your job?'

'Temporarily.'

'Mmm.'

Diane began to get irritated. She'd told herself she wouldn't, but her sister had an uncanny knack of getting under her skin.

'Oh, don't worry,' she said. 'Things will be right back to normal the minute I get away from here.'

'*If* you get away.'

'Well, I'm certainly not staying in Birmingham for the rest of my natural life.'

'Why not?'

'Because you're here for a start.'

She regretted the words as soon as they were out of her mouth. But her sister looked smug, as if she'd scored some kind of success.

'Cheers,' said Angie, raising her bottle in a toast. 'Here's to sisterly love.'

Her sister's attitude made Diane reluctant to think about all the things she'd planned to say. All those questions she'd wanted to ask. *We're going to be all right, you and me?* The moment didn't seem right. Perhaps the time would never be right.

She'd told Rachel Murchison only half the story of their lives. It was true that they'd both been taken into care when Diane was nine and Angie was eleven. And there had been a whole series of foster homes before they landed with the Bowskills. Angie had been trouble wherever she went, though Diane had idolized her in that blind fashion younger siblings sometimes did.

It all went off the rails when Angie began using heroin and left home, not to be seen again by her sister for fifteen years.

Diane was conscious that she and her sister were hardly unique cases. There were sixty thousand children in foster care or local authority homes. Half of those sixty thousand wouldn't get a single GCSE, and would leave school with no qualifications, barely able to read or write, destined for dead-end jobs, if not a permanent place on the dole queue. She was one of the measly two per cent who made it to university. Many were consigned to a life on the street, holed up in a filthy squat or crack house, pissing away their existence. Some care-home children felt unwanted and unvalued for the whole of their lives. Many never formed a normal relationship, because they didn't know how. They'd never been shown.

It was hard for her to think of herself as part of a huge, anonymous mass. But that's exactly what she'd once been – just another statistic in a depressing flow of unwanted children, shuttling to and fro through the back alleys of society. Kids destined never to have a real family, or a real home.

At least for a while it had been Angie and Diane together. That had made fostering a bit more tolerable. But even that had come to an abrupt end.

Fry shut her eyes against the sudden stab of pain. It was a memory that tormented her, even now. That moment she'd realized the unbelievable: Angie had left for good, walked out of their foster home in Warley and disappeared. Ever since then, Diane had thought that she'd make things right by finding Angie. But perhaps the truth was that she had never forgiven her sister for that betrayal, and never could.

'Let's have another drink,' said Angie. 'You're being slow, Sis.'

Diane studied her sister. Yes, Angie herself had changed a lot in fifteen years, yet there was still the familiar rhythm in her speech, the faint buzz of a Black Country accent under the studied flatness. And Diane couldn't avoid noticing a characteristic gesture, a tense lifting of the shoulders that she knew very well because she was aware of doing it herself.

'I don't suppose you've ever kept in contact with Mum and Dad?' she said.

Angie's mouth became a tight line.

'You mean Jim and Alice Bowskill? No, why should I?'

'They were very good to us.'

'They were good to *you*.'

'What do you mean?'

'I was always the disappointment, didn't you notice? I couldn't do anything right in their eyes. You were the one they loved.'

'Angie, you were a nightmare. You made their lives a misery. Just like you did with all our previous foster parents. That was why we moved on so often.'

'Is it? Lucky for you that I left when I did, then. I bet Jim and Alice put everything into you then, didn't they? Of course. They got you through your A-levels, and into university. That must have been the high point of their lives. Little Diane, their great success story.'

'I worked hard for anything I achieved.'

'Right. I bet you were really studious.'

'I was. Angie, I gave you all fifteen years of it. I told you what I did at school, how I managed to scrape through to do my degree. I wanted to get an education. I *needed* it. *And* I told you about our parents coming to the graduation ceremony.'

'Our foster parents.'

'And how they got lost in Birmingham, so they arrived late.'

'And you didn't think anyone was coming, I know. I liked the bit about you getting drunk at a student party and being sick into somebody's window box. I can't imagine you doing that, Sis. You were always so prim and proper. A right stuck-up little prig.'

Diane was beginning to get upset. This wasn't the way she'd pictured it going. The hostility from her sister was growing with every mouthful of alcohol. She wondered if Angie had been drinking before she came, or whether she was high on something else.

'Do you regret making contact with me again?' she asked.

'If you remember, I didn't have much choice,' said Angie. 'Thanks to your Constable Cooper.'

With an effort, Diane controlled herself. She found she was gritting her teeth so hard that it hurt.

'You do know what I'm doing here, don't you?' she said.

Angie took a swig of her drink. 'Oh, yes. I know. It's all about you again, isn't it?'

They went out into Broad Street to look for somewhere to eat. For Diane, it was a relief to get out on to the busy pavement. Angie was getting a little too loud for comfort.

'Hey, have you noticed how Broad Street seems to have become the place for a chavs' night out?' she said.

Diane wouldn't have put it quite like that herself. But, yes – she had noticed.

'I remember Broad Street mostly for the theatres,' she said. 'It used to be where you came for a bit of culture.'

'Nothing cultural about this lot,' said Angie. 'If you dropped a small nuclear device on a Saturday night and took out four or five of these clubs, you'd exterminate the entire chav population from Longbridge to Erdington.'

Young men were hanging out of car windows as they crawled up the road, a youth in white trainers carrying a bottle of Magners ciders was throwing up in the gutter. Further up the street, a group were arguing with bouncers in front of a club, others were shouting abuse at police officers in a riot van. An Asian taxi driver wound up his windows to shut out the racial insults.

Birmingham hadn't seen much excitement since the Eurovision Song Contest and the G8 Summit had come to town in the same week. Back in May 1998, that was. No sooner had Terry Wogan and Ulrika Jonsson left the National Indoor Arena with an army of cheesy pop acts, than Tony Blair was arriving to rub shoulders with Bill Clinton and Boris Yeltsin next door at the ICC.

The International Convention Centre was in use now. That meant convention fodder, hundreds of black-suited sales people filling up the bars and restaurants on Broad Street.

On the pavement, Fry saw a man with a thin, angular face and long grey hair prowling between the streetlights like a wolf. Sharp eyes watching her. Hungry eyes, full of desire for the next fix.

'My God, I bet this is something you don't have in Edendale,' said Angie. 'The range of bars and restaurants in Birmingham is amazing now. We can eat anything we fancy. What do you say to Thai? Caribbean? Mexican?'

Diane was unimpressed. 'Can't we go down to the Balti Triangle?'

'Sis – you'd live in the Balti Triangle, given a chance.'

'Yes. So?'

In the Balti Triangle of south Birmingham, scores of restaurants had combined to put the city firmly on the curry map. In fact, Brum claimed to have invented balti, just as it laid claim to the Mini and HP Sauce. Diane always thought of balti when she heard the bhangra music coming from cars cruising up the Soho Road. Music driven by the dhol drum, food sizzling in a balti dish with cumin and ginger. Both formed by ingredients from the Indian subcontinent.

'K2. Alcester Road,' said Angie at last.

'Okay, then.'

'I'll get a taxi.'

Diane stood in the middle of the pavement, while people dodged around.

'Sis?' she said. 'Will you help me?'

Angie hesitated, with her hand in the air in an effort to attract a passing cab. She looked back at her sister.

'You know I will.'

At that time of the evening, Cooper had reached the Dog and Partridge crossroads, where he turned past the Dovedale Garage towards Peveril of the Peak Hotel in the village of Thorpe.

From the car showroom boomed the unmistakable sound of a cinema organ, someone playing an Irving Berlin medley. Posters announced the Mighty Compton Organ at Pipes in the Peaks. Of course, this was where the organ from the Regal in Derby had ended up, bought and restored by the garage owner, complete with turntable lift and vibraphone effects. The Compton and the cars shared the showroom space.

Even in the dusk, the conical outline of Thorpe Cloud rose beyond the hotel. It always reminded him of a pyramid, there was something so unnatural about its shape. Anywhere else, it would have been taken as man made. But here in the White Peak, among the ancient remnants of the limestone reefs, it was just another eccentric formation in the landscape.

Walking upriver from the Dovedale car park, he soon reached the stepping stones, opposite the outcrop named the Rocky Bunster. Beyond here, a series of weirs broke up the flow of the river, with a small island sitting just upstream of the first weir. Many visitors walked only as far as the stepping stones, while some ventured further on, towards the Twelve Apostles, but they'd start to flag when they reached the top of the long stretch of stone steps and after a rest on Lovers' Leap most would turn back. Only the more active or determined walked the full length of Dovedale, or even reached as far as the packhorse bridge at Milldale.

So this stretch of the river was the most populated – the walk up towards Lovers' Leap, past Tissington Spires and the Twelve Apostles, the Natural Arch and Reynard's Cave, the Lions' Face Rock and Pickering Tor. All familiar landmarks to the tourist.

Hundreds of thousands of visitors came to the dale on summer weekends and at bank holidays. They wobbled backwards and forwards on the stepping stones, picnicked on the grass, took photographs of each other on the edge of the water. At these times, with its manicured slopes and well-worn paths, Dovedale seemed to have been loved into tameness.

But at night, it was a totally different place. Its natural wildness re-asserting itself in the darkness, creeping out of the undergrowth like a shy, nocturnal animal. Sounds that had been only a background to the screaming of children and barking of dogs now grew louder, more dominant, more menacing. The river itself was a roaring, dangerous monster that thundered endlessly down the valley, and could snatch you away at one false step. The crags became looming giants, their white shanks sporadically visible through the trees. Across the water, the Apostles were motionless ghosts, a cluster of jagged teeth against the darkened hillside.

Cooper wondered what exactly Alex Nield had been taking photographs of in Dovedale yesterday. Perhaps one of the money trees. He would have liked the pattern of the copper coins in the grain of the trunk, their shadows on the wood, the glint of sun on their hammered edges.

But surely he would have taken photographs of the stepping stones too? For anyone even remotely interested in photography, it was impossible to visit Dovedale and not capture a shot of the stepping stones. The stones had an irresistible contract between their almost accidental symmetry and the random variation in the angle at which they lay in the water. In sun, each stone produced a slightly different tone – light and shade, light and shade, all the way across the river, with the water forced between them in dark streams.

And any photograph of the stepping stones on a bank holiday had to include people. Would Alex have avoided them for that reason?

On the western bank, the path ended at a pair of ornate wrought-iron gates, blocking the way into the woods beneath the Rocky Bunster. Here, you had to cross the river by the stepping stones, or turn back. Cooper stumbled over mole hills on a muddy bank before reaching Lovers' Leap and climbing the steps that had originally been cut into the bank by Italian prisoners of war. It formed a vantage point opposite the Twelve Apostles. A vantage point, but it had been too far from the water to be any use on Monday.

In Dovedale, even in the daytime, people often spoke in hushed tones, influenced by some kind of reverence for a special place. Tonight, an owl called in the woods on the opposite bank. But that was the only sound, apart from the water.

He thought again about the witness statements taken by Sergeant Wragg and his team. He was trying to imagine where those bystanders would have been placed in relation to the Nield family. It immediately became obvious that some of them must have been screened from the incident by the slope of Lovers' Leap, or by the trees overhanging the bank, dense with summer foliage.

They might have been able to see the middle of the river, where the water rushed over a weir at the angle of a bend. So they might have seen the dog, Buster. He was a golden retriever, a big dog, and he would have caused a lot of splashing. Had anyone really seen the girl, entering the water more slowly, perhaps hesitating near the bank, unsure of the depth? Or had they imagined the rest?

The slabs of limestone lying below the surface were clear even in this light. They gleamed in a sort of luminescence imparted by the foaming water. The water, the stones … it was easy for Cooper, even now, to imagine that he saw the little girl, trying to shield herself from the spray, wobbling, falling, vanishing among the submerged stones.

But he hadn't seen that. He'd just been told that was what happened.

'Yes, I saw the little girl fall and bang her head.' 'She was knocked over by the dog. The rock struck her on the side of the head.' 'She couldn't catch the dog. I saw her slip and float downstream towards the rocks.'

Surely all those members of the public had already heard people talking about the incident before they were interviewed by Wragg's PCs? They could simply be passing on their impressions, saying what they thought they were expected to say.

The only facts he felt sure about were that Emily and her brother had been playing on the bank, throwing sticks for Buster. Their parents must have been with them or nearby. Had they taken their eyes off the children for a while, thinking they were safe?

And had somebody been waiting for exactly that moment, the second when a small girl was unobserved by her parents, by her older brother – a girl in a green summer dress, running after her dog?

Or had it been only one parent who had been distracted? It still wasn't clear where Dawn Nield had been. Was she guiltily staying quiet? Had she, too, seen something? Had she seen the man standing on the bank, his hands raised, fingers dripping water? Her own husband. Or had she seen something else?

Cooper moved further on. The remains of a ram pump still stood on the eastern bank at the foot of Tissington Spires. It had once raised water to the farm above. And here, by the side of the path, hundreds of copper coins had been hammered into a dead tree trunk. More coins covered the surface of stump-like metal spikes. Many of the coins looked very old, others were clearly more recent, certainly since decimalization. A few had been forced

99

into the wood within the past few months – their copper still showed bright and new where they'd bent under the blows. The stump wasn't rotten. It had been a healthy tree when it was cut down, so the wood was solid and hard. It took quite a bit of effort to hammer a coin into solid wood. This was no casual whim, like tossing a coin into water, the way people did at wells and fountains. You had to want luck badly to go to that effort.

Cooper looked up the path. Three more tree stumps ahead bore the same prickly forest of half-buried coins. A lot of people felt they needed luck in their lives.

A movement in the undergrowth made him start. Wasn't he alone, even now?

But it was a fox. Its eyes glowed red in the light of his torch. A narrow, pointed face, and suspicious eyes. After a moment, it slunk away into the darkness and was gone. Off to hunt somewhere else for its next meal.

As the water flowed towards Thorpe, it surged around a fallen tree marooned in the middle of the river like an old shipwreck. He listened to the noise of water rushing over the weir.

Half-submerged objects floated by in the stream of his memory, too. Sometimes he recognized the flotsam, sometimes it swept past his awareness before he could make it out. Every time he thought about the incident, he came back to an image of Robert Nield, hands raised, droplets of water falling from his fingers.

Cooper felt he had to get away from the banks of the river. The water was flowing too close in the darkness. He shivered as he remembered the iciness of it on his body the day before, shuddered at the thought of it creeping towards him now, eager to suck him into its currents and drag his body away on to the rocks. Water and more water, closing over him, entering his mouth, filling his lungs … He had to get away from it.

It was a sharp, steep climb up to the Natural Arch. It was here that he'd seen a figure crouched high on the rock. Hunched up, silhouetted against the sky, his face invisible. A predator on its perch, scanning the valley for prey. Had this been Sean Deacon, scrambling to escape from the scene of the activity, but reluctant to miss what was going on?

Hidden behind the arch was a shallow, mud-filled cave with a small chamber at the back. The cave was approached through a rocky cleft hung with thick jungles of ivy. Streams of water had formed patches of bright green moss on the rock.

Inside the cave, Cooper shone his torch on to the ground looking for traces of recent activity. He found a few footprints in the mud, graffiti scratched on the wall, and a scrap of cloth, which he bagged.

From the entrance to the cave, he had a narrow view through the arch down to the river. The water gleamed with movement in the darkness, surging endlessly through the night. Despite the distance, he could hear its noise. It reached him clearly on the night air, a murmuring, rushing, roaring sound that seemed to grow louder and louder until it filled the cave, bouncing off the walls and echoing all around him until it swallowed him up in roar.

Cooper felt suddenly dizzy, put his hand to the rock wall to steady himself, and touched a patch of soft, cool moss that squashed and slithered under his fingers.

Immediately he was back again in that moment, standing in the rushing water, holding the cold, limp body of Emily Nield in his arms, calling desperately for help but knowing that she was already dead. And all the time the river kept rushing, rushing over the stones, its chill striking deep into his bones and making him tremble uncontrollably.

And finally Cooper let out a long, painful scream. He wanted to hear it bounce off the pinnacles and the limestone cliffs, he needed it to fill the gorge, to drown out the noise of that cold, rushing water. The scream had been inside him for hours, and it had to come out.

Late that night in her hotel room in Birmingham, Diane Fry woke with a jolt, sweating. Another nightmare.

It wasn't the balti, but the presence of her sister that had caused the nightmare, and Rachel Murchison's insistence on talking about her childhood. It had been a big risk, she knew. Just one sound, a single movement or a smell, could trigger the train of memory that stimulated her fear.

Once again, she had been dreaming of the sound of a footstep on a creaking floorboard, a door opening in the darkness. Opening and closing continually, but nothing coming through. She'd been dreaming that she was frightened, yet had no clear focus for her fear. She heard the footstep, and the door opening, saw shadows sliding across the wall. Still nobody came in. She woke with a wail in her throat and the smell of shaving foam in her nostrils – a smell that always made her nauseous, even now.

Fry lay awake, trying to orientate herself in unfamiliar surroundings. Above her, someone was walking around the room upstairs. Perhaps that was what had intruded into her dreams, some guest returning late to the hotel. The closing of a door, the sound of random footsteps.

She got out of bed, made sure the door of her room was securely locked, the catch down, the safety chain on. It was an essential routine if she was going to get some sleep. The voices were right inside her head now.

But as soon as sleep came again, she knew that she wouldn't be able to stop the shadows bringing back the memories that she'd pushed deep into the recesses of her mind. They were memories that were too powerful and greedy to be buried completely, too vivid to be erased, too deeply etched into her soul to be forgotten. They merely wallowed and writhed in the depths, waiting for the chance to re-emerge.

First, she sensed their presence, back there in the darkness, watching, laughing, waiting eagerly for what they knew would happen next. Voices murmured and coughed. *'It's a copper,'* the voices said. *'She's a copper.'*

The memories churned and bubbled. There were brief, fragmented glimpses of figures carved into segments by the streetlights, the sickly reek of booze and violence. And then she seemed to hear one particular voice – that rough, slurring Brummie voice that slithered out of the darkness. *'How do you like this, copper?'* The same taunting laughter moving in the shadows. The same dark, menacing shapes all around, whichever way she turned. A hand in the small of her back, and a leg outstretched to trip. Then she was falling, flailing forward into the darkness. Hands grabbing her, pinching and pulling and slapping. Her arms trapped by unseen fingers that gripped her tightly, painful and shocking in their violence. Her own voice, unnaturally high-pitched and stained with terror, was trying to cry out, but failing.

Nothing could stop the flood of remembered sensations now. The smell of a sweat-soaked palm over her mouth, her head banging on the ground as she thrashed helplessly from side to side. Her clothes pulled and torn, the shock of feeling parts of her body exposed to the cruel air. *'How do you like this, copper?'* And then came the groping and the prodding and the squeezing, and the hot, intruding fingers. And, perfectly clear on the night air, the sound of a zip. Another laugh, a mumble, an excited gasp. And finally the ripping agony, and the scream that was smothered by the hand over her face, and the desperate fighting to force breath into her lungs. *'How do you like this, copper? How do you like this, copper?'* Animal noises and more laughter. The relief of the lifting of a weight from her body, as one dark shape moved away and she thought it was over.

But then it happened again.

And again.

10

Wednesday

Next morning, Ben Cooper received the first anonymous letter of his career. It was addressed to 'Police Officer Cooper', and it had been pushed through the door at Ashbourne section station. It wasn't actually written in green ink, but the writing was difficult to decipher. After a few minutes, Cooper thought he made it out:

You should look into Mr Robert Nield. He's not all he seems. The man is a sinful beast, and the Lord will punish his ways.

Well, the spelling and punctuation was good, anyway. That wasn't what he expected from an anonymous letter. It suggested someone with a decent schooling in English grammar, which wasn't easy to come by these days. An older person, he guessed. Educated in English and familiar with the Bible, if not entirely well balanced.

A shame there wasn't much information in the letter. Cooper wasn't personally familiar with anonymous allegations, but he'd imagined there would be more to go on – a few lurid details of what the accused person was supposed to have done. But here, he had to use his own imagination. And that could sometimes be worse.

Taken together with his unease about the vagueness of the witness statements from Dovedale, and his own instinctive feelings towards the Nields, Cooper had something that he didn't feel able to ignore. He might not have enough to put a case together on paper, but there was sufficient to raise concern, surely?

After a few minutes' thought, he decided to take those concerns to his DI, Paul Hitchens, who was now his immediate line manager.

In his office, Hitchens smoothed his tie anxiously as he looked at the anonymous letter.

'A nutter,' he said. 'We get them all the time. You know that, Ben.'

'I think it might be worth following up, sir.'

'Why?'

'There was a convicted sex offender among the bystanders in Dovedale,' said Cooper.

'How do you know?'

'I recognized him. His name is Sean Deacon.'

'Was he near any children?'

Cooper hesitated. 'I couldn't say for sure.'

'Do any of the witness statements mention him? Or the parents?'

'No.'

'Do you have any reason to suppose that Mr Nield is connected with Deacon in some way?'

'No.'

'Well, if you want to give this Deacon a warning, do that. But the witness statements agree on what happened to Emily Nield.'

'I don't think they do,' said Cooper. 'They're inconsistent. No two statements give exactly the same sequence of events.'

'That's always the way with multiple witnesses,' said Hitchens. 'You know that, Ben.'

Cooper did know that. But he was discovering a stubborn streak in himself. The inconsistencies in the statements felt like a personal failure. He needed to know exactly what had happened to Emily Nield. Exactly. Vague and contradictory statements from confused eyewitnesses weren't good enough.

Hitchens glowered at his intransigence.

'There's no mystery about the death of Emily Nield,' he said. 'It was an accident. The inquest was straightforward, the body has been released by the coroner, and the family will be able to hold the funeral this week.'

'Yes, it's tomorrow morning.'

'Well, there you are. By tomorrow, it will all be over and done with. The family can get on with their lives. Isn't that what we all want?'

'She was so cold. As if she was in shock.'

'She'd been in the water. And that water in the River Dove is cold at the best of times, even though the weather has been so warm. It comes straight down off the hills, you know.'

'Yes, I know.'

'As I understand the matter, it was thought at first that it might have been the shock of the cold water that stopped the girl's heart when she first went into the river. But there was no evidence of that at the postmortem. Her heart was perfectly healthy.'

'And the head injury –'

'She slipped and hit her head on a rock.'

'There's no actual evidence of that.'

'Well? Ben, you're not suggesting one of the parents hit her, or something?'

'It happens. Parents are driven beyond endurance sometimes.'

'They don't all kill their children,' said Hitchens.

'I have a feeling about the father. He's bitter about rival supermarkets. I think business must be bad.'

'So?'

'Well, he's under stress. That could drive him to do something desperate.'

'Like drowning his eight-year-old daughter? You're struggling now, Ben. Grasping at straws.'

'Sir, my instinct is telling me there's something wrong.'

Hitchens sighed.

'Ben, just stop a minute, take a deep breath, and look at the situation impartially. You'll see there's no mileage in pursuing some vague accusation, or even your instinct. Anonymous letters are ten a penny. Ignore it and move on.'

'If we ignore something now that turns out to be significant later on, it will reflect badly on this department.'

'I'm prepared to take that risk. Call it *my* instinct, if you like. And I've been in this job longer than you have, Ben.' Hitchens softened. 'Look, you don't need to find a high-profile case to prove yourself. There's plenty for you to do to show your worth.'

'That's not what I'm trying to do, sir.'

'Are you sure? I know you must see this as your opportunity to shine, with DS Fry out of the way for a while.'

'No, sir. Really.'

'Mmm. Well, take it easy. Don't invent some mystery where there isn't one, all right?'

'All right, sir.'

'Ben, it's not personal, is it? There's no emotional involvement? I mean, I know you were there at the time. Well, more than there, you took action. You –'

'I tried to save her life, yes.'

'Yes, of course. But you have to remain objective. Take a step back, consider this incident as if you weren't involved. I repeat, there's no mystery. Okay?'

'I suppose so.'

'Now start paying some attention to the rest of your caseload. There's Michael Lowndes, for a start.'

'Yes, sir. Michael Lowndes.'

The Grand was the largest hotel in Edendale, a vast Victorian pile designed for the Duke of Devonshire and now owned by a Spanish company based in Majorca. The lobby was certainly grand, with its marble pillars, its chandeliers, and its wide staircase. From outside, the hotel looked French in architectural style, but inside the decoration was almost Moorish.

Cooper had never stayed here, or eaten in the expensive restaurant. But he'd once attended a wedding reception in the Cavendish Suite, and had his photograph taken with the rest of the wedding party on the lawn in front of the cherry trees.

He identified himself at the reception desk, and was taken through to the office, where a duty manager escorted him to the kitchens. They passed along an elegant corridor with gleaming tiles, then through a door marked 'STAFF ONLY' and entered a completely different world, away from the eyes of the guests.

Here they found Sean Deacon dressed in white overalls, mopping the floors. Not exactly Gordon Ramsey, then.

Deacon was almost exactly as Cooper remembered him. A little older, of course, but it was hardly noticeable. An unremarkable face, the face of a middle-aged man with receding hair and a hint of grey stubble, a man who could pass unnoticed in any street. He'd put some weight on around the waist, moved a little more slowly. But Deacon was the same man he'd seen in Dovedale.

'Sean Deacon,' he said.

Deacon undoubtedly recognized the tone, if not Cooper's voice. He had enough experience of the police. He looked up, a sideways glance – wary and suspicious. The eyes left Cooper in no doubt.

They were given a small storeroom to talk privately. Cooper let Deacon sit on the only chair, while he stood over him. Deacon didn't object. He looked resigned, as if he'd gone through all this before and knew where it would end.

Cooper checked his details – his age, his address in Wirksworth. Deacon agreed that he was a registered sex offender.

'What is it that you want?' he said. 'What's happened that you want to implicate me in?'

'Where were you on Monday morning, Mr Deacon?'

Deacon sighed. 'I expect you already know. You people never ask those sorts of questions unless you already know the answers. It gets very tiresome.'

Cooper was taken aback by the way Deacon talked. He sounded well educated, his Derbyshire vowels softened by some other accent. Not only that, but Deacon spoke softly, with a relaxed manner that was more than just resignation. He seemed quite calm. He wasn't what Cooper had expected.

'You were in Dovedale on Monday morning. Is that right, sir?'

'Yes, of course it is.' Deacon looked up at him. 'You were there, too. Your picture was in the paper. They didn't do you justice. What did you say your name was again?'

'DC … I mean, Acting DS Cooper.'

'Forgotten who you are? Join the club.'

Cooper turned and walked a few paces away from him, found he was against the wall, and turned back. Deacon looked at him, smiling gently.

'Thought you were meeting a monster, did you?'

Cooper found he was no longer looking at the man of his memory. This wasn't the watchful predator of his recollection, the figure crouched on the rock above Dovedale. His mind had played him a trick, conjured something out of his imagination. And Deacon was right – he'd come here with an expectation.

'I did my time,' said Deacon. 'But that's not enough, I know. Not enough for society.'

'No.'

A four-year prison sentence meant that Sean Deacon would be permanently on the Sex Offender Register. That was unless he took advantage of a High Court ruling that indefinite registration was incompatible with the European Convention of Human Rights. The court had declared that it denied offenders a chance to prove they no longer posed a risk of re-offending.

Cooper tried to remember the man he'd once interviewed for that attempted abduction, the suspected paedophile slouching from an interview room to a cell in the custody suite at Edendale. That look over his shoulder, the tilt of the head, the distinctive way he moved. This was the same man. And yet he wasn't.

'What were you doing in Dovedale?' asked Cooper again.

'I'd been walking. It's my hobby, when I'm not at work. I was on the moors west of Tissington. I'd parked my car in a lay-by on the A515, and I followed a footpath near Gaglane Barn to look at an old lime kiln in the middle of the fields there. The path comes out above Dovedale, near Reynard's Cave.'

Cooper nodded. It sounded about right so far.

'And then I heard all the noise in the dale, so I climbed up on to the arch to see what was happening,' said Deacon. He looked at Cooper again. 'And that was it.'

'You're sure you weren't near the children at all?'

'Yes, I'm sure. Do you have any witnesses who say otherwise?'

'No, we don't,' admitted Cooper.

Deacon studied him. Now Cooper felt he was the one being assessed, and perhaps failing to live up to expectations.

'I heard about the little girl who drowned,' said Deacon. 'You were the one who tried to save her, weren't you? I read it in the paper.'

'Yes, that was me. But I failed.'

Deacon shook his head sadly. 'It's so often the case, that we either succeed or fail. Society doesn't allow for anything else, does it?'

'I'm not sure what you mean.'

The man stood up slowly. Cooper felt no sense of threat from him at all. In his white overalls, he looked faintly pathetic. Yet he had his own strange air of dignity.

109

'I'll admit there was another reason why I was on top of the arch near Reynard's Cave,' he said.

'What is that?'

'I like being high up.'

'So you can see what's going on? Check out who's around?'

Deacon shook his head. 'No, it's not that. I like the idea of flying. Don't you?'

'I don't think about it much.'

'When I'm high up like that, I think about flying. Or perhaps about falling.'

Cooper looked at him again. Did Deacon have suicidal tendencies? It wasn't uncommon among sex offenders. Their condition was often incurable, and many could see no other way out of a life of constant suspicion.

Deacon smiled sadly. 'Life is all about falling and flying, isn't it?'

'What?'

'Falling and flying. If you're good at what you do in life, you fly. If you're bad at it, you fall. It's as simple as that, Acting DS Cooper. The same with death, really. Up or down, falling or flying. We can only do one or the other. There's no in between, is there?'

It was a pity that his name had appeared in the paper. Cooper picked up a copy of the *Eden Valley Times* on his way back to West Street. The story wasn't difficult to find, since it was on the front page, and they'd dug out some old photograph of him from their archives. It made him look about fifteen years old.

Publicity was rarely a positive thing for an individual police officer, unless you happened to be involved in a community project, helping out at a fun day or giving kids fishing lessons. And then it was pretty much compulsory. When it came to major incidents, contact with the media was best left to the bosses and the Media Office.

But the headline 'Cop's brave bid to save drowning tot' couldn't do much damage, no matter how over the top it was. The subs on the *Eden Valley Times* loved short words, preferably no more than three letters. 'Bid', 'cop', 'tot' made a perfect combination. They hardly needed a verb.

Of course, Edendale would soon be without a local rag altogether. Everyone knew that the *Eden Valley Times* was on its last legs. The paper hadn't been locally owned for years. Its present proprietors were a big publishing corporation based in Edinburgh, who had centralized everything they could think of. They'd moved admin to Peterborough, page production to Chesterfield, and printing to Gateshead. The edition Cooper held in his hands felt flimsy, no more than forty pages, when once it had been more than eighty.

Advertising revenue had fallen through the floor for papers like the *Times*. People got their news from TV or the internet these days. And once the recession cut the legs from under the Property and Motors sections, that was pretty much the last nail in the coffin. There were a few reporters left in the office on the corner of Fargate, but they rarely ventured out on the streets. Everything had to be done by phone when they were so short-handed.

Still, they'd managed to spell his name right, and the subs in Chesterfield hadn't messed up the story too much. He supposed he ought to be grateful for small mercies. The trouble with publicity like this was that everyone he met would want to ask him about it, to pat him on the back and say 'Well done, anyway' or 'Hard luck – you tried.' It wasn't what he needed. Maybe he should keep his head down for a few days until it had all blown over.

Back in the office, everyone was pestering him for attention. They needed his advice, they wanted his signature, they had messages for him, they had questions. Always more questions.

'Want me to follow that up?'

'I can run with that if you like, Ben.'

'The DI wants to know why it hasn't been actioned.'

He really needed some advice. Cooper found himself automatically scrolling to Fry's number on his mobile. At the last second, he remembered that she wasn't around. Well, he could phone her, but she was in Birmingham. She would have no interest in what he was doing back in Derbyshire. And why should she?

Finally, Cooper called a meeting of his team. Gavin Murfin was the senior DC, as the longest serving. Luke Irvine and Becky

111

Hurst made up the rest of the team. They were hardly an army of crime fighters. But they were doing their best, one case at a time.

'So what's the status of the drugs case on the Devonshire Estate? The Michael Lowndes enquiry.'

'Our information says that there'll be another meeting tonight,' said Murfin. 'We could nail them this time.'

'Let's do it, then,' said Cooper.

'Really?'

Three mouths fell open.

'Diane would usually tell us to fill in all the paperwork and do a risk assessment,' said Murfin.

'It was all done the first time, wasn't it?'

'Well, yeah, but –'

'I'll sign it off, then. Let's set up the tasks. If we pull it off, I'd like Becky and Luke to make the arrests. Is that okay with you, Gavin?'

Murfin managed to control his eyebrows. 'No problem, boss.'

While the others busied themselves, Cooper picked up the paper, read the headline again, and sighed. Well, as long as he didn't get all the nutters in Edendale phoning him up and writing him letters in green ink ...

It was only when he read down to the end of the story that he discovered the writer knew far more than they ought to.

'Police are believed to have received an anonymous letter making undisclosed allegations against the Nield family.'

How the heck had the *Eden Valley Times* known that?

A call to the news editor established that the paper had received a copy of the same letter that was sent to the police, and theirs had come in anonymously, too.

So it was used without checking? Was that the standard of journalism now?

'We don't have the staff,' said the news editor.

Don't have the staff? Cooper put down the phone and looked at his team of three. Join the club.

11

The pigeon park. That's what she'd called it when she was a child. She would come here with Alice Bowskill sometimes when they were on a shopping trip in the city. The Bull Ring, New Street, and a stop off here for a sit down. The pigeon park.

In reality, it was the graveyard of St Philip's Cathedral. Conveniently situated near shops and office blocks, it was full of people eating their sandwiches on the benches at lunchtime. Hence the pigeons. Grubby grey pests waddling about the pathways, eyeing up the public hopefully for scraps of bread.

She'd been nervous of the birds as a kid, anxious about their beaks and claws, startled by the sudden clatter of their wings. But she'd been fascinated by them too, in a way. These pigeons seemed to inhabit an entirely separate world of their own – clustering on the tallest buildings at night, stalking the parks by day. They lived apart from people, but took advantage of them when it suited. Now she could see nothing interesting about the birds at all. They were scavengers, pure and simple. They probably carried disease on their scaly feet and fleas in their feathers.

Fry looked up. She'd heard that peregrine falcons were nesting on the roof of the BT Tower these days. If falcons ate pigeons, they were welcome.

A few hundreds yards away stood the West Midlands Police headquarters in Lloyd House, on Colmore Circus. The old *Post and Mail* building used to stand next to it, with a digital clock high on its upper storeys. The last time she'd seen it, the building was in the late stages of demolition, all the journalists having moved out to a vast open-plan newsroom at Fort Dunlop.

Fry checked her phone to make sure there was a signal. It was a habit she'd got into while she'd been living in Derbyshire. Those Peak District hills were a nightmare. But here, she was actually able to stay in touch.

She was waiting for a call to arrange a meeting place. A message had been left at her hotel this morning. An old friend wanted to offer some information. A voice from her past, another reminder of her time here in Birmingham.

On the way to St Philip's, she'd walked through the Bull Ring and into Selfridges, 'the boob tube' building, the Dalek's Ballgown, covered in fifteen thousand aluminium discs in a design inspired by a Paco Rabanne dress. She'd inhaled the smells from the food hall on the ground floor as they wafted their way up through the cat's cradle of escalators.

For a moment, she'd paused in front of Birmingham Town Hall. Its Victorian architects had made it look like a Roman temple, with forty marble columns. Once, on a school trip, a guide had explained that those pillars were modelled on the Temple of Castor and Pollux in Rome. The Temple of Bastard and Bollocks, the kids had called it, giggling among themselves.

Anthony Gormley's *Iron Man* stood nearby in Victoria Square, a twenty-foot mummy figure leaning to one side, as if rising from the tomb.

And then the call came.

'Meet me at the old cemetery in the Jewellery Quarter. Actually, there are two. Make sure it's the southern one, Warstone Lane. There's an entrance from Pitsford Street.'

'A cemetery, Andy?'

'It's quiet at this time of day. And handy for the Metro.'

Fry ended the call and shoo'd away an inquisitive pigeon. The Jewellery Quarter had survived, then. That was a miracle. It was one of the legacies of the city's industrial past, an area of Hockley with dealers and jewellery workshops providing a glimpse into a historic trade. Now it was a tram stop on the Metro line from Snow Hill to Wolverhampton.

There were other monuments still surviving in the city, here and there. Monuments to the 1960s, mostly. The Rotunda. The British Telecom tower. They were antiquities now, mere curiosities in the landscape, just the way that Neolithic stone circles were in the Peak District. History was a pretty elastic concept, wasn't it? All a matter of perspective.

Fry parked her Audi on the top level of the Jewellery Quarter car park in Vyse Street. She'd found the entrance tucked between

114

the Creative Watch Company and the premises of Regency Jewellers.

From the roof level, near the top of Staircase C, she had a clear view up the street towards the exit from Jewellery Quarter Metro station. After a few minutes a train went through, then a blue-and-red Metro tram unit quietly pulled into the northbound platform.

She'd checked out the station earlier. She was confident there was only one exit. Kewley had to cross from the tram stop on a walkway over the railway lines and use the stairs or lift to reach the exit by the ticket office. He would emerge under the giant clock mechanism, near the old cast-iron street urinal that was locked and gradually filling up with rubbish. So he only had one route to choose from the station, which was to come towards her down Vyse Street, past the awnings of the gold and jewellery dealers to the corner of Pitsford Street.

The Cultural Quarter, the Jewellery Quarter, the Irish Quarter, the Convention Quarter. And now there was a designation for the Gun Quarter – and they didn't mean Handsworth, but the industrial area around Queensway and Lancaster Circus, where traditional gun manufacturers were still based. As for the city centre, the latest Big City Plan called this 'The Core'. A core surrounded by quarters? It was just like the planners to come up with some giant fruit metaphor.

A small trickle of people emerged from the station on to the pavement and headed off in different directions. Kewley was the last to come out. She recognized him even from this distance, even with the cap pulled over his eyes and the padded jacket to disguise his shape. There was something about the way people moved that made them recognizable whatever they wore. It took a lot of practice to disguise your body's natural angle and rhythm.

Kewley paused in the station entrance, looked all around him carefully, pretending to check his pockets for something. An old habit, of course. It would have been enough for Fry to identify him, even without the cap.

Andy Kewley was an old street cop. He'd learned to scan every doorway and corner before he made his move. It just never occurred to him to look up.

He reached the corner of Pitsford Street near Bicknell and Sons, and turned down the side of the cemetery. Fry noticed that there was no wall or fence separating their meeting place from the street here, just a low kerb. It would be possible to enter and exit the cemetery at any point, and the row of cars parked at the kerbside would obscure her view. But Kewley continued to stroll dutifully down Pitsford Street until he came opposite a bright yellow wall, then he turned on to a path between two plane trees and entered the graveyard like a respectable citizen going about his business.

Fry knew she would lose sight of him now between the gravestones. But still she waited, watching a red Ford Fiesta and a white Transit van parked on the north side of Pitsford Street. No sign of movement.

'Okay, then.'

She looked at her watch. Kewley was bang on time for their meeting, of course. She, on the other hand, was going to be a bit late. And that was the way she liked it.

Finally, she left the car park, walked down towards the Café Sovereign and stepped through the cemetery entrance. As she approached, she was assaulted by a powerful, sickly sweet smell. Some kind of white blossom on the bushes was filling the air with its aroma. She didn't know what sort of pollinating insect it was trying so hard to attract, but when she breathed in she felt as though she'd been punched in the nose. Oh great, it could be hay fever time.

The rushing sound she heard was the wind hissing through the trees, washing over her.

'Diane?'

Kewley took off the cap, revealing thinning hair streaked with grey. A warm breeze wandered through the plane trees, stirring a lock of his hair. When he raised a hand to push it back, she noticed that it wasn't as steady a hand as it once had been. The cumulative effects of thirty years in the job? Or was Andy Kewley drinking too much, like so many others?

'You've lost more weight since I saw you last,' he said. 'And you were never exactly the biggest lass in Brum, were you?'

'No.'

116

Fry looked around at the site he'd chosen for their meeting. In the middle of the cemetery, they were standing at the top of a terrace of curved brick walls. Two of the walls had rows of small, sealed-up entrances built into them, like arched doorways.

'What is this place? I thought it was a cemetery.'

'Yes, and these are the catacombs,' said Kewley. 'Built into the side of an old sandpit. Don't you think they're interesting? They always remind me of a sunken amphitheatre. You can imagine gladiators fighting to the death down there on the grass. The only difference is, the spectators are already dead.'

'Long since dead,' said Fry. 'These places make my flesh creep.'

Kewley laughed. 'They're harmless. Just our ancestors taking a bit of trouble over their final resting place.'

'Only those who could afford it, I suppose.'

'There's another cemetery to the north of the station – Key Hill. That one has catacombs too. Joseph Chamberlain is buried there.'

'Really?'

Fry wasn't sure who Joseph Chamberlain was. There was a monument of him in Chamberlain Square, of course, and she'd passed a clock tower named after him on the corner of Vyse Street, near the Rose Villa Tavern. She thought there was even a Metro tram with his name on its side. But he was just one more Victorian, wasn't he? Dead beyond living memory. She imagined him with a monocle and mutton-chop whiskers. Part of Birmingham's vanished past.

'I don't like Key Hill so much. It has a campaign group who are busy restoring it. The Friends of Key Hill Cemetery. There are fences and gates, and they lock it up at night to keep people out. Oh and there are too many trees.' Kewley gestured around him. 'This one doesn't have any friends. Just the drunks. Just the dead and the desperate. And you can see who's coming fifty yards away.'

Fry imagined him using this cemetery for years to meet his informants. But it wouldn't be wise to keep coming here after he'd left the job. Too many people might remember. Too many of them might have a grievance to settle. Maybe it was just one of those

117

eccentric fancies that overcame old coppers when they retired. Some had a mad hankering to run pubs, or to look for a quiet life in Northern Ireland. Others chose to hang around in Victorian graveyards.

'They say unhealthy vapours from these catacombs led to the Birmingham Cemeteries Act, which required non-interred coffins to be sealed with lead.'

The upper walkway looked down past two tiers of catacombs to the circle of grass in the centre. From the safety rail, it was quite a vertiginous drop. Lower down, part of the wall had collapsed, scattering gravestones. It was supported by steel props, awaiting some future repair.

The cemetery had been well used. Victorian gravestones marched across the slopes, lurked in the hollows and hid beneath shrouds of ivy. Some memorials were large, horizontal stone slabs that she couldn't help walking over as she found the way down to the lower levels.

On the circle of grass stood two or three dozen memorials under the shade of the trees.

Andy Kewley had been a frontline detective, hardened by thirty years' experience. According to his own story, he wasn't the kind of officer who was afraid of work, but he'd started to want more routine, a bit of stability. The constant changes had unsettled him, made him wonder whether he was appreciated properly. Every officious memo he received had made him count the days to his retirement.

'Sorry to be out of the job, or not?'

'I miss it,' admitted Kewley.

'You know there's still a lot of demand for more civilian staff. Prisoner handling, statement taking, file preparation. There are always cases under review. Any experienced officer can take his full pension and complete his Staff 1 at the same time. Unless you're planning on retiring to the Costa del Sol?'

'I'll bear it in mind.'

His expression said otherwise. He'd probably heard it all before. His eyes suggested that he was a man who'd heard everything before.

118

'Cases under review.' He laughed. 'You can say that again. I wouldn't be surprised if they re-opened the Nielson and Whittle enquiry, just to look as if they're doing something.'

'Donald Nielson and Lesley Whittle? They're just relics of the 1970s, aren't they? Most of the present West Midlands coppers weren't even alive then. The Black Panther is as much ancient history to them as Jack the Ripper. Things move on, Andy. Times change.'

'You can say that again. Brum was a British city once.'

Fry grimaced, but didn't answer.

'I know,' said Kewley, without even having to look at her face. 'I'm not allowed to say things like that. If I was still in the force, you'd report me to the DI and I'd be suspended by tomorrow morning. Probably lose my job and my pension entitlement, too. Just for speaking the truth, eh?'

'Andy –'

'Well, thank God I'm not on the force any more. I got out at the right time, I reckon. It's you poor bloody sods who have to button your lips and take the shit.'

'No, it's not like that, Andy. Not really.'

'Oh? What, whiter than white up in sainted Derbyshire, are you? I thought I heard you had very some active BNP areas.'

'Andy, what did you want to tell me?'

'I thought I might be able to help you.'

'How?'

'Did you know there was an arrest after your assault? I was responsible for that.'

'You produced a suspect?'

'Let's say I provided intelligence. It was good intelligence too, as it turned out. This wasn't one of the primary suspects, but he knew who was involved, all right, and he helped to cover up. A real piece of work. He was as guilty as anyone I ever met.'

'So what did you do?'

Kewley shrugged. 'We needed information, and we didn't want to spend days dragging it out of him bit by bit, with a brief at his elbow telling him to do the "no comment" stuff. So we fast-tracked the interview.'

'Fast-tracked …?'

119

Kewley looked at her, gave her no more than a conspiratorial glance. But she understood.

'I don't want to know any more,' she said.

'No, of course you don't. You wouldn't want to be contaminated.'

'But you got what you wanted to know?'

'Not entirely. We never got the names out of him.' Kewley smiled. 'But if we had … what do you reckon, Diane? Would the ends have justified the means, or not?'

'What was he charged with?'

'Attempting to pervert,' said Kewley. 'Pervert the course of justice, I mean. Obviously.'

'And what happened?'

'Miscarriage of justice. He got a "get out of jail free" card and a few quid in his pocket, and off he went.'

'It's hardly the first time, Andy.'

'No, there's a whole army of them out there.'

Andy Kewley's career could best be described as chequered. In his early days in CID, before she'd teamed up with him at Aston, Kewley had spent some time in the West Midlands Serious Crime Squad. The squad had been disbanded, more than two decades ago now, following accusations that its members had fabricated evidence, tortured suspects, and written false confessions.

For years, lawyers had been demanding fresh enquiries into the scale of corruption, claiming that dozens of innocent people had served time in jail. One had been quoted as saying that the Serious Crime Squad had operated as if they were in the Wild West. *They were out of control.*

'You lost a crucial witness, right?' said Kewley.

'You're well informed, Andy. How do you manage that?'

He ignored the question. 'She pulled out of the case, decided she didn't want to testify after all. The old story, eh? Someone got to her, Diane.'

'One of the suspects?'

'Or maybe their friends.' Kewley shrugged. 'Who knows?'

'She was supposed to be on witness protection,' said Fry. 'How would they have found her?'

'Information. It's easy to get hold of, if you know the right people.'

'Who?'

Again Kewley seemed to ignore the question. Fry remembered this habit of his, recalled how it had often infuriated her. He always wanted to go round the houses before he responded. But later he would drop the answer in casually, as if he'd never been asked.

'There's a real hot potato bothering the bosses around here at the moment,' said Kewley. 'Some of the brass are shitting themselves trying to work out what to do for the best. If you ask me, they're damned whatever they do.'

'What are you talking about?'

He glanced over his shoulder in a ridiculously melodramatic gesture, as if anyone would be lurking behind the gravestones to listen into their conversation.

'Well, you know there's been this recruitment policy in the West Midlands? Quotas for BME officers.'

'Black and minority ethnics.'

'Yeah. Trying to meet government targets.' Kewley looked as though he might spit on the grass. 'Like they say, political correctness gone –'

'Okay, I know.'

'It's turned into a real sensitive issue in Brum, and it's not going away. A couple of years ago, there was a Channel Four documentary, *Undercover Mosque*. The chiefs got that wrong big time. They accused the production company of editing the words of imams to stir up race hatred. But they ended up having to apologize in the High Court.'

Fry remembered it well. One Muslim cleric had been recorded claiming 'Allah created the woman deficient'. But the police had claimed that the programme itself was *Sufficient to undermine community cohesion* and *likely to undermine feelings of public reassurance and safety of those communities in the West Midlands for which the Chief Constable has a responsibility.*

'Now, there are allegations that some Asian officers have sympathies with the extremist elements,' said Kewley. 'That they won't take action over honour killings, for example. You can see how the management are in a bind.'

Fry nodded. She could see it all too well. *Community cohesion.* It was the latest buzz phrase in multicultural societies. You didn't hear it so much in the Peak District.

She looked at the graves of the Victorian dead all around her. According to their memorials, many of them hadn't actually died but had merely 'fallen asleep'. If they woke up now, they'd get a shock. And over there was another one. *Not lost, but gone before.*

'Euphemisms,' said Fry. 'Don't you hate them?'

Kewley looked as though he didn't agree.

'Have you heard the name William Leeson?' he said.

Fry's ears pricked up. This was the way it worked with Kewley. He distracted you with something irrelevant. Then the important information was dropped into the conversation like an afterthought. You had to be paying attention, or you missed it.

'Leeson? No. Who is he?'

'A dodgy lawyer from Smethwick, who used to practise here in the city. I thought you might have come across him.'

'I could have done,' said Fry. 'But hundreds of defence briefs come and go through interview rooms. I don't remember all their names.'

'You might want to remember this one,' said Kewley.

'Why?'

Kewley didn't answer directly. He seemed to be getting more nervous now, and jumped when a motorcycle with an unsilenced exhaust roared by on the Middleway.

'William Leeson first came on to the scene in a big way during all that bother with the Serious Crime Squad,' he said. 'He loved getting the attention, calling for public enquiries and Appeal Court hearings. "Miscarriage of justice" was practically tattoo'd on his forehead, he said it so often.'

'Was he the one who said you were operating like the Wild West?' asked Fry.

'No. But he would have said it, if he'd thought of it. He was always small-scale, though – and he got pushed out by the smarter, more expensive briefs who elbowed their way in when they saw a lucrative bandwagon rolling. Leeson got really pissed off about it. That was why he turned.'

'Turned?'

'He started to give us information.'

'What kind of information?'

Kewley pulled his cap lower over his eyes, and wiped the palms of his hands on his jacket.

'I shouldn't be telling you any of this.'

'Who says? You're retired, out of the force. You're a civilian now, Andy – as a free as a bird. Get used to it.'

'I could still get myself into deep shit. You don't understand.'

The bottom end of the cemetery seemed to back on to the middle ring road. Around it, she could see the commercial buildings of the Jewellery Quarter, the Mint in Icknield Street, a factory chimney, all the places that these affluent Victorians would have made their money.

Fry noticed that the memorials nearest to her had names like John Eachus and Walter Peyton Chance. Strange how names like that seemed to have died, along with the Victorians themselves. She saw defaced angels, tombs blackened with soot. A wire mesh bin was filled with empty bottles of Olde English cider and Frosty Jack, the booze of choice for street drinkers. Nearby, a statue lay broken and beheaded, an empty vodka bottle on the ground at its feet. Many of the memorials had fallen, or had been pushed over. The ground in this part of the cemetery was covered in broken lumps of moss.

And there was that sickly smell again. She would have to get away soon. It was starting to smell like the scent of death.

'I'm just telling you, Diane. There are things you need to know. You could ask someone else, but whether you'll get the truth or not ...'

'Okay, okay.'

'I just want you to know, there are political considerations at play right now. Much bigger issues than a successful conviction in any cold case – and I mean *any* case, no matter who the victim is. You understand me?'

'I'm not sure I do, Andy.'

'Damn it, I can't make it any clearer,' he said irritably. 'Look – anybody can get tossed aside, if it suits them. Justice is a slippery concept these days. You need to watch your back, that's what I'm saying. I gave my statement, Diane, that's all I can do.'

Fry stared at him, wondering whether he'd gone completely off the rails since he retired. Leaving the job took people in different ways. It seemed as though Kewley might have developed some kind of conspiracy obsession, or paranoid delusion. Probably he couldn't cope with the fact that he was no longer on the inside, not a member of the tribe any more. It was that primal instinct again. A desperation to belong. A craving to be part of the game.

Kewley took a breath, looked anxious at his own outburst.

'By the way,' he said, 'who's dealing with your case now?'

'Gareth Blake.'

'Blake? I remember him when he was a young DC, fresh behind the ears. Pain in the neck he was then. I don't suppose he's changed much?'

'I couldn't say. We worked together for a while, but that was years ago.'

'Gareth Blake … a DI now, isn't he? In fact, I hear he's well on his way to making DCI in the not too distant future. Yes, he's definitely got his foot on the ladder, that one. He wouldn't want anything to muck up his pristine record at this point, would he?'

Fry looked at him. 'What are you saying? Has Blake got something to hide?'

Kewley touched the side of his nose – a conspiratorial gesture that he somehow managed to make look obscene.

'You know what they say – the higher a monkey climbs up the tree, the more you see of his arse.'

He laughed, and turned away. It was a signal that she wouldn't get any more out of him on that subject. Not right now, anyway. She might need some kind of pressure she could bring to bear. But that was for another day.

'I'll leave first,' said Kewley. 'If you could just give it a few minutes.'

'Fine.'

Fry turned her back, so that she didn't watch him leave. The head of a broken angel lay at her feet, its blank eyes pressed into

124

the grass, face mottled with damp. A magpie hopped among the graves. An airliner growled overhead towards Elmdon. Counting the seconds till she could get away from this smell, she waited alone in the cemetery.

Half an hour later, Fry stood on the corner of Thornhill Road in Handsworth, and watched Andy Kewley's car turn off the road under a line of maple trees. He pulled up to a set of blue gates on Golds Hill Road. After a moment, his BMW disappeared as it entered the car park behind the Victorian police station.

Thornhill Road, Handsworth. F3 OCU. Why did numbers and letters stick in her mind so well? By the time she'd put in thirty years' service, she'd have a brain clogged with acronyms.

Her phone rang.

'Did you track him?'

'Yes, he went into the nick on Thornhill Road.'

'I thought he looked shifty.'

'Where are you now, Sis?'

'Still at the Metro station.'

'I'll pick you up in a few minutes.'

Angie was a stranger to Andy Kewley. After he left the cemetery, Angie had tailed Kewley back to the Jewellery Quarter Metro station. He hadn't expected to be followed going back. Just one stop north, he'd got off again at Soho Benson Road station, where he'd collected a blue BMW from the car park and driven up Factory Road towards Solo Hill and the white dome of the Gurdwara Nishkam Sewak Jatha.

Diane had picked his BMW up travelling on Soho Road. By then, she'd been pretty sure where he was heading.

She walked back down Thornhill Road, past the glass walls of the Community Roots enterprise centre, and emerged on to Soho Road, the heart of Birmingham's Little India. It was solid with traffic, all the way down from the Gurdwara. The next block was full of Asian shops: Bollywood Connections, Karishma Jewellers, the State Bank of India. A group of Indian girls sat on the wall outside the City College annexe. A Muslim with a long beard came out of Handsworth Library clutching a handful of Urdu books.

125

Fry hadn't felt herself to be so much in a city for a long time. Even the maple trees had something urban about them. There had been a pub here, the Frighted Horse. An M&B house, she was sure. But the building on the corner was boarded up, plastered with posters for a kick-boxing contest. She supposed the pub no longer fit so well among the sari shops, costume jewellers, and halal chicken takeaways.

A few hundred yards down, old men in snow-white turbans and grey beards stood outside the Sikh Gurdwara. Fry thought the complex added a bit of architectural class to Soho Road. They said that anyone could walk in at lunchtime and sit down in front of a metal dish full of chapattis and chickpeas. Inside the Gurdwara, the pages of the Sikh scriptures, the *Guru Granth Sahib*, were recited continuously around the clock, every day of the year.

She picked up a leaflet that someone had tossed aside near the bus shelter. It listed the Five Evils, the *pancadokh* of Sikh Scripture – the major weaknesses of the human personality. Only five? She turned the leaflet over. Oh yes – the common evils far exceeded five in number, it said. But these were the main obstacles in man's pursuit of the moral and spiritual path. *Kam, krodh, lobh, moh* and *ahankar*. Lust, rage, greed, emotional attachment, and ego.

Fry dropped the leaflet into a litter bin. They were weaknesses, all right. All of them. Maybe she should go into the Gurdwara and listen to some readings from the *Guru Granth Sahib*. She might learn something.

But there was another weakness that wasn't mentioned, one that she was as prone to as anyone else.

Too much trust.

12

Examining Fry's desk for some files he needed, Cooper came across the latest issue of *Grapevine* magazine, produced by the British Association of Women Police. He picked it up, feeling a bit guilty about even looking at it, since he was a man.

According to an item on the cover, West Midlands Police had been included in *The Times* list of the 'Top Fifty Places Women Want to Work' for the third year running. Well, if it was such a great organization to work for, why had Diane Fry bothered coming to Derbyshire?

But he knew the answer to that. He'd known it within a few days of meeting her, after her transfer to E Division. She'd blurted out the truth one afternoon on a hillside overlooking a Peak District village.

He hadn't known what to say to her then. He wouldn't really know what to say now.

He wondered how she was getting on in Birmingham, whether she would call anybody in Edendale to keep them up to date. Who *was* there that she might call? Not him, anyway.

In Ashbourne, the Nields looked less glad to see him than they had before. Of course, they'd heard about the anonymous letter, although they didn't get the *Eden Valley Times* here in Ashbourne. Cooper had found that out as soon as he phoned them. They'd been trying to get hold him for hours, they said. Their messages were probably on his desk somewhere.

'A disturbed person,' said Robert Nield, when Cooper was seated in their lounge. 'An attention seeker. It's very sad, really.'

'They need help,' added Dawn, wiping her hands on a kitchen towel. 'When you find out who it is, tell them they should see a psychiatrist.'

Cooper wondered what Mrs Nield had been busying herself with. He bet there was always something that needed doing. And if it didn't, she would do it anyway. Keeping herself occupied.

'That's the trouble,' he said. 'I don't know how we can go about finding who sent the letter – unless you have any ideas yourselves?'

They shook their heads in unison. 'No idea,' said Nield.

'No disgruntled members of staff, perhaps? Somebody you sacked recently?'

'I don't often sack people. Staff members leave occasionally, but of their own accord. We're quite a little family at Lodge's. Any problems we have, we sort them out among ourselves.'

Quite a little family. Cooper looked around the living room, wondering what Mr Nield's idea of a happy little family was, in terms of his staff. Well organized and hard working, no doubt. But whether they were happy – that was a different matter. None of the rooms he'd seen in this house looked as though they'd ever had children in them, other than Alex's bedroom.

'Who's looking after the store at the moment?' asked Cooper.

'I have a good assistant manager. David Underwood. He's perfectly capable, and he knows he can phone me at any time.'

'That's lucky.'

'I believe in delegation. It's part of being a good manager.'

Dawn was turning back to the kitchen, but paused to speak to Cooper. 'Oh, Alex said you should go up and see him again if you came back.'

'Did he?'

'I think you must have showed some interest in what he was doing. I've never understood any of it myself.'

'He attends Queen Elizabeth's Grammar School, doesn't he?'

'Yes, Alex is in Year Nine at the moment. He's very clever, you know. He's already decided what he wants to do next year. He's going to study for a DiDA.'

'I'm sorry?'

'A Diploma in Digital Applications. It's equivalent to four GCSEs. That's one of the reasons we wanted him to go to Queen Elizabeth's, so he had the chance of a DiDA.'

Upstairs, Cooper looked at the closed doors on the landing. One still bore Emily's name on a little plaque decorated with pink flowers. For a moment, he thought about opening the door to peek in, or asking the Nields if he could see their daughter's room. But he decided that he didn't want to see it. The sight of her clothes and toys might turn Emily into a real, living person, and the idea was unsettling.

He found Alex fidgeting expectantly, perhaps knowing that he'd arrived and was in the house talking to his parents.

Unsurprisingly, *War Tribe* was on the screen of his PC, the representation of a city with roofs and battlements. Looking closer, Cooper saw that there was movement in the city. A tiny flag waving on a tower, a soldier pacing up and down, a workman sawing at a bench outside a building.

'How's the game going?' he asked.

'We're going to be in a war,' said Alex. 'Look.'

He clicked a link, and a map appeared, variously coloured blocks on a grid. Cooper guessed they represented other players' cities in the neighbourhood.

'Who are the bright red ones?' he asked.

'Our tribe's enemies. Look, they're near me, on the edge of Continent 34. Turks.'

'Turks?'

'Yeah.

'You mean that's their tribe?'

'No, they're Turks. Aggressive and well organized, those Turks. You can see them starting to expand already, look. They grab the biggest barbs and conquer the tribeless players. They'll be coming for my cities soon, if they think I'm vulnerable. First there'll be scouts to suss me out, and maybe a few raiding parties. Before you know it, they'll be swarming all over me.'

'You're losing me a bit,' said Cooper. 'Barbs?'

'Barbarian villages. The unoccupied ones, that don't belong to any player. You can take those over and expand your empire.'

'I see.'

'If you don't take them, someone else does. And if they get bigger than you, they're a threat. Bigger players try to bully you.'

'Can't you try diplomacy?' said Cooper, though it sounded even to him like a stab in the dark.

Alex shook his head. 'Sometimes. But there's never any point in trying to talk to the Turks. All you get back is gibberish. If they can't speak English, they shouldn't be on the UK server really, should they? That's in the rules. English is the official *War Tribe* language, even if the guys who run it seem to be German, and some of the player guides are in German too. It's a bit confusing sometimes.'

'Yes,' said Cooper. The boy was talking too fast now for him to follow, gabbling excitedly. He might as well be talking gibberish himself.

'Oh, well. Everyone understands battle-axes, whatever language they speak,' said Alex.

'Right. Battle-axes.'

'An army of berserkers will go through any defence. A few battering rams against the walls, and it's rape and pillage all the way. My tribe can really kick some Turkish ass.'

Cooper felt his eyebrows gradually going up, and tried to control the expression before Alex saw it. If the boy thought he was shocked or disapproving, he would clam up. He felt sure, though, that Dawn Nield would not like to hear her clever, studious son talking enthusiastically about rape and pillage, and kicking Turkish ass. This was definitely a private world of Alex's own that he'd been privileged to share for a few minutes.

'If we get our act together, that is,' said Alex. 'We have to work together if we're going to beat off the Turks.'

And that was what it was all about, Cooper supposed – working together. Being part of a tribe. You needed support from your tribe mates when it was your walls that the rams were hitting, your city that the axemen were pillaging. Without support from your tribe, you were dead.

Alex paused, feeling perhaps that he'd said too much.

'Sometimes, it feels like a lot more than just a game,' he said, with a thoughtful tone entering his voice.

Cooper nodded. 'I actually wanted to ask you about your photography while I'm here,' he said. 'I hear you're pretty good.'

'I like playing around, that's all. Doing stuff with the editing programs.'

'When you were in Dovedale on Monday, did you notice the money trees in near the river?'

'What, the ones with the coins in them?'

'Yes. They call them money trees.'

'I saw them.'

'I bet you took some photographs, didn't you?'

Alex nodded. 'Do you want to look at some?'

'Definitely.'

The boy minimized the *War Tribe* screen, and opened some photo-management software that created a slideshow of images. Shots of hillsides slid by. The sky, water, rocks – and the familiar outlines of the Twelve Apostles. They were definitely in Dovedale now. Some of the images had been digitally manipulated – the balance of light and shade altered to accentuate a shape, startling colour adjustments turning the dale into a landscape from another planet. In one striking composition, two images had been overlaid, with the knot holes of gnarled bark creating a ghostly face on a limestone cliff.

Finally, Alex paused the slideshow at a picture of a money tree.

'Do you know why people do that?' said Cooper. 'Hammer the coins into the tree? It's for luck.'

They both sat looking at the photograph. Hundreds of coins banged into the wood over decades, maybe centuries. Generations of people trekking into Dovedale and taking the trouble to add their contribution to the money tree, hoping for some improvement in their lives. Better health, the right partner, an end to some despair that was blighting their existence.

'There's a lot of luck in that tree,' said Cooper.

Alex was silent for a moment. 'Well, there should have been.'

Finally, Cooper thought he detected a sign of emotion, the slight crack in his voice that suggested his younger sister had meant something to him, that her death had been traumatic and was causing him to grieve.

He wondered if the boy's parents had thought about getting him some counselling, or even trying to get him to open up about it themselves – or whether they were too caught up in their own concerns.

Someone ought to suggest it to them. An incident like the drowning of Emily Nield could traumatize a boy of Alex's age, and cause psychological problems months or years down the line. His behaviour could be seriously affected. Who knew what he might do at some future date, if his complex feelings were bottled up and never found a natural release?

Alex had started the slideshow again. Cooper watched more inanimate objects appear and slide by. Patterns, light and shade. Those were the things that interested Alex Nield. None of his images included people, not even his own family. Perhaps especially his own family.

Cooper looked at his watch.

'Well, thanks a lot for your time, Alex. I'm going to have to get back to work now.'

'Okay.'

'I'll see you another time, though.'

'I guess.'

'At least you're easy to find here in Ashbourne. You used to live in Wetton, didn't you?'

And Alex froze. Almost literally. His expression became a mask, all friendliness gone. His face had closed against the world, and particularly against Cooper.

All the time he'd been talking to the boy, Cooper had been aware that he might say the wrong thing at any moment. He'd felt as though he was skating on thin ice. And now he'd fallen through.

Back in the sitting room, he raised the subject of Alex with his parents. They agreed that they ought to consider Alex's welfare and not let him sit alone in his room for hour after hour. 'After the funeral,' said Dawn, pronouncing the words as if she was saying *After the end of the world*. The inference seemed to be that nothing else mattered, or even existed, until that event had been faced up to.

'And you haven't any idea who might have sent the anonymous letter?' said Cooper, looking at the line of framed photographs on the window ledge.

'No, we haven't.'

132

'Or what the letter might have been referring to?'

'No idea,' said Nield, almost snapping the answer. 'It's just somebody with delusions.'

'About Emily,' said Cooper. 'Could she be badly behaved sometimes? A troublesome child?'

'No. What do you mean?'

'Nothing, really.'

A school photograph of Alex was prominently displayed in the window. He was wearing his Queen Elizabeth's uniform, a navy blue blazer and school tie. But Cooper was looking for photographs of Emily. He found a family group, with Robert and Dawn, Alex and Emily – and a teenage girl of about sixteen, with distinctive black eye make-up and a purple streak in her hair.

'Who is the other girl in this photograph with you?' he asked.

There was no answer from either of the Nields. Cooper became aware of one of those awkward silences that seemed to fill a room, as if he'd just broken wind. Was it the result of shock, embarrassment, shame?

He glanced up quickly to catch the expressions on the faces of the Nields. And he met only hostility.

Cooper's return to Edendale had been delayed by a traffic accident. An HGV had toppled into a ditch on the A515 near Sudbury, causing traffic to back up all the way Ashbourne.

Back at his desk, he thought about his visits to the Nields' home. While he'd been sitting in his car listening to traffic alerts about the HGV accident, a recollection had come to him of the Museum of Childhood, just a few miles away in Sudbury.

Among the exhibits at the museum was the Betty Cadbury Collection of Playthings Past. He remembered a three-storey doll's house, made around the end of the nineteenth century. It had nine perfect miniature rooms, with the figure of a Victorian mother downstairs in the kitchen, and Father upstairs in the study with his pipe.

There had been an odd excitement about being able to glimpse the whole life of a house in that way, to know what was going on in every room at the same time. But even then, he'd wondered where the children were, why the bedrooms on the top floor weren't occupied, and the nursery with the toys laid out on the floor was empty. There was no one to play with the rocking horse or the building blocks, no one running in the garden or helping Mum in the kitchen.

He'd always been familiar with the expression 'seen but not heard'– his own grandfather had used it often enough. But children who were neither seen nor heard? That was a house where something was wrong.

'The Nields have an older daughter,' said Cooper when he got back to Edendale and found Gavin Murfin waiting for him. 'Her name's Lauren. It seems they don't like to talk about her very much.'

'Black sheep of the family?'

'Well, let's just say I don't think she came up to Mum's high standards. She looked the rebellious type, even in her photographs. I can imagine she might not have been able to tolerate life in that household.'

Murfin studied the photo. 'A bit Goth, do you reckon?'

'What makes you say that?'

'Too much eye make-up. Black nail varnish. Miserable expression.'

'All teenagers are miserable, aren't they? Especially when they're having their photo taken with Mum and Dad.'

'Yeah, but there's something different about the way a Goth looks miserable. They make it seem as though it's some kind of artistic statement.'

'Existential angst.'

'If you say so.'

Cooper took the photo back. He could see what Murfin meant. 'So how do you know about Goths, Gavin?'

'One of our girls brings her friends home now and then. I asked her why some of them looked like rejects from a Hammer Horror film. She explained to me about Goths.'

'There's more to it than the look, though.'

'Of course. They have a whole culture, if you get into it. They even have their own weekend at Whitby during the autumn.'

'Whitby? Oh, Dracula.'

'Right. But the look seems to be important. Mostly black, but maybe with a bit of red or purple.'

'Lauren has purple streaks in her hair.'

'There you go.'

'It's funny how things like this can make you feel old, Gavin.'

'Imagine what it's like being the parent of one.'

'Is the Lowndes operation set up?' asked Cooper.

'All ready to go.'

As Diane Fry walked through the corridors of Lloyd House, she was sure that she could sense people turning to look at her. She was just being paranoid, she supposed – like Andy Kewley. She wasn't used to being the centre of unwelcome attention, and she didn't like it. The idea that people were talking about her in rooms somewhere made her skin crawl. Never mind what they said about your ears burning, this was an all over hot itch, as if she'd fallen naked into a bed of nettles. Her entire skin felt uncomfortable.

The sudden silences among members of the team were unnerving her. Blake confirmed the bad news later that morning.

'What people don't realize is that the conviction rate is even lower for crimes other than rape,' he said. 'Four per cent for burglaries, one per cent for criminal damage. The number of rape convictions has doubled in the past twenty-five years. But the number of allegations had increased dramatically. The definition of rape has been widened twice, and there's been a push to get victims to report. Those are two good reasons why the number has increased, anyway.'

Fry noticed that Blake could hardly bear to look at her. He was avoiding the real subject.

'The CPS used to insist on independent corroboration before they would take a case to court,' he said. 'But they've been under pressure, too. Now they don't insist on it so much. But that means a case is more difficult to prosecute. A jury is less likely to convict when it's a question of the complainant's word against the defendant's.'

'But in this case, you have DNA,' said Fry.

135

'Right.'

Fry watched him steadily, detecting his unease.

'You do have DNA?'

'Well ...'

'You *do* have DNA evidence, don't you?'

'We have a bit of problem,' he said.

'What's wrong?'

'There seem to have been some procedural issues with the DNA evidence. Contamination.' Blake raised his hands in an appeal for understanding. 'We think the CPS are taking an overly cautious attitude, but you know what it's like ...'

'Tell me the truth,' said Fry. 'What's the strength on Shepherd and Barnes? Have we got a case?'

'Not one the CPS will run with.'

'What about my statement?'

'Its evidential value is limited.'

'Evidential value?'

'Well, okay, Diane – the fact is, as evidence it's practically worthless. But it does give us another lead.'

'Does it?'

'We won't be abandoning the case altogether.'

'Oh, yes? With a hundred other cold cases waiting their turn?'

Fry knew she must be only one of scores of victims waiting for justice. She practically could see Blake's fingers twitching to stamp her file NFA – 'No Further Action'.

'It's just going to take more time, that's all,' he said.

That's all? No matter how many platitudes Blake and Murchison and their team spouted about support, and putting the victim first, they always fell back on the jargon. It was as if they were going through a prepared script, hiding behind a barricade of acronyms and euphemisms. It must be useful to be able to protect yourself from the nasty odours of unpleasant reality with a mask of officialdom, to swat away that irritating fly with a closed case file.

'We can interview pub staff and customers to find out who was at the Connemara that night.'

'So many years ago? You're kidding.'

A splash of coffee fell on to the glass-topped table and began to spread. They both watched it widen, then stop as it lost its impetus. It would stain unless someone wiped it off.

Fry could feel the anger growing inside her now, rushing through her veins in an adrenalin surge. Her hand was shaking as she put the cup back in its saucer. Blake stared at it, responding to the rattle of china as if to the sound of gunfire. Damn cappuccino. She'd never really liked it anyway.

'Paragraph 10.4,' said Fry.

'Sorry?'

'The CPS code for the prosecution of rape cases. The Code sets out the obligations of the CPS towards victims. One of these obligations is to tell a victim if the CPS decides that there is insufficient evidence to bring a prosecution, and explain why they've made the decision. Normally they do it by writing a letter to the victim. But if a police officer notifies the victim, it means the decision not to charge has been during a face-to-face consultation with that officer – without a full evidential report. That's paragraph 10.4. I expect we'll be moving on to 10.5. A personally delivered explanatory letter.'

'Under the CPS/ACPO Rape Protocol –'

'You can stop now,' said Fry. 'Just stop, okay?'

Everything had been done by the book. In this case, the book was the CPS/ACPO Rape Protocol. Snappy title. It could be a best seller.

Fry stood up, pushing her chair back so hard that it scraped on the floor. Blake placed both his hands on the table, as he might do if he was feeling threatened by an aggressive suspect in an interview room. He was still seated and motionless, so as not to provoke more aggression, but poised to respond if necessary.

Fry couldn't deny that she wanted to hit him, wanted to do it so much that it was eating her up inside, needed it so badly that she could almost feel the impact run up her arm as her fist smashed into his smug face. Let him smile with a broken nose, the bastard.

'So they'll escape justice.'

'Well, I wouldn't put it like that.'

'What way *would* you put it? What *is* the politically correct management-speak these days for letting a rapist off the hook?'

'Diane –' he said.

'Don't say any more. Just shut up.'

'But –'

'Shut up.'

The urge to commit violence was slowly passing. In its place, Fry felt a cold determination taking over her heart. Enough was enough.

Diane Fry remembered the immediate aftermath of the attack in Digbeth that night.

In those first few minutes, her thoughts lost in a turmoil of shock and pain and fear, it had been foremost in her mind to say nothing about what had happened to anyone, or not to report it as a rape, at least.

She'd felt so ashamed that it had happened, shuddered at the thought of what people would say – and, worse, what they would be thinking. The idea of going back to the car and telling Andy Kewley, then having to explain it again to her colleagues, over and over again, the way she knew that it went … well, she could hardly bear to think about it.

She recalled standing in the darkness, clinging to the wire fence to support herself, then searching on the ground for her radio handset, finding the pieces crushed into the dirt, feeling in the pockets of her jacket for her phone before realizing that it had been taken.

And then she had sobbed for the first time, feeling herself so desperately alone and helpless in the darkness, terrified of what might be lurking in the shadows, frightened of what lay waiting for her back in the glare of the streetlights. She was scared to be alone, yet more afraid of being with other people. Her skin crawled with disgust, her body's instinct was to shut down, to turn away from the world and curl up in a ball.

She also remembered hearing the sound of water. The dirty brown River Rea sucking against the bricks, thick and sludged with rubbish, carrying away the dirt and detritus of Digbeth. She thought of the river disappearing under the walls of factories, deep in its own tunnel, water swirling in the darkness where no one would ever see it.

Why not another piece of debris, a bit of rubbish used and tossed aside by the world?

It would be so much easier than all the endless hassle and humiliation that faced her. So much more final, so quick, so inviting …

'Do you think it's because you're a cop?' Angie was doing her best. Understanding didn't come naturally to her, but even she was shocked by the suddenness of the blow that had fallen, and the effect it had on her sister.

They were in Diane's room in the hotel off Broad Street, the only place Diane could tolerate for a meeting. Thank God for the anonymity of a hotel, where no one knew who she was, or cared.

'Why would you think that?' she said.

'I dunno. I'm just turning things over in my head, and that's what came out of my mouth. It's just that it all feels, well …'

'Wrong?'

'Yeah. Well, damn it – it's definitely that.'

'Yes.'

Diane flopped back on her bed. They sat silently together for a few minutes. If she closed her eyes, she could picture herself back in Warley as a twelve-year-old, telling her big sister her troubles, waiting for Angie to come up with a solution and make everything right again.

'Diane, you're not going to let them get away with this, are you? What are you going to do?'

Opening her eyes again, Diane found herself staring at the ceiling, saw the winking red light of a smoke alarm and the sprinkler. A hotel room. Oh yes, she'd forgotten. It was entirely up to her to make her own decisions now.

'It's the system,' she said. 'It's as if every victim of rape is given a raffle ticket, and one ticket is pulled out of a bowl. Then the CPS says "We'll take that one to court, we'll not take that one, or that one." The CPS has a lot to answer for. It's no wonder people who don't get convictions stop believing in the system. If I met a rape victim right now, I'd tell her just to have a bath and get counselling.'

'You don't mean that,' said Angie.

Diane sighed. 'No.'

140

She felt so helpless, knowing the men were still out there and would probably do it again. Because most of them did do it again. And so many women who'd gone through the experience still continued to blame themselves. Healing was difficult to achieve. She wasn't sure whether she'd ever be able to describe herself as healed.

She couldn't bear the thought that she'd been reduced to a case file. Somewhere there was a charge sheet, a witness statement, an interview record, a list of key exhibits. She was starting to feel like an exhibit herself. *I present to the jury Exhibit A. Examine it at your leisure.*

The file would also contain a Phoenix print, a PNC print-out of the suspects' previous convictions and cautions. What she wouldn't give to get access to that print-out.

'I might talk to Andy Kewley, see if he knows anything else. I'd like to know more about this William Leeson he mentioned, for a start – what is his connection to this case? He's a lawyer, so has he put some legal block in the way of a conviction? Andy might be able to tell me, if he dares. But he's scared of something. Or somebody.'

'And he's reporting back,' Angie reminded her.

'I know.'

'I don't like this Kewley, Diane.'

'I didn't say I liked him either. But he's useful. And he was my old partner. There ought to be some loyalty there still.'

Diane thought back to her meeting with Kewley in the cemetery. Had he been right, after all? Had she been sacrificed for some purpose she wasn't even aware of? *I mean any case, no matter who the victim is. Anybody can get tossed aside, if it suits them.* Yes, justice was a slippery concept indeed.

Angie shook her head. 'I really don't like him, Diane. And I don't trust him. I think he's dirty. I think he probably always was dirty.'

'Maybe he was. It doesn't matter.'

'Like Hell it doesn't. You suspected him yourself, didn't you? That was why you wanted to follow him. I know this sort of character. Kewley is playing both sides. If you don't watch him, he'll lead you into a trap, Sis. Someone wants you to mess up big time.'

'Angie, we don't have a lot of choice.'

'Well, I don't trust him, and that's that.'

Seeing her sister's stubborn expression, Diane had a momentary shock when she realized that she was the one arguing against Angie's scruples. That shouldn't be the case. It was the wrong way round.

'But who do we trust? Who *is* there we can trust?'

Angie laughed. It was a short, bitter laugh that seemed to sum up decades of hard experience.

'No one, Sis,' she said. 'There's no one we can trust.'

Diane thought about the information that Blake and his team must have, the evidence that she'd never been given access to. She was the IP, the victim. She didn't get that sort of information.

But somewhere there were names in a file – the names and addresses of suspects, and of witnesses. There were DNA profiles and results from a database search. Even the medical examiner's report on her injuries after the assault. Her file would consist of at least forty pieces of paper, probably over a hundred. It was all there, if she knew how to get hold of it. But then, if she did get her hands on that information, what would she do with it?

Diane's muscles tensed and her fists clenched as her body responded to the thought.

'What are you thinking, Sis?' said Angie. 'I don't like the look on your face. You're scaring me.'

Diane sat up. 'I need to know the names of those witnesses. Why did the key witness change her mind and decide not to testify? If only I could get my hands on their statements.'

'Is that all?'

'No. I need to get details of those two men – Marcus Shepherd and Darren Barnes. Addresses, aliases, their known associates. And photographs. I need photographs.'

'You can get that sort of information from the police computer, can't you?' said Angie.

'The PNC, yes. But I can't do that here in Birmingham. I can hardly go to Gareth Blake and ask him to look it up for me.'

Angie nodded. 'Right. Well, it's a pity you can't just nip back to Derbyshire, then. Or … have someone up there do it for you?'

Cooper was surprised to get the call from Diane Fry. He'd thought about trying her number a couple of times, but changed his mind when he considered how unlikely it was that she'd want to talk to him. Now, when he took the call, he was so taken aback that he thought she must have the wrong number.

'You've been wandering around Birmingham?' he said. 'On your own?'

'Yes, why?'

'Is it safe?'

'Yes, of course it's safe. You just need to have your wits about you, that's all. 'Besides, I'm not on my own.'

'Oh, is that West Midlands DI with you?'

'Gareth Blake? No, not him. I meant Angie.'

'Oh.'

Cooper felt cold at the idea of Fry teaming up with her sister in Birmingham. He wondered if Fry really knew what she was doing.

'Actually, I'm calling to ask for a favour,' she said.

'Oh?'

Fry asking him for a favour? Had things really come to this?

'Why do you need me to do this? What's wrong with your friends in the West Midlands?'

'Ben, I just want it done discreetly, okay?'

That sounded more like the Diane Fry that he knew. He could hear the edge of irritation in her voice, the tone that she almost always used to him. Back to normal.

Fry explained to him what she wanted. It was a simple enough request, details that he could access easily enough.

But Cooper was frowning when he put the phone down. Something didn't feel right about this. Diane Fry had always insisted on doing things by the book, and she was his supervising officer. If he'd done this on his own initiative, he would have been in trouble. Being asked to do it by Fry was completely counter to his experience.

Was it safe? Fry laughed at the recollection of Ben Cooper's ignorance. She could almost see the pictures that had been going through his head. The mean streets, violent drunks and aggressive vagrants, junkies and psychopaths. Drug dealers with nine millimetre Glocks shoved down the waistbands of their baggy trousers. The Peak District had ruined him. Cooper would never now move into the twenty-first century.

Angie had left the hotel, gone back to wherever it was she came from. Still she hadn't offered any information about herself. She never said where she went or where she came from, what part of the city she was living in, who she might be sharing her life with. Her sister was determined to keep a distance between them. And that was perfectly okay with her.

Fry hated sitting around, doing nothing. But what was there that she could do while she waited for information?

She dialled the number in Perry Barr, picturing Jim Bowskill on the doorstep in his Harrington jacket, sorting out his wheelie bins.

'Dad?'

'Hello, love. How are you doing?'

'I'm okay,' she said. 'I just wondered if you could tell me where Vince lives now.'

'You're planning to go and see Vincent?'

'Yes.' She tried to detect the tone of his voice, and wished she could see his face. 'There's no problem with that, is there?'

'No, no. He's around. I'll find you the address.'

He put the phone down on the table, and Fry heard him fussing about the room, then saying something quietly, Alice's voice replying. She wondered if Jim really needed to go and look the address up. His memory wasn't that bad yet, was it?

'Yes, here we are,' he said cheerfully, when he came back. 'He managed to get a flat in one of the old tower blocks, Chamberlain Tower. Flat 1620. That's quite a way up, on the sixteenth floor.'

Fry made a note. 'Thanks, Dad.'

She could hear him breathing, trying to think what else to say. She wondered whether she could prompt him to get whatever it was off his chest. Or would she just make him clam up?

144

'Diane, are you sure you want to go and see him?' he asked finally.

'Yes, of course. I haven't seen Vince for ages.'

'Well, you ought to know then ...'

'Yes? What, Dad?'

'You see ... he has this girl living with him.'

Fry laughed. 'Is that all? I thought it was going to be something terrible. So Vince has got himself a girlfriend. That's perfectly normal.'

'Yes,' said Jim. 'I suppose so.'

Cooper could not explain the sudden surge of pleasure at being asked for his help by Diane Fry. It was something he had thought would never happen. Probably that was why it meant so much – the pure rarity value of it.

Some of the information she wanted was easy enough to access. Marcus Shepherd and Darren Joseph Barnes were well documented on the PNC. Intelligence provided their addresses, known associates, and aliases. These two were called S-Man and Doors by their friends. He printed out their previous convictions. There were photographs, too. He hoped it was what Fry needed.

The solicitor, William Leeson, was more difficult. He only had an expired conviction for minor fraud, and a note of disciplinary action taken against him by the Law Society.

Cooper did a search on the Law Society's database, found several Leesons practising around the country. But most of them were female, and almost all of them partners in firms in London or the South of England. It looked as though William Leeson had been struck off.

He tried for a while longer, but failed to come up with anything else. There was no William Leeson in the phone book, or on any of the electoral registers for the West Midlands. He wasn't listed at Companies House as a director of any company. Left the country, perhaps. Taken his ill-gotten gains and fled to the Costa Brava. Well, it happened.

If Diane Fry had been here with him in the office, he could have talked it over with her, bounced ideas around, asked questions, challenged each other's opinions. It had always worked well in the past.

But Fry wasn't here. She was a long way from Edendale. And without her, he was only operating like half a man.

14

Vincent Bowskill lived in a tower block near Yellow Park. Fry arrived as the setting sun was casting its shadow right across the low-rise housing in Gordon Avenue.

High-rise towers. Not much community cohesion here. It seemed to Fry that decades of short-sighted architectural policies had done more to destroy communities than any amount of immigration could. For years, Birmingham had been known as the ultimate concrete jungle. The inner ring road had created a cement collar separating the centre from the rest of the city, and driving pedestrians underground. At least it was reversing its direction now, trying hard to rid itself of that concrete image.

Poor maintenance and social issues had resulted in the residents becoming unhappy with the towers. Rivalries had broken out among groups of residents, and many were uneasy about people suffering from HIV/AIDS living in the towers. A report in one daily newspaper had quoted a resident who said that she wore protective gloves when she touched the buttons on the lift, for fear of contracting the disease. Birmingham City Council had been deluged with complaints about waste facilities, and about a man who had previously threatened suicide being re-housed on a high floor of one of the towers.

And this was the Chamberlain Tower. That was a man who got everywhere. Fry had a feeling there used to be a hotel called the Chamberlain Tower, too, on Broad Street. It probably had a different name now, rebranded for new corporate owners. Or to avoid confusion with this place.

Estates like this were a policing nightmare. The main problem was the grassing code. Reporting someone for a crime brought vilification and harassment. Yet any experienced copper knew that many of those who claim to adhere to the code would sell out their friends in a heartbeat under the right circumstances, to get a hit of heroin or to save their own skin.

In Perry Barr, Fry knew she was standing on the edge of gang country. To the west, Handsworth and Hockley were the territory of the notorious Burger Bar Gang, while Lozells, Aston and Nechells to the south and east were the patch of the Johnson Crew.

Somewhere near here was a spot known as Checkpoint Charlie – if you crossed it at the wrong time you might end up dead. It was the disputed frontline between two of Birmingham's most ruthless criminal gangs.

The Burger Bar Boys had become nationally infamous after a gunfight with the Johnson Crew left two girls dead at a New Year party in Birchfield Road – seventeen-year-old Letisha Shakespeare and eighteen-year-old Charlene Ellis. The attack was carried out as retribution for the murder of a Burger Bar member, Yohanne Martin. And so the cycle went on.

Last year, a report produced for Birmingham City Council had listed more than eighty schools described as recruiting grounds for violent street gangs. Children whose families had a gang connection used it as a badge of honour in the playground. It was a world away from anything that Jim and Alice Bowskill had experienced, and alien to the lives of most parents, thank God. But there were many families right here in the northern districts of Birmingham who were faced with the daily reality of teenagers growing up with only one ambition – to become a member of the Burger Bar Boys or the Johnson Crew, or one of the many other gangs who operated in Birmingham. The Blood Brothers, Real Man Dem, the Ghetto Hustla Boys – the list was endless. Police intelligence systems creaked under the pressure of untangling all the links; when feuds flared up, allegiances were broken, and brothers could end up on opposing sides.

As a child, Fry hadn't quite realized that everyone dreaded finding themselves on the outside, not a part of the gang. She thought it was her own weakness of character that drove her to seek acceptance from her peers. It made her wince now to think of her teenage self, hanging around in the corridors of her comprehensive school, trying to attach herself to a group. It was only as an adult that she'd learned it was the same for most kids of her age. Some were so desperate to belong that it became a question of any gang that would have them.

Being a member of the herd was a primal instinct – probably the deepest, most powerful instinct of them all.

But here, it was all about drugs. That was where the money and the power came from. And that was in spite of the fall in street value. In the right area, you could buy a gram of coke for a couple of tenners, enough for twenty lines. Cheaper than a latte at Starbuck's, they said. Well, it was cheaper because most of that coke was actually baking soda, or crushed powder from painkillers like Phenacetin and Benzocaine to simulate the numbing effect of cocaine. Analysis had shown that some street coke was as low as nine per cent pure. Sometimes it contained worse than baking soda. Cockroach insecticide and cat worming powder, for example.

As Fry walked towards Chamberlain Tower, a black youth passed her in the doorway He was wearing a green T-shirt, marking him out as a member of BMW, Birmingham's Most Wanted. 'Stay Mean, Stay Green' was their slogan. He probably had it tattooed on his biceps. She knew not to look him in the eye.

Inside the tower block, she reluctantly entered a lift. Battered stainless-steel walls, graffiti still visible where someone had tried to clean it off. Obscene messages surrounded her like ghostly writing.

And as soon as the doors closed she remembered the smell. No matter how often a lift like this was cleaned, the enclosed space would never lose its distinctive odour, that stale stench of desperate humanity, people leaving their mark like territorial animals. *I woz here. F*** off.*

The sixteenth floor. As the stinking lift juddered open, she felt as though she was about to enter a graveyard, to disturb the dead by knocking them awake. She was reminded of the cemetery at Warstone Lane, the tiers of catacombs, each of the burial chambers sealed up and forgotten. But behind these doors weren't the long dead of Victorian society. These were the modern living dead, the forgotten detritus of twenty-first century Britain. She pictured the residents of Chamberlain House sitting comatose in front of their TV screens, the volume turned up to drown out the real world. Eyes glazed and brains in neutral. Zombies, or sleeping vampires. It was probably best not to disturb them from their graves. Not unless you came mob-handed, and armed with a stake.

She found herself walking empty corridors and cold landings, with long rows of doors on either side. She sensed eyes at spy holes, heard dogs growling behind closed doors, a distant scream echoing down a stair well.

Flat 1620. A scarred door like all the others. She felt sure the spy hole was being used in the pause before her knock was answered.

'Oh boy, look who it is.'

'Hello, Vince.'

'Di, you're looking good.'

'Oh, sure. Can I come in?'

'I guess.'

Vincent Bowskill had put on weight since she saw him last. He was too chubby now to walk the way his mates did, like the youth who'd passed her downstairs – the arrogant swing of the hips, the jut of the shoulders. He didn't wear his clothes they way they did any more, either. Of course, Vince was well into his twenties now, no longer a youth.

'Have you been to see the old folk?' he said, leading her from the hallway into a tiny sitting room.

'Yes, they gave me your address.'

'And you thought you'd call and see if I was behaving myself. Cool.'

Fry tried not to look too hard at the contents of Vincent's flat. Not because she might be shocked, but because she was doing her best not to be a police officer. It was nothing to do with her if Vincent had left signs of drug use lying around his sitting room. Like a crude crack pipe, converted from a Ventolin asthma inhaler. She hadn't seen that at all.

Vince's mother had been Irish, his father Jamaican. But he was as Brummie as anyone she knew, and spoke like it. The mix of genes had given him a honey-coloured skin and dark eyes that could have been his fortune in other circumstances. But Mum had died of undiagnosed breast cancer, and his father hadn't been seen around for some years before that. Vince had already been adopted by the Bowskills when she arrived at their home in Warley with her sister.

150

Fry supposed he must be around twenty-eight now. And he'd never had a career – not a proper one, anyway. She was baffled by people who didn't know what to do with their lives. But if she asked Vince about his plans now, he would only get irritated.

'So – are you working?'

Oh, it came out anyway. She just couldn't help herself.

'Yeah. I got a job.'

'Really?'

'I work at a restaurant in Handsworth.'

'A proper restaurant?'

'It's Indian. Is that proper?'

'Yes. Well, that's great, Vince.'

'Glad you approve.'

A woman came out of the kitchen. A blonde with black roots, wearing a T-shirt and jeans, with bare feet and bright red toenails.

Vince gestured at her. 'Oh, this is Candy.'

'Candy?'

'It's my professional name,' she said.

Vince laughed. 'Don't say too much to Di, she's a fed.'

'What?'

'The filth, the Old Bill. She's a copper.'

Fry cringed inwardly when he said the last phrase. It came unexpectedly, and she wasn't prepared to hear those exact words again, spoken in Vince's Brummie accent.

He was looking at her oddly, maybe wondering why she wasn't the same Diane he'd known.

'So, you want a brew, right?'

'No, thanks.'

'A beer?'

'I'm okay.'

Fry could hear a TV set babbling in the background. She wasn't quite sure whether it was in the bedroom, or in the next flat, audible through the thin walls.

'Are you all right living here, Vince?' she said.

'Oh, it's a palace, Sis. You're just not seeing it at its best.'

'I'll take your word for it.'

Hearing him call her 'Sis' felt good. They had never been all that close, she supposed. But they had shared part of their lives, living the same experience for a few years. It was enough to create a bond, even between two people who were so different. She was glad that Vince remembered it.

'They said they were going to demolish these flats years ago,' he said. 'Then they ran out of money. So we're still here.'

'I remember.'

Yes, a few years ago, Birmingham City Council had paid out more than a million pounds in compensation for a mass high-rise eviction that need never have happened. Five thousand pounds was paid to each tenant to clear these tower blocks after they were earmarked for demolition. But after two years of the flats standing empty, the authority had said residents could move back in, as the need for social housing soared during the recession.

'They'll get around to it, I suppose,' she said.

'Yeah, right. Still, it's cheap. I'm not exactly rolling it, as you can see. And there's a great view from up here, if you like other tower blocks.'

Fry knew he was speaking differently to her than he would if he was talking to his friends, the young men he hung out with on the streets. He wasn't uneducated – the Bowskills had seen to that. He could adapt his language to the circumstances, could get a decent job if he wanted to.

And she was glad of his ability to talk to her in a way she understood. There was never any point in trying to learn the street language. It changed from estate to estate, from tower block to tower block, each little community developing its own particular argot, its own terms for the police, for money, for crack cocaine. It meant they were only completely understood by people from the same small area, from the same background, maybe only by those in the same gang. Now *that* was community cohesion.

'Jim and Alice worry about you,' she said.

Vince lowered his head. 'Yeah, they've been good to me.'

'I hate to see them disappointed.'

He waved his hands. 'No, look, I'm doing okay. I left all that other stuff behind.'

'Are you sure, Vince?'

'It's for kids, man. Kids who don't know any better. Too many people get hurt with that shit. You know what I mean?'

152

'Of course I do.'

He stroked the girl's arm. 'Besides, I got other things on my mind now.'

'Will you stick with the job, though?'

Vince shrugged. 'There's not much else, Sis, until they sort this country out. There are loads of young lads around here who want to work. But, you know, what they want to do is bricklaying, plumbing – that sort of job. A good trade. But right now, if you want to sign up for a plumbing course, there's a twelve-month waiting list. What use is that? The papers talk about this "broken Britain" thing, don't they? Well, if you don't want a broken Britain, if you don't want a broken Birmingham, you got to give these kids the chance of a job.'

Before she left, Fry couldn't resist another sweep around the room. The makeshift crack inhaler had magically disappeared.

Vince opened the door and checked the corridor before he let her out of the flat. The screaming in the stairwell had stopped. Fry wasn't sure whether that was a good thing, or not.

'Sis?' said Vince quietly, as they stood outside his door. 'Are you okay now? You're doing all right, aren't you?'

She looked at his face. His dark eyes were full of worry. He badly wanted some reassurance.

'Yes,' she said. 'Yes, don't worry. I'm doing all right.'

'Cool. Take care, eh?'

'Sure.'

Fry heard the door close and bolts shoot home as she walked down the corridor. She wanted it to be true that Vince would turn out okay. He was a good-looking boy. She hoped that he wouldn't end up with his pretty face immortalized in a crime-scene photograph.

She took the stairs all the way down. Yes, it was sixteen floors. But she would have walked sixty to avoid being shut in that lift again.

Night was falling fast on the estate. The tower blocks stood as dark monoliths, the open spaces harboured invisible dangers.

Heading back into the city, Fry could see the lights of the Expressway. Cars streaking through the darkness, like insects flitting through the dusk. They said it was a jungle out there. The smaller animals hid in their burrows, desperate to stay safe. But larger beasts still stalked the streets, calling to each other in the night.

15

Eighty miles away from Birmingham, Ben Cooper bumped his Toyota down the track to Bridge End Farm, twisting the wheel at familiar points along the way to avoid the worst of the potholes. Matt repaired the track regularly with compacted earth and stones, but the first heavy rain of winter always washed it all away again. When the water came rushing down from the hillside, it turned the narrow track into a muddy river.

His wheels rattled over a cattle grid and into the yard, tyres splashing through trails of fresh-dropped cow manure left by the herd coming down to the milking shed from their pasture and back again after afternoon milking.

At this time of year, there would normally be some calves waiting to go to Bakewell Market, but their pen was empty. Matt used to have a vintage tractor tucked away in the implement shed, an old grey Fergie that he loved to tinker with in any spare minutes. But that had gone now, sold off to make a bit of money. Farming was one constant battle against cash-flow problems.

Standing in the tractor shed was the solitary big green John Deere. Its bulky shape usually made Ben smile – it looked so much the way his older brother did in his green overalls, with his big shoulders and barrel chest.

But for some reason he didn't feel like smiling tonight. He was conscious of so many other things that he had to do, which were being neglected. And he was starting to get anxious about what might be wrong at the farm. He'd experienced too many family traumas to bear the thought of facing another so soon. His father, Sergeant Joe Cooper, had been everybody's favourite local bobby until he was kicked to death in the street in Edendale by a gang of drunken yobs. His mother had suffered from schizophrenia for years, putting the whole family through nightmare scenes until the final release of her death. Was it wrong to wish that people would only bring him good news about the family, and keep their problems to themselves?

But he loved his two nieces. Amy was thirteen now, the same age as Alex Nield. In some ways, she'd been strangely adult since the age of eleven. Ben had started to feel sorry for the teachers at Amy's new school. She could be mercilessly outspoken if you were boring her.

And Josie ... well, maybe she still kept that imaginary friend in her head, but at least she'd stopped talking about her, and that had allowed Matt to stop worrying about Josie inheriting her grandmother's mental illness.

Ben entered the big farmhouse kitchen through the back door and gave his sister-in-law Kate a kiss. The girls weren't around, presumably doing their homework or whatever girls got up to in their own rooms.

'So what are you working on at the moment?' asked Matt.

'All kinds of things,' said Ben, picturing the paperwork on his desk rather than what he had actually been spending his time on. 'I was in Ashbourne today. The little girl who died in Dovedale.'

'Oh, the drowning,' said Matt. 'Was there something funny about it?'

'I couldn't say.'

'I've got a friend who farms in that area. Brian Dyott. I met him through the NFU. Odd sort of place, isn't it? It seems to be important what other people think about you. When you talk to Brian, you'd think his greatest ambition was to be featured in the farming pages of the *Ashbourne News Telegraph*.'

'Really?'

'When they had Jonathan Dimbleby and *Any Questions?* at the grammar school last year, Brian tried to ask about the single farm payment scheme. Not because he thought anyone would be interested. It was just so he could get his name mentioned. They didn't pick him.'

'Is he standing for election to the town council, or something?'

'Maybe. Anyway ...' said Matt, carefully not looking at him, 'he might know the family of that girl.'

Ben didn't react to the hint. While it was useful to get information from any source he could, it was never wise to involve his own family, even peripherally.

'What's the problem at home, Matt? You didn't explain in your message.'

'Well, it's about Amy,' said Matt.

'What has she been up to?'

'I'm not really sure she's been up to anything. She seems to be having trouble at school. The teachers say she's been bullying other pupils, but I don't think that can be right. You know Amy – she's more likely to be the one that's getting bullied. But if she loses her temper and retaliates –'

'Has she hurt somebody?'

'There was a complaint from some other girl's parents,' admitted Matt. 'They're talking about sending her to a counsellor or something. The parents wanted to report it, just because Amy made the girl bleed a bit. I mean, it's not as if she's a criminal. She's not going to turn into a serial killer, just because she had a bit of a teenage spat with another kid. It's ridiculous.'

'What does Amy say?' asked Ben.

'Well, that's the problem. She won't talk to us about it. And God knows, we've tried, both of us.'

Ben felt suddenly angry. He stared at his brother, his red farmer's face so complacent, his mind so bound up with his own concerns that he saw nothing of anybody else's problems. He was as isolated from the realities of life in the outside world as his farm was from the streets of the town.

'Matt, what exactly do you expect me to do?' he said. 'If she won't talk to her mum and dad, she's not going to talk to me, is she?'

'Well, I thought you might –'

'You thought what? Jesus, Matt, don't you think I've got better things to do? Have you any idea what's going on out there in the real world? On Monday, I held a dead girl in my arms.'

'Yes, we heard –'

'Right here, in my arms, Matt, and I couldn't save her. And now I don't know if she was killed, or who killed her. Don't you think that's more important than your petty worries about some upset in your perfect little family? Wake up, man. I'm your bother, not your keeper.'

157

Ben could feel the flush that had been rising from his neck into his face, the surge of unaccustomed rage seething through his veins. It felt wrong, but he couldn't help himself. He saw his brother's face change from shock to a grim hostility. He saw Kate turn and stare at him in horror.

'I'd better go,' he said. 'Before I say any more.'

'Yes, Ben,' said Matt. 'I think you better had.'

At home that evening, Cooper kept thinking, not about his own family, but about the Nields. There was definitely something not right about the father. He was hiding something, but it was impossible for him to say what, without more information.

The idea of Robert Nield being responsible for the death of Emily was starting to recede from Cooper's suspicions. It didn't seem likely. Besides, Dawn had been right there with the family on the bank of the river. There were some instincts that even centuries of civilization had failed to suppress. One of those was the 'tiger mother' instinct – a killing rage against anything that threatened her children. She would never have stood by and let her daughter die, if there had been anything she could do to stop it. So what had Dawn been doing while it all happened?

Cooper was finding that he couldn't trust his own memory. And if he couldn't trust his memory, he couldn't trust himself. He no longer felt able to rely on his own instincts.

This frustrating ambiguity of his recollections was like the first stages of some degenerative brain disease. The events in Dovedale had happened only two days ago, yet they were beyond his grasp. On the other hand, when Diane Fry had asked him about his childhood, he'd summoned up perfectly clear images from thirty years ago or more. Was he becoming like those old people who could recite every word of some wartime song, but failed to recognize their own children from the day before? Or was this some short-term effect? He felt perfectly okay. But who knew when your mind might decide to play tricks on you?

As for Alex … well, Cooper suspected Alex was much the same sort of boy that he'd been himself at that age. His withdrawal took a different form, that was all. These multi-player online games hadn't existed when he was growing up, in the days before broadband access and game servers. It seemed decades ago now. Well, he'd played *Doom* and *Myst*, but those were essentially solitary games. This ability to meet, befriend and bully other online users was a fairly recent development – but it had drawn in millions of players all around the world.

Cooper switched on his laptop and idly googled for references to multi-player online role-playing games. He was sure there would have been some analysis of the effects the games had on participants, or the types of person they attracted.

And indeed there was. In one sociological study, it was found that just over one in five gamers said they preferred socializing online to offline. Significantly more male gamers than female said they found it easier to converse online than offline. It was also found that fifty-seven per cent of gamers had created a character of the opposite gender – an online female persona providing some positive social attributes that individuals lacked in real life.

He came across something called the Bartle Test, which had classified multi-player RPG players into four psychological groups. There were the Achievers, who preferred to accumulate points, levels, and equipment as measures of success in a game. On the other hand, the Explorers liked to dig around, discover new areas, and create maps to put their world into some kind of order. Many were Socializers, who chose to play for the social aspect, rather than the actual game itself, gaining enjoyment from interacting with other players, and making online friends. And then there were the Killers, who thrived on competition, preferring fighting, carnage, action, and destruction. They were the individuals who liked to depart from the norm of being 'the good guy' and play on the side of evil.

Cooper found a link directing him to the major online games, including *War Tribe*. It was the easiest thing in the world to click through and find himself on a page urging him to sign up and start playing straight away. Well, why not? Perhaps it would be a way of discovering that other side of Alex Nield, the one his parents never saw.

He soon figured out the basics of the game. It seemed to be all about building up your cities, making your defensive wall strong and training as many soldiers as possible. Then you could go out raiding, plundering the resources of neighbouring cities or conquering them with your chieftain. With many thousands of players signed up, the permutations of the conflict were endless. You could experience betrayal and conspiracy. You could make friends, enemies, have spies and allies, take part in wars, destroy and pillage to your heart's content.

Cooper could imagine the sort of messages that must go back and forth via the instant messaging function. Vicious arguments, threats of destruction, the curses of the destroyed. He supposed there would have to be some in-game rules to control the abusive language and threats of real physical violence. He felt sure it would be that serious. If a fraction of the players put as much time and commitment into the game as Alex Nield did, they would have a huge emotional investment in their cities.

When his city was created, Cooper switched to the map view. He saw all the Turks on the edge of Continent 34. Aggressive and well organized, those Turks. And there was never any point in trying to talk to them. Oh, well. He didn't expect to last very long in the game. A few battle-axes would finish him off.

Then he found Alex's cities on the map and clicked on his profile. The artwork on his profile page was dominated by a huge sword created from multiple ASCII characters – slashes, back slashes, hash marks, and some symbols that Cooper didn't even know the name for. It must have taken hours to get that right. And an awful lot of patience, too.

There was a screed of text below the sword. Cooper picked out a few expressions and acronyms.

i just took ur city
wtf u goin to do?

That was pretty clear, if you knew what WTF meant, which Cooper reckoned he did. But there were other lines he was baffled by, like:

im s0 1337 taht i pwn ur @ss n00b!!!

The last word looked a version of 'noob', the derogatory term for a 'newbie' – or a new, inexperienced player who didn't know how to play the game properly. Someone like him, in fact. An idiot who asked stupid questions, made mistakes all the time, and was easy prey for the more experienced player.

There were plenty of threats, too. That was to be expected, he supposed – your profile was all about bravado and pretending that you were a tougher guy than your neighbours.

if u dare to touch my cities u wr born wrong, and u must die!!!!!!

Lots of exclamation marks featured pretty much everywhere. A minimum of six at the end of every line. That made the threats more scary, perhaps.

Alex's log-in name was SmokeLord, but his cities had strange names. They ought to have been called Smoke Screen, or Smoke and Mirrors. Oh, and Smoke on the Water, of course. Those would have been Cooper's choices, if he was going for a cool theme.

But Alex Nield hadn't done that. Cooper scrolled through the list. His city names included Engine House, Dutchman, The Folly. His capital seemed to be Engine House, the biggest of his cities by the number of its points, so its walls were probably high level and almost impregnable, the numbers of defensive troops stacked up. That made sense, he supposed. It would be the engine room of his expanding empire.

There was a lot of repetition of symbols in the profile. Cooper couldn't make head or tail of some of them. In fact, he wasn't sure whether they had any meaning or were just for decoration. One sequence of characters was repeated several times. It said:

£0$7

Some kind of money obsession? Though how much £0$7 was, he had no clue.

Beneath a representation in ASCII characters of a sort of cartoon baby face, the sequence occurred again.

£0$7
£0$7
£0$7
£0$7 Я1√32

And finally at the bottom, Alex's profile ended:

brb
kk??

He was in need of a translator. Like other police forces, Derbyshire Constabulary spent many thousands of pounds every year on translation services, to help deal with suspects who had a poor command of English. But he didn't think this particular language would be offered by the translation service. It could only be described as geek.

Cooper had always thought of himself as pretty technically literate. He knew about iPods and iTunes, and Facebook and Spotify. But Alex Nield was making him feel old and out of touch. He had no idea what some of this stuff meant.

So how could he make real contact?

Finally, he clicked on Alex's user name and a message box came up. He wrote: *'Hi, mate. Can I join your tribe?'* and sent the message.

As soon as he'd sent it, Cooper realized that he probably shouldn't have included so much punctuation. He'd automatically used capital letters and a full stop. A comma, even. That would give him away as someone outside the age range of Alex and his friends. He ought to have just stuck to lower case and lots of exclamation marks.

Nevertheless, he wondered if he would get accepted into the tribe. It was strange, but acceptance in this fictional world already seemed important to him. Because that was what it was all about – being part of a tribe. You needed support from your tribe mates, from your substitute family. Without their support, you were dead.

And Alex Nield was right. It felt like a lot more than just a game.

He sat back, drank a bottle of beer from the fridge, thought about calling Matt and Kate, and apologizing for his outburst. It had been unforgivable. Now that he'd cooled down, he couldn't explain to himself why he'd lost his rag over something like that. He cared for Amy a lot. He wanted to help, if he could. But now Matt probably wouldn't even speak to him about it again.

Then he thought about calling Liz. She would be expecting to hear from him. In fact, she'd been amazingly quiet today with the text messages. But the cat took the opportunity to jump up on his lap, and began purring with instant pleasure. And he found that he couldn't get up to reach his phone, even if he'd wanted to.

Just before he switched off his laptop for the night, Cooper saw that he already had a reply to his message on *War Tribe*. Alex Nield was online then, sitting in his bedroom at home in Ashbourne, occupying his fantasy world.

Cooper clicked on the link to see how Alex had responded to his request to join the tribe.

In the message box, the boy had typed just two words:

die, n00b!

16

Thursday

The funeral of Emily Nield was held on a morning of cool mist. The sun had been promising to break through since dawn, but didn't quite make it until after the soil had been scattered on the coffin.

Crowds of people had streamed through the gothic entrance gates towards the tall central spire of the church. Watching the mourners, Ben Cooper wondered how many of them actually knew the Nields, let alone their eight-year-old daughter. In communities like these, there was a general instinct to turn out to show support and sympathy.

Cooper could see the faces of people closing as he passed. Everyone knew he was a police officer. Perhaps they were aware that he was the officer who'd failed to save Emily Nield's life. And there was no question that most people would have read the story about the anonymous letter and the police investigation. As yet, no one had any idea who'd written the letter, or who'd leaked.it to the paper. The clever money was on it being the same person. Someone with a grievance, and determined to give it a public airing, just in case the police didn't act.

Considering what everyone would be thinking about him made Cooper feel like turning round and walking back to his car. But that would be cowardice. That would be another failure.

In any case, these were nice, respectable people. No one would say anything. They might ignore him, or give him dark looks behind his back. They might shake their heads in disapproval at his presence. But no one would point a finger at him. They wouldn't start shouting and screaming. Not here. His reception would be a cold, uncomfortable silence. That was the respectable way.

While Cooper waited, he found himself examining the wreaths. There was always a kind of poignant fascination in reading the message cards and trying to guess who the wreaths were from. Some of the messages were baffling, but no doubt they had some personal meaning – an intimate link between the dead and the bereaved. Take this one at the end of the front row, for instance. A large spray of roses and carnations, with a green ribbon. Cooper bent closer to read the card, and frowned a little.

Remembering 30th June for ever.

But today wasn't 30th June. Nor was the day that Emily Nield had died. So what was the sender of the wreath remembering for ever?

And there was no name on the message, which was odd. Part of the ritual when someone died was this conspicuous display of grief in the form of giant displays of dead flowers. The bigger the wreath, the more you'd paid – and therefore, the more you cared. Wasn't that the way it went? Leaving your name off the message card broke with the ritual. It meant the sender wasn't concerned what other people thought. She'd sent the wreath entirely for her own reasons.

Cooper watched the mourners starting to file back towards their cars. He realized he'd already started to picture the sender of the anonymous wreath as a 'she'. Well, it seemed a very female thing to do. Could it have been one of these women leaving the church in their black skirts? Or would this particular mourner have stayed away from the funeral altogether, preferring to remain as anonymous as the card on her wreath?

With an exasperated sigh at the way his own mind worked sometimes, Cooper turned away from the flowers. His imagination loved fruitless speculation. The chances were, of course, that the date and the absence of a name on the card had just been a mistake made by the florist.

He saw a woman coming towards him. She was dressed not quite in funeral black, but in a subdued grey suit and white blouse, with blonde hair pulled tight back. A woman in her mid-forties perhaps, with an air of competence and confidence. No shyness about approaching him with this one.

'You're the policeman,' she said. 'Not in uniform, though. Don't want to be recognized?'

'I'm CID,' said Cooper.

'Oh, yes. You were in the paper, you know.'

'I saw it.'

165

'I'm sure you did your best. The rest of it – well, it's not your fault, is it?'

'Thank you.' Cooper looked at her more closely. 'Are you a relative of the Nields?'

'God, no. Work colleague. You sort of have to come, when he's the boss.'

'You work at the supermarket, then? Lodge's.'

'I'm checkout supervisor. The name's Marjorie. Marjorie Evans.'

Cooper kept an eye on the porch of the church for the Nields themselves coming away from their formal examination of the flowers.

'Is Mr Nield a good boss to work for?' he asked.

She sniffed. 'It depends what you mean. He runs the store all right, keeps the profits coming in, from what I hear. Difficult times, but still. And he's fair with the overtime and that. Not too much favouritism, no matter what the others say.'

She gave him a sly look to judge his reaction. Cooper took the cue.

'All right. So what do the others say?'

'I couldn't possibly pass on gossip. That would be wrong. And at a funeral and all. The poor little child.'

Cooper watched a small party of relatives coming down the path towards them from the church.

'Marjorie, if there's something you think I ought to know –'

She seemed to be about to walk away, as if suddenly nervous about being seen talking with him.

'I shouldn't have said anything. Forget it.'

'If you don't talk to me now, I could come to the store and talk to you.'

'You mustn't do that.'

'So …?'

'All right, look. You ought to talk to David – he's the assistant manager. Or Yvonne, on Customer Service. That's all I'm saying. I'm not accusing him of anything.'

'Thank you.'

She slipped quietly away from him before Robert Nield turned to look their way. But Nield's eyes were dull, and his attention was focused on his wife, who was barely able to walk without his support. He hadn't noticed Cooper talking to one of his staff members. Or if he had, it didn't register in his face. Cooper wasn't yet sure how practised Robert Nield was at hiding his feelings.

And there was Alex standing behind his father, awkward in his black suit, a little too big for him. No thirteen-year-old boy had a black suit, so it was either borrowed, or bought specially for the occasion.

The boy showed no interest in the flowers, or in the other mourners. Cooper saw him gazing at the nearby graves, tilting his head to one side as he studied the moss-covered memorials and Celtic crosses. Some of the oldest graves were close to the church entrance, and he gradually edged away from his parents towards a massive stone tomb, commemorating some notable Ashbourne family. He seemed to like the shape of it, the suggestion of a giant stone coffin with an inscribed slab for a lid.

Well, Alex Nield was thirteen. He and his friends had probably watched lots of horror films. Zombies and vampires were back in fashion in a big way these days. The world was full of evil creatures coming back from the dead, scrabbling their way out of a grave or sitting up in a velvet-lined coffin with blood trickling from their mouths.

But in the real world, the dead weren't evil. There was no reason to be afraid of them. In fact, they were pretty boring and mundane – they just lay around doing nothing for the rest of eternity. Alex Nield's curiosity was actually rather healthy. He looked as though he wished he had his digital camera tucked in the pocket of that black suit, so he could pull it out and take a few shots, catch the patterns of the gravestones, the light now casting the shadow of the spire across the grass.

Cooper shook his head as he watched the Nields ignoring their son, unaware of what he was doing while they talked to friends and relatives.

But perhaps he shouldn't blame them. Grief affected people in different ways. Sometimes, the greatest effect was shock, which seemed to numb the emotions. The death of a child in a tragic accident was the biggest shock of all. And this had been a girl of eight, drowned in a few inches of water on a bank holiday outing.

Of course, the dynamics of most families were difficult to understand from the outside. Some were inexplicable on the inside, too. He'd seen families whose way of living wouldn't be considered normal in any society, who seemed to be held together by hatred and cruelty rather than any other form of blood tie. In fact, the complexities of their relationships were enshrined in the crime figures. Most murders happened within the family. Only ten per cent were committed by someone who was a stranger to the victim, and the figure was even lower for serious assaults and rapes.

Far too many parents seemed to get so caught up in the business of earning a living, paying the bills and bringing up a family, that they forgot what it was like to be children themselves. That, or they wanted revenge for their own miserable childhoods.

As for Alex Nield, his absorption in the online game was undoubtedly a retreat from reality. Cooper suspected he'd become as addicted as a junkie, with *War Tribe* his drug of choice. If left to run out of control, it could destroy his ability to handle real life as surely as shooting heroin into his veins. So the question became – what particular aspect of reality was he retreating from?

Cooper watched the boy's parents walking towards him now. The father, cool and distracted, the mother fidgeting anxiously with her coat. Outside of school life, they represented Alex's reality.

He turned to find a girl watching him. About seventeen years old, black eye liner, black lipstick. Black clothes, of course. A funeral was a place she fit right in.

'Load of pious hypocrites, aren't they?'

'That's not fair.'

'Isn't it? I bet there isn't one of them who believes the words.'

'Ashes to ashes, dust to dust?'

'Oh, that bit's all right. I meant "in certain hope of the resurrection to eternal life". That's not true, is it?'

'I don't know.'

'Yes, you do. When someone's dead, they're dead.'

The girl gazed back at him, her Doc Martens planted firmly on the gravel.

'And who are you?' asked Cooper.

'It doesn't matter.'

But Cooper knew who she was. He'd been a bit slow at first, might have noticed her earlier but for the predominance of black clothes. Gavin Murfin's comment came back to him, and it clicked.

'You're Lauren.'

The girl turned on her heel and began to stamp away.

'No, wait,' called Cooper.

But Lauren ignored him, and carried on walking. Cooper ran after her, pulling a card from his pocket.

'At least take this.'

Reluctantly, she accepted the card. And in another moment she'd stepped through the gothic gates on to the street and was gone.

A cavalcade of cars went back to the Nields' house for the funeral lunch, lining the streets on the estate. Outside the house, Cooper met Marjorie Evans again, getting out of someone's estate car. He stopped at the end of the drive, noticing something different about the house. He turned to Marjorie with a question.

'Why are the curtains closed?' he said.

She gazed at the front windows. 'Well, it used to be customary. When there was a death in the family, I mean.'

'But no one does that now, do they?'

She shrugged. 'Some folk hang on to traditions. They might feel it was expected of them.'

'By who?'

'By the community.'

Cooper looked around the estate. Streets of executive homes, each house separated from the next by hedges and drives, cars safely locked away in their double garages, no one visible on the pavement. Any activity was taking place around the back, each family in its own private space. Not much community here. Surely no one cared whether the Nields kept their curtains closed or not? Those ideas of respectable behaviour had vanished decades ago.

But Marjorie was reminiscing.

'I remember once, years ago, my gran went mad,' she said. 'Jut because we kids went out on the street with no shoes on, in the

169

summer. She said people would think we were ragamuffins. It was okay in our back garden, but not on the street. Not respectable, you see.'

'When was that?'

'About 1968.'

'But the sixties are long gone,' said Cooper.

She smiled.

'In some places,' she said.

During the funeral lunch, Dawn Nield seemed to spend most of her time in the kitchen, despite the fact that she had friends and relatives to help. Cooper was getting a feeling about her now. She was one of those people who needed to be in control of everything, as though no one else could be trusted to do things right. He saw her straightening the plates on the table, brushing up the slightest crumb. A little bit obsessive. And probably quite difficult to live with at times.

Even while he was talking to people in the dining room, he could hear Dawn's footsteps clacking backwards and forwards on the ceramic tiled floor. The sound never seemed to stop. Back and forth, back and forth she went. Clack, clack, clack. He sneaked a glance at Robert. But that was a man who didn't reveal his feelings very much. If he was aware of his wife's absence from the room, he didn't show any concern.

Cooper pictured Dawn Nield doling out carefully measured amounts of food to her family, as if she were a prison warden, or an aid worker in a famine-stricken Third World country. Her manner suggested that supplies were strictly limited, that the recipient ought to be grateful. There even seemed to be a slight pause before she handed over a plate, as if she were waiting to see how each individual would express that gratitude. Cooper recognized that Dawn had found her role, a function where she could exercise power over those around her.

Why did the way she smiled so possessively at the family waiting at the table remind him of his childhood? And why did the way she watched each person eat with a sharp eye make him feel guilty about leaving a bit of potato salad at the side of his plate?

He noticed that she hardly ate anything herself, but spent her time passing dishes, rushing off to the kitchen for more bread, more sauces, or an extra plate.

He gravitated towards the kitchen to get a closer look. The units seemed to be brand new. Too new to have been in the house when it was built, even though it was no more than twelve years old. But some people insisted on installing a new kitchen every two years, as if they only lasted that long before they became infested with germs. He could see Dawn Nield being one of those women.

In the middle of the kitchen, the granite-effect U-shaped preparation surface was spotless. Although it must have been in use all day, it gleamed as if it had just been polished. Cooper glanced at the appliances – an integrated Electrolux dishwasher, a Smeg gas hob with an eye-level double oven. It all looked brand new.

Part of the preparation surface formed a kind of peninsula dividing the breakfast area from the kitchen proper. Dawn stood on one side of the peninsula, gently ushering back visitors who attempted to stray towards the sink with an empty plate or glass. The message was quite clear – this was her territory, and she was the absolute ruler.

Following the flow of people towards the back door, he noticed Alex standing in the utility room. He had the internal door to the garage open, and seemed to be examining his father's silver grey Volkswagen Passat.

Outside, the garden was screened by close-boarded timber fencing, making it as private as it could be on a modern estate. A paved terrace and gravel paths were bordered by ornamental trees and shrubs, which stood almost regimentally erect, as if prepared for inspection.

Cooper had never liked gardens that were too neat or formal. He preferred to see nature allowed in. A garden like the Nields' felt too sterile, too artificial. Those shrubs might as well be made of plastic.

The only sign of real life was the dog – a large golden retriever lying disconsolately on the path. This must be Buster, the dog who'd chased the stick into the River Dove, and who'd been followed into the water by Emily Nield. According to some accounts, anyway. Cooper could hardly ask for an eyewitness statement from the animal itself.

The dog looked up and wagged a shaggy tail half-heartedly when it heard his footsteps, but lowered its head again when it failed to recognize him.

Cooper heard splashing, and walked towards the corner of the house. A small water feature tinkled at the end of the sun terrace. Water poured from the mouth of a twisted stone face. A god or gargoyle, he couldn't tell.

But, even as he watched, the flow stopped suddenly. The mouth dried up, and the trough began gradually to empty. Puzzled, Cooper looked around for the source of the water. He couldn't see a hose pipe, so presumably the supply came straight from the house.

Shrugging, he walked back in through the back door, and saw Alex still in the utility room. He smiled at the boy.

'You need to get away from the crowds some time, don't you?'

'I wish they'd all go,' said Alex.

'I understand. Have you got some time off school?'

'They've said I can take as long as I want.'

Cooper could practically see him itching to get back to his computer, to disappear into the security of his online world. He wondered if Alex was worried about getting ejected from his tribe if he stayed offline too long. How long did you get until you were kicked out, anyway? What was the leeway before you turned yellow? Or was Alex simply itching to destroy that stupid noob who'd just asked to join his tribe?

'Alex, I think I saw your sister at the funeral this morning,' said Cooper. 'Your older sister. Lauren, isn't it?'

The boy kept his head down. 'Yeah, I saw her.'

'When did she leave home?'

'I dunno. About two years ago, I suppose.'

'Alex, does the thirtieth of June mean anything to you?' asked Cooper.

'No, why?'

'It isn't Emily's birthday, or anything?'

'No, her birthday is in March.'

172

'And Lauren's?'

'November.'

'Thanks.'

Alex began to edge away, trying not to meet his eye.

'Two years ago,' said Cooper. 'That would be while you still lived in Wetton?'

The boy nodded, then slunk off. Cooper still hadn't got the chance to ask him more about what happened in Dovedale. But now wasn't the time, either. He would have to find another excuse to visit the Nields. Another question, for another day.

When he was gone, Cooper noticed that the boy been standing in front of a tap that controlled the flow to the water feature in the garden. So that explained it. Alex had been the one who turned it off.

Back in the house, the family and some friends were huddled over a collection of photographs. Not the type that Alex took, though. These were family snaps, the history of the Nields captured on glossy paper. Dawn was showing off Alex's class photo, three rows of children lined up in their navy blazers.

She pointed out other people's sons, surnames that seemed to mean something to her, but passed Cooper by. The more respectable families of Ashbourne, no doubt. He did notice that all Alex's classmates seemed to have biblical names – Joshua, Daniel, Jacob, Gabriel. At one time, a child called Alex would certainly have been Scottish. And Gabriel would have been a character in the school nativity play – a role taken by a girl, too.

Cooper recalled his brother, Matt, complaining that all his daughters' male classmates were called Jack, and that Amy and Josie treated him as if he was stupid for not knowing which one they were referring to. Well, according to the newspapers, Jack had been the most popular choice of a boy's name for sixteen years running. That must be causing chaos in classrooms by now. But where were the Jacks among Alex's friends?

'Which of those are his closest friends, Mrs Nield?' he asked.

'I'm not sure. He doesn't mention any of them very often.'

'Don't any of his friends come to the house?'

173

'They have been here, now and then. But they don't come often enough for us to get to know them.'

'That's a shame.'

'Yes, he seems to prefer those solitary games he plays on his computer.'

'Well, they're not really solitary,' said Cooper.

Dawn screwed up her eyes. 'What?'

But before he could explain, she was drawn away to speak to someone else. Cooper realized that she didn't know the difference between a game on a PlayStation and the kind of multi-player online world that Alex inhabited. In *War Tribe* he had many friends – allies, tribemates and neighbours, from all over the world. But he also had plenty of enemies.

Cooper said his goodbyes and left the Nields' house. He had more than enough to do. He had a phone call to make to Diane Fry in Birmingham, for a start. She would be waiting to hear from him, and he didn't want to let her down.

As he reached the end of the drive, Cooper heard footsteps running behind him. He turned and found Alex coming round the side of the house from the garage. He looked furtive, as if he'd just sneaked through the door from the utility room without his parents knowing that he'd left his room and was away from his computer.

'Alex?' said Cooper.

The boy held out a sheet of paper. 'I printed this out for you. I thought you should have it.'

'What is it?'

'I have to go back.'

Cooper watched the boy run back into the garage and dodge past his father's car. He unfolded the paper, and saw a colour image. The printing was poor quality, probably done on the small photo printer he'd seen in Alex's room. But it wasn't the quality that mattered. It was the subject.

The image was clearly one of Alex's series from Dovedale. But it hadn't been part of the slideshow on his computer, and Cooper could see why. The subject was quite different – the first picture he'd seen with people in the shot. The spires of the Twelve

Apostles were visible in the background, and opposite the steep scramble up to the arch in front of Reynard's Cave, with a glimpse of glittering water where the River Dove flowed in between.

There might have been an intended pattern in the shot, the juxtaposition of the two sides of the dale. But the composition was spoiled by the accidental human subjects. On the bank of the river stood two figures, distant but recognizable. They were recognizable to Cooper, anyway.

One of them was Robert Nield, tall and slightly stooping, dressed in the blue shirt and cream slacks he'd been wearing at the hospital that day. He was talking to another man, older and less tall, one shoulder slightly raised as he turned towards Nield, an expression of appeal on his face. That other man was Sean Deacon.

17

When Fry awoke in her hotel room that morning, she knew from the state of the bedclothes that she'd been dreaming. Dreams always made her toss and turn restlessly, kicking out at the duvet and crumpling the bottom sheet. She had a dim recollection of being lost in a strange city. No, that wasn't right – it wasn't a totally strange city, it was like Birmingham in some ways, but unlike it too. She'd known where she wanted to get to, but couldn't find the way. All the roads had changed, and none of them went where she expected them to. As a result, she'd been getting further and further away from her destination instead of nearer to it. And of course, she'd been running out of time. In every dream she ever had, she was always short of time. Forever in a hurry, and always destined to be late.

As she exercised and showered, Fry slowly began to realize that fragments of real memories had been scattered through her dream. They were elusive recollections, pebbles in the sand, which slithered away when she tried to grope after them. Like the drops of water bouncing off her body, they had pinged against her mind and whizzed away again.

Was this what Rachel Murchison had meant when she talked about hidden memories? But these were more than hidden. These memories were playing a game with her, continually sneaking close enough to be almost within her grasp, then eluding her like slippery balls of soap.

Of course, you brought along a lot of baggage as you went through life. Some of it clung to you so persistently that it weighed you down for years. But surely there was even more baggage that you left behind, wasn't there? Memories and experiences, and failed relationships, that you shrugged off and left at the roadside when you moved on. She pictured a mass of sagging cardboard suitcases, sealed with grubby parcel tape and bulging at the corners. A long row of them, standing at the edge of a pavement, as if awaiting collection by the binmen, but destined never quite to reach the tip. There wasn't ever any point in going back and poking open the lids to look at what you'd left behind. The accumulated mould was likely to choke you, the dust to get in your eyes.

Now her body craved action, something to focus the pent-up tension, some target to hit out at. Her old *shotokan* master in Warley had taught her to recognize that feeling and use it. Very soon, she would have to get that release, or the dark well of anger would boil over and the wrong target would be in the way.

An hour later, Fry had eaten her usual light breakfast and was standing on the walkway over the fountains, near the eye-shaped Costa Coffee outlet in Central Square. Office workers in dark suits strolled through the square, past the steps in front of the Italian-style arcade of the 3 Brindleyplace office block.

It was unseasonably warm again. More like July than early June. The weather shouldn't be quite so humid this early in the summer, not in England. But maybe this was the climate change they'd been warning her about for years, and Birmingham was turning into the new Provence. Soon there'd be vineyards on the slopes of the Lickeys, and olive trees growing on the banks of the Rea.

Well, not really. There'd just be more office workers sweating in their glass towers. Mosquitoes swarming on the scum of the canal. Huge, pale women showing far too much flesh in their halter tops and baggy shorts. Brum would never be Cannes, no matter how much it tried.

Tower blocks were going up again in Birmingham. But now they were high-rent, city-living apartments. The inhabitants of the Chamberlain Tower would never be able to afford to live on the top floors of the Beetham, above the Radisson SAS. She could imagine them having a good laugh when Beetham Tower residents' cars were trapped in their underground car park for three days by a breakdown in the computerized access system.

When Angie arrived, she was carrying a black shoulder bag.

'Not here,' she said. 'Can we go to your hotel room?'

'Yes, if you like.'

They went back to the hotel, checking that the housekeeping team had finished with her room, and locked the door.

177

'There's some stuff for you,' said Angie.

Diane looked at the folder she put on the table.

'Stuff?'

Angie flicked it casually. 'Oh, names and addresses, witness statements, signatures of investigating officers, PNC print-outs. Forms and more forms, I don't know what.'

'A copy of the case file? You're kidding.'

'You'll be able to tell what it all is, I suppose. I hope it's what you need.'

Diane opened the file, and read the cover sheet. 'How on earth did you get hold of all this?'

'I have my abilities. I'm always unappreciated, of course.'

Leafing through the file, Diane felt her sense of astonishment fighting with a feeling of guilt – guilt at the knowledge she was handling confidential information that should never have left Colmore Circus.

'I suppose I shouldn't ask,' she said, hardly able to look her sister in the eye.

'That's usually the best advice.'

'Are their Phoenix prints here?'

'Probably. You'll have to look, won't you?'

Diane closed the file. She had hardly read a word of it, simply scanned the headings. Case summary, Witness Statement, Record of Interview. And on all of the pages was the familiar black bar – 'RESTRICTED WHEN COMPLETE'.

'I'm not sure I can take them,' she said.

'This stuff has all the names, doesn't it? You've seen enough to tell that. Suspects, witnesses, alibis – it's all there, I know it is.'

'Angie, I'm sorry, but it goes against the grain even to handle something like this, when I know it's been obtained illegitimately.'

Throwing herself back on the bed, Angie blew out one long, exasperated breath. 'Oh, you have got to be kidding. What – you're suddenly going to go all upright and honourable again? You don't want to put a foot wrong, in case you upset your bosses? That's the old Diane. Things have changed, Sis. Haven't you noticed? We're not playing this game by the rules any more. And that was your decision. Don't forget that.'

Diane shook her head.

178

'Okay, so what are you going to do? Shop me? Betray the only people who are trying to help you? Because it's either that, or you become an accessory.'

Angie stood up. Finally, Diane forced herself to look at her.

'Where are you going?' she asked.

'I'm going to leave you to think about it. There's the file. It's all yours. Now it's up to you whether you read it or not.'

'Angie –'

But her sister was on her way to the door.

'You know how to get hold of me, if you want to talk about it.' Angie paused in the doorway. 'But if you don't want to, Diane – well, that's fine too.'

So Angie knew someone who worked West Midlands Police headquarters in Lloyd House. She knew them pretty well, too – well enough to persuade them to break every rule in the book.

Fry supposed she ought to feel grateful that someone was on her side, and that person was willing to help her buck the system and achieve proper justice. She touched the front of the file where it lay on the table. She couldn't quite figure out why that feeling of gratitude didn't come.

Now she didn't know what to do. She'd always tried to go by the book, to follow procedures and not put a foot wrong. It was the way she'd planned to advance her career, having sussed out the restrictive times the police service was going through. An insensitive or imprudent comment could damage an officer's prospects permanently.

Yet she saw officers breaking the rules all the time. And not just back in the nineties when she first joined up. Even now there were people willing to bend the rules, play the system, or totally cross the line. Sometimes they did it for their own benefit, to fund a gambling addiction, or to help out a friend who happened to be on the wrong side of the law. Other times, though, they did it for reasons they might claim were good and honourable ones. Reasons like loyalty, justice, the righting of a wrong that the court system alone couldn't deal with.

So which situation was this? Was there some honourable justification she could claim for implicating herself in a breach of the rules? Did it really make any difference? The outcome would be the same, if she was found out.

Besides, what was she planning to do with the information? If she'd obtained these names in any other way, what were her intentions? Nothing that was within the rules. She acknowledged that fact to herself for the first time, accepting that a determination had been growing slowly inside her, a bloom of anger that needed an outlet, and which cared nothing for correct procedure.

From the moment she faced that fact, and accepted her own failing, she began to feel an awful lot better.

And who had done this to her? Who had been the Satan who placed temptation in front of her, the person who was so much inside her mind that she knew the exact moment when Diane wouldn't be able to resist? Who would get their satisfaction from corrupting her principles?

Diane went to the window of her room, looked down into the central square with its fountains. She watched her sister walking away towards Broad Street, striding confidently, not glancing to either side as the bag swung on her shoulder.

After all this time, Angie Fry was no longer the figure that Diane remembered from her past, the older sister she'd worshipped. Now, she was a totally different person. Another broken angel.

Fry opened the case file. The various forms were numbered in order, from MG1, in accordance with the Manual of Guidance.

> Form MG1
> RESTRICTED WHEN COMPLETE
> FILE FRONT SHEET
> File Type: Expedited
> CPS Office: Birmingham
> Anticipated guilty plea? No

And then there were two sections for the defendants' details:

Defendant's full name: Darren Joseph Barnes
DOB: 19/07/1981
Male X
Persistent Offender? No
Occupation: Unemployed
PNC Ethnicity code: IC1
Nationality: British
No of TIC(s) (if applicable)
Previous convictions? Yes
Previous cautions/final warning/reprimands? Yes
Defendant's full name: Marcus Shepherd
DOB: 07/03/1980
Male X
Persistent Offender? No
Occupation: Unemployed
PNC Ethnicity Code: IC3
Nationality: British
No of TIC(s) (if applicable)
Previous convictions? Yes
Previous cautions/final warning/reprimands? Yes

Fry had already committed the names to memory. Barnes and Shepherd. When she first heard them, they'd sounded so innocuous somehow. So rural, even. When she looked at their dates of birth now, she could see that they'd both been teenagers at the time of the attack.

According to their PNC ethnicity codes, one of them was white and the other black. At least, that was the opinion of an arresting officer entering their details on to the Police National Computer. She couldn't have testified to that herself. It was a detail beyond her recollection.

MG1 concluded with a dated declaration:

I certify that, to the best of my knowledge and belief, I have not withheld any information which could assist the defence in the early preparation of their case, including the making of a bail application.

At the bottom it was signed by Gareth Blake as the 'officer in case', and by his supervising DCI. Fry turned to the second page, Form MG5. The Case Summary.

Regina v. Shepherd and Barnes

There are three witnesses. One independent witness Louise Jones had an unobstructed view of two males seen running from the scene of the incident. At a subsequent ID parade, Miss Jones made a positive identification of Darren Barnes as one of the males. A second witness Miss Tanya Spiers states that she encountered Shepherd and Barnes at a club later that night with a group of other males, when they boasted that they had 'done a copper'. Shepherd and Barnes were both previously known to her. The third witness is the IP, who is unable to make an identification.

Officers arrested Darren Barnes and Marcus Shepherd. Barnes stated in his first interview that he had not been with Shepherd at all that night, but said he had heard about the incident. Shepherd stated in interview that he had been with Barnes in the general area, but they had been drinking in a local pub and had not left until around 21.30 hours, when they visited the Sub Zero club in Broad Street, Birmingham. On re-interview, Barnes stated that he had seen Shepherd at the club, but had not been with him at the pub in Digbeth.

I submit this file for review.

There was more, lots more. MG11s for the witness statements, several pages of MG15, the Record of Interview.

WITNESS STATEMENT

(Criminal Justice Act 1967, section 9)

Statement of: Louise Jones

182

Occupation: Editorial Assistant

This statement signed by me is true to the best of my knowledge and belief and I make it knowing that, if it is tendered in evidence, I shall be liable to prosecution if I have wilfully stated in it anything which I know to be false, or do not believe to be true.

I am the above-named person and reside at the address overleaf.

My name is Louise Susan Jones DOB 05/05/1979. At approx 12.15 a.m. I was leaving my place of employment after an evening event. As I walked to my car I looked down the street. I had a clear unobstructed view. I saw two males running away from an area of wasteland near the Connemara pub. The first male was white, skinny build, I would say probably approx five feet eight inches tall. He was wearing a dark sweatshirt and jeans. The second male I would describe as much larger in build than the first male and probably six feet tall. He was black. I could not tell what he was wearing, other than a baseball cap. I would recognize the first male if I saw him again. If required to do so I am willing to give evidence and attend court as a witness.

Signed: Louise Susan Jones

Fry was impressed with Miss Jones' observation. She seemed to have identified the white male. That would have been Darren Barnes, the IC1.

MG15
RECORD OF INTERVIEW
ROTI
Person Interviewed: Darren Joseph Barnes
Place of Interview: Queens Road Police Station
Interviewing Officer(s): DI Blake

Other persons present: DS Sandhu, Solicitor Mr Alderton
DI Blake: Introduction and Caution in accordance with PACE. DI Blake reminds Barnes that he was arrested in connection with an alleged rape near the Connemara pub, Digbeth. Barnes gives his account of his movements on the night.
Barnes: I wasn't in Digbeth. I wasn't at the pub. I met up with S-Man (Marcus Shepherd) at the club in Broad Street. No matter what he says.
Blake: We have a witness who states that she saw you running from the scene, Darren.
Barnes: She's wrong then.
Blake: Did you attack a woman in Digbeth that night?
Barnes: No comment.

Fry flicked impatiently to the end of the interview. Once the 'no comments' started, it was a waste of time. Though it wasn't stated in the transcript, the solicitor must have intervened to steer his client's responses. With an experienced suspect, it only needed a shake of the head. Nothing that would be recorded on tape.

She checked back to the beginning again. The solicitor was Mr Alderton. She had half expected to see the name of William Leeson printed there. There must be some significance to him, or why did Andy Kewley mention him? The same law firm as Alderton, maybe. She could probably check.

Barnes: No, I told you it weren't me.
DI Blake: This interview will now be concluded, however, we need to make further enquiries and will be further interviewing you later. Interview concluded.

When Cooper's call came through, Fry was sitting with the case file closed on the table in front of her, wondering whether she was right to have read it. Had it helped her at all? Had it made her feel any better? She was really no closer to knowing who these people were, these individuals who had become inextricably entangled in

184

her own life. Darren Barnes, Marcus Shepherd, Louise Jones. And the mysterious William Leeson. Not forgetting him.

She drew a pad of the hotel stationery towards her and jotted down the information Cooper gave her.

Marcus Shepherd, also known as 'S-Man'. A last-known address in Handsworth Wood, a string of cautions and convictions from the age of twelve, but just one spell in prison.

'There's a lot of other stuff,' said Cooper. 'Date of birth, ethnicity codes.'

'You can skip those.'

Darren Joseph Barnes, also known as 'Doors'. Another Handsworth address, an even longer conviction record. Barnes had started his career in crime early, with prosecutions for criminal damage and anti-social behaviour at the age of ten – the youngest you could be charged with a crime in this country.

'Street names,' said Fry. 'They both have street names. Are they members of a gang?'

'I don't know, Diane.'

And Fry felt irrationally disappointed that there was so little on Leeson.

'What was the name of his firm?'

'I don't know. I couldn't find him. That means he's not currently practising.'

'Okay.'

'So,' said Cooper. 'Have you got what you needed?'

'I really need to know what the problem is with the DNA evidence. What Gareth Blake means by contamination. And what matches were made on the database. But I can't ask you to get involved any more, Ben. You've done your bit. I'm already way out on a limb as it is.'

'Are you sure?'

'Yes. Thanks. I appreciate it.'

'See you back home some time, then?' said Cooper.

'Sorry?'

'Back here, in Edendale.'

'Oh right. Yeah. And, Ben – you're not worrying about this incident on Monday? The girl who drowned?'

'No, of course not. I've got far too much else to do.'

185

Fry looked at the case file again. She'd been told that a cold case hit had resulted from an arrest of one of the suspects – a routine swab taken from him when he was processed through the custody suite, linking him to the rape years previously through a DNA profile match.

There were two types of sample at issue here. There was a Criminal Justice sample, the DNA collected by rubbing a buccal swab inside a suspect's cheek to collect skin cells. And there were SOC samples, taken from evidence recovered at a crime scene – blood, hair, semen, saliva.

When a new Criminal Justice sample was added to the National DNA Database it was checked against all Scene of Crime profiles on the database. When a new SOC sample was added, it was checked against all CJ and SOC records. Any that were compatible were reported as a match.

Fry wondered if she knew too much about this process. She wasn't the average IP, totally ignorant of the criminal justice system, her knowledge of forensics limited to what she'd picked up from *CSI: Las Vegas*. Most victims would accept what they were told.

But it was true that current DNA profiling methods were very sensitive. It was possible to detect very low levels of DNA, equivalent to approximately fifty cells, and even to detect the DNA present in a single cell.

Fry knew that because of that high sensitivity, there was an increased chance of detecting DNA from more than one person in samples. It might be background DNA, which was everywhere in the environment and couldn't be avoided. It might be DNA deposited inadvertently by police officers attending the scene after an incident, or collecting samples for analysis. Her own DNA profile was already on the PED, the Police Elimination Database, designed to eliminate DNA left innocently at a scene.

And it went further. DNA could be shed by scientists involved in the analysis, or even by the people involved in production of the laboratory materials. DNA could be accidentally transferred from one item to another somewhere along the line.

DNA from all of these sources was referred to as contamination. That was what Gareth Blake had said – 'contamin-

186

ation'. Well, that sort of contamination was easily detected in CJ samples and the profile wouldn't be loaded on to the database. It was less easy to detect contamination in a DNA profile from a crime-scene sample. Contamination at the scene could compromise the lab's ability to interpret a DNA profile from an SOC sample. Despite all the precautions, contamination still happened.

Contamination. What a wonderful word. If anything or anyone had been contaminated in this process, it was her.

She looked at the notes she'd taken from Cooper's phone call. 'S-Man' and 'Doors'. Street names were significant. If these two were members of a gang, they would be well known to West Midlands Police. But she needed access to the police intelligence systems to find that out.

'No, don't be ridiculous,' she told herself.

Fry almost laughed. She wasn't on the inside now, she was an outsider. She couldn't turn to the PNC any more, and she couldn't consult the intelligence officer. If she wanted information, there was only one thing to do – ask the right person.

18

A man with white hair was playing a guitar in the Shaw Croft Centre near Boots the Chemist and the Co-op. He was performing a version of 'A Nightingale Sang in Berkeley Square'.

Near Victoria Square, St John Street still had its famous gallows-style pub sign spanning the street. It bore what must be one of the longest pub names in England – The Green Man and Black's Head Royal Hotel. It sounded like three pubs, but was actually only one. Mounted on top of the sign was the head of the black boy himself. Seen from the Dig Street end, he was grinning like an idiot. But from the other side, his painted red lips were turned down in mock sadness. The guide books still referred to him as the 'blackamoor'.

Heavy lorries were struggling to get past a keg delivery at the pub. Of course, it was no longer a brewery dray, but a lorry owned by Kuehne & Nagel drinks logistics.

Cooper realized that he might have chosen the wrong day. It was market day in Ashbourne, and parking spaces were in high demand.

The market itself was only a small one, nothing like the size of Edendale's. But people from the surrounding area were in town doing their shopping, or having tea at Spencer's the Bakers tea rooms in the Market Place under the antique Turog sign.

Lodge's supermarket was located in the southern half of the town, near the corner of London Road and Blenheim Road, just down from the Quality Inn and the Black Sheep Bar. Across the road were commercial premises on the Airfield Industrial Estate. Alruba Rubber, Artisan Biscuits, Vital Earth Organic Compost. The mixture of smells must be interesting over there. A forklift truck bumped up the road, carrying a stack of pallets to an engineering works.

The assistant manager of Lodge's was David Underwood, a man in his thirties with a neat goatee beard and the sort of red hair that suggested distant Viking ancestors. When he met Cooper in the office, he was just removing a white coat.

'I was about to go off shift,' he said. 'Perhaps you could give me a lift home? I only live just up the road. I normally walk.'

'Fine,' said Cooper. It would be a better place to talk anyway. He could see members of staff already looking their way, wondering what his visit was all about.

Underwood lived in a nice post-war semi-detached house on Old Derby Road. Lots of hedges and larch lap fencing. Handy for the golf club, if you were interested. And Cooper noticed that all the streets in this area seemed to be named after plants – Rowan, Poplar, Chestnut, Lime. On Willow Meadow Road, they passed the Pinecroft Stores.

David Underwood invited him in.

'So what can I do for you?' he asked. 'Is it anything to do with the death of Bob Nield's little girl? We've all been very upset about that. A lot of the staff took time off to go to the funeral.'

Cooper remembered Robert Nield describing the Lodge's staff as a big family. But was that entirely true?

'Yes, I met one of your staff after the service. Marjorie Evans.'

'Our checkout supervisor. She's been at Lodge's for years. We couldn't manage without her.'

'Are all the staff so loyal and contented?'

Underwood looked at him sideways. 'I suppose Marjorie said something to you, did she? She's a lovely woman, but she can be a bit of a gossip. Likes people to think she knows things they don't, if you understand me.'

'So if I asked you your opinion of Robert Nield, would it be an entirely positive one?'

With a smile, Underwood turned to gaze out of his front window at Old Derby Road. 'It depends on how persistent you're planning to be. I could say the two of us see totally eye to eye, and you might go away satisfied. But if you're intending to talk to any of the staff, you'd get a different story. And then you would know I was lying.'

'Well, it's probably best not to start by telling any lies then, Mr Underwood,' said Cooper.

'Well, the fact is, we've had a few disagreements about the running of the store. Business isn't good at the moment. The

189

competition is too intense. If we don't adapt and change, we'll go down, like so many other businesses. That's my view, anyway.'

'And Mr Nield is more of a traditionalist, perhaps?'

'He's very conservative,' said Underwood. 'He says Lodge's have unique values, and we've got to stick to them. But that's not what customers look for these days, is it? They shop on convenience and price. The only value they want is value for money. Special offers – three for twos and BOGOFs. Locally sourced products are good, but it's not the priority, if we're going to survive.'

'I can see you're both probably quite passionate about it.'

'We are. Bob Nield has a vested interest in the store, of course. But it's my livelihood, too. I want a career in retailing. I don't want to be part of a failing operation.'

'Do you have disagreements about the staff too?' asked Cooper.

Underwood shrugged. 'Oh, sometimes. But, to be fair, Bob has a good eye when it comes to hiring staff. He can assess people pretty well. And, once they're on the payroll, they become part of the family. He treats everyone like an uncle. That's the part of the job he really loves, I think. Presiding over his family. The trouble is – some of his family know that he's leading them towards disaster.'

Cooper nodded. It wasn't an uncommon story. Nield sounded like a man who was giving far more attention to his work family than to his real one back home.

Perhaps that was because he had more control in the workplace, the power over the pay packet, the ability to hire and fire. In the Nields' home, Cooper suspected that Dawn was the one in control.

He turned back to Underwood.

'You don't happen to know a man called Sean Deacon, sir?'

'I'm afraid so.'

Cooper was surprised. It had been a bit of a shot in the dark.

'You do?'

'He worked for us for a while.'

'At Lodge's?'

190

'Yes, Bob Nield gave him a job. I think he felt sorry for the man. Deacon wasn't long out of prison then. He was trying to get his life back on track, he said. He seemed genuinely to want to work – though I would have said he was a bit over qualified for stacking shelves. He used to be a teacher, I think. But that profession is closed to him now.'

'Did you have trouble with him?'

'No, he was a perfectly good member of staff. Honest, punctual, hard working …'

'Is there a "but"?'

'There's always a "but",' said Underwood. 'It was other people who had problems with him. I mean, when it got around the area that a convicted paedophile was working at the store. You can imagine what that was like. Some of our customers were up in arms, and said they daren't bring their children into the store while he was here.'

'I see.'

'All nonsense, of course. Complete hysteria.'

'Do you have any children yourself?' asked Cooper.

'No.' Underwood looked at him. 'Oh, I see. You mean I can't really understand how parents might feel in those circumstances. Well, perhaps you're right. Anyway, Bob Nield had to let Deacon go in the end. I suppose we were being tainted by association. It was a real shame, though. The guy seemed absolutely genuine to me.'

'Yes, I met him.'

'Did he get another job?'

'Yes. But I'm not sure it's any better than stacking your shelves.'

'Pity.'

'Were there any anonymous letters written to the store at the time?'

Underwood hesitated. 'Yes, a few.'

'Did you report them to the police?'

'No, we didn't take it too seriously. And we're hardly going to take our customers to court over something like that. Business is difficult enough as it is.'

'I wonder if you kept any on file?'

'No, I'm sure we didn't. Why are you asking?'

'Because we had one about Robert Nield, after the death of his daughter,' said Cooper. 'You haven't heard about it? The letter was mentioned in the *Eden Valley Times*.'

'We don't get it here,' said Underwood. 'It's the good old ANT – the *Ashbourne News Telegraph*.'

'Of course. Well, if I had any idea who wrote it, that would help me.'

Underwood sighed, and looked faintly guilty.

'I'm afraid that would probably be my mother. She has religion issues.'

'How bad?'

'Oh, bad. Basically, she believes that she's one of the chosen. When the Apocalypse comes, she'll get called up to Heaven in the Rapture, leaving nothing but an empty heap of clothes and the rest of us poor buggers burning in Hell.'

'That affects her social interactions, I suppose.'

'Oh, yeah. She won't hardly speak to you, unless you're among the chosen. You know, the way she looks at people sometimes – it's as if they're already burning, and she's quite content that they deserve every second of the agony.'

'Not the most congenial of neighbours, then.'

'No.'

Then Underwood started to chuckle to himself.

'What are you laughing at?' asked Cooper.

'Just a thought that popped into my head. They talk about "neighbours from Hell", don't they? But maybe a neighbour from Heaven could be every bit as bad.'

'Is she at home?'

'No, she works at Moy Park – the poultry company on the industrial estate over there.'

'If I could be sure it was her …'

'Handwriting that looks like a spider's crawled across the page? Threats that God will wreak his vengeance on the wicked sinners?'

'That's about it.'

'I'm sorry,' he said. 'She took a major objection to Bob Nield over the Sean Deacon business, blamed him personally for

192

introducing wickedness. Getting rid of Deacon wasn't enough for her. She practically crossed herself with garlic every time she saw Bob. You know, like you do with the Devil.'

'Vampires maybe,' said Cooper.

'Funny that,' said Underwood, with a small smile. 'I always thought Bob Nield had a look of Christopher Lee about him. He'd make a good Count Dracula.'

Robert Nield looked at the photograph Cooper showed him, the shot of himself and Sean Deacon standing a few feet apart on the banks of the River Dove, below the limestone spur.

'It's not possible,' he said. 'That never happened.'

'The evidence is there, sir.'

'Where did you get this from?'

'Does that matter?'

Nield was sweating inside the car. They were sitting in Cooper's Toyota at the Dovedale car park. It had seemed preferable to making a nuisance of himself at their home in Ashbourne again, where he was starting to wear out his welcome. This might be something that Dawn and the rest of the family didn't need to know about. There was no point in piling on the agony when it wasn't necessary.

'It's true that I helped Sean Deacon out when he needed a job,' said Nield. 'He came to the store for an interview, and I was impressed with him. He was always open about his background. I did my best for him, but it didn't work out. That's all.'

'But you've been in contact with him since then, haven't you?'

'No. Well ...'

'Yes, sir?'

'He phoned me at home last night. He was pretty upset. He told me he'd lost his job at the hotel.'

'They sacked him from the Grand?'

'Yes. He said it was because he'd been interviewed by the police again.'

'That would have been me,' said Cooper.

'Well, he said people were talking, and the management didn't like it. The same old story, I'm afraid. He'll never be able to put his life back together, no matter how hard he tries.'

'Why did Deacon phone you?'

'Because I'm the only person who's ever tried to help him.'

Cooper wondered if it was as simple as that. Could there be more to the relationship between Deacon and Nield, a comradeship made from shared interests? Paedophiles and child abusers had to find their friends where they could get them. They forged strong bonds in the face of adversity, like soldiers under fire.

He tapped the photograph again. 'But you met him here in Dovedale on Monday, didn't you sir? There's hardly any point in denying it.'

Nield opened his mouth to speak, closed it again.

'Are you going to arrest me?' he said. 'Because if you are, I'm not saying anything until I can speak to a solicitor.'

'Of course not. We wouldn't want it any other way, sir. We have rules here, you know. Codes of Practice, the Police and Criminal Evidence Act. All for your protection.'

Nield looked confused. He'd probably watched too many detective dramas on TV, and been misled by all those scenes where the suspect was left sweating in a bare room, bullied and shouted at until he broke down and confessed. Sometimes those TV programmes were useful. They raised false expectations, and people were disorientated when they encountered the real thing. Many a first-time offender had discovered that police officers were real human beings, who treated you with politeness and consideration, brought you a cup of tea and asked how you felt. The British character couldn't resist that treatment. It was only fair to be polite in return and tell the nice policeman what he wanted to know.

There were regulars who knew the score, of course. Hard cases who were doing the 'no comment' bit even before you got them in the van. But Robert Nield wasn't one of those. Cooper was willing to bet that he'd never been in a police station in his life.

'Look,' said Nield. 'If you're not going to arrest me, let's walk along the river to the place where that photograph is supposed to have been taken.'

194

Cooper hesitated. He didn't want to go near the river again. The thought of it was disturbing, the water seemed to fill his eyes and mouth the moment he thought about it. He shuddered, knew that what Nield was suggesting made sense.

'All right.'

They walked in silence past the stepping stones, alongside the weirs, and skirted the grassy spur of Lovers' Leap to reach a spot close to the Natural Arch and Reynard's Cave. Cooper stayed as far as he could from the bank, trying to shut out the sound of the rushing water.

'About here, I think,' said Nield.

'Yes, I think so.'

'You know, these rocks in used to be coral reefs, when this part of Derbyshire was under a tropical sea. It took millennia for water and wind to eat away the limestone and form those caves and arches, and leave the harder rock projecting from the valley. That arch was originally the mouth of a cavern until the roof fell in.'

'Your point is?' said Cooper.

'It used to take thousands of years to change the shape of a landscape like this. Now we can change it in a few minutes – with the help of a computer.'

'What?'

'Compare your photograph to the real thing.'

Cooper located the position that Nield had been standing by an oddly shaped outcrop of rock nearby. To the left of it on the bank was a stand of trees, and one of the ancient stumps with coins hammered into its cut surface. A money tree.

Then he held up the photo. The oddly shaped rock was there, just to the left of Nield. But the money tree wasn't there. Behind Sean Deacon was a background of grassy bank, slightly blurred in the print. In fact, the closer he looked, the more blurred the grass seemed, as if it had melted.

He looked at Robert Nield, remembering his son's digitally enhanced photographs, the face superimposed on the limestone cliff. It would be perfectly possible for Alex to merge two images and tinker with the background to make them look like one. It was a trick performed all the time by the professionals.

195

And Alex had three days to come up with this. If he'd shown Cooper the image on his computer screen in higher definition, the line between the two halves might have been more obvious. But the low-quality print-out had been enough to fool him. He had only focused on the people, not the background – just as Alex had expected him to. He knew that Cooper would fail to see the pattern of the landscape.

'I suppose you've guessed where I got this from, Mr Nield,' said Cooper.

'Yes. My son is very talented. I did tell you that.'

'Yes, you did. But why would he deliberately try to get you into trouble?'

Robert Nield shrugged and raised his hands, as if appealing to the river and the spires of the Twelve Apostles.

'Who knows why teenage boys do these things? Their minds are a mystery to me.'

'Why are you still pursuing this, Ben?' asked DI Hitchens when Cooper reported to him at West Street.

'I'm convinced there was someone else there,' said Cooper. 'Someone nearby when Emily Nield drowned. Possibly Sean Deacon.'

'The photograph was just a prank by the teenage son, wasn't it?'

'Yes.'

'And there's no other evidence?'

'None of the witnesses is specific about it, but if you read between the lines in their statements ...'

As soon as he said that, he knew it was a mistake. The CPS didn't read between the lines of a statement. Nor did a judge and jury. They only read what was there, the words that had actually been said by a witness. No one read between the lines, except a police officer who'd become obsessed and was trying too hard to make a case out of nothing.

'All right, you don't need to tell me, sir,' he said.

Hitchens looked relieved. 'Thank God, Ben. I'm glad you see sense. We can't have you going off the rails, can we? Not right now.'

'No, sir. Not right now.'

Cooper tried a smile, and Hitchens rubbed his hands together, a sure sign that he thought the conversation was at an end.

'Let it be then, eh? Leave the Nields in peace.'

In the CID room, Cooper tried to concentrate on something else. He'd remembered an old acquaintance who had been serving with the RAF Police until recently. Carol Parry was a local woman, who had ~~had~~ often talked about applying to Derbyshire Constabulary for a job when she finished her time in the RAF. Derbyshire would have welcomed her with open arms – officers with her experience were vital to balance the number of new recruits who were filtering into the ranks.

But, in the end, Parry had met a man from Coventry and had applied to join West Midlands Police instead, so they could be together. She was a loss to Derbyshire. But she might still remember him.

He called her and chatted to her for a while before explaining what he wanted.

'Okay, Ben, I'll do some asking around. Details will be a bit hard to come by, you know – but I might get a general idea of what's going on.'

'That's brilliant, Carol. I owe you one. Thanks a lot.'

Then Cooper turned his attention to the transcripts of the interviews with Michael Lowndes and his associate from the Devonshire Estate, who were now both under arrest.

Luke Irvine and Becky Hurst had done a good job with the interviews. But reading over the transcripts again, Cooper could see that there were some questions which had been leading. Irvine had almost put the answers into Lowndes' mouth, so that he knew what he was expected to say. Awareness of that tendency in yourself came with experience.

For a moment, Cooper thought about the statements from witnesses in Dovedale. He realized that many of those individuals had been asked questions that could have influenced their subsequent memories. 'Where were you when the girl fell into the water?' 'Did you see her bang her head on the stone?' Anyone who'd been asked those questions would have no doubt that the girl had fallen, would believe that they'd actually seen the stone on which she hit her head. Careless phrasing during the interviews could have planted the images in their minds. It was called 'verbal overshadowing'. It was a mistake to underestimate the power words had to affect the mind.

Cooper could still remember what it was like when he was a new, wet-behind-the-ears detective constable just learning the ropes. It didn't seem all that long ago, really. But the years had passed quickly, and DC Luke Irvine was from a different generation.

His family were from West Yorkshire, some village between Huddersfield and Barnsley. Denby Dale? Wasn't that the place they had giant pies? Irvine had once confided that his father used to work in the mining-equipment industry, but his job went when all the pits closed down. So he got a job at Rolls-Royce in Derby, and the family moved down to Derbyshire. He was only five at the time, so he didn't remember much about Denby Dale, except for visits to his grandma. It sounded odd to Cooper. So many people seemed to be displaced. Was it all that unusual now to stay in the area where you grew up?

And Irvine had another quality that might come in useful. He was a bit of a computer geek in his spare time.

'Well, you might call it geek language,' said Irvine when Cooper showed him Alex Nield's profile. 'But some of this stuff is leetspeak.'

'What?'

'Leetspeak.'

'Luke, I have no idea what you're talking about.'

'You don't know what leetspeak is?'

'Not a clue. And I bet the Nields haven't either.'

'It's a kind of cipher that you only come across on the internet. Originally, it began with users of the old bulletin board systems in the 1980s. If you had "elite" status, you could access special chat rooms, things like that. Elite became "leet", you see.'

'Right.'

'They used these mis-spellings and ASCII characters to get round text filters, so they could discuss forbidden topics. They became a sort of code. Now, young kids use it to show off how knowledgeable they are. Everyone wants to be thought of as "leet".'

'So it would be used to show off, and to stop outsiders understanding what you're saying?'

'Yeah. And to mock newbies, of course.'

'Noobs.'

'That's it.'

Irvine looked at the profile again.

'Some of it is just text language, though. Like using "u" instead of "you", or "n" instead of "and".'

'Those are the parts I can get,' said Cooper.

He scrolled down to the sentence that had disturbed him most.

u were born wrong n u must die!!!!!

'I've seen a lot worse than that,' said Irvine. 'They can get pretty nasty, these kids. The general rule is, the nastier they talk, the younger they are. How old is this kid?'

'Thirteen.'

'About right.'

'So what about this one?' said Cooper.

im s0 1337 taht i pwn ur @ss n00b!!!!

'Okay, that's easy,' said Irvine. 'A zero is used in place of an "o". That's an obvious one – so "n00b" instead of "noob".'

'Yes.'

'Common mis-typings come into leet – so "taht" is deliberate, not a mistake. So is "pwn" which originally meant "own", the "p" being next to the "o" on the keyboard. And the "@" symbol replaces an "a".'

'Okay so far,' said Cooper.

Irvine looked up. 'It feels strange just explaining this letter by letter. It's not what you're supposed to do with it. The idea is, you either understand it straight off, or you don't. You're either leet literate, or you're not. There's no in between.'

'Well, I think I'm getting there,' said Cooper. 'Of course, "ur" is "your", yes?'

'Correct.'

'But what's this "1337"? What's the significance of the number?'

'Well, that's leet,' said Irvine.

'I know, but –'

'No, I mean "1337" is leetspeak for "leet".'

'Say that again.'

Irvine grinned. 'The numbers stand for letters, Ben. The one is "l", the three is "e" …'

'… and the seven is a "t".'

'You got it: "1337" is "leet" in leetspeak.'

Cooper blew out a breath, as if he'd been working physically hard for the last few minutes.

'It makes your brain hurt a bit.'

'So the sentence reads …?' asked Irvine.

'*I'm so leet that I own your ass, noob.*'

'*w00t!!!!!*'

'What?'

'That's a leet expression. *w00t!!!!!* It's an exclamation of joy, or success.'

'You should use it with lots of exclamation marks, I imagine,' said Cooper.

Irvine laughed. 'Yes, I did.'

'You're enjoying this, aren't you, Luke?'

'It's good to get a chance to show off your talents.'

'*I'm so leet that I own your ass, noob.* A bit American, but I suppose we get the message.'

'The kid probably copied a lot of this stuff from someone else's profile, you know.'

'Probably.'

'Right down at the bottom, we've got *brb kk??* You see those a lot in messages – "brb" is "be right back". You say "brb" when you're ending a conversation. Sometimes you're not coming back at all, it's just a way of getting rid of someone you don't want to talk to. And "kk??" is just "okay?"'

'Some of it is just decoration, though,' said Cooper. 'The sword and the face.'

'Yeah, just ASCII art.'

'Art?'

'That's what they call it.'

'These city names don't mean anything to you, do they? Engine House, Dutchman, The Folly.'

Irvine shook his head. 'Can't help you there. They're plain vanilla. Ordinary English. They must have particular meaning for the user.'

'And is this just for decoration? It looks like something to do with money.'

Cooper pointed at the repeated characters.

£0$7

£0$7

£0$7

£0$7

£0$7 Я1√32

'No, that's leet,' said Irvine. 'A slightly different use of the character set, but you would do that to confuse the issue.'

'Successfully, in this case.'

'You see, the pound sign stands for an "l" …'

'Maybe,' said Cooper, 'you could translate the words, rather than doing it letter by letter.'

Irvine shrugged. 'Okay. This is what it says.'

He drew a message pad towards him and wrote it out in big capital letters that could be understood even by the most ignorant noob.

Cooper ripped the paper from the pad and stared at it. It read:

LOST

LOST

LOST

LOST RIVER

19

The Indian restaurant was having a busy evening. Its windows were steamed up with hot breath and curry, the front was propped open to let a waft of curry drift out on to the pavement.

On a warm night like this, doors and windows would be standing open all over the city, everyone desperate to get a bit of cool air. Not many in Birmingham thought it worthwhile to install air conditioning. Well, some of the smart new office blocks down by Holloway Circus had it, perhaps. But not here in the streets of Handsworth. Here, everyone expected grey clouds and rain, even in the summer. Anything else took the entire city by surprise. Ironic really, that even the original generation of Asian migrants had forgotten the heat of the Indian subcontinent so thoroughly. Birmingham certainly got into your blood, didn't it?

But those open doors and windows were also an invitation. Burglars everywhere wouldn't believe their luck tonight.

Diane Fry saw a wino sheltering in the doorway of an off-licence. A ghetto blaster on wheels roared past, doing well over the speed limit for a city street. But you could never find a police officer when you needed one, could you?

Outside a bank, a woman was using the cash machine, hunched over the hole in the wall while a friend stood cavey, eyes alert for skimmers or an opportunist mugger. Safe? Of course the city was safe – provided you were sensible, and took a few precautions.

Fry remembered her old bus route to college at Perry Barr. The number 51 or 16, she wasn't sure. But she recalled with absolute clarity that the route had seemed to pass through all the scariest parts of the city. Aston, Handsworth, Lozells, Newtown. All the places she would have avoided in any other circumstances. Some of those streets she would never have walked down alone. She only viewed them from the top deck of the bus, surrounded by other passengers, eyes glued to the greasy windows as she stared at the people on the street, as if she were a visitor to a wildlife park, observing the big cats at a safe distance. Travelling home on the bus at night could be quite an adrenalin ride. Maybe that was why she'd always wanted to go back and do it again.

Vincent Bowskill was waiting for her in the entrance to an alley full of grey city council wheelie bins bursting with plastic bags. He was smoking a cigarette, his face washed sickly green by the restaurant sign. Through the plate-glass window, Fry glimpsed gold-embossed wallpaper, tables covered in plum-coloured cloth and sheets of glass, a few customers mopping up curry with their naan bread.

The streets were all yellow glare and deep shadow. A pair of black ghosts moving soundlessly between the streetlights turned out to be two women in black burqas, their eyes covered by concealing grilles. They wore the full Afghan chadri – the type some Pakistanis called a 'shuttlecock burqa'. Purdah clothing.

Fry had passed a row of shuttered shops, barricaded against the possibility of riot or ram-raid. On the corner, there used to be bullet holes visible in the concrete wall, at the scene of another notorious shooting. But the wall itself had been pulled down now. One more re-development site.

In some parts of Handsworth, fear prowled the streets like more black ghosts. If you lived in a place like this, it was best to keep your head down, filter out the things you don't want to see. Close your eyes, and the world looks better.

'There are lots of serious gangs in Birmingham,' said Vince. 'Not just the Johnnies and the Burgers. Your lot ought to go after some of them Asian gangs – the Lynx, and the Panthers.'

'Right.'

'Oh, but I forgot. You won't take on the Asians.'

'It's nothing to do with me any more.'

'Oh, yeah. You got out, didn't you? Left it all behind. Lucky you.'

'The local gangs, Vince.'

'They're not all bad, you know. Those crews have been around the city for a while. There's two hundred members in the Johnnies, and they're not all out shooting innocents on the street. Some of them are safe.'

The Johnson Crew was widely accepted as being the more organized of the two main gangs, having made loose affiliations with the local Asian heroin gangs in Aston as well as with Jamaican-born Yardies, until the Jamaicans became increasingly marginalized in the city. Despite being numerically inferior, the Burger Bar Boys had taken advantage of their small, tight-knit community and were seen as the more ruthless.

The UniSeven Studio shootings were in retaliation for the murder of leading Burger Bar Boy Yohanne Martin, who died behind the wheel of his silver Mercedes in West Bromwich High Street.

And it wasn't just a bunch of testosterone-charged youths proving their manhood and earning respect. Girls were being drawn into the nightmare now. The suspects charged with the shooting of Yohanne Martin were seventeen and eighteen – and both of them were female.

The gangs got their names from two cafés in Handsworth where black youths congregated in the late eighties and early nineties. The Burger Bar was on the Soho Road, while the Johnson café was in Heathfield Road.

Legend had it that both gangs were originally friendly, but fell out over a bet on who won a game of *Streetfighter* on the PlayStation. By the late nineties, their street fighting had moved off the computer screen and out on to the streets. And it was no longer a game.

The killings began in the last days of 1995 as the young men fought off Yardie gangsters, and then turned on each other in a bloody turf war. Betrayals, executions and tit-for-tat killings. Bodies on the streets of North Birmingham. Fry knew gangsters' lives weren't glamorous. They were full of fear and paranoia.

'I want you to make contact with two men,' said Fry. 'Marcus Shepherd and Darren Barnes. They're known on the street as S-Man and Doors.'

She could see by his expression that he knew them. Or had heard of them, at least. A spasm of fear passed across his face, before he forced his features back into that sullen mask.

'Do you know which gang they're in?'

He shifted uncomfortably. 'Yeah, the M1 Crew. But I can't do this. They'll think I'm baiting them up.'

'Setting them up for arrest?'

'Yeah.'

'But I'm not working with the police here, Vince. You don't even need to tell them that I'm a police officer. I'm sure you can think of something to persuade them.'

'I suppose.'

She watched him smoke his cigarette and think about it. Across the road, a drug dealer was operating openly, small plastic packages changing hands in full view. There would be lookouts at each end of the block, and a car arriving each day to distribute the drugs to the street dealers.

Being a civilian gave Fry an exhilarating sense of freedom. As a police officer, if she'd wanted Vince Bowskill to become an informant, she would have had to do everything officially. There was no such thing as a detective running his own snouts any more, with their names known only to him. Those days were long gone, swept away in the desperation to clean up any suggestion of corruption or dodgy practices.

Now, she would have to make Vince sign a contract and leave all contact with him to a properly appointed handler. In documents, he would be referred to as a CHIS – a Covert Human Intelligence Source.

Immediately, her brain began to churn with extracts from the code of practice relating to Section 71 of the 2000 Regulation of Investigatory Powers Act. According to the code, she would have to get authorization from a designated authorizing officer, who would provide authorization in writing. Using the standard application form, she would have to provide details of the purpose for which the source would be tasked, the grounds on which authorization was sought, the level of authority required, a summary of who would be affected, details of any confidential material that might be obtained. She would have to keep detailed records of every task, and be prepared to account for her actions to the Chief Surveillance Commissioner. She would have to carry out a risk assessment on the deployment of her source. A risk assessment, for goodness sake.

She was amazed that she could remember all this stuff. It was even more incredible that, right at this moment, she could forget the whole bloody thing.

'So will you help, Vince?' she said.

'Yeah, okay. Well, it's family, right?'

Angie had taken on her own jobs. Diane wasn't entirely sure why her sister was so keen to get involved, but she wasn't in a position to turn down help. What she needed most was someone to talk to, a person she could open up to and bounce questions off.

Right now, the only person who came close to filling that role was Angie. She wouldn't have been Diane's first choice, but this was all she had. She was waiting when Diane got back to her hotel in Brindleyplace.

'This first witness, Louise Jones,' said Angie. 'She doesn't work for the publisher any more. She left them months ago. They don't have a current address for her – but they say she moved away from Birmingham.'

'If she was on witness protection, she wouldn't be giving out her address,' said Diane.

'No.'

'But it seems someone got to her, nonetheless. Everyone is out to put the knife in. It feels as though the whole world is against me.'

'There are people on your side, Diane. They're trying to help you.'

'I don't know who they are.'

'Well, where do you think I got a copy of the case file from?'

'I don't know.'

Angie shook her head. 'Gareth Blake. He rates you.'

'He told me to clear off home. Almost in as many words.'

'He had to say that in front of his sergeant.'

'Maybe.'

'Well, what about this other witness?' said Angie. 'Tanya Spiers. Where does she work again?'

'Some place called the Rosebud Massage Parlour.'

'A massage parlour? Oh, great. There are so many massage parlours in Birmingham it's a miracle they haven't caused a worldwide shortage of baby oil.'

Diane agreed. Oh, a few of them were genuine, of course. They administered a good, healthy pummelling to get the stress out. Not a bad idea, either. But the others …

She pictured a grimy flight of stairs and a dim bulb. The sweet smell of cannabis creeping under a door, unmasked by the scent of incense and aromatic oils. An overweight died blonde in a low-cut lurex top and skin-tight leather. A fake-fur rug and a price list on the back of the door. Sex and the City? Forget the glammed-up Hollywood version. The real thing was quite different.

She had no doubt that trafficked women still worked in the massage parlours of Lozells and Digbeth. Young girls fresh off the plane at Birmingham International, flight BA305 from Bucharest. They came believing they had a job in the hotel business, speaking little English and carrying even fewer possessions. And instead of going into a job, they were passed from hand to hand, deprived of their passports, beaten and intimidated by a succession of new 'owners' until they accepted their fate, became resigned to a grinding day-by-day degradation. And, of course, they were told over and over that the police couldn't be trusted. So no one was going to come forward with information.

But there were lots of other places, officially licensed as massage parlours, where sensual massages and special services were openly advertised. These places were rarely raided, unless there was a problem. As long as the girls were called Chelsea and Holly, everyone turned a blind eye. And maybe Tanya, too.

Angie was leafing through a copy of Yellow Pages that she'd found in a drawer.

'Yep, it's listed.'

'Nothing like being up front. I'll phone them.'

'And say what?'

'I'll think of something,' said Diane.

But the woman who answered the phone said that Tanya didn't work at the Rosebud any more. Another missing witness, like Louise Jones? If Diane had been a man, she guessed she would have been offered someone else's services at this point, probably received the hard sell. But that didn't happen.

'Have you got Tanya's home address, please?'

The woman sounded outraged. 'No, I soddin' haven't.'

'You must keep addresses on file. It's one of the conditions of your licence.'

'There was a moment's silence. 'You're the police aren't you?'

'Yes.'

'Why didn't you say so? I always co-operate with your lot. Are you trying to catch me out, or something?'

'If you could just give me Tanya's address …?'

Angie had been listening with interest, and stood up when she'd finished the call.

'Where, then?'

'Off the Hagley Road.'

'Naturally.'

At one time, prostitution in Birmingham used to be concentrated around Balsall Heath. A campaign by local residents and businesses had succeeded in driving most sex workers out of the area. But, of course, the problem just went somewhere else.

That somewhere else was the Edgbaston area, in several streets off the Hagley Road. It seemed to reach its peak near the Plough and Harrow. There were also reports of girls still operating around Speedwell Road, Hockley, and even in the Jewellery Quarter. Competition and a dependency on drugs had driven the going rate down to twenty pounds for a quickie in the back of a car. Surveys suggested that most people didn't really mind the sex trade, as long as it went on behind closed doors, rather than on their street corner. The problems that residents had with prostitution were based on needles and condoms being left in places where they shouldn't be, and vehicles driving aimlessly around looking for girls.

West Midlands Police now had active patrols in those areas and were taking a tougher line with the problem. Once happy to caution a driver for kerb crawling they were now arresting the offender and carting them off to the police station. A call was then made to their home address to verify the person's identity, and the police would press charges.

The police said they were acting in the interests of both the girls and local residents. Many of the sex workers were beaten up, abused by pimps, and addicted to drugs. Some had even been murdered. Many were under age. But there were plenty of massage parlours in Birmingham offering sexual services, and these were seldom raided unless problems occurred. The girls at a massage parlour were less likely to be abused, less likely to annoy the locals, and far less likely to be taking drugs.

And getting girls off the streets of Birmingham only moved the problem from one place to another – in this case, the Black Country. Some said that Walsall had become the sex capital of the West Midlands.

'How do we go about being unobtrusive in that area?' said Diane. 'Especially at this time of night. I'm not going to walk up and down Hagley Road like a prostitute. I couldn't do it.'

Angie looked at her oddly. 'I could.'

Diane studied her sister. A denial was on the tip of her tongue, but something made her stay silent. She was seeing Angie from a different perspective, picturing her standing on a street corner, looking available, trying to catch the eye of a passing motorist. Yes, she was right. Angie could do it, and wouldn't look too out of place. Given the right clothes, anyway.

'I know just what I'd need,' said Angie.

Not for the first time, Diane wished her sister would stop reading her mind.

'Forget it', she said. 'I'm going on my own anyway.'

20

At Five Ways, the road that had been Broad Street crossed the Middleway and became Hagley Road. This was the very northern end of Edgbaston, bordering on the reservoir – a long way from the cricket ground and the Priory Hospital.

J.R.R. Tolkien had lived around here somewhere. They said that the Two Towers were inspired by Perrott's Folly and the nearby waterworks. There was a Tolkien Trail, *Lord of the Rings* postcards, and a Middle Earth weekend every May. Fry was glad she hadn't arrived during that event. Imagine being surrounded by crowds of orcs and hobbits with bad breath and Birmingham accents. Wasn't that one of Dante's Nine Circles of Hell? Somewhere between Violence and Heresy.

As a rule, enthusiasms didn't come naturally to Brummies. They were usually careful to avoid emotional extremes, an attitude reflected in their accent. Other urban voices sounded strident, but the natural Brummie tone hovered somewhere between bewilderment and despair. And that was an understandable way of looking at the world, when you thought about it.

Fry could see a couple of tom carders working the phone boxes, sticking up adverts for massages and personal services. There were plenty of people glad to earn a few quid for work like that. So as quick as the council took them down, the cards were replaced. It was all the old stuff.

Andy Kewley called her back while she was standing outside a little Asian-run supermarket called Safebury's.

'I'll talk,' he said. 'But not on the phone, obviously. I want to tell you about William Leeson.'

'What is it about this Leeson?'

'He's the man who's up to his neck in everything. It's amazing that he's survived this long, to be honest. I'd like to see you bring him down, Diane. You could be the person to do it.'

'Okay. When do you want to meet?'

'Tonight. Late, while there's no one about.'

'Andy, you're getting really paranoid.'

'You understand, Diane,' said Kewley. 'You know the score.'

'No, I don't think I do. Explain to me.'

'Well, you know what they say about things you don't like being generally best swept under the carpet?'

'I don't have carpets in my house, Andy. I like nice, clean tiles.'

'Diane, I want to help, I really do. But there are complications. Just take what I can give you and accept it as it's intended. Don't ask me too many questions. Trust me, it's for the best.'

Fry grimaced. There was that word again. Trust. She had a negative reaction every time she heard it.

She sighed. 'It's the cemetery again, I suppose?'

'Unless you've got a better idea.'

'Oh, no. It's becoming my favourite place.'

Tanya Spiers had an address in a City Estates flat near Perrott's Folly. As Fry passed the Church of the Redeemer, a black youth stopped her to ask for twenty pence to buy a bag of rice at Safebury's. For once, she forked out. It was a novel excuse, and twenty pence was hardly enough reward for his imagination. There was always a chance that he was telling the truth, too.

A powerful smell of blossom reached her from the gardens around Perrott's Folly, reminding her of the cemetery at Warstone Lane.

At least these weren't tower blocks. These flats were built on a more human scale. But Tanya Spiers wasn't home – or at least wasn't answering her door. Maybe she took a pill and slept through the day.

Fry pulled out one of her cards and scribbled a message on the back before pushing it through the letter box. The steel flap was on a powerful spring. The slam as it closed echoed mockingly down the hall.

Outside the flats, a familiar silver grey Hyundai was parked at the kerb under a streetlight. Detective Sergeant Gorpal Sandhu leaned against the bonnet, his arms folded, a smile on his face. DI Gareth Blake was in the passenger seat, his mobile phone to his ear.

Coming face to face with Sandhu reminded Fry guiltily of what Andy Kewley had said in Warstone Lane cemetery about some of the Asian officers here in the West Midlands. Had he been hinting something about DS Sandhu in particular? Or was it just part of the smokescreen created by his obsessions?

'We want a word,' said Sandhu. 'Please get in the car.'

Blake's face was creased with concern, his eyes steady and sincere. Fry recognized that expression. This was the face of the caring, sharing, modern police service. A face that couldn't always be believed.

'Diane, you know the department really wants to be supportive. Especially in the circumstances ...'

'Thanks. Although I think I hear a "but" coming.'

'Well, we were wondering ... I mean, to put it bluntly, why are you still here? We thought you would have headed back to Derbyshire by now. Isn't your BCU missing you? I imagine they're always short-staffed up there in the sticks.'

'Oh, they're coping,' said Fry. 'In fact, I'm sure some of them will be quite happy to have me out of the way for a while.'

Blake smiled. 'Oh, is someone stepping up in your place? I should watch your back, if I were you, Diane. That's always good advice.'

Fry looked away. Gareth Blake was no fool. She'd almost forgotten that. Like all the best detectives, he could read between the lines. And he could listen between the words, too. Damn it, she'd have to be more careful.

'I don't get back here very often,' she said. 'I've just been catching up with a few people. West Midlands Police don't have any objections to that, do they?'

'No, of course not. In fact, it might help you, Diane. Help to put things behind you, I mean.'

Was it her imagination, or did he put a little more emphasis on the phrase 'behind you' than was strictly necessary, or natural? Fry felt she was being given a hint. A gentle hint for now, but it might turn into a warning very quickly.

'You know what it's like with people from your past. When you meet them again, you remember why you didn't keep in touch with them. You realize you have nothing in common.'

'That's right. You've moved on, Diane. That's good. A nice, clean break is probably best for all concerned.'

Fry opened the door and stood on the pavement. She watched them drive away before she went back to her own car. Best for all concerned? Was it? She was sure there were some people who'd be very happy if she just gave up and walked away. DI Gareth Blake might be among them. So why was he warning her off, yet helping her covertly at the same time?

And how could Blake have known that she would be in Edgbaston? Surely he wasn't having her followed? She would have noticed – her guard wasn't down that much. And besides, he would never have got surveillance approved. She knew how these things worked. There was no justification for such an operation, let alone enough spare cash in the budget. Unless Blake had been following her himself on some lone crusade, it was impossible. And he wasn't the loner type.

So who was he in contact with who might have been giving him information?

Well, there was only one person. And if she couldn't trust her own sister, who could she trust?

The frustration that was growing inside her made Fry feel reckless. If she wasn't very careful, she would do something stupid. There was no one here to restrain her, to offer the quiet word of advice, or make the sensible suggestion.

In Derbyshire, a Traffic unit had taken a shout on the M1. Several calls had come in that night reporting an obstruction on the northbound carriageway, midway between junctions 28 and 29.

Ben Cooper heard the news on his radio as he was leaving West Street. He'd been working late into the evening, trying to catch up with all the jobs he hadn't done, and perhaps not wanting to go home. He'd phoned Mrs Shelley and asked her to go round and feed the cat. At least that was one thing he wouldn't have to feel too guilty about.

But the message about the motorway incident caught his attention. Last time an obstruction was reported on the M1, it turned out to be a human body. Admittedly, it would have been almost unrecognizable by the time the later callers saw it. The log had showed eight minutes thirty seconds between the initial call

213

and the final one, when the first response car was already on the scene.

Cooper had still been in uniform then, just on the point of transferring to CID. He and his partner had been diverted to the scene to help out.

It had been evening rush hour, he remembered. From the squashed and bloodied look of the body, it seemed that every vehicle in the middle lane had hit it before Traffic officers managed to close the carriageway. By then, it was just another bit of roadkill stirring gently in the slipstream of a lorry.

'A drunk,' one of the Traffic officers had said. 'Drunks and motorways are a bad mix.'

Then Cooper found himself being called up on the radio by the control room.

'Traffic have an incident on the motorway, between junctions 29 and 30.'

'I heard,' said Cooper. 'But that's C Division. What has it got to do with me?'

'Your attendance has been specifically requested, DS Cooper.'

'I'm on my way.'

Cooper jumped into his car and headed out of Edendale. Frowning, he contacted the Traffic officer whose name he'd been given by Control, the officer in charge at the scene. It was a man he knew, a long-serving member of the Roads Policing Unit who had probably been present at similar incidents, possibly even the one that Cooper remembered.

'Another one?' he said. 'A jumper? Between 28 and 29?'

'It's that bridge on the B road near Tibshelf Services. Do you know where I mean?'

'Newton Wood Lane?' said Cooper.

'That's the one. It's the quietest spot you can pick, if you're really going to do it. The bridge on the A38 is bigger, but it's much too busy. You're likely to get some Good Samaritan stopping and interfering.'

'It still has nothing to with me,' said Cooper, but less certainly.

'We were lucky. We got an ID straight away.'

'An ID on the body?'

'No, he hasn't actually jumped yet. You know what it's like, Ben – we got a load of contradictory reports and it came out all garbled. We arrived expecting a dead one, and he's very much alive.'

'And now ...?'

'And now he's on the bridge, and he's threatening to jump any minute. He says his name is Sean Deacon.'

'Oh,' said Cooper. 'So it *is* to do with me, after all.'

Sean Deacon had resisted all attempts to talk him down from the parapet of the bridge. He was precariously balanced, and everyone could see that a move too close would send him over. Bizarrely, Deacon had a briefcase clutched in one hand, the other braced against the top of the parapet, which was barely wide enough to stand on.

'We've closed the outside lane underneath him,' said an officer in a yellow high-vis jacket. 'But it won't do him much good if he goes over.'

A few yards away, paramedics were waiting, and a crew in a fire-and-rescue appliance. It was clear that Deacon had been waiting for Cooper to arrive. He smiled briefly when he saw Cooper approaching the bridge, walking into the headlights of a police car.

And then Deacon jumped to his feet, ran ten yards towards the opposite carriageway, balancing like a tightrope walker, before leaping out into the air over the motorway. He seemed to glide through the air, his silhouette caught in the flickering lights of the oncoming traffic, his jacket opening out around him like wings. For that one moment, he was a bird soaring.

Cooper began to run across the bridge, footsteps pounding after him. He saw Deacon's briefcase falling into the traffic, picked out by the headlights of a lorry, bouncing and cartwheeling, forcing cars to swerve in a terrible cacophony of horns and screeching tyres.

Deacon had taken them all by surprise. He'd run so far along the parapet and jumped so hard that he'd landed on the grass banking just beyond the hard shoulder. For a moment, Cooper glimpsed him, crumpled against the base of a tree. Incredibly, he still seemed to be alive. Perhaps the undergrowth had softened his landing. Cooper saw him beginning to move, to sit up against the trunk, a hand pushing himself off the ground, his white face staring into a blinding light.

Then something hit the tree with a shocking impact. Cooper could tell from the noise that it was more than just metal hitting solid wood. It was more like the crunch of a boot crushing a snail. Splintered shell and ruptured flesh. The sound turned his stomach.

When they scrambled down the banking, the emergency services found Sean Deacon pinned to the tree by the grille of a Transit van that had swerved off the carriageway. A paramedic went to him, shook her head at Cooper, opened her kit, and injected Deacon with painkiller.

'Why did you do this, Sean?' asked Cooper.

'I just came to the end of the line,' he said. 'There's no point in going on. It's better this way.'

Cooper didn't know what to say. Deacon gripped his arm.

'Can I tell you something?' he said.

'Of course. Anything.'

'I never intended to do any harm.'

And somehow, Cooper knew that he meant it.

He held Deacon's hand so tightly that it would have been painful, if it hadn't been for the diamorphine flooding through the man's collapsing veins.

'Let it go, Sean,' he said. 'Let it go. It'll be all right.'

Finally, he felt the grip relax. Deacon released a long, rattling breath that came from deep inside his body somewhere. It was more than just carbon dioxide escaping from the lungs, more than just a simple exhalation. It was the dying breath.

'Let it go. Don't struggle, just let it go.'

Cooper looked up at the paramedic and stood aside for her. His mind numb, he began to walk away, with no idea where he was heading, just walking away from the scene. Don't look back, he thought. There's no need to look back.

Behind him, he heard the fire and rescue service start up their cutters. It was too late for Sean now, but it had to be done. All these things had to be done.

At the top of the banking, he reached a fence, and stopped. The Derbyshire landscape stretched out in front of him – the village of Tibshelf, Woolley Moor, and the higher hills around Matlock in the distance. Roads glittered like strings of jewels as they snaked across the moors. Villages lay sleeping in the darkness all across the Peak District.

Cooper wondered whether Sean Deacon was flying now, or falling. Was his spirit whispering across the sky, somewhere high above those night-time hills? Or was that Deacon's voice he could hear, screaming faintly in the dark as he plunged into a deeper blackness?

Flying, or falling?

Well, perhaps it was all the same, in the end.

A 1920s red-brick pub stood on the corner of Warstone Lane and Vyse Street in the Jewellery Quarter, near the Chamberlain clock. The Rose Villa Tavern, it was called. A Mitchells & Butlers pub, drinkers sitting among decorative tiles.

Fry looked at her watch again. Andy Kewley was late. That was unlike him. But maybe he'd needed a stiff drink before their meeting. She glanced up Vyse Street towards the Rose Villa, considered walking up to see if she could find him propped in the corner of the bar with a whisky, staring morosely at the tiles.

But that picture wasn't right. It didn't fit Kewley's personality. He was much too careful for that. Much too cautious.

Fry entered the Warstone Lane cemetery. Hundreds of Victorian gravestones marching across the slopes, lurking in the hollows, hiding beneath shrouds of ivy. Tiers of catacombs, defaced angels, tombs blackened with soot. And that powerful, sickly sweet smell, still strong on the night air.

An engine revved noisily nearby, and a car raced away on the Middleway. It was very dark away from the streetlights, and Fry pulled a small torch from her pocket. She looked down from the top tier of the catacombs to the grass circle below, the centre of the amphitheatre.

For a moment, Fry thought the vandals had struck again since her last visit to the cemetery, that another memorial angel had been toppled to the ground. In the light of her torch, she saw blank eyes pressed into the grass, a face mottled with damp.

But when she looked again, she knew this was no angel. The face was pale, but it wasn't stone. The eyes were blank with the stare of death. And the mottled dampness was much too dark. It was dark as clotted blood.

21

Friday

The next morning, Ben Cooper drove through endless red-brick suburbs, streets so identical that it made him wonder how thousands of Birmingham commuters ever found their way home.

On the map, Birmingham looked like a giant spider's web, a dense network of roads radiating out in a ragged pattern to absorb the surrounding motorways, M42, M5 and M6. Between the roads, the ground was thick with houses.

Cooper took a wrong turning somewhere as he left the Expressway. He thought he'd probably come off too soon, and was driving through some apparently nameless suburb. He stopped to look at the *A to Z* and turn round, and found himself sitting in front of a bay-windowed semi in an empty, tree-lined street. Cooper looked around him. Acres of brick and leaded glass. Bitumen-stained fencing, and flower beds full of pansies. This place was so suburban it was almost a caricature of itself. It might look comforting if you belonged here. But it was pretty damn weird if you didn't.

He knew there must be thousands and thousands of homes like this, out there in the spider's web. Suburb upon suburb, making up a vast brick blanket that covered most of the West Midlands. Warwickshire had been here once, and part of Staffordshire. Now great chunks of them had been absorbed into the urban sprawl.

While he was stopped, he called Fry's mobile number.

'Diane, are you at the hotel?'

'No.'

'Where, then?'

'What do you want to know for? What's going on, Ben?'

'I'm coming to see you.'

'What? Where are you?'

'I'm in Birmingham. I'm not sure exactly which part.'

'At the risk of sounding dim – why?'

'I've got something to tell you.'

'And you couldn't do it on the phone? You're not turning into another paranoid, are you?'

'Sorry?'

'Never mind. Come to Hockley. Warstone Lane, in the Jewellery Quarter. You'll find it easily enough. Just follow all the police cars.'

A few minutes later, Cooper finally reached the city centre. Its tower blocks, streams of traffic and crowds of pedestrians made him feel he was nothing but a single ant in the middle of a seething ant heap. Well, one insect might be insignificant. But at least that meant it went pretty much unnoticed by the rest of the heap.

It had always seemed to Cooper that city people lived in a permanent sodium twilight. It never really grew dark here, and the stars were invisible. The sky was only a dim void, way up there beyond the tower blocks.

And in the daytime, it didn't seem to get properly light in the shadow of those high-rise buildings. Streets running west to east were too narrow for the sun ever to reach the pavement. So shoppers and office workers gravitated to the open spaces to soak up some rays in their lunch breaks. The cathedral gardens were crowded with people escaping the shadows.

His departure on his rest day hadn't been popular, particularly when he'd told Liz about it.

'I've got to get right away for a few hours,' he said. 'The incident last night really shook me up.'

'I understand, Ben. It's been a tough week.'

'You could say that.'

'Maybe you ought to take more time off than just a few hours.'

'No, I'll be all right. Too much to do.'

'So where are you going?' she asked.

'Birmingham.'

'Birmingham? You're kidding. Is this actually work?'

'Well … I can't say, really.'

And she didn't sound happy with the reply.

'Ben,' she repeated, 'why are you going to Birmingham?'

'Liz –'

'Do you think I don't know that Diane Fry is there?'

Cooper could have kicked himself. Of course she would know that. He bet that Fry's trip had been the subject of office gossip for days. It might have been better if he'd lied. She would have found him out though, and then it would have been even worse.

But what could he say to Liz now that would smooth things over, yet wouldn't be a lie?

'Diane needs my help,' he said. 'It's as simple as that.'

'Simple? You might think so, Ben. But I'm not sure it is.'

DI Blake looked seriously troubled now. His face was creased with disappointment, as if Fry had let him down somehow.

'Diane,' he said, shaking his head, 'I remember you as a first-class colleague when we worked together in Aston. Straight as an arrow – that was DC Fry. Always going by the book.'

Fry said nothing. He hadn't asked a question, so there was no need for an answer. Silence was a weapon that worked both ways.

She'd already been interviewed by members of the Major Incident Unit attending the scene of Andy Kewley's death. Blake must have been alerted at an early stage, because he arrived before she'd even finished making her initial statement.

Fry watched the West Midlands forensic scene investigators in their white scene suits and blue latex gloves combing through the cemetery, picking among the cider bottles on the moss-covered tombstones. They would be looking for fingerprints, fibres, blood or hair, searching for footprints or weapons. She wished them luck in the tangled undergrowth and broken memorials.

She and Blake were standing at the outer cordon near the RV point. They were prohibited from the scene itself, excluded as unnecessary personnel.

Fry thought of the three principles of crime-scene management – protect, record and recover.

The potential for contamination must be immense. If an item of evidence was vulnerable, the chances were that everyone was going to walk over it. She might have walked over something herself, crushed some fragment of vital trace evidence into the dirt.

'How was he killed?' asked Fry. 'It looked like a head injury to me. But they won't tell me anything.'

'Yes, blunt instrument.'

'He can't have been dead for long. He liked to be on time.'

'And you didn't see anybody?' asked Blake.

'No.'

'So was there some particular reason you were meeting him?'

'Because he called me and asked me to, that's all. I covered it all in my statement to the MIU.'

'Yes, you're right – it's not my enquiry. But I worked with Kewley for a while too, don't forget.'

Fry shook her head. 'I don't understand. Who would want to attack Andy Kewley?'

'Well, we get all kinds of people hanging around in places like this. Sociopaths, drunks, drug addicts. Individuals who ought to be in secure accommodation, but who've fallen through cracks in the system. They're drawn to disused areas like old cemeteries.'

'Oh, I see. You mean it was a random assault? Just some harmless homicidal crank?'

'I don't know, Diane. I don't have any information. What do you think?'

Fry didn't answer the question. 'Somebody must have seen Andy arrive, at least.'

'Uniforms are doing a trawl for witnesses, but my guess is it will be a short list.'

Fry saw Ben Cooper arrive at the outer cordon, looking bewildered by the extent of the activity in and around the cemetery. She also thought he appeared particularly dishevelled today. His hair fell untidily across his forehead, and she wasn't sure that he'd even shaved properly this morning.

'So did this sort of thing always happen when you lived in Birmingham?' said Cooper when Fry explained the activity.

'I didn't live in Birmingham,' said Fry. 'I never lived in Birmingham, even when I was at college in Perry Barr, and even when I worked in Aston. I lived in the Black Country, at Warley.'

'Okay. There's a difference?'

'You bet there's a difference.'

'I'll try to remember.'

'And another thing to remember, Ben – now you're in the city, you can't just go around being nice to everybody you pass in the street here. They don't know who you are, and they won't like it. You're liable to get yourself killed.'

'Stop being nice? Okay. I'll try to be more like you, then.'

Fry thought she'd misheard him. 'What?'

But Cooper ignored it.

'So what do you think is going on, Diane? With your case, I mean.'

'I really don't know. I don't have enough information.'

'What's your instinct?'

'It's too late for instinct, Ben. Much too late.'

Fry looked at him. For the first time, she noticed that he didn't look well. It wasn't just untidiness. He was pale, and there were dark rings under his eyes, as if he hadn't been sleeping properly for days. His hand shook when he brushed back a lock of hair. She had never seen his hands shake before. Never. He seemed fidgety, and he kicked out irritably at a pigeon which came too close. She wondered what had really made him set off and drive to Birmingham this morning. Was he trying to escape from something back in Derbyshire? Because, if so, he seemed to have brought it with him.

'How is the new role going, Ben?' she said. 'Acting DS.'

'Oh, fine.'

But he sounded so unsure that he might as well have said the opposite.

'You can ask me for advice, you know, if you want to. It's not an admission of weakness.'

'Well, it's not the job. It's just something I'm worried about. The family of this dead girl.'

'The drowning accident on Monday?'

'Yes.'

'It's been bothering you all week, hasn't it?'

'Yes, but the DI thinks I'm worrying about nothing.'

'Oh no, don't tell me – you've found another lost cause to champion.'

'I knew you wouldn't listen.'

223

Hearing his irritation, Fry immediately regretted her response. She didn't want him to go away again.

'No, I'm sorry, Ben. Go on. What about this family?'

Standing near the incident command unit, Cooper told her about the Nield family, and his suspicions, about the ambiguity of the witness statements and his fear that their memories of events couldn't be relied on. Exactly as he knew it would, just telling Fry about it all helped him to get things clear in his mind. He could detect the weaknesses in his own arguments by watching her face and reflecting on his words.

When he'd finished, he knew what he should be doing next, what questions he should be asking. And Fry had hardly needed to say anything.

'Thanks, Diane,' he said.

'I didn't do anything.'

A woman stepped out from behind the van. Cooper wondered if she'd been there all the time. Fry introduced her as Rachel Murchison, a member of DI Blake's team. But he could see that she didn't really look like a police officer.

'I'm sorry, I couldn't help overhearing,' said Murchison. 'You were talking about interference theory, which is an interest of mine.'

'I didn't mean to suggest that the witnesses had been deliberately interfered with,' said Cooper, wondering if he'd said too much in public.

'No, I know. It's just a name for it.'

'Are you a psychologist?' he asked.

Murchison smiled. 'Let's just say, I know the theory.'

'I've been wanting to ask someone about this – the way witnesses perceive things. Why their memories of an incident might contradict each other.'

'Well, our memories of what we've seen are often inaccurate. I mean, they might not actually be what happened. Everyone knows this. When it comes to a court case, your witnesses always contradict each other. Some of them are better left out of the

224

witness box, because they only muddy the water, and then no one knows what to believe.'

'But they're not lying,' said Cooper.

'No, of course. They're not lying, just mistaken. Some witnesses see what they want to see. Or they remember what they think you want to them to remember. In a nutshell, that's interference theory.'

'So the interference is self-imposed?'

'In a way,' said Murchison. 'As with all memories, our eyewitness memories can be distorted by what we previously knew, which is pro-active interference, or what we subsequently learn – retroactive interference. The distortion of memories has been widely studied. Retroactive interference can result from police questioning, which is well intentioned but can lead to difficulty in accurate recall. Unfortunately, poor interview techniques are all too common.'

'Yes, I'm aware of that,' said Cooper.

He looked at Fry, then looked away again, hoping she didn't think that he was referring to her abilities.

'If you're interested,' said Murchison, 'the classic study on this subject is Loftus and Palmer. They showed eyewitness memory was vulnerable to post-event distortion. In their experiment, it came down to a difference between the questions "How fast were the cars going when they smashed into each other?" or "How fast were the cars going when they hit each other?" Participants asked the first question were convinced they'd seen broken glass. The use of the word "smashed" affected their recollection.'

Cooper nodded. 'It makes sense. It was what I was thinking anyway.'

'And you,' said Murchison. 'How is your short-term memory?'

Now Cooper was taken aback. He hated being so transparent. But people often said his feelings were written on his face.

'Not good,' he admitted. 'Not during these past few days. I get confused about what I saw and what I didn't.'

'It's the result of trauma – that is, of experiencing the child's death in the river, and being helpless to save her. Short term, you may have re-experiences – flashbacks. You may also get adverse reactions to anything your brain associates with the traumatic event. In this case, water, perhaps?'

Cooper remembered his reluctance to go too near the river in Dovedale. He nodded cautiously, wary of admitting a weakness.

'It's perfectly common,' said Murchison. 'It should pass in time.'

'Does it always pass?'

'Well, not always. If left unacknowledged and untreated, it can develop into full-blown PTSD, and the effects of that can last for years. Occasionally, serious psychological disturbances may result from traumatic experiences in the past. But that's quite rare.'

Now Cooper was interested.

'Tell me,' he said. 'Would it be more common in a child?'

'Oh, yes. Certainly.'

A few minutes later, Murchison took Fry aside for a quiet word. They stood at the corner of the cemetery, just outside the cordon.

'Diane, your colleague has a problem,' she said.

'You noticed?'

'There are a lot of small signs.'

'It's the incident earlier this week that he just mentioned. The death of the little girl he tried to rescue from drowning.'

Murchison nodded.

'There should be early intervention after a traumatic incident like that. It can prevent acute stress reaction from developing into full-blown PTSD. What was the level of your critical incident stress management?'

'I don't know. I wasn't there.'

Murchison shook her head. 'Someone should have taken responsibility. Isn't this officer part of your team?'

Fry looked across the cemetery at Cooper.

'Do I still have a team?' she said.

When Fry was released by the Major Incident Unit, she took Cooper back to her hotel. He looked as though he needed a cup of coffee or two, maybe some food.

'Ben,' she said, as they parked their cars in the Brindleyplace multi-storey, 'how much do you remember of your childhood?'

Cooper turned to her in surprise as he keyed the locks on his Toyota. 'I remember lots of things.'

'I mean, what are your earliest memories? How old were you at the time?'

'Oh, well. There's a vague memory of crossing a street somewhere in town, with Mum and Matt. It must have been during the summer, because Matt had a wasp land on his hand. I have this picture of him standing there, with his finger out as if he was pointing at something. And he was screaming. He was terrified of getting stung by wasps as a child. I think it's probably the sound of him screaming that impressed the memory on me.'

'Matt was a child? But he's five years older than you, isn't he?'

'Yes.'

'So you must have been …?'

'Well, Mum was standing behind me. I was in a pushchair.'

'You weren't even walking? That means you were, what … two or three years old?'

'I suppose so.'

'My God.'

Cooper stopped in the exit to the car park and looked up at the office blocks in Brindleyplace.

'Why are you asking something like that, Diane?'

'Well, I realized a strange thing. I don't have any early memories at all. Nothing as early as you. I don't even remember my first day at school. That's a bit odd, isn't it?'

He shrugged. 'Not necessarily. I think you remember things that were particularly traumatic or especially enjoyable. I don't remember my first day at school either. But I remember the second day – I didn't want to go, and I kicked up a real fuss at home that morning. But Mum tricked me into walking past the gates so we could look at all the other children who were having to go in, and then she pushed me into the arms of a teacher. I cried then. That was a real trauma, I can tell you. But I can't actually remember why I didn't want to go in the first place.'

'I can't picture you crying because you didn't want to go to school.'

'I bet you can't picture me in my school shorts and cap either.'

'I'd rather not, thanks.'

Cooper gestured at the hotel. 'Is this where you're staying?'

'Oh. Yes. Come on in.'

'So what brought this on suddenly, Diane? Has your Birmingham visit turned into a trip down Memory Lane?'

'Sort of. I just keep noticing that other people seem to remember far more than I do. Their memories are clear, right down to the smallest details. I don't know how they do that. For me, anything that happened more than ten years ago is just a blur. I've always taken the view that your memory can only hold a certain amount of information, so it gradually ditches all the old stuff that you don't need any more.'

'But there must be some things you remember.'

'Yes, of course.' Fry hesitated. 'Yes, of course there are. A few things.'

'No happy childhood memories? Well, maybe I shouldn't ask …'

'Considering the sort of childhood that I had? No. Well, I suppose you have happy memories of long summer holidays playing in the garden with your pet dog.'

'Playing on the farm among the cows. But, otherwise, yes.'

When they were seated in the hotel lounge, Cooper looked around to see who was within earshot, reminding Fry too closely of Andy Kewley, whose body now lay in the mortuary.

'Anyway, I've got some news,' he said. 'An old friend came up trumps and passed on some information.'

'Yes?'

But Cooper jumped as someone walked up to their table. Fry looked up and saw Angie.

'Well, look who it is,' said Angie. 'What a surprise.'

Diane couldn't bear the smile on her sister's face when she saw Cooper. Angie pulled up another chair and joined them at the table. She looked as though she might start questioning Cooper, or making some joke that only she would find funny. She had to prevent that.

'Ben was just telling me that he had some information.'

'Right.'

Cooper looked at her with one eyebrow raised, and she nodded. Angie had to be allowed in.

'Okay,' he said. 'Well, apparently, the cold case team put all the evidence samples from your assault through the lab again for fresh DNA tests.'

'Yes, that's right.'

'And, as a result, it seems they got a new hit – a familial DNA match.'

'What does that mean?' asked Angie.

'They widened the search criteria on the national database. Although they didn't find a direct match to the person who left the scene of crime sample, they identified a family member.'

'Wait a minute. That means a close relative who was already on the database.'

'Yes. Probably someone who'd been arrested at some time. A CJ sample taken from a buccal swab. They didn't even necessarily have to be charged, let alone convicted. They would still be on the database.'

'It could be an innocent person, then.'

'Well, maybe.'

Fry knew the DNA database had its own internal algorithms for identifying immediate relatives on the basis of similar profiles. A one-off speculative search approach was used for conducting familial searches, which could throw up parents, siblings, or offspring. This type of search could be used to pursue two lines of enquiry – the identity of an individual who could be a sibling of the offender, or the identity of the offender's parent or child.

Some time in the not too distant future, she expected that a DNA profile of someone arrested could be statistically linked to more and more relatives like uncles, aunts, cousins, many of whom would not have been arrested.

'So who was traced by the familial match?'

'I don't know,' said Cooper.

'Was it Shepherd, or Barnes?'

'It doesn't seem to have been either of them.'

'What? It must have been one or the other. A familial match means either Shepherd or Barnes has a father or brother on the database – that's what happened, surely?'

'It seems not, Diane.'

'But theirs was the only DNA recovered from the scene. Unless …'

Cooper nodded. 'Yes. The new series of tests produced a third DNA profile. Techniques have improved a lot over the last few years. Analysis is much more sensitive now.'

'A third person at the scene,' said Fry. 'A third person.'

Her mind re-ran that confused memory – a figure crouching over her, with a different feel and smell. There was no other way she could disentangle that one recollection from the rest, because it was caught up in the overwhelming flood of sensations – the pain and shock, and fear, the vicious sharpness of the gravel, the bite of the barbed-wire fence, the suffocating darkness.

She had always known there were other figures in the background. She had seen their shadows in the streetlights, heard their voices in the dark. But a third taking part in the attack? Well, there could have been. A third member of the gang, drawn into the assault, urged on by the others. A third person leaving his DNA.

'A familial match could still mean they linked the third person to Shepherd or Barnes.'

'I don't know,' said Cooper. 'It could have been that. Those are all the details I've got so far on the DNA evidence. I'm sorry it isn't more, Diane.'

'No, that's great. You've done really well, Ben.'

Angie looked sideways at Cooper before turning to her sister. 'Did you leave that file in your room, Di? Is it safe?'

'I left a "Do not disturb" sign on the door.'

'By the way, I have these, too,' said Cooper.

He produced the PNC print-outs for Marcus Shepherd and Darren Barnes, with all their details – addresses, dates of birth, ethnicity codes, criminal records. There was also a photograph of Tanya Spiers, obtained from the police computer system. She was the witness who claimed to have known both the suspects, and heard them boasting at a club.

'Why was she on the PNC?' asked Fry.

'She was arrested at some time for soliciting, and outraging public decency,' he said. 'Actually, I feel sorry for her.'

'Why?'

'She looks as if she's gone through a lot of tragedy in her life. It's her eyes – they're very sad.'

Angie laughed. 'No, Ben. It's too much crack and vodka that makes your eyes look this way.'

Cooper lowered his head, as if embarrassed by Angie's laughter.

'So what's next?' he asked.

'Yes,' agreed Angie. 'That's a good question. What's next?'

Diane gazed out of the hotel windows at the fountains splashing in the square, and the office workers moving backwards and forwards in front of 3 Brindleyplace.

'Andy Kewley was killed because he knew something, and was about to give it away,' she said. 'And, if Andy was right, there's one person central to all this. His name is William Leeson.'

22

It had begun to rain by the time they got to Digbeth. Warm, summer rain – but heavy enough to make pedestrians run for cover.

The entrance to the sprawling Custard Factory arts complex was hidden away opposite the Peugeot dealer on the Bull Ring Trading Estate. An ancient half-timbered pub stood by the traffic lights on the corner of Heath Mill Lane – the Old Crown, its fourteenth-century origins written on the back wall. Fry noticed a martial arts academy in a yard under one of the railway viaducts, close to the campanile of Father Lopes' Chapel.

The buildings of the Custard Factory were painted in pastel colours. Blue, green, pink. A metallic dragon guarded a small lake. A giant living tree statue of a green man loomed over Pagan Place, with empty eye sockets and rain water dripping from his mouth.

Some entrepreneur had taken a massive punt on this project. Scattered around the area now were trendy venues and exhibition spaces. Barfly, Vivid, the Medicine Bar. All tucked in among the old factories, like wild flowers blooming in a desert.

'Louise Jones was leaving the publisher's offices in the Custard Factory,' she said. 'They'd been holding some kind of public event – a book launch party, or something like that. People had been drinking until quite late. Miss Jones probably stayed behind to help clear up.'

'And to chuck out the drunks, from what I hear about publishing.'

'Maybe.'

'And as she came out to get her car, she looked down the street, and she saw two males running away from the patch of wasteland.'

'That's it. One black male and one white.'

'Marcus Shepherd and Darren Barnes.'

Fry looked around. 'That means they must have been on the other side of the river, though.'

As they went up the steps into Heath Mill Lane, the paving under the walkway was treacherously slippery after the fresh rain.

'What was the piece of wasteland?'

'I don't know. Some old disused factory yard, or a demolition site.'

The Connemara wasn't the only pub in this area. She noticed the Floodgate Tavern standing on the corner of Floodgate Street and Little Ann Street.

'So, if the DNA results are correct, there must have been a third person.'

'I do have a vague recollection, but it's too confused for me to be certain.'

The entrance to the car park on Heath Mill Lane was bordered by a twenty-five-foot wall made of compacted cars – crushed engine mountings, ripped tyres, even the old carpets from footwells, still full of the debris left by their drivers. Another symbolic statement of some kind?

In the nearby streets, taxis were parked by the kerbside waiting for repair. A small engineering workshop stood under the arch of the railway viaduct, now hung with weeds and saplings re-colonizing the brickwork. Every yard and alley was protected by steel security fencing.

'I'm not sure this is going to help,' said Fry.

'Memories emerge gradually. The more reminders you get, the better.'

Fry stood on the brick steps leading down to the river, watching the oily flow, touching the tall stems of the wild plants that she knew would burst into purple flowers later in the summer. She turned the page of her *A to Z*, trying to trace the river's route. It wasn't an easy task – the line on the map was narrow, and broken in places, weaving between a network of roads and canals.

She found the Lickey Hills to the south of Birmingham. It was from here that the Rea came into the city, meandered its way through Canon Hill Park, skirted Edgbaston cricket ground, and crossed Belgrave Middleway, before being swallowed up by the industrial belt.

From there, it was pretty much a forgotten river – visible only from derelict factories, or glimpsed from the car park of Maini's cash and carry. Even train passengers might fail to notice it as they crossed the viaduct over Floodgate Street. Boaters on the Grand Union Canal might be aware of the dirty brown river flowing beneath their aqueduct at Warwick Bar. But within a few metres it had disappeared again under the freightliner terminal in Montague Street.

Somewhere north of Washwood Heath, the Rea finally merged with the Tame under the shadow of Spaghetti Junction. Along the way, the river had picked up a tide of industrial debris, sucking the grime out of miles of crumbling brickwork and nineteenth-century foundations.

The purple flowers were rosebay willowherb, she recalled – a weed that had been the bane of life for her foster parents, who'd run a plant nursery in Halesowen, a bit too close to a railway embankment that had been allowed to run wild. All of those clumps of weed were an unwelcome intrusion from the countryside. Their seeds must drift in on the wind from the Lickeys, or cling to the feathers of birds roosting in the parks. Maybe they even floated in on the rivers too, swept past Longridge and under the factories of Digbeth on the muddy surface of the Rea. Left to itself, she supposed willowherb would re-colonize the city, cover the whole of Birmingham in purple flowers and clouds of white seed-heads.

Thank goodness for the parks department with their back-packs full of weed killer, spraying a barrier of poison against the forces of nature.

Fry looked round for Cooper. Angie had backed out of coming with her on this visit, claiming that she had other things to do.

'Does that mean I have to do this on my own?' Diane had said.

But Cooper had stepped forward. 'I'll come with you.'

And that had been that. Fry hadn't commented on her sister's attitude, but Cooper couldn't resist.

'I would have thought that Angie could be with you,' he said. 'Now, of all times.'

Fry had shrugged then.

'You know, Ben,' she said, 'I don't care any more.'

Fry gestured at the water as Cooper came alongside her.

'There you go,' she said. 'That's the River Rea. Birmingham's forgotten treasure.'

Cooper was startled by the change in her. This wasn't the Diane Fry he knew. The look she gave him when she said 'I don't care any more' was almost a challenge, as if she wanted him to provoke her, to push her too far. She was turning into a different person in front of his eyes, and he wasn't sure that he liked it. Perhaps he hadn't really got to know her very well in these past few years. This side of her had been pretty well hidden, anyway.

Now, standing in Digbeth, he looked down at the dirty brown water, trying to see it as a treasure. But the River Dove was still in his mind, clear and cold, flowing down from the hills.

'People associate London with the Thames, Liverpool with the Mersey, and Newcastle with the Tyne. But to generations of Brummies, the River Rea is a mystery. Most of them don't even know their city possesses a river. They think they just have canals.'

'To be honest, it's not very impressive,' said Cooper.

'Maybe not,' admitted Fry. 'But it's not the river itself that's important, is it? It's what's on the banks of the river that matters.'

Fry's phone rang. She could see from the caller display who it was.

'Do I want to talk to her?' she said out loud.

'Who?' asked Cooper.

'My sister.'

'Perhaps you'd better.'

Cooper walked away a few yards, to give her some privacy. Perhaps he thought they were going to have a row. If so, he was disappointed.

'You need a bloke called Eddie Doyle,' said Angie.

'Who's he?'

'William Leeson's partner. Or ex partner, at least.'

'How did you find that out?'

'I looked him up on Facebook.'

'What?'

'Well, ask a stupid question …'

Fry turned impatiently, scowled at Cooper as if it was his fault. 'What was that name again?'

'Eddie Doyle. They say you might find him at the Irish Club, if the bar's open.'

'Thanks, Angie.'

'You didn't sound all that pleased to hear from me, Di. Were you expecting someone else?'

'I was hoping for a call from Vince. He hasn't been in touch yet about getting me within arm's length of Shepherd and Barnes. He agreed to do it, but I suppose he's got cold feet.'

'Vince? I wouldn't rely on him. He was never the toughest kid on the block.'

'No.'

Fry finished the call and gestured to Cooper. He ambled over, too slowly for her liking. She felt like telling him he was in the city now. People here moved at a pace that was a bit faster than a ruminating sheep.

'Where are we going?' he asked.

'To a little bit of Ireland.'

The Irish Club stood in a prominent position on Deritend High Street. Here, the River Rea formed the dividing line between Digbeth and Deritend. At Deritend Bridge was the very spot where Birmingham had first developed. Someone once told her that the early settlers had just called this stretch of water 'the river', and nothing more – 'rea' was a word meaning river in Anglo Saxon. That was good Brum, calling a spade a spade.

Drum and accordion music drifted from an open fire door at the Chapel House Street entrance of the club. There was a dance going on in the main hall. Fry glimpsed middle-aged couples swinging each other around the floor.

In the lobby, old Gaelic Athletics Association posters were framed on the walls. Carroll's GAA Allstars of 1974. A bit of nostalgia there, definitely. Posters in the windows advertised wrestling matches and concerts by two singers called Sean Nenrye and Mick Flavin. In their publicity photos they looked so similar they could have been twins. The same Irish twinkle, the same hazel eyes.

'Want me to go in and ask?' said Cooper.

'What? Do you think you'll pass as Irish?'

'Better than you will,' he said. 'Anyway, you might want to keep an eye out front here, in case he legs it.'

'Legs it? Like he's a suspect?'

'Well, I'm just thinking – nobody else seems to want to talk to you at the moment, Diane. Mr Doyle might be no different.'

Fry nodded. 'Okay. Let's do that.'

Standing at front of the club, near the pedestrian crossing, Fry looked towards the city centre. The clean light after the spell of rain lit a panorama of contrasting buildings – the blue sheen of the Beetham Tower, the Paradise Circus multi-storey car park, the spire of St Martin's in the Bullring, the Rotunda, the shimmering aluminium curve of Selfridges.

Cooper came out a few minutes later.

'They know Eddie Doyle pretty well, but he's not here at the moment. They suggested trying a pub called the Connemara.'

Well, the Connemara wouldn't feature very highly in the tourist guides to Birmingham. It stood a few hundred yards too far east to be part of the gay scene, and it hadn't quite made enough effort on its food or décor to attract the cultural crowd from the Custard Factory. And from what she'd heard, all the really beautiful people went to the Rainbow in Deritend High Street anyway. So the Connemara was left with the flotsam and jetsam, the type of hardened drinkers who still gravitated to old-fashioned back-street pubs, no doubt for their own good reasons.

When Fry worked in the West Midlands, there had been a thousand pubs like the Connemara, magnets for petty criminals and prostitutes, the scenes of regular Saturday-night brawls, and the occasional all-night lock-in. But there weren't many of these places left now, even in Birmingham. Times had changed, and people wanted more than a packet of cheese-and-onion crisps and a pint of Double Diamond on a damp beer mat. Customers expected food and cocktails, and a bit of an ambience. If they didn't adapt to changing demands, these back-street pubs were doomed. During the past few years, they'd been closing down faster than teashops in a street full of Starbuck's.

There was a reason she hadn't remembered this pub at first. It had changed its name a few times. Leaded windows and ornate Victorian brickwork, red and white, with a top storey like a half-timbered Elizabethan addition. Spotlights. Above the hanging baskets, a CCTV camera enclosed in a steel cage to protect it against vandalism.

'Let's do it the other way round this time,' she said.

Cooper shrugged. 'Whatever you like.'

'Give me five minutes. If I don't come out, you can follow me in.'

'Sure.'

Fry walked through the door, and the atmosphere hit her immediately. Stale beer and body odour, no longer masked by cigarette smoke. Or was it?

My God. It was the second decade of the twenty-first century, and she still felt uncomfortable going into a pub on her own. Well, going into the Connemara she did. It was probably something to do with the distance she'd put between herself and civilization the moment she walked through the door. She caught the powerful odour of spilt beer, sour as if it had been spilled last week and no one had bothered to wipe it up. And wasn't that cigarette smoke she could see hanging in the air in front of the dartboard? Maybe she should just pretend it was a trick of the light.

She asked at the bar, and a man sitting on his own in the corner was pointed out to her.

'Eddie Doyle?'

He jumped as if he'd been shot.

'Jesus and Mary! Who the Hell are you?'

Fry sat down across the table from him.

'A bit jumpy, sir?'

He wiped a splash of whisky off his shirt.

'You don't creep up on people like that around here. Jesus.'

Eddie Doyle was small and flabby, and had grown a brown moustache in an attempt to make his face look more interesting. It wasn't working. The sly look in his eye was more reminiscent of a

238

salesman, calculating the odds, weighing up his chances of closing a deal.

He reminded Fry of a part-time college lecturer she'd dealt with once. He was some kind of expert on the history of the industrial revolution. He'd spent a lot of his time poking around in the back streets of Digbeth, admiring the contour of a factory wall, excited by a line of brickwork on a railway viaduct.

The lecturer had been a heavy drinker, too. He'd run an elderly woman over in his car on a pedestrian crossing, his blood test showing that he was nearly three times the drink-drive limit. He'd got a custodial sentence for causing death by dangerous driving. He might still be in Winson Green now.

Doyle peered at her through watery eyes.

'No, I don't know you. Are you on the game? You don't look like a tart.'

'I'm looking for William Leeson,' she said.

Doyle took another drink. 'You still haven't told me who you are.'

Fry drew further away from Doyle. Stale alcohol seemed to leak out of his skin in place of sweat.

'I don't need to tell you anything,' she said.

'Snap.'

'You don't sound very Irish, Mr Doyle.'

'I'm third generation, which makes me practically royalty among this lot.' He nodded at a crowd of men round the bar. 'Look at these plastic paddies. Listen to them all, over there in the Irish Club, singing their pathetic rebel songs. They think the old country is some kind of romantic paradise. *Tir na nog*, the land of the ever young. A Shangri-la out in the west, on the edge of the world. My God. Have you been to Ireland recently?'

'Yes, as a matter fact.'

'And what did you see?'

'A lot of pink bungalows, and new shopping developments,' said Fry.

'Exactly. And it's as bad out west in County Galway as it is in Dublin. The Irish government got a shedload of European money, and they spent it building as much tat as could be fit into Ireland.'

Doyle was smiling at her, which she didn't like. Fry was starting to wish Cooper would appear. How long had she told him to wait? Could he actually tell when five minutes were up, or was he still on country time?

Taking advantage of her silence, Doyle leaned closer.

'Some of these people started drinking here when another Irish pub up the road was burned down in an arson attack a few years ago.'

'Oh? Terrorism came a bit close to home, did it?'

'Ah, well. No one was ever convicted of arson, so it might just have been kids, you know?'

'Sure.'

'No, really,' said Doyle. 'It was a decent place. Full of Brummie Irish, of course, but it served the best pint of Guinness in Birmingham.'

'I'll take your word for it.'

Doyle snorted.

'Plastic paddies,' he said. 'You know what they say – a typical Brummie is the one wearing a shamrock in his turban.'

'Very funny. You know what, Mr Doyle – I'm starting to get tired of the atmosphere in here.'

'No, don't go. We don't get much female company in here.'

'I can't imagine why.'

Doyle looked past her shoulder and nodded resignedly.

'Oh, how typical. You didn't say you'd brought the boyfriend with you.'

Cooper stood over him, saying nothing. He did that pretty well, Fry thought. Maybe it would be better if he said nothing more often.

Nervously, Doyle stared into his glass. 'I suppose you're the police.'

'You want to see our warrant cards?'

He flapped his hands anxiously. 'No, no. Not in here. Let's keep it friendly, all right?'

'Suits us,' said Fry. 'Perhaps we could buy you another drink? That would look really friendly, wouldn't it?'

'Okay.' Doyle looked up at Cooper, and tried a smile. 'A malt whisky. Laphroaig would be lovely.'

Cooper didn't smile back. His fixed stare and slightly unshaven look made him look a bit intimidating, as if he was a borderline psychopath who might lose control at any moment. He was getting good at that, too.

'You could see if they've got anything non-alcoholic for me,' said Fry.

Doyle waited until he had his drink, and took a swig of whisky that added an extra flush to his face.

'So. Is this about the ex-copper who got killed last night?'

'What do you know about that?'

'Nothing, nothing,' he said quickly. 'It's just what everyone seems to be talking about today. So I thought … well, obviously I was wrong.'

'If you do know anything …' said Fry.

'Of course.' He took another sip of his Laphroaig. 'I'll be a helpful citizen.'

Fry didn't altogether believe him. But the news of Andy Kewley's death had undoubtedly been on the local news today, and would be in the evening papers later on. The murder of a former police officer was likely to create a few waves. It was certainly enough to take everyone's attention off her for a while, which was a good thing right now.

'So …' said Fry.

Doyle frowned at her, as if he'd forgotten the original question.

'William Leeson. That's who I asked you about.'

'Oh, yes. Will Leeson used to be my partner,' he said.

'We know that.'

'Leeson and Doyle. We were small scale, never likely to be among the big boys. But I was quite happy with that. A steady criminal practice, it kept me in whisky. There's no shortage of crime in Brum.'

'Tell me about it.'

'But Leeson wasn't happy with that. He had big ideas, got greedy. You've no idea the sort of people he got involved with. Anyone who had money, no matter what they did to earn it. He made a lot of enemies, did Will Leeson. And some worse friends.'

'He got struck off, didn't he?' said Fry.

241

'Damn right. It was only a matter of time. Trouble was, he took me down with him. Bastard.'

'Tell me some of the people he was involved with.'

'No way. I want to live.'

'I can't think why.'

Doyle snapped. 'There were some of you lot, for a start. Dirty coppers. Birmingham was full of them. Maybe still is.'

'Names?' said Fry.

He shook his head. 'Bollocks.'

Fry could see that one more drink would put Doyle beyond use.

'All right. I need to talk to William Leeson. Tell me how I can find him, and we'll leave you alone with your plastic paddies.'

Doyle looked from her to Cooper, and drew a beer mat towards him. Fry handed him a pen, and he scrawled an address and a mobile phone number in an unsteady hand.

'That's all you're getting.'

Fry read the address. 'It'll do.'

Then he peered at her again, his eyes suggesting that his brain cells might finally be working properly.

'I know who you are now,' he said. 'Listen – you're better off staying out of it. Don't chase after Will Leeson. You'll regret it.'

'Thanks for offering the legal advice, Mr Doyle. But I just dispensed with your services.'

He sighed.

'All right, it's up to you. Only – don't punish the monkey, okay?'

Cooper hesitated on the pavement when they left the pub.

'"Punish the monkey"? What did he mean?'

'I've no idea, Ben.'

But Fry thought about it as they walked back to the car. There was an expression that people used when they didn't want to deal with a minion, but only the boss. *I'll talk to the organ grinder, not the monkey.* Was that what his reference meant? *Don't punish the monkey.* Was it his way of saying that he was only a minion, doing what he was told? A bit like *Don't shoot the messenger.*

Okay, then. But if Eddie Doyle was only the monkey, who was the organ grinder?

23

'So how are you going to follow this up?' asked Cooper. 'You don't know William Leeson, and he doesn't know you.'

Fry wasn't so sure about that. She had a feeling that Leeson knew who she was, only too well. She suspected that the mention of her name might send him running. And would he recognize her if he set eyes on her?

'This is going to be a big favour, Ben,' she said. 'I'll understand if you want to bail out now. You've done more than enough.'

'Just ask,' said Cooper.

She gave him the beer mat with the mobile phone number scrawled on it. 'He definitely won't know who *you* are.'

An hour later, they were sitting in Fry's car on Lodge Street, near Winson Green Prison. Leeson had told Cooper that he would be 'at the Green'. It didn't mean much to Cooper, but this was a familiar to location to Fry.

In fact, Winson Green prison was synonymous with Brum in certain parts of society. Recently, the old Victorian institution had undergone an investment programme and was now officially known as HMP Birmingham. Its capacity had been expanded to cope with the influx of prisoners sent there by judges and magistrates on the regional circuit. There were fourteen hundred prisoners currently enjoying the benefits of a new sports hall and health-care facilities while they counted down the days to their release.

'Is there a lifer unit here, then?' asked Cooper.

'No. The highest level is Category B.'

'No convicted murderers serving their time?'

'Not here. They're shipped out of Brum.'

In fact, Fry knew that most of the Green's population were unconvicted, prisoners on remand or awaiting trial. There were some convicted Category B and C men, and a few retained Cat Ds. But since society had become so celebrity-obsessed, the only thing many Brummies knew about Winson Green was that Ozzy Osbourne had served a couple of spells there in the 1960s, and during his stay had tattooed smiley faces on his knees to cheer himself up.

She told Cooper this while they were waiting.

'Is that Sharon's husband?' he said.

'Right. I supposed I should have known you're not a Black Sabbath fan.'

Oh, and the prison had accommodated Fred West too, who'd hanged himself in his cell one New Year's Day. You could consider him a celebrity of sorts, she supposed. Serial killers were the kind of people who had books written about them, after all. She supposed she ought to call him an 'alleged' serial killer, since he never came to trial. Unlike Ozzy Osbourne, West was one of the unconvicted.

Fry could see the bright red-brick walls of the prison, and the two blue pepper-pot towers either side of the main entrance on Winson Green Road. Somewhere beyond those walls was the cell where West had sat polishing his boots, waiting for his trial and planning how to end his life. Hated by every thug in the prison, and fearing that a life sentence would actually mean life in his case. She wondered if his ghost still haunted the prison. Or did a place like the Green not even need a ghost?

It was three o'clock on a Friday – visiting time at Winson Green. Family members would already have booked in at the visitor centre and had their identities checked, their photographs taken, their personal belongings stored away in a locker. Only loose change to be carried into the prison. And God help you if that dog got a sniff of drugs about your person.

If you wanted a taste of what life in jail was like, all you had to do was find someone on the inside to visit.

On Lodge Road, a cricket ground stood in front of the psychiatric hospital, almost in the shadow of the prison wall, with a children's play area backing on to the canal. The play area was deserted now – the younger kids weren't home from school, and the older ones hadn't yet arrived to hang out for the night.

'He definitely said he would meet you?' said Fry.

'Yes, I persuaded him,' said Cooper. 'Calm down, Diane.'

He was right, of course. She was starting to get edgy, and she couldn't explain the reason for it. William Leeson has begun to take on a form in her mind, a shadowy figure that she believed she might have seen before, but only in the darkness, an indistinct outline lurking in the shadows of her memory.

'He said he'd be at the Green, visiting a client,' said Cooper. 'But he's going to meet me outside the prison when he's finished.'

'He shouldn't have clients any more,' said Fry.

'I'll ask him about that, if you like.'

Fry watched a narrow boat glide past on the canal, passing under Asylum Bridge to Winson Green Wharf. She looked back at the walls of the prison, traffic passing under the two towers.

Oh, Lord – was that the number 11 bus again? Was the thing haunting her? Of course, the number 11 was the legendary Outer Circle route, more than twenty-six miles long, taking over two hours to ride, delivering passengers undiscriminatingly to Cadbury World, Birmingham University, and Winson Green Prison. They said it was the longest route within one city anywhere in the country. The only bus route with its own website. A joke and an icon at the same time. People hated it, and loved it. But that was Brummies for you.

Fry had seen the number 11 at Perry Barr, at Aston, at Handsworth, and now at Winson Green. She remembered it from living in Bearwood, where the route diverged briefly into the Black Country. The one she was looking at now was the 11C, the clockwise service, heading for all the places she'd already been to. And there were bound to be two more behind it. Three buses always came along at once.

'It's nearly time,' said Cooper. 'What do you want to do?'

Fry opened the car door, suddenly anxious to be out of sight.

'I'll wait over there, by those trees. He won't see me, but I'll be able to hear what's going on.'

Cooper looked at her quizzically, but said nothing.

She was hardly in position before a man walked down the road from the prison, paused at the entrance to the cricket ground and walked towards the car. She'd chosen a bad spot, because she could only see his back as he approached Cooper. He was a tall man, dressed in a dark suit, carrying a file case like a real professional. Cooper spoke clearly, so that his voice reached her.

'Mr Leeson?'

'Yes.'

'Acting DS Cooper.'

'I'd say it's a pleasure, but I'm not sure whether it is, yet.'

'So who were you visiting at the prison?'

'A client. I can't say any more than that.'

'But you don't have clients any more, Mr Leeson. You're not practising, according to the Law Society.'

'I don't represent clients in court, so I'm not bound by the Law Society's rules any more. I'm an independent legal advisor.'

'Those are just words, aren't they?'

Leeson laughed. 'Words are my stock in trade, Detective Sergeant. It's what the law is all about, the interpretation of words. You know that, I'm sure.'

Listening to the conversation, Fry decided she didn't like his laugh. But perhaps she was already prejudiced against him.

'First, I'm afraid,' said Leeson, 'I'll have to ask to see your identification.'

Cooper produced his warrant card. Leeson spent a few moments looking at it. 'Derbyshire Constabulary,' he said. 'What an honour. And to what do I owe this pleasure, Acting DS Cooper?'

Fry took a step away from the tree, making sure Cooper saw her.

'I have a friend who's anxious to talk to you,' he said.

Leeson turned, and saw Fry walking across the ground towards him. Their eyes met for the first time. And Fry was disappointed.

Though he was probably no more than sixty, William Leeson was gaunt and pale. The jacket of his dark grey suit hung from his shoulders without making any other contact with his torso. His height and gaunt cheeks made Fry think of an undertaker, but the impression was spoiled by a mane of fair, wavy hair, thinning at the front but left to grow too long at the back. His bony fingers moved restlessly against the file case, as if reading a Braille inscription on the black leather.

And Leeson knew her. She could see it in his eyes, that moment of shock and recognition. And, best of all, she saw his expression turn to fear.

'I'm sorry, but I'm not stopping for this,' he said.

He turned quickly away, and almost broke into a trot, stumbling on the grass verge as he took the most direct route away from her. When he reached the road, he pulled out a phone and pressed it to his ear, gesturing with his free hand.

Fry stood next to Cooper, and they watched Leeson striding back towards the prison, without a single glance over his shoulder.

'So,' said Cooper. 'That went well.'

Fry drove back into the city in response to a call from her sister. A short diversion took them through the Jewellery Quarter, where she glimpsed the crime-scene tape and the police vehicles still closing off the streets around Warstone Lane cemetery.

'What was your friend's name again?' asked Cooper. 'Kewley?'

'Yes,' said Fry.

It was on the tip of her tongue to deny that Andy Kewley had been her friend. That wasn't the way she had ever thought of him. A colleague, once. An ex-colleague. But a friend? No.

She held her tongue, though. She sensed it would be the wrong thing to say to Cooper just now.

'Who do you think killed him?' he asked. 'Any theories?'

'No idea, Ben. I have a feeling he was mixed up with a lot of people, and probably knew too much. Andy always liked to know things. When he was in the job, he hoarded intelligence like a miser. I suppose it made him feel important.'

'And out of the job?'

'He still wanted to feel important. Andy was dropping all kinds of hints to me the day before he was killed. I'm willing to bet he did that with other people too.'

'So if he knew something about the wrong person, or they thought he did ...?'

'They wouldn't trust him not to share it around. I wouldn't trust Andy Kewley myself, come to that.'

'Really?' said Cooper. 'But he was your partner.'

'Ye-es.'

Cooper was silent for a moment as she negotiated the traffic to get on to the inner ring road.

'Diane,' he said finally. 'Do you trust me?'

For a second, Fry opened her mouth to laugh. Then she stopped herself. She was surprised by the knowledge that her own instinctive reaction was wrong.

'As a matter of fact, Ben,' she said. 'I do.'

Satisfied, he stayed quiet as Fry managed to find her way across Digbeth via a few back streets behind the wholesale markets, past warehouses that mostly seemed to be occupied by Chinese bean sprout suppliers.

At the end of Lower Essex Street, workmen were still dismantling the main stage after the Birmingham Pride parade. Cleaners were sweeping up small mountains of brightly coloured streamers and balloons.

Fry had helped police Birmingham Pride once. The parade had set off from Victoria Square on a Saturday afternoon, following an official civic send-off in front of the art gallery. The procession had headed down New Street towards the main shopping area, but had diverged on to Temple Street and returned to the square via Colmore Row, passing the cathedral along the way. When the parade had dispersed, most of the participants made their way half a mile south to continue the celebrations. Many simply walked down Hill Street and crossed Queensway in a sort of ragged, bizarrely dressed crocodile.

And this was the area they had all been heading to – Birmingham's gay village. Hurst Street and the roads around it, full of bars and clubs, sex shops, the Hippodrome and the National Trust. The council had widened the pavements here to let the bars put tables outside, and they'd planted trees and shrubs, aiming for a more cosmopolitan feel. Barcelona was said to be the model they were aiming for. If only there was a bit of sun.

The bar they wanted was next door to an ex-catalogue furniture warehouse. Inside, a drag act by the name of Lola Lasagne was performing a medley of James Bond theme songs. 'Diamonds Are Forever', 'The Spy Who Loved Me'. Posters advertised next week's coming attractions. Lady Imelda, Topping and Butch, Miss Thunder Pussy. *This is a gay venue* said the signs just inside the door.

Cooper stopped suddenly.

'Diane –'

'What?'

'Oh, nothing.'

Fry laughed. 'We could just wait for her to come out, if you like.'

A few minutes later, Angie opened the car door and slipped in.

'Well?' asked Diane.

'Vince is going to get one of them to a meeting tonight.'

'How did you persuade him to do that?'

Angie smiled. 'I threatened him.'

'What with?'

'Now, Sis, you're better off not knowing that.'

'Was he surprised to see you?'

'You might say that. He looked as though he'd seen a ghost. You didn't tell him I was dead, did you?'

'I don't think so.'

'Anyway, he's set up Darren Barnes for us. The one they call Doors.'

'Good.'

'We ought to be careful, Di. According to Vince, this bloke has been a hardened criminal since birth.'

Fry's eyebrows rose. 'Since birth? Oh, really?'

'Well …' Angie shrugged. 'Maybe he stabbed his midwife with the forceps. I don't know.'

'Okay, so this isn't some casual tea-leaf. What difference does it make?'

'He'll have the contacts, that's the difference. You don't spend a lifetime in crime without bumping into a few serious players along the way. He's had several spells inside, for a start. He'll know pretty much anyone who's anyone in the Winson Green old boys club.'

'Including Ozzy Osbourne, then?'

'What?'

'Never mind.'

'Sharon's husband,' said Cooper.

'I said never mind.'

'What is this, anyway?' asked Cooper. 'Who's Vince?'

'My foster brother, Vincent Bowskill. He has contacts in some of these street gangs.'

Cooper looked concerned. 'What are you getting into, Diane? This sounds very dangerous.'

'Gangs control everything that goes on in some of these areas, Ben.'

'Yes, I know that. I've heard of some of them. The Johnson Crew, the Burger Bar Boys ... they shoot people on the streets. Innocent bystanders, sometimes.'

'Congratulations, you've read the *Daily Mail*.'

They left Angie heading for the gay village Tesco Express on the corner of Hurst Street. An emergency point was located at the bottom of Kent Street, a CCTV camera pointing up the road, ready for trouble. But not even Angie could get into much trouble in Tesco's.

'I'd better get back to Derbyshire,' said Cooper. 'I have lots of things to do tomorrow.'

'Fine. I'll take you back to your car. And thanks for coming, I guess.'

'No problem. You're pretty much finished here, aren't you?'

'Do you think so?' said Fry, tempted to cross her fingers behind her back. He really didn't need to know what she was going to do next.

Earlier she'd told Cooper that she trusted him. And that was true, wasn't it? The knowledge made her feel guilty that she wasn't telling him everything. One day soon, she would have to sit down with him and tell him the whole story. He was, after all, the only person she could do that with. It had taken her a long time to come to the realization. And now was the wrong time for it.

'I mean, you're not going to do anything?' said Cooper.

'I'll probably just say goodbye to a few people,' she said.

Cooper frowned. 'Well, okay. I'll see you back in Edendale, then.'

'Probably.'

Cooper turned to look at her, halfway to his car. He shook his head, as if brushing off an annoying fly, and climbed into his Toyota to drive back to Derbyshire.

Cooper steered his car towards the Aston Expressway and the M6. His last sight of Birmingham was the concrete pillars supporting the tangle of slip roads at Spaghetti Junction.

Diane Fry might think the violent gang culture of the city was something alien to him that he would never understand. But gang warfare had come to Derbyshire. Less than two years ago, the first killing had happened in the city of Derby, when a fifteen-year-old boy died in a drive-by shooting, blasted twice in the chest at close range as he walked into a park with friends. The first fatality in a dispute between the Browning Circle Terrorists and the A1 Crew.

Cooper shook his head. If that sort of thing happened in Edendale, if the world ever changed so much, he would have to think about leaving, finding somewhere else to live. Scotland, maybe. The Faroe Islands. St Kilda. He had no idea where.

But, right now, the Peak District felt like a sanctuary. Well, at least a place where people killed each other for a reason.

Speaking of which – he would have to face Liz when he got back to Derbyshire. He had no idea what she was going to say to him about this trip. But he felt sure she'd been working on it all day.

Driving northwards out of Birmingham, Cooper saw hills in the distance, touched by the colour of a slowly setting sun. He wanted to just sit and watch the hills for a while, like a man who'd been given a glimpse of paradise. It already seemed years since he'd seen real hills.

But he was heading towards them now. So he put his foot down, and kept going.

24

Diane Fry tapped the steering wheel of her car as she watched the dusk fall in Digbeth. It had turned into another warm evening. Humid as only a city could be. A stale smell bubbled off the pavements, and the factory walls oozed a sour, grey fluid, as if the city's industrial lifeblood was being sweated right out of the brick.

One thought kept going through her mind. Was this really what she wanted to get herself into? Things were starting to get very complicated now. Soon events would reach a point where there was no going back, and she was afraid she might not recognize the time when it came.

She glanced at her sister's expressionless profile. In fact, they might have reached that point already.

Diane realized she'd lost count of how many rules she'd broken. It no longer mattered, though. She was a civilian, after all. Not a part of the enquiry team, just the IP, the victim betrayed by the system, the one person whose actions couldn't be predicted or controlled. The strange thing was, breaking all the rules had made her feel more alive than at any time she could remember in her life.

Angie was looking at her now, with that faint, sly smile on her face.

'This is really cool, isn't it?'

Diane tried not to show what she was thinking, even to her sister. She always had that lurking fear that her feelings might be used against her.

Best change the subject. This long half-hour sitting in her car might be the only chance they had to talk.

'Sis,' she said. 'There's one thing I've always wanted to ask you.'

'Yes?'

'After you left home, all those years ago, did you … go to somebody?'

'What, to a bloke? No.'

'I thought there must have been someone you fell for.'

'I've been with men here and there, over the years,' said Angie.

'No one you fancied particularly?'

'Get real, Sis. You don't go with a bloke because you fancy him. You go with him because he's there, because there's nothing better on offer. Or because you want to get your own back on his girlfriend.'

'So you were alone all that time, then?'

Angie shrugged. 'I've always been on my own, one way or another.'

'But –'

Diane stopped. She didn't really want to hear the answer to her next question. Why would she want to have her suspicions confirmed, to reinforce that nagging feeling that the relationship between them had never been an equal one? As a teenager, she had worshipped her older sister, been devastated when Angie ran away from their foster home and never came back.

But she must have known, if only at the back of her mind, that Angie didn't care as much about her in return. She would never have left in the first place, would she? She would never have stayed out of touch for so long. She would definitely have found some way to let her little sister know where she was all those years. But she hadn't done that. There had been nothing, only that silence, the pain of not knowing.

Diane knew that if she hadn't figured this out for herself by now, she would have to be stupid. But figuring it out and accepting it were two different things. It was easy to sink yourself into a delusion, and ignore the evidence to the contrary.

So whatever Angie's reasons now for being around, they surely weren't because she cared about her sister's welfare. Angie didn't think of them as a partnership, as two people working together. She had always been on her own, she said. And she was on her own now.

Which meant that Diane was on her own, too. No one could ever share what went on inside her head, the dark world she really lived in, re-imagined from those fragmentary memories of her past.

'The car is black, that's good,' said Angie. 'Not too flashy. No one will take any notice of us.'

'Two women sitting in car at night? We might attract the wrong kind of attention.'

'Well, okay. Try not to look too attractive, then.'

'At least I actually have to try.'

Angie smiled. 'Cow.'

Diane nodded. That was better. That was the way it always used to be. Sisters together.

'And, Sis ...' she said.

'What?'

'No heroics. They never work. All you do is leave somebody else with a mess to clean up.'

'I wasn't planning on any heroics,' said Angie.

'That's your trouble. You don't plan things, you just do them.'

'A lot you know about me, then.'

'I know you're a junkie bitch.'

'Sod you, filth.'

Diane felt her resolve harden. Her sister always knew which buttons to press.

That night, some kind of event was taking place at the Custard Factory – an exhibition opening at the Vaad Gallery, or a performance poetry night. The parking area on Heath Mill Lane was full, the wall of crushed cars surrounding and mocking the smart town cars and four-wheel drives. Tonight, the message was clear: *You might be someone's pride and joy now, but this is the way you'll all end up, every one of you. Get used to it.*

Diane still wasn't sure what she hoped to achieve. She didn't expect to get any answers tonight. There was too much fog obscuring the truth – a fog of her own making, she supposed. But all the more impenetrable for that. Still, there were times when you had to do things without any hope of a measurable outcome. Action was a release, a way of finding out more about yourself, if not about the rest of the world.

Earlier, she'd picked up a copy of the *Birmingham Evening Mail*, and found the story she'd been expecting on the front page. She read through a series of tributes to former Detective Constable Andrew Kewley from his colleagues, including one from the Chief Constable, who had never even met him. Kewley had become a hero, now that he was dead.

255

The details she was looking for were sparse. Police were appealing for witnesses. They were also looking for the rider of a motorcycle seen leaving the scene at the time of the murder. She had given them that lead herself. But what she hadn't done was tell the Major Incident Unit everything she and Andy had talked about the previous day. She felt sure there were individuals in West Midlands Police who knew more about Kewley's connections than she did, anyway.

'S-Man and Doors,' said Angie. 'What do they call this gang again? The one Marcus Shepherd and Darren Barnes are in?'

'The M1 Crew.'

'M1? As in the motorway?'

'I expect so.'

'Unless it's after the rapper.'

'Rapper?' said Diane. 'You've lost me.'

'I guess you're not up on hip-hop music. Never heard of Dead Prez?'

'You got that right.'

'Dead Prez are a political hip-hop duo. M-1 and Stic Man.'

'Well, I suppose that could be it,' said Diane. 'Or the M1 carbine. But that's an antique weapon, World War Two vintage. Not the sort of thing our Birmingham gangsters are likely to use, when they have access to MAC-10 machine pistols.'

'No. It would be far too uncool.'

The Connemara was spilling out customers into the night. There were lights at the end of Heath Mill Lane, but they only made the railway viaduct looked blacker, the shadows of the factories darker. A stretch of fence by the waste ground glittered like a pattern of slug trails. The river ran under the road here, but you would never know it existed.

'So, would you be able to get hold of a gun, if you needed to?' asked Diane.

'What? Can't you?'

'Well, not officially.'

'You mean an illegal firearm, then?' said Angie. 'Is that it, Di? And you think I might have the contacts, I suppose.'

'I hear it's not too difficult, if you know the right people.'

Angie gazed out of the window. 'No, it isn't. Everyone knows you can get hold of a gun in a couple of hours. It's a piece of cake.'

Diane felt she ought to be reading something into the tone of her sister's response.

'What's wrong?'

'Nothing,' said Angie. 'I've just realized that you're finally starting to know me a bit better.'

A man walked past their car, stopped, and looked back. He hesitated for a moment, then hurried on, his neck hunched into his collar, as if to avoid the evil eye.

'So, did you actually want a gun?' asked Angie.

'No.'

'I'm glad to hear it.'

'Illegal firearms are too easy to trace now,' said Diane. 'There's a NABIS hub right here in Birmingham.'

Angie laughed uneasily. But a few moments later, she seemed, to pick up on the train of thought.

'Diane, it's supposed to be just Darren Barnes, but you know …'

'His mates might not be far away, of course. The first rule is not to trust anyone. He'll know that.'

'If this goes wrong, we're dead.'

'No,' said Diane. 'You're not dead until three minutes after you stop breathing.'

'That's good to know. Oh, and by the way, it's getting near time.'

'Okay.'

Diane twisted in her seat and strapped on the scabbard for her extendable baton. Police officers called the baton an ASP, after the name of the American manufacturer. It consisted of six inches of heavy-duty steel, extending to sixteen inches when fully racked. It was supposed to have an unparalleled deterrent effect.

Most CID officers simply carried the weapon in their pocket, but on Diane's slender build the bulge of the closed ASP was noticeable. So she'd bought herself a back pocket scabbard with a Velcro flap which stopped the baton falling out when she ran. When she put on her jacket, the outline was barely visible.

She'd brought the baton with her from Derbyshire. But the one thing she didn't have with her was a stab vest. She realized she was thinking like a police officer again now, performing a mental risk assessment before an operation. It felt wrong to be putting her sister in jeopardy, just as she would worry about sending one of her team into a dangerous situation without proper back-up and the right equipment. Once you learned those ways of thinking, they were difficult to get out of. Habits were so hard to break.

She had no personal radio tonight either. But a mobile phone turned to vibrate was almost as good. She looked at her sister. Whether she could rely on her back-up, she wasn't so certain. She ought to accept that she was alone from the word 'go'.

'I'm not sure we're doing the right thing,' said Angie. 'But I'm trying to think of it as restorative justice.'

Angie looked at her sister, surprised by her silence, and blinked at her expression.

'Diane, say something. You're scaring me again.'

Trouble was waiting for Ben Cooper when he arrived home in Edendale. Liz was in his flat in Welbeck Street. Had she used the front door key he'd given her, or had Mrs Shelley let her in? He didn't get a chance to ask.

Liz stood up when he came in. Her body was tense, her eyes challenging. She had come ready for an argument.

'So. What's going on, Ben?'

'Not even a hello?' said Cooper.

'Answer me.'

He wanted to move towards her and put his arms around her. It was what he would normally have done. If he could do it now, everything would be all right. But her attitude held him back. It was as if she'd erected some kind of force field between them that pushed him away.

'I've been to Birmingham,' he said. 'I told you.'

'No you didn't.'

'Yes, I –'

'No. You haven't told me the truth. I know you too well, Ben. I can tell when you're keeping something from me. I'm just wondering now how long this has been going on.'

Her face was a mask, her lips set in a hard line. Cooper could feel the chill in the air. He looked around for the cat, but it was hiding somewhere. Sensible animal.

'How long what's been going on?'

'You tell me. That's what I'm here for.'

Cooper tried to think of a way of getting Liz to relax, to persuade her to sit down at least. There had to be a means of defusing the situation somehow. Otherwise the conversation would follow a predictable script, accusation following denial, suspicion becoming anger, until it had degenerated into an exchange of insults.

'Look, Liz, let me get you a coffee. A drink, maybe? And then we can talk about things calmly.'

'I *am* calm.'

'No, you're not.'

Her voice was beginning to rise. Cooper winced as a shrill edge entered her tone. He paced the room nervously, hoping against hope that she wasn't going to throw the one accusation at him that would take the situation beyond recovery.

'I want to know about you and Diane Fry,' she said. 'I know there's something going on. Ben, I want to know whether it's the end of the road for you and me.'

And then Cooper knew there was nothing he could say that would avoid a blazing row.

On a back street in Digbeth, Angie Fry sat up suddenly, adjusting the car's rear-view mirror to look over her shoulder.

'He's here,' she said.

'Are you sure it's him?' asked Diane.

'Well, he doesn't look as though he's going to the poetry reading.'

'How many?'

'Just him.'

'Darren Barnes?'

259

'If Vince has done his job right.'

'Well, he's not exactly Mister Reliable.'

Diane remembered the description in Louise Jones' witness statement. *The first male was white, skinny build, I would say probably approx five feet eight inches tall. He was wearing a dark sweatshirt and jeans.* She recalled that the other man, Marcus Shepherd, had been much bigger, a six footer, and more powerfully built. She hoped Vince had made the right choice.

Barnes had parked down the street, beyond the pub and the car park. His vehicle looked like some kind of convertible.

'Can you make out the registration?' said Diane.

'No.' Angie put her hand on the door. 'Do you want me to …?'

'No. Stay where you are.'

'Why?'

'Remember what I told you – no heroics.'

'I was only going to get a sodding number plate.'

'Well, wait.'

Maybe it had been a mistake to let her sister come with her tonight. 'Loose cannon' was an expression which fit her perfectly. If there was going to be trouble, Angie would cause it.

Diane watched the man cross the road, stare through the fence, and stop at the bridge to light a cigarette.

'Okay.'

She got out of the car and began to walk towards the bridge. It wasn't the walk she'd imagined making when she came to Birmingham. She'd pictured herself taking that long walk down the corridor from the witness room to take the stand in a crown court trial. Only a few yards, but a million lonely miles when you were going to face your own demons.

Barnes took no notice of her, even when she came right up to him. She stood carefully a couple of steps away, the best position for defence.

'Darren Barnes?' she said.

'Maybe.'

'Or should I call you Doors?'

'And who the hell are you?'

'You don't recognize me? Well, no – you wouldn't. I was never a person to you, was I?'

He looked at her then. 'You know what? I have no idea what the fuck you're talking about.'

'Let me explain.'

'No, no explanations. I heard there was something in this for me, right? Or am I being fed some crap?'

'I want information from you.'

Barnes smiled. His eyes were half closed as he peered at her through his cigarette smoke. He smelled of some expensive deodorant or hair gel.

'Oh, information is it? I don't know who you are, but you've come to the wrong guy with your bullshit. The last bloke who messed with us ended up in that canal. They needed three bin bags for the bits. You get me?'

'It's a river,' said Fry.

'What?'

'It's not a canal, it's a river.'

'Like I care. This is some kind of joke, right?'

Fry could read the contempt in his face. He took the cigarette out of his mouth, and blew the smoke towards her. Then he spat towards her foot.

'I'm going to ask you some questions,' she said.

'You,' he said, 'ain't going to do shit.'

Before Fry could react, Angie's voice came in her ear.

'Diane, we've got more company.'

'Damn. Don't leave the car.'

Quickly, Diane turned, and Barnes laughed.

'Hey, where you going? I was just getting to like you, kind of.'

She ignored him, moving back across the waste ground to the wall. Though she'd brought a torch, the narrow pool of light it cast only seemed to emphasize the blackness outside its reach, to make her isolation total and threatening. From beneath the railway arches, the shadows had begun to sidle towards her, bringing back the memories. They were memories that were too vivid to be erased, too deeply etched into her soul to be forgotten. They merely wallowed and writhed in the depths, waiting for the chance to re-emerge.

Standing back in the darkness, watching, laughing. Voices murmured and coughed. 'It's a copper,' the voices said. 'She's a copper.'

She'd always known those old memories were still powerful, and ready to rise up from the darkness. Desperately, she tried to count the number of dark forms that loomed around her, some of them mere smudges of silhouettes.

The memories churned and bubbled. Brief, fragmented glimpses of figures carved into severed segments by the streetlights, the sickly reek of booze and violence. And then that rough, slurring Brummie voice that slithered out of the darkness. 'How do you like this, copper?' The same taunting laughter moving in the shadows, the same dark, menacing shapes all around. Hands grabbing her, pinching and pulling. Her arms trapped by fingers that gripped her tightly, painful and shocking in their violence.

Then she saw that Angie had left the car and was surrounded, dark shapes on all sides of her. Diane began to run across the waste ground, feeling the energy pouring into her limbs, drawing in the deep breaths that expanded her lungs and quickened her muscles. The group turned towards her, astonished at her charge.

'Who's that?'

'It's another woman.'

She could smell them in the darkness, see their shapes moving towards her as her brain began to flood with the memories. It was the same old film that had run through her mind constantly, no sooner reaching its climactic end than it would start all over again. A great rage came over her, swamping her resistance, and she badly needed something to hit out at.

Automatically, her hands closed into fists, the first two knuckles protruding, with her thumbs locked over her fingers. Concentrate. Pour the adrenalin into the muscles. Get ready to strike.

The men were grinning. They weren't taking her seriously, even though she was now within reach. One of them turned to reach out towards Angie, and Diane reacted. She hit him in the kidneys, swept his legs from under him and split his nose with the edge of her hand.

With a startled shout, a second man came at her from the left. But he had hesitated too long, and she diverted his fist with a forearm block. She swivelled, cracked his kneecap with a side kick.

Then an arm closed round her throat as she was grabbed from behind. The third man was strong and much heavier than she was. The impact of his body forced her up against the factory wall, trapping her arms and banging her forehead on the bricks. Her face to the wall, she clutched at the sweating brickwork, felt her fingers slither on the greasy surface.

When she was firmly pinned, her attacker shifted his grip. The possibility she was most afraid of was a knife. A miasma of beer fumes filled her nose, and his breath pressed hot on the back of her neck. The feel of his body pushed up against hers and the smell of his sweat-soaked hands brought back all the remembered terrors.

Now panic drove her. She took a deep breath through her nose before folding suddenly forward at the waist, kicking backwards into his groin with her heel and driving her elbow hard into his solar plexus. He grunted in pain, and his grip loosened. She spun round, using a full rising block to break his grip completely.

She found herself facing Darren Barnes again. Diane drew her ASP, and opened it with a flick of the wrist.

'Do you know who I am now?'

'You're the copper.'

'Who was the third person that night?'

'You know who it was, though. Right?'

'No.'

'You're a cop. The cops know.'

'Tell me anyway.'

He gasped, struggling to get his breath as he stared at her, sweat running down his face. He was far too unfit for this. He relied too much on the presence of his friends to protect him.

'Well, I couldn't give a shit,' he said. 'It was the lawyer guy.'

'William Leeson?'

'Yeah, yeah, him. Leeson. We had a meeting set up with him, at the pub.'

'In the Connemara.'

'Right. He was working on something big for us. He was our guy, you know.'

'That's what you think.'

He shook his head, as if she was talking a different language that he didn't even want to understand.

'When we came out of the pub he was right behind us. The guy was hammered. He'd been on the lash with his partner.'

'Doyle.'

'Whatever. Then he came to us for his Charlie. He's a complete coke head, you know?'

'No, I didn't know that. So he was with you when you came out?'

'Like I said, he was right behind us. That guy was completely off his tits. He was pissing himself laughing.'

'Laughing?'

'Oh, yeah. I reckon some of the boys were playing it up, just for him.'

Diane recalled figures back in the darkness, watching, laughing. The reek of booze and violence. But there was no memory of Leeson.

'It was weird, you know?' said Barnes. 'It was like, if he hadn't been there, it might not have happened.'

'Oh, so it wasn't your fault? You didn't know what you were doing?'

'All I'm saying is, you ought to go after him. Otherwise, a bloke like that will never get what's coming to him.'

Angie called to her, and Diane turned. While her attention was distracted, Barnes made a grab for her. That was a mistake. She took hold of his arm, straightened it out, and whipped him off his feet so he sprawled across the parapet of the bridge.

'Keep struggling,' she said. 'It would give me quite a lot of pleasure to break your arm. I'll make you beg in front of your mates. I'll let them see you crawl to a woman.'

'Fuck you.'

Then she let him go. She heard a crunch, the crash of a body falling through the broken fence, and a loud splash as something hit the water. The River Rea had swept up more of the city's debris.

Her sister stood a few yards away, watching her. When Diane saw the expression on her face, she dropped her ASP in the dirt in despair.

'Angie,' she said, 'I can't do this any more.'

25

Saturday

This morning, Cooper was taking a trip into the past of the Nield family.

Last night had been exhausting. He'd come home from Birmingham already tired, and the bust-up with Liz had ended badly, with tears and the slamming of his front door. It had been inevitable from the moment he walked into his flat.

Soon, he would have to do something about his relationship with Liz. He felt like a coward to be avoiding the issue right now. But a day or two might make a difference. Things would be calmer, at least. Meanwhile, there was work to do.

To reach Wetton, Cooper had to drive past the turning to Dovedale and through the estate village of Ilam, with its Alpine-style cottages and the sound of sheep where other villages had traffic. Coaches from Norfolk and Birmingham were parked up at the Dovedale entrance. A farmer on a quad bike moved his flock up the road.

For more than twenty-four hours now, he'd been haunted by the content of Alex Nield's profile on *War Tribe*, his secret little messages that could be intended for no one except himself. In his online world, well away from the eyes of his parents, the boy seemed to be revealing his obsessions, the inner turmoils that were troubling his teenage life.

u were born wrong n u must die!!!!!

What had put that idea into his head? It was more than just an idle threat, it sounded like something he'd heard, or words that had been said to him personally. Who must die? Who had been born wrong?

And there was the final bit of code:

LOST
LOST
LOST
LOST RIVER

It could be a reference to the River Dove, to the events in Dovedale last Monday.

Cooper had no way of knowing when Alex might have updated his profile. But his instinct told him there was something much deeper here, and much older. It dated to the Nields' time in Wetton, the village whose name Alex Nield couldn't even bear to hear spoken.

Despite its Ashbourne postal address, Wetton was actually in Staffordshire. Strictly speaking, that meant it was out of Cooper's jurisdiction. But, of course, the people involved in this case were very much his.

This was a typical limestone village, an old farming community with pretty cottages, converted barns, and a scattering of B&Bs. A few holiday lets were owned by the Chatsworth Estate, the Duke of Devonshire's tentacles reaching even here. In the centre of the village stood a pub, Ye Olde Royal Oak, famous for originating the annual Toe Wrestling Championship. Another quirky English sport, like the Ashbourne football game on the smallest of scales.

Like the streets in Ashbourne, most of the cottages seemed to be named after plants. Vine, Laburnum, Sycamore, Rose. It was funny how little things gave away the fact you were in a different area. Here, it was the brown wheelie bins of Staffordshire Moorlands, replacing the green of Derbyshire Dales.

The Nields had lived on a quiet lane at the Leek Road end of the village. The house wasn't far from the village hall, which looked as though it had once been the village school. Probably another casualty of falling numbers, families forced out of the villages by rising house prices.

Stable House was solid and stone-built, with a double frontage and big sash windows. It had that wonderful Georgian symmetry that gave even the most humble home a bit of character. The slopes of Wetton Hill rose behind it. Given a choice between this and the executive home in Ashbourne the Nields occupied now, Cooper knew which he would go for.

The Ashbourne to Alstonefield bus passed through Wetton, the Glovers 443 route. But the morning and afternoon runs for Queen

Elizabeth's School didn't travel as far as Wetton. They stopped at Ilam Cross.

For a child like Alex Nield that would mean a walk home of … what? Nearly four miles, he guessed. Up Ilam Moor Lane, through the hamlet of Stanshope, and across the Wall Ditch before you'd even come in sight of Wetton. Not very likely. Country kids might have done that at one time, but not in this day and age, with too much traffic on those narrow roads and the dangerous temptation to accept a lift from the wrong person. No, there would have to be someone to pick a child up from Ilam Cross. A car waiting at the roadside near the bridge.

But the lack of a school bus was because Wetton lay in Staffordshire, of course – and therefore outside the Queen Elizabeth's catchment area. This might have been the Nields' reason for moving into Ashbourne, to qualify Alex for attendance at a better school. Parents moved house for those reasons all the time. Well, maybe.

There was no point in talking to the people who lived at Stable House now. Chances were, they had never known the Nields, except as names on a conveyance. The neighbours were the folk he needed to speak to.

Next door, separated by a garden, was a house called Oak Tree Cottage. This had been part of a farm, too. There were still derelict outbuildings behind the house, windowless, with grass growing from the gutters. Cooper sniffed. Someone nearby had a wood-burning stove. The smell was so distinctive, and so evocative.

Cooper walked up the path to Oak Tree Cottage. He took no notice of the mock Georgian front door. In these parts, front doors were just for show. The truth was always round the back.

The woman who answered the door introduced herself as Mrs Challinor. She'd lived in Wetton all her life, and her parents before her. She'd married a local man, too. Generations of her ancestors probably lay in the churchyard over there. And she remembered the Nields very well. Of course she did. It was only two years since they left.

'They live in the town now, don't they?'

'Yes, that's right,' said Cooper.

'Is this to do with the little girl's accident?'

'In a way, yes.'

'They must be devastated.'

'It's been very upsetting for them.'

'I never talked to the parents all that much. He was out all day, and sometimes in the evening as well. She was a bit quiet, too. But then, she had the children.'

'Alex and Emily. And the older girl …'

'Lauren,' said Mr Challinor. 'That was her name.'

'Yes, Lauren.'

'A bit wild, she was. But that's teenagers for you, isn't it?'

Cooper was in her kitchen, feeling too warm in front of the wood-burning Esse.

'What exactly do you mean by "wild"?' he asked.

'Oh, I couldn't say really. But I know they had some problems with her. I could hear the arguments from here sometimes.'

'Lauren arguing with her parents?'

Mrs Challinor frowned. 'More the parents shouting at each other. It disrupted the family altogether, I think.'

'But Lauren left eventually, didn't she?'

'Yes. I believe she walked out and never came back. Very sad.'

'What about the boy? Alex?'

'He always seemed a perfectly normal little boy. Friendly, inquisitive, lively.'

'Really?'

'Well, until the older girl left. He seemed to change then. I suppose he was very close to her. Family bust-ups can have a bad effect on small children, can't they? Very, very sad.'

'So did you see much of the children when they were here?'

'Well, they were all at school, of course.'

'What about during the summer holidays?'

'Oh, they used to spend all their free time by the river.'

'The river?'

'Down at Wetton Mill.'

Cooper tried to picture a map of the local landscape in his head. The courses of rivers were unpredictable in this area, but he was pretty sure he'd come about three miles west of Dovedale to reach Wetton, crossing the plateau over Ilam Moor.

'Wetton Mill? That wouldn't be the Dove, would it?'

269

'No, it's the River Manifold. It runs past Wetton Mill, and joins the Dove at Ilam.'

'Yes, thank you.'

As he left, Mrs Challinor came to the gate with him.

'Can I ask you something?' she said.

'Yes?'

'Why don't you leave them alone?'

Cooper shook his head. 'It's too late for that.'

But sometimes things *were* best left alone. Like the 'do not disturb' sign Fry had hung outside her hotel room. Don't ask too many questions, don't dig up the memories. Let the past rest in peace. Should he do that?

As he walked back into the centre of the village, Cooper considered what his next move should be. He could do what DI Hitchens had told him to, and leave the whole thing alone. It would be the best thing for his own career. But it wouldn't help him to resolve the craving inside him for answers, the need for an explanation that had lodged in his brain from the moment he held Emily Nield's body in his arms.

Alex Nield needed to do that, too. He couldn't go on escaping into his fantasy online world for ever. One day, he would have to face reality. And, if he wasn't prepared for it, reality could destroy him.

Cooper wished he'd found out more from Lauren. He ought to have kept her back and stopped her disappearing from the churchyard in Ashbourne so quickly. He badly wanted to ask her whether she was the person who'd left the unnamed floral tribute. He felt sure that she was, but craved confirmation.

And there was another question he longed to put to her. What had happened on the thirtieth of June, that she would remember it for ever?

But it had been the wrong place and the wrong time. And now he might never track Lauren down again. He could only hope that she'd be drawn out of the woodwork again by something she'd heard.

His phone buzzed, and a number came up he didn't immediately recognize. He answered it anyway.

'Oh, Carol. Hi. Thanks for getting back to me again. Have you got some more?'

He listened to Parry for a few moments, a frown forming on his face.

'Really? That doesn't seem to make any sense. Are you sure? Well, okay. Thanks.'

Cooper ended the call thoughtfully, making a mental note to contact Fry with this piece of news soon. At least he would seem to be helping. But not just now. He had a feeling she wasn't going to like it one bit.

In Wetton, the clock of St Margaret's church was discreetly chiming the half-hour. A dog barked, and children laughed in the play area.

At the top of Church Brow was a working farm, judging by the rumble of tractor engines and the smell of slurry. But their barns had been converted to holiday cottages.

Beyond the farm, he saw a walkers' trail headed over the hill towards Ecton and the remains of its copper mines, which had once supplied half the world's demand. Ecton Hill was almost unique in this area. Well, a copper mine in the middle of lead-mining country? To those old miners, it must have seemed like a miracle, a red fountain in the midst of a grey landscape. Even now, its existence was an anomaly.

Ecton's copper mines had been a real money spinner, too. But of course, the land owner had made all the profit. In this case, it had been the Duke of Devonshire, a man who was literally the owner of all he surveyed. The proceeds from the mines in the eighteen century were enough to enable the fifth Duke to build the Georgian crescent at Buxton.

If he moved to Wetton himself, Cooper supposed he would choose to live in the Old Police House near Ewe Dale Lane, where a blue lamp still hung over the door and a set of stocks stood in the garden, decorated with shackles. Those were the days.

Seeing it reminded Cooper of the previous night, when he got home to Edendale. In his flat, it had occurred to him to log on to his *War Tribe* account, to see if he'd been accepted into a tribe. But he'd been punished for being such a noob. SmokeLord had already slaughtered his soldiers, knocked down his wall, and conquered his

271

city. It was now part of Alex Nield's growing empire. He'd renamed it Powder Hut. That was probably some obscure insult.

The drive from the village down to Wetton Mill was quite a white-knuckle ride. Cooper found a narrow single-track road all the way, through dense banks of cow parsley and meadow buttercup, camouflaging the dry-stone walls on either side. The road was barely wide enough for the Toyota to pass without swiping lumps off the vegetation. On this kind of road, it was best to keep an eye out for passing places. And pray that you didn't meet a car coming the other way.

At the bottom of Leek Road, he drove over the bridge at Redhurst Crossing and through the open pastures below Ossoms Hill to the Manifold Trail. It was incredible to think that this narrow pathway alongside the Manifold had been a rail line once. It was a re-surfaced section of the old Leek and Manifold Light Railway, which had carried milk churns from Ecton Diary and passengers to the tourist attractions along the route. High on a limestone crag, he glimpsed one of those attractions – the dark mouth of Thor's Cave.

Cooper pulled the car over at the first bridge and parked it off the road. He would have to walk from here to see the river properly.

As soon as he got out of his car, he felt the hairs on the back of his neck go up. Something was wrong, but he couldn't put his finger on it. The scene was very quiet and peaceful. The only sounds were the chattering alarm call of a blackbird that he'd disturbed from the bushes, and the whirr of a pheasant on the hillside above.

He looked around, wondering if he was sensing the presence of someone else nearby. But there was no one around, not a soul. Not a car, nor even a bicycle. No one walking the Manifold Trail – not within sight or earshot, anyway. So why did he feel so uneasy?

Walking towards the first bridge, he couldn't shake the feeling off. His own footsteps on the trail sounded wrong. It was as if the whole of the valley was holding its breath, waiting for him to do

272

something, to speak, shout, make some kind of noise to break the spell.

Then he came round the bend and looked over the parapet of the bridge, and saw the reason for it. The absence of noise should have warned him earlier. It wasn't exactly a silence, but a sound that had been missing from the background for the past few minutes. And now it was absent from the foreground too. Without the sound of rushing water, the call of the blackbird sounded more piercing, the whirr of the pheasant so much louder. It was unnatural.

In Wetton, Mrs Challinor had talked about the River Manifold running through here. But Cooper could see there was a problem. He was looking at an empty river bed. It was bone dry, littered with desiccated branches and dried-out boulders. Its stones were as dry as if they'd never seen water.

The muddy edges told a different story, of course. There *had* been water here once. But right now, the fact was inescapable. The river had gone.

26

Diane Fry sat on the bed in her hotel room, trying to work out how she felt. Somehow, she'd slept through the bad hours. As a result, she'd woken this morning feeling disorientated, and strangely deprived. It was as if something was missing from her regular routine, that jolt of fear that she usually woke to, the dry mouth and tangle of bed clothes. She opened her eyes and saw not only a strange room, but a different psychological landscape.

And now, after a shower, she felt much better. Her muscles ached, and the skin was scraped off the knuckles of one hand. But she felt positive, energetic, and ready for more action. The world out there was waiting for her to make decisions.

Having got hold of William Leeson's address, she wasn't sure what she intended to do with it. She was reluctant to confront anyone on their doorstep. She was too far out of her patch, and too exposed. But she'd already taken plenty of risks. She'd reached that point of no return. There was no turning back from the truth now.

One decision had to be made quickly. A message was waiting for her on her phone. An officer from the Major Incident Unit would like her to come in again to help them with their enquiries into Mr Kewley's death. They had some more questions to ask her. Would this morning suit? Well, actually, no.

The address that Eddie Doyle had given her was way out in the leafier suburbs near Solihull, where the trees grew denser and street signs were few and far between.

Fry pulled her car on to the grass verge near a field gate and looked at the sweeping drive beyond the wrought-iron gates. She could see a CCTV camera and an entry phone. This was a man who took his security seriously, then. It suggested a past that might be expected to catch up with him one day. An uneasiness about who might come calling.

Well, she could sit right here in her car until Leeson decided to emerge from his house, which might be hours or days. Or she could try the field, and see what security was like at the back.

There were cows in the field, a black-and-white herd, lurching ponderously about and munching the grass. But Fry had seen plenty of cows before, thanks to her time in Derbyshire. She knew all about cow pats and dung flies, midges and thistles. She knew to be wary of mad-eyed bovines whose rear ends gushed like fountains. These things held no mystery for her any more.

The animals watched her with lethargic movements of their huge heads, jaws rotating slowly, ears and tails twitching to keep off the flies. Fry reached a small copse of trees fenced off with barbed wire to keep the cows out. She could see that the far side of the copse overlooked the back garden of William Leeson's house. Another fence there, of course. But the undergrowth was dense enough to give her a concealed vantage point.

When she reached the back fence, she realized that one of the trees was close enough to provide a handy overhanging branch. That was remiss of someone. Whoever was responsible for maintenance should have been doing some trimming back to maintain the security of the premises. If she was the local crime prevention officer following up reports of a burglary, she'd have words of advice to give. Now, she considered their oversight from a different angle.

A few minutes later, Fry felt gravel crunch under her feet as she reached the edge of the drive. Ornamental shrubs had provided cover most of the way across the sloping lawn, close-mown grass muffling the sound of her feet. She hoped Leeson didn't possess a guard dog. She didn't like dogs, especially those big ones with teeth like tombstones.

From here, the drive swept around the back of the house towards a row of garages. The doors of one garage stood open, revealing a soft-topped sports car of some kind. Fry's mind was completely blank on models of sports car, but this one looked old. A classic car, she supposed. Something with leather seats and a noisy exhaust. Not the sort of car you'd leave parked on a street in Handsworth.

She found a set of French windows looking on to a patio. They stood open, too. The warm weather was working to her advantage, the way it did for burglars.

Fry slid through and surveyed the room. It had a desk and bookshelves, a laptop standing temptingly open. Then she heard the creak of a handle as a door swung slowly open.

When she turned, she was staring into the barrel of a handgun. William Leeson was pointing it directly at her head. He held the weapon professionally, in two hands, his body braced to achieve a steady aim. Someone had given him training.

'So you're going to shoot me, Mr Leeson?' she said. 'Seriously? That will look good.'

'I have special protection measures in place at this property,' he said. 'There's an alarm which links directly to the police station.'

'And have you activated it?'

He hesitated. 'Not yet.'

'Which means you're not going to. Put the gun down, Mr Leeson.'

He lowered the weapon.

'It was perhaps a bit melodramatic,' he said. 'I wasn't expecting the intruder to be you. Not our Detective Sergeant Fry. You're not known for breaking and entering. You're supposed to be the one who goes by the book.'

'I think that was the old me.'

Leeson put the gun in a drawer, and sat down at his desk.

'How did you get in here?' he said.

'Perhaps your gates are open. Have you checked them recently?'

She watched his skeletal hands. When she looked a bit more closely, Fry could see that his face was even greyer than his hair. The skin looked fragile – brittle, as if it might flake away at any moment and expose the bone. She wondered what was wrong with him, what pernicious illness was sapping his energy and draining the colour from his skin.

But then she realized that she didn't actually care.

'I suppose I should have talked to you at the prison yesterday,' he said. 'It was inevitable, really, that we would end up having this conversation. But you took me by surprise. I don't like that.'

'And what do you think our conversation is going to be about?' asked Fry.

Leeson gave her a small smile.

'Blood,' he said. 'That's what we have to talk about, you and I. It's all about blood.'

She looked at his grey skin and skeletal hands, and remembered Darren Barnes calling Leeson a coke head. She pictured him snorting cocaine through a rolled-up twenty-pound note, absorbing it through his mucous membranes. A more direct hit than smoking it, the way Vincent Bowskill did.

'What blood?' she said.

'Mine. It was my blood at the scene of your assault in Digbeth.'

'So, what? You got a nose bleed from snorting too much cocaine?'

'The first thing you don't know, Diane, is this – I was trying to help you.'

'Don't lie to me.'

'It was my blood at the scene. My blood the police got a DNA profile from. I pulled one of those boys off you, and he punched me in the face. I cut my hands on the fence, on the barbed wire. It was my blood, Diane. My blood was on you.'

'I don't believe you.'

'You know what they say, Diane. Blood is thicker than water. You might not believe it right at this moment. But you'll learn the truth soon enough.'

The truth? Fry didn't expect to be overburdened with too much of that. But if she got a straight answer, it would be a start.

'Mr Leeson, what is your relationship with Darren Barnes and Marcus Shepherd, and their crew?'

'Relationship? That's not exactly it.' With one thin hand, he made a gesture which seemed to encompass the whole of Birmingham beyond his wrought-iron gates. 'There's a very delicate balance of power on the streets of this city at the moment. The M1 Crew are in danger of being wiped out, if it gets out of control. They've made themselves a target for rival gangs, who have far more firepower at their disposal. They've been encroaching on other people's territory. That just isn't done.'

'I won't weep for them,' said Fry.

'They've been very useful to us.'

'Us?'

Leeson folded his lips closed as if he'd already given away too much.

'There are people on your side, Diane,' he said.

'I've been told that. But I haven't seen much evidence of it.'

He shrugged. 'I'm sorry, then. There are bigger issues to be considered.'

'I've heard that somewhere before, too.'

'Seriously, Diane. You could ruin everything. Don't interfere with Barnes and Shepherd and the M1 Crew.'

Diane felt the rage building inside her. Who was this man to dismiss her so casually, to tell her not to interfere? Her hands trembled as the adrenalin surged through her body, her fingers itching to latch on to a target.

'Perhaps you should call the police, after all,' she said.

'Why?'

'Because you're in real danger now.'

But Leeson made no move. 'You have no idea what's going on, do you? You're totally focused on yourself.'

'Aren't we all?'

'No, you were always worse than anyone else. That single-minded ambition you had, that drove you for years. A pity it came to this.'

Fry stared at him. How was it that this man seemed to know her so well?

'As I said, there are more important issues at stake. Control of the streets, preventing more young people from dying, I can't say any more.'

'So you're some kind of crime-fighting super hero?'

'No. I'm just a flawed human being who found himself in these circumstances.'

'Barnes and his crew think you're their man.'

Leeson smiled then. 'Everyone thinks what they want to think. That's the reason we so often put our trust in the wrong people.'

'I'll tell you what I think,' said Fry. 'I think you're the cause I was sacrificed for, the reason my case will never go ahead. I think this whole charade has been about saving your pathetic skin. Well,

278

I guess you must have the right bits of dirty knowledge about the right people in this city. Am I close?'

But Leeson was gaining confidence now. He stood up from his desk, and looked over her shoulder towards the French windows. Fry's muscles tightened. She hoped he would make a wrong move, so that she could react. She only need one ounce of justification.

'Didn't you bring Angie with you?' he said. 'That would have been nice.'

And that was the final straw.

'What do you know about my sister?'

Fry found she had hold of his arm and was twisting it. She wasn't sure how it had happened, but now that she'd made physical contact with him, she wanted to punish him, to make him bleed, to see that blood flow again that he talked about.

'You're hurting me,' he said.

'Good. I could hurt you a lot more.'

She spun him round and bounced his face against the wall. She saw the blood then – a trickle of it running from his nose, bright and shockingly red.

'You know, Diane, I always thought Angie was the ruthless bitch of the family. But I got that wrong, didn't I?'

His face twisted with pain, as she unconsciously tightened her grip.

'Do you know what? I think she's actually worse than me.'

'No, she's a pussy cat compared to you. You'd kill me, if you could. If you thought you could get away with it.'

'No.'

'Oh, don't pretend. You're no different from the rest of us. Everyone has it in them.'

Fry bit her lip. It was something she'd thought herself often enough. Everyone had the ability to commit murder, in the right circumstances. Or the wrong circumstances. Perfectly ordinary people could be pushed over the line by the most trivial of provocations. Some of them did it, and regretted it. Others would go through their entire lives without encountering the right situation. Those were the lucky ones.

'Shut up,' she said.

He smiled, as if he'd struck a blow home and achieved some kind of satisfaction.

'The trouble is, Diane, you're too familiar with the consequences, aren't you? You can't help thinking about what happens afterwards. How you'd ruin your career, and all that stuff. It's thinking too much that stifles the real you, that kills your emotions. It's what makes you less than human.'

'I told you to shut up.'

'Go on, go on. Do it. You know you want to.'

Fry tensed, but held back. His almost insane grin was the only thing that stopped her. She recognized a desperate attempt at provocation when she saw it. This man wanted her to hurt him. *Really* wanted it.

She let him go and took a step back.

Fry knew it was time for her to leave the house. She could sense some awful event about to happen, something that was completely out of her control. She made her way towards the French windows, checked the patio and the drive. The garage door still stood open, and the car was inside. No sign of security guards, or armed police. Not even the dog with tombstone teeth. It all seemed quiet. She stepped out on to the gravel.

And then her phone rang. It was Ben Cooper.

'Ben, your timing is terrible. This had better be *really* important.'

'Yes. It's very important, Diane. It can't wait.'

'Out with it, then.'

'That familial DNA match. I got some more information from my friend. This took quite a bit of arm-twisting on her part. I think.'

'So? Do we know whose the third DNA profile at the scene was?'

'No. Like I said, there was no CJ sample on the database to make a direct comparison with or the third person would have been identified immediately. But that third person had a relative who was on the database. That means he was a close family member, Diane. A brother, father, or son.'

'And do we know whose DNA this familial match was made to?'

'Yes, we do,' said Cooper.

'Whose?'

'The victim's.'

'What?'

Though she got him to repeat what he'd said, the words still didn't seem to make sense to Fry. The victim wasn't some unconnected person, not in this case. It was wrong, completely wrong. An error in procedure. Contamination. Was this why the prosecution had been dropped?

'What are you saying, Ben?'

'The third DNA profile was a familial match to the victim's. It belonged to a close family member. The familial DNA – it was a match to you, Diane.'

'It's impossible,' she said. 'I don't have a brother, or a son. You know that.'

'Yes, I know.'

Reading the rest into his silence, Fry went slowly back to the French windows and looked at William Leeson.

Now she was feeling the memories collide and merge. A presence in her room as a small child, the smell of shaving foam, the creak of a door handle, a figure held in a shaft of light from the landing. A form crouching over her in the darkness of a patch of wasteland in Digbeth, his features blurred against a barbed-wire fence, but a familiar smell and touch. Too familiar.

Fry watched the blood trickle from Leeson's nose and coil into his mouth, forming a slow, glistening spiral.

She had seen a lot of blood in her life. She knew it could run in unpredictable ways. It spurted and glistened, darkened and congealed, formed pools and jagged rivulets. A bubble of fresh blood would burst and collapse, a gush split into scores of crimson trickles. Your body's fluid spread much further than you'd imagine. It could turn into an ever-expanding stain, a creeping edge that reddened everything it touched.

And your family could be a stain, too. Damaged genes spread through generations, darkening everything they came into contact with. Like death and taxes, your lineage was inescapable. It was bred in the bone, and it poisoned the blood. Some strains could run pure and free. But others formed thickening pools that soured and congealed, releasing the stink of heredity.

Fry had often thought about the genes she'd inherited. She'd wondered time and again what heredity had been inflicted on her, whose poisonous nature ran in her blood. She could feel that blood pump through her veins now. It was cold and alien, eating her flesh with its acid. She fought a momentary urge to slash open her wrists and let the blood drain away, to cleanse her body finally of the venom.

Leeson watched her calmly, his face giving nothing away. There was no suggestion in his expression that he was even aware of the feelings that were going through her.

Cold and insensitive, that's what he was. A cruel, unfeeling, twisted bastard.

And he was her father.

27

Well, it was summer. Below ground, limestone sucked the water down like a thirsty giant, leaving the river bed dry and choked with dead weeds. Here, the river had vanished, gone from the face of the earth.

This was what they called a *karst* landscape, shaped by the dissolution of layers of rock. The geology meant that rivers responded rapidly to rainfall variations. In dry weather, water sank into the ground via swallets, and the surface rivers ran dry. During wet weather, water often burst back through resurgences, as the subterranean passages filled up. Then rivers flowed at the surface again.

Here, only a solitary stagnant pool was left in the shade of a sycamore, swarming with midges and mosquitoes. A crow picked its way between the rocks on the dry river bed. The big rhubarb-like leaves of gunnera were encroaching gradually from the banks. A weir stood bare and useless a few yards from the bridge.

Cooper pulled out his iPhone, and called up Google Maps. He zoomed into the Ashbourne area and scrolled across to Wetton. On the satellite image, the bends of the River Manifold formed an outline like a giant face superimposed on the landscape. The curve of a cheek, the jutting angle of a nose, trees fringing the shape like hair.

The Manifold had only one tributary, the Hamps. In summer, the Hamps also disappeared. It re-appeared, like the Manifold, at Ilam Risings four and a half miles to the southeast. And just downstream from there, in Ilam village, the Manifold met the Dove.

On the way to Ilam, Cooper stopped briefly to pass Carol Parry's information on to Diane Fry, though Fry had hardly seemed to be concentrating on what he told her. Maybe he was just out of step now and she had moved on to something new. She might tell him eventually. Or, of course, she might not.

So that was what he was thinking about as he walked down into the grounds of Ilam Hall and across the Italian Gardens to St Bertram's Bridge, once the main crossing of the River Manifold. Upstream of the bridge there were two weirs, and just above the second were the boil holes, where the water from the Manifold and Hamps surged back to the surface. Further upstream, there was nothing but a few stagnant pools.

A path emerged from the trees and moved away from the river bank. Paradise Walk, created for hall guests to take their exercise. In these surroundings, an obscure hole in the rock on the riverside walk probably went mostly unnoticed. Here, the rivers that had flowed underground through a series of caves and passages burst up to the surface in their boil holes. The Manifold had travelled out of sight for four and a half miles from Wetton Mill to re-emerge in a small grated grotto.

Currents spread outwards into the river as the Manifold and Hamps re-emerged into the daylight and gushed downstream towards their meeting with the Dove. Cooper noticed that the water in the rock pool was full of coins. Everywhere he saw that old superstition, the longing that something, anything, might bring a bit of luck. And again he had the sound of the water in his head.

He watched the bubbling currents, listened to the sound of gushing water. That sound took him back to the morning in Dovedale so clearly. A white face, hair floating, the blood washed clear by the stream, a green summer dress tangled on the body like weeds. Limbs flopping, a head lolling back, water cascading from her dress and oozing from the sides of her mouth.

Cooper closed his eyes, and saw another image. Robert Nield standing on the bank, his hands raised, water dripping from his fingers. Like a priest, performing a blessing. Or a funeral rite. But the scene only seemed to exist there, in the space behind his eyes. Had it never happened in reality? Was his memory so unreliable that his experience in Dovedale had created a false image? He supposed it was possible. The mind was a mysteriously murky pool.

So how had a river affected Alex Nield? Cooper felt sure there was a river involved in Alex's real life story. And not just any river – a lost river.

The sound of the water was driving him away from this spot. And it was more than just a memory, an echo of the River Dove. This location just wasn't right. Here was where the rivers re-emerged, where the Manifold and Hamps came back from the lost, bursting up to the surface. Ilam Risings were about rebirth, not loss. He was in totally the wrong place.

Getting his bearings, Cooper remembered that the bridge he'd stopped at was Redhurst Crossing, at the bottom of Leek Road. A short distance away, the first bridge south from Wetton Mill was Dafar Bridge. According to the map, the swallets lay on the section between the bridges. Wetton Mill Swallet, and Redhurst Swallet.

To the north, the Manifold Way diverged on to the River Hamps at Beeston Tor and ran upstream towards Waterhouses. To the south, the Manifold headed into Ilam to join the Dove at St Mary's Bridge, close to the Izaak Walton Hotel.

Cooper drove back up the road towards Wetton Mill, part of the route merging into the Manifold Trail. The light railway had run for more than eight miles down the valley of the Hamps as far as Beeston Tor, before turning up the gorge of the Manifold, and through to Hulme End. The line had a large number of stations in its short distance. Even Thor's Cave was said to have had its own station, with a waiting room and refreshment room. Today, it was obvious from a walk along the path that the line had crossed the Manifold dozens of times – including nine bridges in the short section between Sparrowlee and Beeston Tor.

Wetton Mill was a focal point for visitors to the Manifold Valley. The mill house itself was owned by the National Trust, with a tea room, shop and toilets. The bridge here was built by the Duke of Devonshire for packhorses carrying his copper from Ecton before the arrival of the railway.

If the Nields had spent their leisure time here as a family, he imagined they would have visited the tea rooms, walked across the stone bridge, maybe had their photographs taken in front of the stone arches. They'd have sat eating their picnic on the shelves of rock by the water, tried out the rock that had been carved to look like a throne. Those were the sorts of things families did.

285

Or had the children come here on their own, walking or riding their bikes, getting away from their parents for an afternoon? When he was ten or eleven years old, Alex Nield had gone through an experience that changed him so much his next-door neighbour had noticed. That was such a critical age. A traumatic event could affect his psychology for ever, if it was never dealt with.

Here at the mill, the river was flowing well, its water as clear as the Dove where it rattled over stones and foamed into pools under the limestone cliff. Yet within a few yards it had vanished. Just downstream, on the next bend, the bed was completely dry.

So somewhere near here were the actual *swallets*, the holes in the earth where the river disappeared, sucked up by the thirsty limestone.

Looking at the river, Cooper recalled standing with Diane Fry in Digbeth the day before, staring at the muddy River Rea. The Rea was hidden from sight, too – though not as a result of natural forces, like the Manifold. It had been channelled by human beings, who always wanted to control the flow of water, the way they controlled everything else.

But that wasn't the most important thing. Cooper was remembering Fry's comment as they stood above the Rea. It had seemed to mean very little at the time, a reference to Digbeth's industrial past.

So what was it she'd said exactly?

'But it's not the river itself that's important. It's what's on the banks of the river that matters.'

Cooper parked at Wetton Mill and hurried back down the Manifold Trail on foot. Almost opposite a field barn, he came to a crumbling, dilapidated gate. If he hadn't been looking, he would never have noticed a tiny sign on the gate post, marking a Staffordshire RIGS geotrail. So there was a regionally important geological site here.

As far as he could see, only an empty pasture stood beyond the gate. Through the deep, lush grass, someone had left a clear trail, the long stalks of grass flattened in the direction of the river. But there was no sign of a trail coming back.

He crossed the field, pushed his way through the deep banks of gunnera and cow parsley, and found himself standing on the bank of a dry river bed. At certain times of year, the River Manifold flowed through here, but the limestone had swallowed it up. A single shoe, an orange Croc, lay abandoned on a pile of stones in the middle.

Carefully, Cooper stepped down on to the river bed. Dry rocks clattered under his feet like broken pottery. A faint smell reminded him of seaweed left on a beach by the ebbing tide. It suggested vegetation that had once grown in water, now decomposing in the open air. Within a few yards, he found a spot under a beech tree on the far bank, where water gurgled down a hole in the rocks, rushing below ground as if to escape from the daylight. Nearby, a smear of brown scum had gathered where a smaller rivulet slowly swirled and vanished.

Standing on the river bed, he realized he was out of sight of the road, and of the mill too. No sound reached him of the children playing on the bridge. Here, there was only the murmuring river in one direction, and dry, silent stones in the other. In front of him was a sheer, unclimbable limestone cliff, with jackdaws calling and circling overhead. And below the cliff, a steep slope dense with ivy ran right down to the edge of the river.

He followed the last trickles of water until he found a swirl like the suction of a plug hole under a wedge of stone near the opposite bank. He had to balance carefully to be able to step right on the spot where the water vanished beneath his feet. Then he leaned over to the bank, pulled back a branch of the beech tree and peered up into the ivy.

The earth had been scraped away from the roots of the tree. The soil was too thin here to conceal anything from a fox scavenging for carrion. The scent of a dead carcase would be strong enough to draw wild creatures down from the woods above the river.

There were just a few bones left, scattered on the surface among the twisted roots and white tendrils of ivy. At first, Cooper thought someone had buried a dog or a cat. He'd never asked whether Alex Nield had owned a pet when the family lived at Wetton, a predecessor to Buster. Could his father have drowned a puppy in the river and disposed of the body on the bank? Was that what Alex had been so upset about, the incident that had traumatized him and turned him against his father?

Cooper knew that some children could become obsessively attached to a pet, and might make an animal the focus of all the affection they ought to be sharing with other human beings, particularly with their family. Had Robert Nield forced Alex to watch the execution, ensuring that the awful memory would be etched into his son's mind for ever? It would explain a lot.

Balancing with one knee on the bank, Cooper tugged back a clump of ivy to clear the earth around the bones. He found the skull, shrouded with mould, ran a hand over the dome of the cranium, brushed soil and dead leaves out of the eye sockets.

And then he knew for certain that he wasn't looking at the bones of a dog.

28

Strain, line, breeding, blood. It was strange how those words could sound like a curse. Fry trembled with unreleased emotion as she made her way back to her car.

There had been little left to say to William Leeson once she'd realized the truth. Oh, there were plenty of questions she could have asked him. But there were no answers he could have given her that she would have believed. This was the man she and Angie had been taken away from as children, the man who had abused her sister. His name was the one missing from her birth certificate, the reason she carried her mother's surname. And this was the same man who was now setting about wrecking her life in some way that she didn't even understand.

'I thought I'd better tell you all this, Diane,' he'd said. 'It's time to be honest about things.'

'You're telling me because you know the truth is going to come out anyway. That's not a conscience you've suddenly developed – it's a defence mechanism. It's the response of a cornered animal.'

'Everything you've ever done is wrong. You never had any concern for other people.'

'So you're moralizing now? Spare me. I know lots of ways to kill you. It would just be a question of whether to make it quick … or whether I want you to suffer.'

He smiled, a slightly nervous smile. He was trying to show that he knew she was joking, while deep down he wasn't quite sure if she was serious.

'You don't understand a thing,' he said.

'I wish people would stop telling me that.'

There was only one feeling that Fry was left with as she climbed back into her car and drove away from Leeson's house. Hatred. It was the most corrosive of emotions. If it found no outlet, hatred would eat you up, bit by bit. It could drip acid into your heart and gnaw your brain to useless wreckage, like a self-inflicted cancer. Hatred would kill you in the end. Now and then, it killed someone else along the way.

Within a couple of miles, she began thinking of some of the things Leeson had said to her during the time in his house.

'You know what they say, Diane. Blood is thicker than water. You might not believe it right at this moment. But you'll learn the truth soon enough.'

And there had been something else.

'Everyone thinks what they want to think. That's the reason we so often put our trust in the wrong people.'

She called Angie, who had taken the case file away from her hotel room for safety.

'Can you bring the file and meet me? I'll be back in the city in half an hour.'

'Yes, no problem.'

Diane swept into the hotel lobby in a hurry. Angie jumped up from a chair, sensing her urgency. She had the file clutched under her arm. 'Di, what's going on?' she said.

'Are the PNC print-outs there that Ben brought?'

'Yes.'

'Read the details of Darren Barnes to me again.'

Angie began to read hesitantly. *Darren Joseph Barnes, also known as 'Doors'.* She went though his address, date of birth, and ethnicity codes, and got to his conviction record.

'Stop. Go back.'

'To which bit?'

'The ethnicity codes,' said Diane.

'Really?'

'Yes, go back and read them again.'

'This is for Darren Barnes. *Ethnicity Code. PNC: IC1. Sixteen point self-determined system: M1.* That's mixed race, White and Black Caribbean.'

'I knew that,' said Fry. 'Damn it, I knew that. And Marcus Shepherd? Is he the same category?'

'*Ethnicity Code. PNC: IC3.*'

'So he's black?'

'No, wait. Under the self-determined system, he's M1 too. They're both classified as mixed race, Diane.'

'They class themselves as mixed race. Although, to the arresting officer, one looks white, and one looks black.'

'I guess we're talking shades of colour here.'

'Shades of colour, right.' Diane jumped up. 'Oh, Christ. I don't believe it.'

'What?'

'The M1 Crew.'

'What about them? Where are you going?'

But Diane was already on her way out of the door, not even looking back to see if her sister was following.

'Diane, where are you –'

Tower blocks looked even worse in the day time. At night, they had a certain mystery, a brooding presence, the curtained windows of their flats forming a pattern of light against the sky. Now, in the daylight, the Chamberlain Tower looked grubby and forlorn, the cracked concrete and graffiti'd walkways oozing despair, all its flaws exposed by the sun.

Vincent Bowskill was alone this afternoon. He was unshaven and bleary eyed, as if he wasn't long awake. His flat smelled like a derelict laundry, full of unwashed clothes. But underneath it was that sweet, faint chemical odour of recently smoked crack.

'Diane,' he said. 'What do you want?'

'I need to talk.'

'I did what you asked me to. There was no need to send Angie round. She's mad, that one. Dangerous, you know? I don't want her coming to mine again. Keep her away. I could get in deep shit here, you understand. Some of these guys don't mess around.'

'Vince, shut up.'

He ran his fingers nervously across his mouth as he looked at her face.

'What? What?'

'The M1 Crew.'

'What about them?'

'The name is nothing to do with motorways or rappers, is it? It refers to the sixteen-point ethnicity code, the self-determined system. It's what you describe yourself as when you're stopped by the police. Your say you're mixed race, White and Black

Caribbean. They put you down on their stop-and-search forms as M1.'

'Everybody knows that.'

'You hate being put into a category by the system. So you decided to categorize yourselves. I understand that, I really do. It's a way of taking back control, asserting your own identity. Everyone needs an identity. You have to belong to a group, a family, a tribe. Or a gang.'

'So?'

'You wanted to get into the M1 Crew, didn't you? You badly needed to be part of the gang, to feel you belong. But they weren't really like you at all. Were they, Vince? They thought you were much too soft, a kid with no street cred. You couldn't get their respect. So you made them a gift. Was that the deal you made?'

Fry recalled Andy Kewley's words. This wasn't one of the primary suspects, but he knew who was involved all right, and he helped to cover up. A real piece of work. He was as guilty as anyone I ever met.

Vince shook his head. 'It wasn't me. You didn't see me there.'

'But you were there that night.'

'You don't understand anything.'

'I understand you, Vince.'

'No way. You can't ever understand. You're a copper.'

He stopped and stared at her, as if suddenly scared by her expression.

And so he should be. A vivid memory had come to her now. No confused images or blurred impressions any more. She almost had it last time, stood here in this flat, but she'd been distracted by the crack pipe, the blonde girlfriend. She remembered that shudder when she heard him say, 'She's a copper.' It wasn't just the accent. The voice was the same. A familiar voice, coarse and slurring. Of course it was familiar. She'd lived in the same house with him for years.

'Vince,' she said, 'I didn't see you. But I heard you.'

Fry sat for some time in her car, staring blindly at the traffic on Birchfield Road, streams of motorists hurtling past Checkpoint

Charlie, oblivious to the fact that they were crossing the borderland in the deadly turf war between Birmingham's street gangs.

She couldn't have said how long she sat there before she finally turned on the engine, wound down the windows, and swung out on to the underpass, heading for Perry Barr.

Jim Bowskill answered the door in his slippers, with his sleeves rolled up to expose white forearms. He looked as though he'd been cleaning, or doing the washing up. The impression of domestic banality turned her heart over.

'Your mum's not here,' she said. 'She's a doing a bit of shopping.'

'Good. It's perhaps better this way.'

'You should have let us know you were coming, love. I'll put the kettle on. Alice won't be more than half an hour or so. She popped across to the One-Stop. She said we needed some fresh meat. I don't know why, when we've got plenty of stuff in the freezer. Would you like tea, or coffee?'

'No, Dad. Don't bother.'

Why did people talk so much when there was nothing to say? Fry wondered if they felt they had to fill the silence with noise to prevent reality from leaking into their minds, as if the truth was hiding in the pauses.

'Can we sit down for a minute? There's something I want to tell you.'

'Of course, love. But are you sure you don't want –'

'No, Dad. Sit down.'

They sat opposite each other, Jim in his usual armchair, but perched anxiously on the edge of the seat, Fry on the settee like a visitor.

'We've never really talked about this before,' she said. 'I mean, the night of the assault.'

Even now, she felt reluctant use the word 'rape' when speaking to Jim Bowskill. It was as if she had to protect him from the harsh world out there, the one he didn't seem to see passing his window.

'We're always here if you want to talk,' he said. 'Your Mum would love –'

293

'I know,' said Fry. 'I know that, Dad. Thanks, really. But there's something … a bit of information that I've only just realized myself. It affects you personally, Dad. You have to know about it.'

He gazed at her steadily, a look of concern crossing his face. Or was it an expression of fear? Fry hesitated now. Was she about to turn Jim's world upside down?

'Go on, love,' he said.

'It's about Vincent. He was one of the group that night. In Digbeth, you know. He was part of the gang involved in the assault.'

Jim Bowskill didn't say anything, but lowered his head and looked at his hands. They lay in his lap, strong hands but with slightly swollen knuckles, a result of his years spent working at the engineering factory. He was grasping his fingers together, and Fry saw that he was trying to stop them from shaking.

'Dad? Are you all right? I didn't think you would be so upset about Vince. You must have known what sort of company he'd got into.'

He shook his head, and Fry was shocked to see a tear break free from his cheek and plop on to the back of his hand.

'Diane, I'm sorry,' he said. 'We're both really sorry. We didn't know what else we could do.'

He spoke in a very small voice, as if it was painful for him to get out the words. At first, Fry didn't understand. She wanted to go over to his chair and comfort him for his distress, but something was holding her back. Somehow, she knew that his words were more than just an expression of sympathy. That had all been said before, years ago. This was something more, something much bigger. These were words that would change everything. Jim Bowskill was apologizing.

'Dad?' she said. And then she asked the toughest question of all. 'You knew?'

'Yes, Diane,' he said. 'We knew.'

29

Once again, Cooper allowed himself to be swept up in the activity, the arrival of the whole caravan in response to his call. The field had been taped off, and a scene-of-crime tent stretched across the dry river bed to the opposite bank, though it was much too late to worry about protecting the remains.

Sergeant Wragg had attended from Ashbourne, and DC Becky Hurst arrived from Edendale, close behind the medical examiner. There was nothing for Cooper to do at the scene now, so he moved himself out of the way.

Only now, when he stood back on the roadway, did Cooper notice the limestone cliff above the swallet hole. Crevices and fissures in the rock had formed the crude outline of a face, like a primitive wall carving. Two eyes, a nose, and a narrow cleft for a smiling mouth.

No, not a wall carving. It was just like a cartoon face, drawn by a child.

The medical examiner brushed dirt off his gloves as he walked back across the field.

'You'll need a forensic anthropologist for a specialist opinion,' he said. 'The pathologist won't be too interested in this one. Not enough flesh or soft tissue left on the bones. Well, there wasn't much there to start with.'

'Meaning, Doctor?'

'A neonate. It was a new-born baby. No more than a few hours old, I'd say. Perhaps it was never even alive.'

'Will we be able to tell that?'

The ME shrugged. 'Well, a birth is considered live if the child breathes after being born. Since most killings of neonates occur immediately after birth, before the ingestion of food or healing of the umbilical stump, the only method of determining whether a child was born alive is by examination of the lungs.'

'The lungs?' said Cooper.

'A hydrostatic test.' He stripped off his gloves and gestured with his hands. 'Basically, you take out the lungs and put them in water. If they sink, we can presume the child was stillborn. If the lungs float, the child was born alive and breathed. A bit like the test for witchcraft, I always think.'

'What? Oh, yes. If you float, you're guilty. If you drown, you're innocent.'

'That's it. But obviously, there's a problem here. The remains are too decayed, from exposure to the air. There are no lungs.'

Cooper turned away. He'd seen and heard enough here.

'You haven't asked me how long the remains have been here,' said the ME. 'Don't you usually want to make unreasonable demands for my estimate on the time of death?'

'I don't think I need to ask that,' said Cooper. 'It would be around two years ago, I imagine.'

The ME raised his eyebrows. 'A very good guess, DC Cooper.'

'Acting DS.'

'I'm sorry. Promotion obviously improves your speculative abilities.'

'Actually, I'd go a bit further,' said Cooper. 'I'd say this child died on the thirtieth of June.'

Cooper was walking slowly back down the trail towards his car when his phone rang. He heard a young woman's voice.

'Hello. You gave me your card. At the funeral.'

'Is that Lauren?' said Cooper.

'Yes. How did you know?'

'It wasn't too hard to figure out. Where are you?'

'I'm not sure I want to say.'

'But you do want to talk to me?'

'Alex told me you'd been asking questions,' she said.

'So you've been in touch with Alex?'

'I emailed him. We keep in contact that way. Then he can delete my messages, so Mum never finds out.'

'Of course,' said Cooper. 'I suppose I ought to have guessed that.'

Cooper watched the activity taking place around the dry river bed.

'Lauren …' he said hesitantly.

She seemed to detect a seriousness in the tone of his voice.

'You've found out something, haven't you?'

'Yes. I'm near Wetton Mill right now. At the spot where the river goes dry. You know where I mean, don't you?'

'Yes, I know.'

'Lauren, we found the remains.' He paused to let it sink in. 'Please, tell me – whose baby was it?'

There was a long silence, and for a while Cooper thought he'd lost her. But he could hear her faintly in the background. She had either put down the phone, or taken it away from her ear so that she didn't have to hear what he said next. She sounded to be having trouble breathing. He heard a ragged sob, and wondered if she was totally on her own somewhere, with no one to comfort her.

'Lauren, don't go. Where are you? I'll come and meet you anywhere. Lauren?'

'I'm still here,' she said.

Cooper could barely hear her, because her words were almost swallowed by her sobbing.

'It's all right, Lauren. Everything's okay. I just need to know –'

'Yes,' she said. 'The baby was mine.'

Cooper drove through Ashbourne, negotiating another busy market day to reach Church Street, and heading towards some of the oldest buildings in the town – the alms houses, the original grammar school. At least they were made of stone. It made him feel a bit more at home.

Lauren was waiting for him near the entrance to the churchyard, a dark figure in black clothes that swung as she turned to meet him.

'The same place that we met before,' was all she'd said. Of course, here was where her sister Emily had been buried. Perhaps Lauren's floral tribute still lay here somewhere, too. *Remembering 30th June for ever.*

Lauren's Doc Martens crunched on the gravel as they walked towards the newest gravestones and stood for a moment in front of Emily's gleaming, pristine memorial.

'I don't know how you managed to keep it quiet,' said Cooper.

297

She shrugged, feigning indifference now.

'It wasn't that difficult. I wore a lot of baggy clothes, so nobody would notice for a while. It helps when nobody expects you to dress in the latest fashions. And, to be honest, I was a bit on the big side then, anyway. I put a lot of weight on when I got to my teens. I think I was stress eating. I hated myself for it, but Mum just kept putting more food in front of me.'

'It's her way, I think.'

'Right. I wouldn't have got away with it much longer, though. I would have had to go down with some illness or other, even though I was due to leave school about then. But the baby came early. Very early, actually.'

'Your mother must have known about the baby, Lauren.'

'Oh, yes. She knows everything, or she thinks she does.'

'And when the time came?'

'We had to dispose of it. That's what Dad told me. He said –'

She looked up from the grave, no longer able to get out the words.

'He said it was born wrong and it had to die,' suggested Cooper.

'How did you know that?'

'I got it from your brother. I think Alex must have heard it somehow.'

'Oh, Alex knew was what happening. He was the only person I could tell. Me and Alex, we were really close at one time. It's funny to think that, I suppose. We're so different.'

'He was only eleven, Lauren.'

'I know. I'm not sure he understood everything.'

'Did it occur to you what it might do to him?'

'I'm really sorry.'

'No,' said Cooper. 'It's not your fault.'

Two women entered the churchyard with fresh flowers to place on a grave. Cooper and Lauren moved on to stay out of earshot. They walked down past the front of the church hall and came to a path along the side of the Henmore Brook.

'You could have got the morning-after pill,' said Cooper. 'Didn't they do that at your school? Or you could have gone to a clinic. To your GP.'

She shook her head. 'I was terrified people would talk, or they would ask me who the baby's father was. You don't know what it's like in a place like this.'

'Surely if it was just some boy at your school –'

'A boy?' Lauren looked at him and laughed bitterly. 'You don't know everything then, do you? You're not quite as smart as I thought you were.'

Cooper stopped walking. Down here, there was no sound, except for the trickle of the brook, a few birds calling in the yew trees in the churchyard.

Lauren strode on a bit further, then she stopped too. Instead of turning towards him, she stayed with her back to him, her head down, hair falling over her face, the purple streak incongruous against the trees. She seemed to be staring at her boots, as if the pattern of the laces and steel hooks had some significance.

Cooper had a sudden realization of the full horror in that phrase her father had used. *It was born wrong and it had to die.* There could only be one meaning. Why had he been so stupid? Lauren was right. He really wasn't all that smart.

The girl looked up at him now, to see if he understood.

'It didn't feel like a baby, you know?' she said. 'Just some dirty little secret that I had to keep quiet about and hide from the world.'

'How did it happen?'

'He came into my room one night. I was really upset about something, you know? But I can't remember what it was now. Isn't that stupid? It was something so trivial that I can't even tell you what it was all about. It seemed *so* important to me at the time, but now it's just … a big nothing in my memory. Meaningless, because of what came after.'

'And your father forced himself on you?'

'He was trying to comfort me. I think he meant well. At first, anyway. Mum was away that night. Not that she would have been any better. She's no use in situations like that. She doesn't like things being out of control. It would have ruined her routine.'

Cooper shook his head in despair. 'I can't understand how he would do something like that.'

'Well, he'd been drinking on the way home from work. Things had started going badly at the store. It must have been about the

299

time the new supermarket moved into town, and he thought it was all over. He told Mum he thought he was going to have to lay off all his staff, and go on the dole himself, for the first time in his life.'

'It doesn't excuse –'

'Anyway, he was really stressed, you know?' she said. 'He didn't usually drink, so it affected him badly when he did. I don't think Dad knew what he was doing that night. Honestly, I don't think he did.'

She must have seen the doubt in his eyes. Cooper suspected she was about to start putting the blame on herself again. That wouldn't do anyone any good.

'I've always felt guilty about it,' she said. 'Guilty about everything.'

'You shouldn't. What your father did was very wrong. It was rape.'

'But was it?'

'Yes, of course it was. You were under age.'

'Well, it's got to be partly my fault. I suppose I was lucky it wasn't worse.'

'You mustn't talk like that.'

Lauren's black eye make-up was running now, streaking her pale cheeks.

'I did something bad to Alex, though,' she said. 'Didn't I?'

Cooper thought she had, but he couldn't explain to her quite what. He didn't really know what had been going on in her brother's mind.

'I suppose you told Alex where the baby was buried?' he said.

'I took him there, and showed him the place.'

'What? Oh, Lauren.'

She wiped a sleeve across her face, only making the streaks worse.

'I had to. It was like a memorial service, just me and him. It was the only way my baby's death would ever be remembered.'

'Well, Alex remembers it all right,' said Cooper grimly. 'How did he react?'

'He was a bit strange, you know? He went right down on to the river bed, stood on the exact spot where the water disappeared through the ground. I think he had to do that, to make it real. He was very quiet afterwards. But then, he always was a bit withdrawn.'

'Was the baby born alive, Lauren?' asked Cooper.

'Does it matter?'

'Yes, it does.'

She shrugged hopelessly. 'Not to me.'

They walked slowly back towards the church, Cooper allowing Lauren to walk a little way ahead. Following her black coat, he felt like a mourner in procession to the grave. When they got back to the gate, she spoke to him again, more composed and reflective now.

'Some people say Dad looks a bit like Dracula,' she said.

Cooper nodded. 'I've heard that.'

'Well, it's true, in a way. He sucked the blood out of me.'

For a moment, Cooper paused and looked back across the graves, beyond the churchyard and the Henmore Brook.

It was so difficult to understand what went on in families. How had the Nields reconciled themselves to a situation like this? What compromises had they made with each other, what rationalizations had gone on in their minds? As time passed, did they convince themselves that nothing was wrong, that they could all just go on as normal? And all for the sake of keeping the family together.

It was a twisted kind of loyalty, a sense of allegiance that shut out the rest of the world, and rejected concepts of conventional behaviour. Whatever went on in your own home was the reality you had to live. No one else could understand it, so you didn't tell them.

As he surveyed the view over Ashbourne, Cooper noticed the site of the old Nestlé factory across the brook, now rapidly becoming a new housing development. In the other direction, towards the town centre, the car park of Sainsbury's was busy with shoppers.

Cooper wondered if Lodge's supermarket would stay open without Robert Nield to keep his little family together. Probably not. He'd destroyed one family, and the other would surely follow.

30

The Nields were at home that afternoon, entirely unaware of what had being going on. Cooper met up with Becky Hurst outside the house off Wyaston Road. This wasn't a visit he could do on his own. While he waited for her, he gazed down the street at the outline of Thorpe Cloud, where it stood guard over the entrance to Dovedale. The hill was a silent watcher, hardly less valuable as a witness than any other.

'Okay,' he said, when Hurst had arrived. 'Let's get it over with.'

Robert and Dawn Nield were surprised to see him. But they sensed immediately that something was seriously wrong. It was remarkable that they could do that, in a week when so much had already gone wrong for them.

Cooper explained to them about the remains found on the banks of the River Manifold, and Lauren's admission that the baby had been hers. He hesitated before going any further. There was always a possibility that Lauren had been lying about the rest of the story.

Cooper looked at Dawn Nield first. She was clutching a tissue in a trembling hand, and her face was flushed. A glaze was spreading in her eyes, like a slow welling of terror.

'Do you know who the father of that child was, Mrs Nield?' he asked.

She shook her head. 'We never knew. Lauren wouldn't say.'

'I see.'

Cooper held her eye for a moment, then looked at Robert Nield.

'Is that your answer too, sir?'

The briefest of pauses left an uncomfortable silence in the air.

'Yes.'

But his response had come too slowly. Before he spoke, Nield had met Cooper's eye briefly, then looked away. It was a fleeting glance, done reluctantly, as if he'd been forced into it. But for that one moment, Nield just had to look into Cooper's face. He needed to see if Cooper knew the truth.

'The child, sir. It was yours, wasn't it?'

Nield ran a hand over his face, as if attempting to restore the colour to his skin, which had suddenly turned grey. His mouth sagged, and for a moment he seemed to have lost the power of speech.

'You know we can do DNA tests, Mr Nield.'

'Tests?'

'On the remains. We can match your DNA to establish parentage.'

In fact, Cooper wasn't entirely sure that anything usable still existed. The flesh had gone from the bones, had decomposed and fallen away, been carried away by scavenging animals, or deteriorated with exposure to the weather. There might just possibly have been something under the body that could produce a result in the lab. A fragment of skin that had been preserved from the air. And that was presuming a SOCO found it, examined the leaf litter carefully enough when the bones had been lifted. The bones themselves might yield a DNA result, of course – if anyone thought the tests were worthwhile.

Yes, it might be a long shot. But Robert Nield wasn't to know the odds.

'Were you the father, Mr Nield?'

Nield lowered his head. 'You know already.'

'How could you do that?'

'I don't know.'

Cooper flinched as a great sob was ripped from Dawn Nield. Her face was contorted beyond recognition. She might be repressed, might feel the need to be in control. But that control was failing her now. He could see her whole façade cracking, as the false world she'd constructed around herself began to crumble.

'It wrecked our family,' she said. 'Lauren left us after … after the baby died.'

'And it resulted in the death of Emily, too,' said Cooper. 'You do realize that?'

'What? That was an accident.'

Cooper recalled what Rachel Murchison had told him. His own stress caused by the experience of the child's death in the river, and being helpless to save her. Short-term adverse reactions to anything his brain associated with the traumatic event. In this case, water.

'It's perfectly common. It should pass in time.'

'Does it always pass?'

'Well, not always. If left unacknowledged and untreated, it can develop into full-blown PTSD, and the effects of that can last for years. Occasionally, serious psychological disturbances may result from traumatic experiences in the past. But that's quite rare.'

'Would it be more common in a child?'

'Oh, yes. Certainly.'

'The truth is,' said Cooper, 'that only one person saw Emily die. And he was the one person who no one ever asked for his account of the incident. There was no point in putting him through it, was there? Everyone thought there were enough witnesses, even though not a single one of them saw what actually happened. As usual, Alex wasn't needed.'

'Alex?'

'And the worst thing is, I was there,' said Cooper. 'I was there myself. But I didn't see it.'

'Didn't see what?' asked Dawn. Her voice was distant, distorted, ghostly – the sound of a woman withdrawing from reality. Cooper knew he wouldn't get much else from her now.

'It was Alex who pushed his sister down in the water, hit her head on the stone and drowned her. No one saw that, did they? Except you, Mr Nield. You pulled him out of the river. That was how you got wet.'

'Is Alex so disturbed?'

'Yes, I think so. The memory of the river pushed him over the edge. He needs help very badly.'

Nield hung his head. His shoulders had dropped, and his whole body was bent like a man who had fallen in on himself, his internal organs collapsed, his heart torn away.

'Why couldn't he talk to us?' asked Dawn.

Cooper lowered his eyes. 'That's not for us to answer, Mrs Nield.'

And suddenly she was out of her seat and standing in front of him, her body swaying dangerously, her arms flying so violently that Cooper ducked back out of the way. Her face had passed from flushed red to deathly white, and her chest heaved with enormous, painful breaths. An awful, indistinguishable noise came from her throat, as if an animal was trapped in the room.

Shocked, Cooper stood uncertain what to do. The whole room seemed frozen, Robert Nield gaping from his chair, Becky Hurst giving a startled intake of breath behind him.

Then Mrs Nield staggered, and Cooper stepped forward to prevent her falling. And that broke the spell. Hurst moved in and helped him steady the woman and get her back into her seat.

'It's all my fault, isn't it?' whispered Dawn as she began to recover.

'No. Why should you feel that way?'

'Because I failed,' she said. 'I failed Emily. I've failed all my children.'

Cooper felt guilty at his inability to call up the degree of sympathy she was asking for. Somehow, Dawn Nield had made it all seem to be about her. The tragedy hadn't happened to Emily, but to her mother.

'Why didn't we see that Alex wasn't coping?'

'I think we did,' said Nield. 'But he shut himself away with it, and we thought it would pass.'

Cooper turned away from Mrs Nield to face him again.

'It doesn't pass unless it's dealt with,' he said. 'He needed someone to talk to.'

'We couldn't take him to a doctor. If he got referred to a councillor or therapist, it would have come out what upset him so much.'

'There's such a thing as patient confidentiality. A reputable therapist wouldn't pass on information like that.'

Nield shook his head. 'We couldn't take the risk.'

'So you sacrificed your son's psychological health,' said Cooper. 'And, ultimately, the life of your youngest daughter.'

'It all started with good intentions. From a moment of weakness.'

'Weakness? How could you do that to your daughter? Lauren would have been fifteen at the time.'

'It was a mistake,' said Nield.

'A mistake?'

Cooper had heard enough.

'Robert Nield, I'm arresting you. You do not have to say anything. But it may harm your defence if you do not mention when questioned something which you later rely on in court. Anything you do say may be given in evidence ...'

Cooper put Robert Nield in the car, and asked Becky Hurst to stay at the house until help arrived. Mrs Nield needed a doctor, and Social Services would have to be involved with Alex.

'I think I understand him, though,' said Nield, as they drove back through Ashbourne.

'Really?'

'He's very like me when I was his age. When I was about twelve, I had a Swiss Army knife I was very proud of. I used to play with it all the time, opening and closing the blades. One day, while I was watching TV, I slashed the leather sofa I was sitting on. It was just because the blade was in my hand, and that was what it was made for.' Nield smiled sadly. 'My father didn't accept that explanation. I got a good smacking for it.'

'I don't see the connection,' said Cooper.

'Have you never done something for no particular reason? Just found that you'd destroyed an object without even thinking about it? Let me tell you, it's as if your hands act on their own, while your mind is somewhere else entirely. There's no question of intention – that doesn't come into it. It's a sort of ... physical unreasoning.'

'You make it sound as if it was nothing more than tearing up a sweet wrapper.'

'There are impulses we can't control.'

'But this isn't an object we're talking about. It's a person.'

'The principle is the same.'

'I don't think so.'

'It takes a bit of imagination to understand.'

Cooper shook his head. 'We all have impulses. But we don't always act on them. Maybe when they happen, it's because our mind allows them to.'

'Still, it's a shame that Alex lied to us.'

'He didn't want to lie. He wanted to tell the truth. But there was no one who could be bothered to listen to him.'

'I can't really blame him for lying,' said Nield, as if he hadn't heard. 'Teenagers lie to their parents all the time. It's a miracle if they tell us the truth now and then. The only view we get of what's going on in their heads is the impression we have from the outside, and what they tell us. The truth can be something completely different.'

Cooper knew that was probably true. But Alex was only putting into practice some of the things he'd learned from his father.

'But he isn't mad, you know.'

'I said "disturbed".'

'You don't have to be mad to do something horrible. Malice is natural to the human soul – just as natural as kindness. Being bad is part of being alive.'

Cooper didn't want this conversation. He tried not answering, hoping it would shut Nield up. It didn't work.

'It's true what I said, though,' said Nield. 'No one thinks of the consequences of that moment.'

'Are you speaking about the conception of Lauren's child now?' asked Cooper. 'Or the killing of your daughter Emily?'

The question Cooper asked himself now was, what would happen to Alex? The boy was thirteen years old. At one time, Alex Nield would have fallen into a legal grey area, where children aged between ten and fourteen were presumed not to know the difference between right and wrong. In those days, they could only be convicted if the prosecution proved they were aware what they were doing was seriously wrong. Under the age of ten, children weren't considered to have reached an age where they could be held responsible for their crimes at all.

Now, though, the law had changed. At thirteen, Alex Nield was considered fully responsible for his actions, in the same way as any adult. He couldn't vote until he was eighteen, and he couldn't legally have sex until he was sixteen. But at the age of thirteen he was well within the age of criminal responsibility. The law would say that he knew perfectly well what he was doing.

Yes, Alex might be exactly like his father was at the same age. It was ironic, then, that if Robert Nield had committed a serious crime when he was thirteen, he might have escaped prosecution. But this was the twenty-first century. Alex would have no such luck.

Cooper recalled the four psychological types identified in that study of online gamers. Achievers, Explorers, and Socializers. And what was the name of the fourth group?

Oh yes, that was it. The Killers.

A call came in from Becky Hurst, still in Ashbourne.

'Social Services have arrived,' she said.

'Good. Where is Alex? Still in his room, I suppose? He'll be on his computer, oblivious to everything.'

'No,' said Hurst. 'That's the bad news. We can't find him. Alex has disappeared.'

31

There were more officers at the Nield house now. Uniforms in the garden, checking along the back fence, talking to the nearest neighbours. Two social workers were with Mrs Nield in the sitting room.

'We've looked everywhere,' said Hurst. 'He's gone. Disappeared without a word. He must have gone out of the back door when we arrived to talk to his parents.'

'If not before that,' said Cooper. 'They wouldn't have noticed that he'd gone.'

'I'm sorry.'

'It's not your fault.'

Why did everyone keep wanting to take the blame? Cooper looked around desperately for clues.

'Did he leave a note? A message? A text?'

'Nothing,' said Mrs Nield. 'We've got to find him. He's only thirteen, you know.'

'Okay, so where would he go?'

'I don't know.'

'We'll have to get a full-scale search under way, Becky. He has quite a head start.'

'I'll get onto it.'

No message, that was bad news.

Cooper turned to the only person who Alex might have been in touch with. His older sister. At least he now had a phone number for her.

'Lauren, has Alex contacted you?'

'I got an email a little while ago,' she said.

'Of course you did. What did he say?'

'It was really short. He just said "brb kk?"'

Cooper thought again of Alex's online profile. That terse final line: *brb kk?*

Literally, it meant 'Be right back, okay?' But Luke Irvine had explained that it often signified something quite different. It was a way getting rid of someone if you didn't want to deal with them.

You were telling them you'd never be coming back. It was saying goodbye.

A few minutes later, Cooper stopped his car and looked out over the country along the border between Derbyshire and Staffordshire. He saw Dovedale snaking off to the east, the dry valleys of the Manifold and The Hamps to the west. In between, there lay a scatter of villages, with Wetton in the centre, and Ecton Hill just visible beyond it.

He was trying to see the landscape in the way that Alex Nield would. Alex lived in a virtual world, moving around a continent populated by enemies – Saxons, Romans, Vikings. They all had to be confronted and dealt with. His was a world where you fought constantly for survival. Kill or be killed, that was the rule of the game.

But then, each player had his own castle, didn't he? He established a defensive stronghold, a place of safety where he could resist attacks. Walls to keep out the rest of the world.

Yes, a place of safety. It was something that Alex Nield had never possessed in real life.

Or had he?

If he was Alex, Cooper knew he would have somewhere to go. At Bridge End Farm, there had been an old field barn that wasn't used any more. Most of the roof had fallen in, except for the far corner, where it was dry and sheltered from the wind. It was a good three fields away from the house, so no one would ever find him, unless they really knew where to go looking. Having those stone walls around him gave him a sense of reassurance, as if the cold winds of insecurity would bounce off the stones with the rain.

So where would Alex go? Given that he couldn't physically retreat into the world of *War Tribe*, there must be somewhere.

Cooper tried to recall the exact details of the boy's profile on *War Tribe*. Not the Lost River part, the names of his castles. All the players seemed to choose names that they thought were cool, or had some specific meaning known only to them. But Cooper's memory was failing him now. He wished he was back in the office in Edendale, with a PC and internet connection, so he could check.

But wait. He didn't need that. He had an iPhone.

Cooper looked around, hoping that for once there was a decent signal. At least he wasn't in a valley. He was on the plateau between the two rivers, close to the edge of Wetton Hill.

He likes patterns. Of course he does. From his behaviour, Alex might even be mildly autistic. Unsocial, solitary, slightly obsessive. Alex was always looking for patterns – in his online world, and in real life. Patterns in the bark of a tree, or in the lichen on a rock. So one river meant another river. Water that flowed in the same direction, faces in the rock, a pattern in events as there was in the landscape.

His hands shaking now with the urgency, Cooper used his phone to access the internet and logged on to *War Tribe*. It was much slower connecting than on his laptop at home, but finally he was clicking on Smoke Lord's profile, scrolling down the names of Alex's cities. Engine House, Dutchman, The Folly. And his latest city, conquered but not yet built into a castle. Powder House.

'I get it,' he said to himself. 'I'm not such a noob, after all. I get it.'

A tiny side road led him to Back of Ecton, where footpaths snaked off to the old mine workings. He left his car in a gateway and walked to a trig point on the summit of Ecton Hill.

The Manifold Trail ran below him, diving through a tunnel at Swainsley, to the old station at Hulme End, a wooden-framed brown-and-cream building now housing a shop. In its day, the light railway must have been like a toy train set, its station platforms only six inches high, its trains running at fifteen miles an hour, stopping to pick up passengers on the footpath. A dairy had once stood at Ecton, making Stilton cheese. And below Ecton Hill, the loading platforms for the old copper mines lay along the route of the trail, though the railway had come too late for the future of the mines.

Beyond Ecton village, one of the public footpaths passed through an area on the hillside where the mines breached the surface. Here were the adits, the drift entrances that enabled miners to get access to the copper without the need for a long descent. Cooper saw a moss-covered tree, and behind it seven vertical iron bars with darkness beyond. A drift entrance, sealed off against the curious or foolhardy.

About seventy mine workings were scattered over Ecton Hill, including about fifty vertical shafts. The chief mines were the Duke of Devonshire's Deep Ecton, Dutchman, and Chadwick mines, and the Burgoyne family's Clayton and Waterbank. And down in the valley the smelting works and dressing floors were situated between the river and the road, along the slopes of the hillside. Only the mine manager's house, sales room and offices were left, all used as dwellings. A castle-like folly with a copper spire dated from much later.

At their peak, these mines had reached three hundred yards below river level. Although the deep workings were now flooded, those above the level of the river were still accessible. They rose from deep inside the hill to the site of one of James Watt's first steam engines, housed on the hilltop.

The slopes below him were too steep to descend safely. But as he approached the mine along the top of the ridge, Cooper saw a number of open shafts. They had been fenced off, but some of the fences were the worse for wear. Walkers would need to take care if they went too near the shafts. Too many accidents had happened in the past, small children disappearing into the earth as the ground crumbled beneath them.

He came to a halt. He'd strayed off the path somehow. In front of him was a fence, strands of barbed wire snagged with clumps of wool.

The fence followed the contours of the land to the east, then veered away from him. Beyond it, he glimpsed the remains of an old water tower, a rusted iron ladder dangling from the base of the tank like tendrils of blighted ivy. The fence was protecting something, or keeping walkers away. There must be an open mine shaft here, an entrance to the old copper workings above river level.

And then he saw, ahead of him, the limestone walls of James Watt's engine house. The steam engine had once raised massive buckets full of copper out of the Deep Ecton Mine. The engine was long gone, and all the other machinery broken up when the mines ceased to be viable.

Engine House. That was the name of Alex Nield's main city in War Tribe, his heavily fortified castle where he could be safe from his enemies. He needed a place of security in the real world, too.

The stone chimney was no more than a stump. Half-tumbled walls, ash tips grown over with grass. And what were these raised areas either side of the engine house? Cooper tried to remember the basics of the physics involved. The heavy ropes in the deep shaft had needed a balancing weight to raise them, so two shafts at the same height.

Pacing the ground around the engine house, Cooper glimpsed a scrap of colour below a tumble of stones on the edge of one of the shafts.

'Alex? Alex? Don't move.'

The boy was close to the edge of the shaft, motionless. Was he dead or unconscious? Or only frozen, afraid to move in any direction? Cooper felt the ground slither and crumble under his feet, a stone dropped away into darkness. He never heard the sound of it hitting the bottom. These shafts had gone down three hundred yards, way below river level. Without the drainage pumps and soughs, water would have filled up the lower levels centuries ago.

Sensing his rising panic, Cooper inched gingerly closer, until he could grab a handful of fabric. He'd lost two people in the last week. He wasn't going to lose this one.

With a heave, Cooper drew Alex's weight up from the edge, remembering all too clearly the feel of Emily Nield's cold, limp body in his arms.

But this body was warm. Alex Nield was alive.

32

Monday

The weather had changed on the morning Diane Fry drove back to Derbyshire. Clouds rolled across the landscape, touching the tops of the hills. A stiff wind blew across the motorway, making a caravan in front of her sway dangerously. She turned off the air conditioning in her car. Was it the end of summer already?

Monday seemed to have come round too soon. Her Sunday had been spent trying to get everything straight in her mind. In the evening, she'd decided on a drink in the Pitcher and Piano at the Water's Edge. She hadn't realized how hungry she was until she passed Tin Tin and Shogun Teppan-Yaki on the way to the pub. Choosing between Chinese and Japanese food would have seemed like too big a decision earlier in the week.

But last night, as she sat eating Mongolian lamb in the Tin Tin, Fry had finally realized that she was worrying about all the wrong people. Why should she concern herself about the fate of William Leeson, or Darren Barnes and Shepherd? Or even Andy Kewley, or Vincent Bowskill?

The concrete city belonged to the past now. Her foster parents, her old home in Warley, her career with West Midlands Police – it all belonged to the past. Birmingham was no longer the same place she'd worked in, and her history had been flattened by those bulldozers. It was a blue-glass city now. Brum was moving on. There was no reason why she couldn't do the same.

This morning, Fry felt as though she was waking from the horror of a bad dream. For the first time in years, she seemed to have discovered a peaceful place in her own mind. It was here now, inside her – an ocean of calm. She could imagine it blue and warm, glittering with sunlight, stretching endlessly to that horizon.

As she was passing the outer suburbs of Walsall, she switched on her radio and found she was still tuned to BBC WM. The presenter's voice was giving way to a news bulletin. According to the lead item, two members of the notorious M1 Crew had been killed in a drive-by shooting in Handsworth. They were executed, it was believed, in a revenge attack by a rival gang. The victims had been named as Marcus Shepherd and Darren Joseph Barnes.

Maybe someone was on her side, after all.

In Edendale, Ben Cooper had just left the Superintendent's office. Somehow, things had gone right for him this week. He didn't really understand why, but he wasn't going to fight it. Two arrests, and a missing child recovered alive – those had helped. And he'd even earned credit for giving the young DCs their head, allowing them the chance to show what they could do with the Lowndes enquiry on the Devonshire Estate. Another successful outcome.

As a result, Branagh had offered him a permanent promotion to detective sergeant. Well, he was hardly going to refuse. For some reason, the Super seemed to like him.

And there was another reason to feel good today. Last night, as soon as he was free, Cooper had climbed into his car and turned it towards Bridge End Farm without even thinking where he was going. The time he'd spent with the Nields had reminded him of something that he should never have forgotten – that the worst thing you could do was destroy your own family.

Where had he read that *A person's enemies will include members of his own family*? He had a feeling it was in the Bible somewhere. But that should never be the case, should it?

Matt had been surprised to see him. But as they faced each other on the threshold of the farmhouse, the words had almost been unnecessary. His apology, when it came, had felt like a huge release.

'It's okay,' Matt had said. 'It's okay, Ben. We're always okay, you and me.'

Sitting at his desk, Cooper smiled at the memory. But there was just one more thing left to do, and he'd been putting it off. He might have put it off too long already. After the row with Liz on Friday night, the situation was coming to a head. He'd heard nothing from Liz over the weekend, not even a text message. That put the responsibility on to him. He had to sort it out. A decision had to be made, one way or another.

When Diane Fry called the office a few minutes later, he could tell she was in her car from the amount of road noise. She would be hands free, of course. Fry always followed the rules.

'Well, I'm on my way back,' she said.

'Great. So how are you feeling about things now?'

'It's strange. I feel good – though logically I shouldn't. I learned one thing, Ben, if nothing else.'

'What's that?'

'The people who you think are on your side always turn round and betray you. No one sticks by you all the way. No one.'

Cooper felt his heart thump painfully with the need to speak. But he held his tongue. Now wasn't the time. But then, would it ever be the time? Their relationship had been unpredictable ever since she transferred to Derbyshire.

To an outsider, it might seem that he had no reason to feel any affection for Diane Fry. And yet, when she asked, he had felt no hesitation in giving her his help. Had she forgotten that so quickly? Or was this just typical of the Diane that he knew, saying honestly what she thought?

'I should have known, I suppose,' she said. 'It's always the people closest to you who cause you the most harm. Always your family who wreck your life.'

'I didn't know you were that close to him, Diane,' said Cooper. 'I don't think you ever mentioned him, even.'

'Who?'

'Vincent Bowskill.'

'Oh, Vince. Well, it was years ago, Ben. Years ago.'

She ought to sound as weary as ever. Yet there was a different quality in her voice. Something must have happened to her in Birmingham, in connection with her past. Cooper supposed it was nothing to do with him, and he might never know what it was. The passage of time could turn a person into someone you didn't recognize. But that was true the other way round, too. Sometimes, you couldn't relate to the person they'd been in the past, either.

'Ben,' said Fry, 'Angie wants me to come back to Birmingham. I mean – for good.'

'But … I thought Birmingham held bad memories for you.'

'Memories disappear in the end. They do, don't they? It just takes time.'

'Oh, well. I suppose that's where you feel you belong, Diane. And there's no reason for you stay in Derbyshire. Is there?'

'Nothing too important.'

'So what have you decided to do?'

There was a silence at the other end of the line, apart from the hum of tyres on tarmac. Cooper listened. He listened as hard as he could, until he became aware that he was holding his breath because he was straining so hard to hear. He needed to hear something. Anything. But still, there was silence.

'Diane? So what have you –'

But now there was no road noise either. It was the silence of a lost signal.

When she reached Edendale, Fry called first at her flat in Grosvenor Avenue. After just a few days away, her furniture had turned into some kind of huge dust magnet. She wondered why she had ever thought the place was fit to live in.

The house was completely quiet, too. All the students were at college, and the restaurant workers sleeping. A scatter of envelopes lay behind her door. Junk mail to welcome her home. There was no point in staying here.

An hour later, she walked into the CID room at West Street. Gavin Murfin was eating a meat-and-potato pie over his paperwork. There was an officer she didn't know sitting at the rickety desk in the corner. The window nearest her was spattered with bird droppings. She already felt as though she'd stepped into a parallel universe, where the twenty-first century ceased to exist.

She tried to work, to plough her way through the mountain of memos and bulletins, to read a few of the emails filling her inbox. But, within a few minutes, Fry felt stifled.

Cooper stopped by her desk and looked at her anxiously.

'This William Leeson,' he said quietly. 'He was your real dad?'

'No. He might be my father. But he was never my dad.'

Fry thought about what she'd just said. For years, she'd considered Jim and Alice Bowskill her mum and dad. They were

317

the people who'd brought her up when she was a teenager, given her the stability she needed at a critical time in her life. It was true that there had always been the knowledge that they were not her real parents. How could it be otherwise? And always there had been that nagging question – why had they never adopted her, as they did Vince?

Maybe it was because she'd already been too old when she came to them, or perhaps it was their experience with Angie. But there had been a lack of commitment she'd tried not to resent when she looked at Vince, a hint that they might have expected her to move on somewhere else after a while. Perhaps they'd been surprised that she'd stayed with them so long.

The questions were endless. She really had no way of imagining what it was like, either to have children of your own, or to be caring for someone else's children. What sacrifices did you have to make, what compromises, what denial of your own feelings?

She stared out of the window at the same old view. The stand of Edendale Football Club, the roofs of the town, a vague line of hills on the horizon. She gazed around the CID room. Ben Cooper, Gavin Murfin. The two young DCs, Irvine and Hurst. DI Hitchens walking down the corridor towards his office. She'd been here in Edendale for years, made herself part of the life of the Peak District, in her own way. Or had she?

She turned to Cooper. 'Ben, is there any chance we can get out of here for a bit?'

'Yes, why not?' he said. 'Gavin can manage. I think I can get away with taking an hour off. I'm in the good books at the moment.'

Now was Fry's chance to sit down and tell him everything, the way she'd promised herself she would. She'd said she trusted him, and it was true. There was just one thing she wasn't sure of – whether Cooper would be able to understand hatred.

Edendale's river was too shallow for anyone to drown in. Even the mallards were able to stand up to their feathers in the water as it rushed over their feet.

Cooper still felt reluctant to get too close to the water, so they walked slowly along the path where tourists sat enjoying the sun. Fry listened while he told her about the Nields.

'That family is destroyed now,' he said. 'There is no family. Yet some people have the idea that crimes committed on behalf of their offspring are morally justified.'

'Do parents think like that?' asked Fry. 'This man lost his child. If you're a parent, I would have thought your own children would be the most important thing in the world to you. Your own flesh and blood.'

But she sounded uncertain, as if it was a subject she wasn't qualified to speak on.

'Four,' said Cooper. 'This is a man who's lost four children, for different reasons.'

'What? How?'

'He lost the baby, he lost Emily – and he'll lose Alex, at least for a while. And Lauren took herself away from home two years ago, so she might as well be lost.'

'She might go back,' said Fry.

'You think so? How could she forgive her father?'

'People do.'

Cooper nodded. Well, people did all kinds of things that he could never understand. Of course, DI Hitchens had been right. Parents who killed their children were in the minority. But there was a fine line between the people who did those things and the rest of us.

'The witness statements were so confusing,' he said. 'No one saw the right thing, not even me. They all thought they knew what they'd seen, yet everyone saw something different.'

'One person's truth is someone else's lie,' said Fry. 'We all know that.'

'I suppose so.'

'Ben, you remember me asking you about your childhood memories?'

'Yes. And you didn't have any.'

'No. Well, I realized my most accurate memories consisted of sounds and smells.'

'You're right. Mine too. There are certain sounds that are still inside my head, long after the event.'

'Do you get that as well?' asked Fry. 'I thought it was just me.'

Cooper smiled. 'It's probably everybody, Diane. We're not unique, are we?'

'Far from it.'

Hearing the tone of her voice, Cooper looked at her. He was changing his mind. He decided he quite liked this new Diane Fry, after all.

'Didn't you once tell me that you and Angie were taken into care because of allegations of abuse?' he asked.

'Yes.'

'Then he ought to have been listed on the Sex Offenders' Register, like Sean Deacon.'

'It was too long ago. The register was only created in 1997, and it wasn't retrospective. There could be lots of Sean Deacons and William Leesons walking about still. Men who have been able to leave their past behind.'

When they reached the bridge under the High Street, Cooper turned to her. He had the strong feeling that there was more she wanted to tell him. If only he could find a way of getting her to relax and talk to him properly. There were few opportunities, and this seemed like one of them. Too valuable a moment to miss.

'So?' he said. 'Are you going home, or do you want to come for a drink?'

But Fry was watching the river flow past, her eyes following the water as it came into the town from the hills to the west and headed out again, out beyond the borders of Derbyshire, where it didn't stop until it finally reached the sea. She had the air of someone experiencing a revelation.

Then Fry looked at him, with a softer expression in her eyes than Cooper had ever seen before. It was a look, almost, of apology.

'Home, I think,' she said.

Cooper sighed. 'Okay, Diane.'

For a moment, Fry stopped in the car park to allow a coachload of tourists to pass.

'A permanent promotion, then,' she said. 'I bet you're happy, Ben.'

'It will help,' said Cooper. 'The extra money makes a difference. And the security.'

Fry nodded. 'It will help you plan for the future. You and Liz probably have ... well, lots of plans.'

'Maybe,' said Cooper.

But Fry was gazing at Edendale as if she was seeing it for the first time. Or perhaps for the last.

'Well that's great,' she said. 'So you got what you always wanted.'

Cooper watched her get into her car. She had started the engine and was already driving away down West Street, well out of earshot, before he could think of an answer.

'Did I?' he said.

* * * * THE END * * * *

<u>Author's note:</u>

LOST RIVER was the 10th novel in the Cooper & Fry series. As I wrote it, there was a sense of some events and story lines coming 'full circle' from the first book, BLACK DOG. In particular, it allowed me to explore long-running issues in the life of DS Diane Fry.

As a result, this was also the first book in the series to be set outside Derbyshire to any great extent. Although Fry had been back to the West Midlands on two previous occasions (in BLIND TO THE BONES and THE KILL CALL), they were brief visits - and she had the added encumbrance of being accompanied by DC Gavin Murfin! In LOST RIVER, she's able to re-visit all her old haunts in the city of Birmingham and look up her foster family as she investigates the incident which blighted her life.

I make no apology for using so much of Birmingham. I think it's a fascinating city, with a unique character. Despite its potential, it's woefully under-used in crime fiction. For me, it provided a dramatic contrast to the Peak District - counter-pointing the urban with the rural, the ever-changing cityscape with the eternal appeal of the countryside.

I was a student in Birmingham back in the 1970s. In fact, Diane Fry studied at the same institution as me - which is now the City of Birmingham University. While I was at college, a new Central Library opened in Brum. I remember it being 'state of the art', the first library in the UK to have computerised checkout. Now, that library is about to be closed. It's considered out of date and obsolete, and will be replaced by a brand new building which is itself 'state of the art'. This is Birmingham, constantly rebuilding itself and sweeping away anything more than forty years old!

But the Peak District is always a presence in the Cooper & Fry series. In this case, the extraordinary Dovedale and the lovely town of Ashbourne provide plenty of scope for Ben Cooper. Dovedale is one of the most popular areas in the national park, a so-called 'honey pot' which attracts many thousands of visitors. Don't go there on a bank holiday weekend and expect it be peaceful.

Because of the significance of the physical settings in LOST RIVER, and because I know how much readers like to check out the locations from the books, I created two internet Google maps - one for locations in Birmingham and one for Derbyshire. There are photos and some local information. In many places, you can even zoom in using StreetView and see exactly what Ben Cooper or Diane Fry would find (though in Dovedale you can only get as far as the car park - it's all on foot after that).

The maps can be accessed here:

Google Map Birmingham: http://tiny.cc/g2f0dw

Google Map Derbyshire: http://tiny.cc/m3f0dw

I hope you enjoy the tour!

Stephen Booth

If you enjoyed LOST RIVER, why not try more novels in the Cooper & Fry series? The series so far:

1.   BLACK DOG
2.   DANCING WITH THE VIRGINS
3.   BLOOD ON THE TONGUE
4.   BLIND TO THE BONES
5.   ONE LAST BREATH
6.   THE DEAD PLACE
7.   SCARED TO LIVE
8.   DYING TO SIN
9.   THE KILL CALL
10. LOST RIVER
11. THE DEVIL'S EDGE
12. DEAD AND BURIED (2012)

There's also a Ben Cooper novella: CLAWS

And a standalone crime novel by the same author: TOP HARD

The most recent title in the Cooper & Fry series is
THE DEVIL'S EDGE:

In his most gripping case yet, newly promoted Detective Sergeant Ben Cooper investigates a series of lethal home invasions in the Peak District. During the latest attack, a woman has died in an affluent village nestling close under the long gritstone escarpment known as the Devil's Edge. Despite seething enmities between neighbours in the village of Riddings, the major lines of enquiry seem to lead to the nearby city of Sheffield. But before Cooper and his team can crack the case, the panic spreading throughout the area results in an incident that devastates the Cooper family. And the only person available to step into the breach is Ben's old rival, Detective Sergeant Diane Fry...

Here's a sample to give you a taste:

THE DEVIL'S EDGE

Stephen Booth

CHAPTER ONE
Tuesday

A shadow moved across the hall. It was only a flicker of movement, a blur in the light, a motion as tiny and quick as an insect's.

Zoe Barron stopped and turned, her heart already thumping. She wasn't sure whether she'd seen anything at all. It had happened in a second, that flick from dark to light, and back again. Just one blink of an eye. She might have imagined the effect from a glint of moonlight off the terracotta tiles. Or perhaps there was only a moth, trapped inside and fluttering its wings as it tried desperately to escape.

In the summer, the house was often full of small, flying things that crept in through the windows and hung from the walls. The children said their delicate, translucent wings made them look like tiny angels. But for Zoe, they were more like miniature demons with their bug eyes and waving antennae. It made her shudder to think of them flitting silently around her bedroom at night, waiting their chance to land on her face.

It was one of the drawbacks of living in the countryside. Too much of the outside world intruding. Too many things it was impossible to keep out.

Still uncertain, Zoe looked along the hallway towards the kitchen, and noticed a thin slice of darkness where the utility room door stood open an inch. The house was so quiet that she could hear the hum of a freezer, the tick of the boiler, a murmur from the TV in one of the children's bedrooms. She listened for a moment, holding her breath. She wondered if a stray cat or a fox had crept in through the back door and was crouching now in the kitchen, knowing she was there in the darkness, its hearing far better than hers. Green eyes glowing, claws unsheathed, an animal waiting to pounce.

But now she was letting her imagine run away with her. She shouldn't allow irrational fears to fill her mind, when there were so many real ones to be concerned about. With a shake of her head at her own foolishness, Zoe stepped through the kitchen door, and saw what had caused the movement of the shadows. A breath of wind was swaying the ceiling light on its cord.

So a window must have been left open somewhere - probably by one of the workmen, trying to reduce the smell of paint. They'd already been in the house too long, three days past the scheduled completion of this part of the job, and they were trying their best not to cause any more complaints. They'd left so much building material outside that it was always in the way. She dreaded one of the huge timbers falling over in the night. Sometimes, when the wind was strong, she lay awake listening for the crash.

But leaving a window open all night - that would earn them an earful tomorrow anyway. It wasn't something you did, even here in a village like Riddings. It was a lesson she and Jake learned when they lived in Sheffield, and one she would never forget. Rural Derbyshire hadn't proved to be the safe, crime-free place she hoped.

Zoe tutted quietly, reassuring herself with the sound. A window left open? It didn't seem much, really. But that peculiar man who lived in the old cottage on Chapel Close would stop her car in the village and lecture her about it endlessly if he ever found out. He was always hanging around the lanes watching what other people did.

Gamble, that was his name. Barry Gamble. She'd warned the girls to stay away from him if they saw him. You never knew with people like that. You could never be sure where the danger might come from. Greed and envy and malice - they were all around her, like a plague. As if she and Jake could be held responsible for other people's mistakes, the wrong decisions they had made in their lives.

Zoe realised she was clutching the wine bottle in her hand so hard that her knuckles were white. An idea ran through her head of using the bottle as a weapon. It was full, and so heavy she could do some damage, if necessary. Except now her finger prints would be all over it.

She laughed at her own nervousness. She was feeling much too tense. She'd been in this state for days, maybe weeks. If Jake saw her right now, he would tease her and tell her she was just imagining things. He would say there was nothing to worry about. Nothing at all. *Relax, chill out, don't upset the children. Everything's fine.*

But, of course, it wasn't true. Everyone knew there was plenty to worry about. Everyone here in Riddings, and in all the other villages scattered along this eastern fringe of the Peak District. It was in the papers, and on TV. No one was safe.

Still Zoe hesitated, feeling a sudden urge to turn round and run back to the sitting room to find Jake and hold on to him for safety. But instead she switched on the light and took a step further into the kitchen.

She saw the body of a moth now. It lay dead on the floor, its wings torn, its fragile body crushed to powder. It was a big one, too - faint black markings still discernible on its flattened wings. Was it big enough to have blundered into the light and set it swinging? A moth was so insubstantial. But desperate creatures thrashed around in panic when they were dying. It was always frightening to watch.

But there was something strange about the moth. Zoe crouched to look more closely. Her stomach lurched as she made it out. Another pattern was visible in the smear of powder - a section of ridge, like the sole of a boot, as if someone had trodden on the dead insect, squashing it onto the tiles.

Zoe straightened up again quickly, looking around, shifting her grip on the bottle, trying to fight the rising panic.

"Jake?" she said.

A faint crunch on the gravel outside. Was that what she'd heard that, or not? A footstep too heavy for a fox. The wrong sound for a falling timber.

This was definitely wrong. The only person who might legitimately be outside the house at this time of night was Jake, and she'd left him in the sitting room, sprawled on the couch and clutching a beer. If he'd gone out to the garage for some reason, he would have told her. If he'd gone to the front door, he would have passed her in the hall.

So it wasn't Jake outside. It wasn't her husband moving about now on the decking, slowly opening the back door. But still she clung on to the belief, the wild hope, that there was nothing to worry about. *I'm perfectly safe. Everything's fine.*

"Jake?" she called.

And she called again, louder. Much louder, and louder still, until it became a scream.

"Jake? Jake? *Jake!*"

Six miles from Riddings, Detective Sergeant Ben Cooper turned the corner of Edendale High Street into Hollowgate and stopped to let a bus pull into the terminus. The town hall lay just ahead of him, closed at this time of night but illuminated by spotlights which picked out the the pattern in its stonework which had earned its nickname of the Wavy House. Across the road, the Starlight Cafe was doing good business as usual, with a steady stream of customers. Taxis were lining up for their busiest time of the day. It was almost ten o'clock on an ordinary August evening.

The pubs were even busier than the Starlight, of course. Cooper could hear the music pounding from the Wheatsheaf and the Red Lion, the two pubs on either side of the market square. A crowd of youngsters screamed and laughed by the war memorial, watched by a uniformed PC and a community support officer in bright yellow high-vis jackets, the pair of them standing in the entrance to an alley near the Raj Mahal.

Even in Edendale, there were often fights at closing time, and drug dealers operating wherever they could find a suitable spot. On Friday and Saturday nights, there would be a personnel carrier with a prisoner cage in the back, and multiple foot patrols of officers on the late shift. A change came over the town then, a place that had looked so quaint during the day, with its cobbled alleys and tall stone buildings, revealed its Jekyll and Hyde nature.

"Hey, mate, shouldn't you be out arresting some criminals?"

"Ooh, duck, show us your baton."

328

Looking round at the shouts, Cooper saw that the bus was a Hulley's number 19 from the Devonshire Estate. Oh, great. He took a sharp step back from the kerb, turning his body away towards the shop window behind him. There were too many eyes gazing from the windows of the bus, and the likelihood of too many familiar faces, people he didn't want to meet when he was off duty. Half of the names on his arrest record had addresses on the Devonshire Estate. He didn't recognise the voices, but there was no doubt their owners knew him.

Well, this was his own choice. Many police officers chose to live outside the area they worked in, for exactly this reason. When you went for a quiet drink in your local pub, you didn't want to find yourself sitting next to the person you'd nicked the day before, or sharing a table with a man whose brother you'd just send to prison. But Cooper had resisted moving to a neighbouring division. He could easily have travelled into Edendale every morning from Chesterfield or Buxton, but that wouldn't be the same. He belonged here, in the Eden Valley, and he wasn't going to let anything push him out. He intended to stay here, settle down, raise a family, and eventually turn into a cantankerous pensioner who rambled on about the good old days.

That meant he had to put up with these awkward moments - the looks of horrified recognition on faces, the shying away as he passed in the street, the aggressive stare at the bar. It was all part of life. *All part of life's rich pageant.* That was what his grandmother would have said. He had no idea where the expression came from. But he knew the phrase would stick inside his head now, until he found out. He supposed he'd have to Google it when he got home. He seemed to be turning into one of those people whose minds collected odd bits of information like a sheep picking up ticks.

As he walked, Cooper checked his phone in case he'd missed a text message, but there was nothing. He carried on towards the end of Hollowgate, ignoring the loud group of youngsters. Not his business tonight. He'd only just come off shift, at the end of a long drawn-out series of arrests and the execution of search warrants. With six prisoners processed through the custody suite at West Street, there wasn't much of the evening left by the time he finally clocked off.

At the corner of Bargate he stopped again and listened for the sound of the river, just discernible here above the sound of the traffic. The council had been talking about making Hollowgate a pedestrianised zone, like neighbouring Clappergate. But of course the money had run out for projects like that. So a stream of cars still flowed down from Hulley Road towards the High Street, forming Edendale's version of a one-way system. 'Flow' wasn't exactly the right word for it. Half of the cars stopped in front of the shops to unload passengers, or crawled to a halt as drivers looked for parking spaces, the little car park behind the town hall already being full at this hour.

Cooper studied the pedestrians ahead. There was no sign of her yet. He glanced at his watch. For once, he wasn't the one who was late. That was good.

He decided to wait in front of the estate agent's, looking back towards the clock on the Wavy House to make sure his watch wasn't fast. There was always a smell of freshly baked bread just on this corner, thanks to the baker's behind the shops in Bargate. The scent lingered all day, as if it was absorbed into the stone and released slowly to add to the atmosphere. It was good to have somewhere in town that still baked its own bread. For Cooper, it was these sounds and smells that gave Edendale its unique personality, and distinguished it from every other town in the country, with their identikit high streets full of chain stores.

He turned to look in the estate agent's window, automatically drawn to the pictures of the houses for sale. This was one of the more upmarket agents, handling a lot of high-end properties, catering for equestrian interests and buyers with plenty of spare cash who were looking for a country residence. He spotted a nice property available not far away, in Lowtown. An old farm house by the look of it, full of character, with a few outbuildings and a pony paddock. But six hundred and fifty thousand pounds? How could he ever afford that? Even on his new salary scale as a detective sergeant, the mortgage repayments would be horrendous. He had a bit of money put away in the bank now, but savings didn't grow very fast these days, with interest rates still on the floor. It was a hopeless prospect.

"So which house do you fancy?" said a voice in his ear.

It was totally different voice from those that had shouted to him from the bus. This was a warm voice, soft and caressing. A familiar voice, with an intimate touch on his arm.

Liz appeared at his side, laid her head against his shoulder, and slipped her hand into his. He hadn't seen her approach, and now he felt strangely at a disadvantage.

"What, one of these?" he said. "Chance would be a fine thing."

She sighed. "True, I suppose."

Cooper looked beyond the the pictures of houses and caught their reflections in the glass. The pair of them were slightly distorted and smoky, as if the glass was tinted. Edendale's traffic moved slowly, jerkily behind them, like a street in an old silent film. And, not for the first time, it struck him how well matched they looked. Comfortable together, like an old married couple already. Liz looked small at his side, her dark hair shining in the street lights, her face lit up with a simple, uncomplicated pleasure. It delighted him that she could respond this way every time they met, or even spoke on the phone. Who wouldn't love to have that effect on someone? It was a wonderful thing to bring a bit of happiness into the world, to be able to create these moments of joy. A rare and precious gift in a world where he met so much darkness and unhappiness, so many lonely and bitter people.

"Kiss, then?

He bent to kiss her. She smelled great, as always. Her presence made him smile, and forget about the gaping faces. Who cared what other people thought?

They crossed the road, squeezed close together, as if they'd been parted for months. He always felt like that with Liz. At these moments, he would agree to anything, and often did.

"So, any progress on the big case?" she said.

"The home invasions, you mean?"

"Yes. The Savages. That's what the newspapers call them."

Cooper grimaced at the expression, sorry to have the mood momentarily spoiled. It was typical of the media to come up with such a sensational and ludicrous nickname. He knew they were aiming to grab the public's attention. But it seemed to him to trivialise the reality of the brutal violence inflicted on the victims of these particular offenders.

"No, not much progress," he said.

"It must be awful. I mean, to have something like that happen to you in your own home."

"The victims have been pretty traumatised."

The gang of burglars the papers were calling the Savages had struck several times this summer, targeting large private houses in well heeled villages on the eastern edges. E Division was Derbyshire Constabulary's largest geographical division by far, and the edges marked the furthest fringes, the border with South Yorkshire.

Cooper wondered how he'd feel if he owned that nice home in Lowtown, and someone broke into his house. He'd been told that owning property changed your attitude completely, made you much more territorial, more aggressively prepared to defend your domain. Well, he'd seen that at first hand. Because it had certainly happened to his brother. He'd watched Matt turn into a paranoid wreck since he became responsible for the family farm at Bridge End. He patrolled his boundaries every day, like a one-man army, ever vigilant for the appearance of invaders. He was the Home Guard, ready to repel Hitler's Nazi hordes with a pitchfork. That level of anxiety must be exhausting. Was owning property really worth it?

"Do you think the Savages are local?" asked Liz, voicing the question that many people were asking. "Or are they coming out from Sheffield?"

There were few people he could have discussed details of the case with. But Liz was in the job herself, a scenes of crime officer in E Division. She'd even attended one of the scenes, the most recent incident in Baslow.

"They know the area pretty well, either way," said Cooper. "They've chosen their targets like professionals so far. And they've got their approaches and exits figured out to the last detail. At least, it seems so - since we haven't got much of a lead on them yet."

They had a table booked at the Columbine. It was in the cellar, but that was okay. In Edendale, there wasn't much of a choice of restaurants where last orders were taken at ten. And even at the Columbine that was only from May to October, for the visitors.

Edendale people didn't eat so late.

Cooper was looking forward to getting in front of a High Peak rib-eye steak pan fried in Cajun spices. Add a bottle of Czech beer, and he'd be happy. And he'd be able to forget about the Savages for a while.

They opened the door of the restaurant, and Cooper paused for a moment to look back at the street, watching the people beginning to head out of town, back to the safety of their homes. If anyone's home was safe, with individuals like the Savages on the loose.

"Well," he said, "at least they haven't killed anybody yet."

In Riddings, a figure was moving in the Barrons' garden. Barry Gamble was approaching their house cautiously. The last time he'd been on the drive at Valley View, it hadn't been a happy experience. Some people just didn't appreciate neighbourly concern. He hoped there was no one hanging around outside, no chance of seeing any of the Barrons. He would just have a quick check, make sure everything was okay, then get back to his own house a few hundred yards away in Chapel Close.

Gamble shook his head at the roof trusses and window frames stacked untidily against the wall. That was asking for trouble, in his opinion. It gave the impression the house was empty and vulnerable while construction work was going on. The Barrons' improvements seemed to have stalled, though. The area that had been cleared behind the garage was supposed to be an extension for a gym and family room, so he'd heard. But the foundations were still visible, the breeze block walls hardly a foot high where they'd been abandoned. Perhaps the Barrons had run out of money, like everyone else. The thought gave Gamble a little twinge of satisfaction.

He wondered if some item of builder's materials had made the noise he'd heard. A dull thump and a crash, loud on the night air. And then there had been some kind of scrabbling in the undergrowth. But he was used to that sound. There was plenty of wildlife in Riddings at night - foxes, badgers, rabbits. Even the occasional deer down off Stoke Flat. The noises animals made in the dark were alarming, for anyone who wasn't used to them the way he was.

Gamble skirted the garage and headed towards the back of the house, conscious of the sound of his footsteps on the gravel drive. He tried to tread lightly, but gravel was always a nuisance. He'd learned to avoid it whenever he could. A nice bit of paving or a patch of grass was so much easier.

He began to rehearse his excuses in case someone came out and challenged him. *I was just passing, and I thought I heard... Can't be too careful, eh? Well, as long as everything's all right, I'll be getting along.* He couldn't remember whether the Barrons had installed motion sensors at Valley View that would activate the security lights. He thought not, though.

The house was very quiet as he came near it. The younger Barron children would be in bed by now. He knew their bedrooms were on the other side of the house, overlooking the garden. Their parents tended to sit up late watching TV. He'd seen the light flickering on the curtains until one o'clock in the morning sometimes.

Gamble peered through the kitchen window. A bit of light came through the open doorway from the hall. But there wasn't much to see inside. No intruders, no damage, no signs of a break-in or disturbance. No one visible inside the house, no soul moving at all.

In fact, there was only one thing for Barry Gamble to see. One thing that made him catch his breath with fear and excitement. It was nothing but a trickle. A narrow worm, red and glistening in a patch of light. It was a thin trickle of blood, creeping slowly across the terracotta tiles.

* * * * * *

THE DEVIL'S EDGE is published by Little, Brown under their Sphere imprint.

Stephen Booth is a multiple award winning UK crime writer. He is best known as the creator of two young Derbyshire police detectives, DC Ben Cooper and DS Diane Fry, who appear in twelve novels, all set in England's beautiful and atmospheric Peak District. Stephen has been a Gold Dagger finalist, an Anthony Award nominee, twice winner of a Barry Award for Best British Crime Novel, and twice shortlisted for the Theakston's Crime Novel of the Year. DC Cooper was a finalist for the Sherlock Award for the best detective created by a British author, and in 2003 the Crime Writers' Association presented Stephen with the Dagger in the Library Award for "the author whose books have given readers the most pleasure". The Cooper & Fry series is published all around the world, and has been translated into 15 languages. The latest titles are THE DEVIL'S EDGE and DEAD AND BURIED, published by Little, Brown.

For the latest news, visit the author's website:
http://www.stephen-booth.com

or stay in touch on Twitter:
http://twitter.com/stephenbooth

on Facebook:
http://www.facebook.com/stephenboothbooks

or the Stephen Booth Blog:
http://stephen-booth.blogspot.com

Chat to other readers on the Forum:
http://www.stephen-booth.com/Old forum

or visit Stephen Booth's channel on YouTube
http://www.youtube.com/watch?v=1ssD8g65LK8

Made in the USA
San Bernardino, CA
15 April 2014